D1708403

THE BRIAR
AND THE ROSE

THE BRIAR
AND THE ROSE

LAURA
MILLS-ALCOTT

Five Star • Waterville, Maine

This novel is a work of fiction. Names, characters, places and incidents are either the product of the author's imagination, or, if real, used fictitiously.

First Edition
First Printing: November 2003

Set in 11 pt. Plantin.

Printed in the United States on permanent paper.

Library of Congress Cataloging-in-Publication Data

Mills-Alcott, Laura, 1964–
    The briar and the rose / by Laura Mills-Alcott.
    1st ed.
    Published: Waterville, Me. : Five Star, 2003.
      p. cm.
    ISBN: 1-59414-089-8 (hc : alk. paper)
    Notes: "Loosely based on the ballad Barbara Allen and the Irish folktale The briar and the rose"—p. [8].
    "Five Star first edition titles"—T.p. verso.
    1. Women domestics—Fiction.   2. Lookalikes—Fiction.
  3. Nobility—Fiction.   4. Amnesia— Fiction.   5. Ireland—Fiction.
  6. Regency fiction.   7. Love stories.   I. Title.
PS3613.I59B75 2003

2003060137

DEDICATION

I tried very hard to think of one person to dedicate this book to, and found the task impossible, as there are so many people whom I must thank or give credit, and who each, for different reasons, deserve this dedication.

First, I would like to dedicate this book to my mother, Carol: you encouraged me to spread my wings, even when you didn't always agree with my destination. Thank you for believing in me and teaching me to believe in myself.

To my stepfather, Chuck: thank you for being there and for being you.

To my children, Jared, Jordan, and Jacob, who have all traveled this road with me and who deserve a special award for their support and cheers while I wrote this book and then re-wrote this book and who never complained too loudly when dinner was microwaved leftovers because Mommy had to write some more.

To Collette Captain, my friend in Dublin since we were both in sixth grade, for patiently answering all my questions about Ireland.

To Dolly Parton, whose music has always been a source of inspiration.

To Emma Jensen, Lori Soard, Sally Painter-Kale, Nancy Richards-Akers, Eileen Charbonneau, and all the other writers who never failed to lend a shoulder, an ear, encouragement, or research tidbits while I wrote this book.

To Geroid Ó Maonaigh for his help and Proinsias Ó Maonaigh for his Gaeilge translation of the ballad.

To Curt, Revis, and Mark, for your friendship and the countless hours of conversation over coffee, trivia, and wings, and the laughter, tears, and political debate we shared during this time in my life.

To my editor, Russell Davis, for your patience and all your help on this project.

To Pamela Harty, my agent, for your faith in this book and perseverance.

To Andy, for the good times, bad times and all the times in between, and for those times you were my hero. We miss you.

And, as always, to my father, Richard Williams, the inspiration for Lord Richard Windham, for teaching me the true meaning of unconditional love. I know you're watching over me. I love you, Daddy.

From the bottom of my heart I thank each and every one of you, and thank God that our paths have crossed. My love to you all.

A QUICK GAEILGE PRIMER

Is sea: equivalent of "yes", though there is no word for
   "yes" in Gaeilge
Maime: another name for mother
Dia dhuit: God be with you, used as a greeting
Táim: I am
Mo chara (mo hara): My friend
Mo stór: My treasure or my darling
Mo ghrá: My love
Tír Na n-Óg: Western Isle, the equivalent of the afterlife in
   Irish mythology

HISTORY

The Briar and the Rose is loosely based on the ballad "Barbara Allen" and the Irish folktale "The Briar and the Rose." The haunting ballad was brought to America by immigrants and passed down from generation to generation. Today, it is still one of the most widely known of the old ballads, as well as one of the most beloved. I was so moved after hearing the ballad on the Dolly Parton album *Heartsongs*, that I researched the ballad, finding many versions, as well as the poem published by Thomas Percy in 1765.

"The Briar and the Rose" is a tale that has been told in Ireland for centuries, about a young woman named Mairéad, and her lover, Séamus.

In 1760 Thomas Percy, later Bishop of Dromore, visited Ireland and heard the tragic tale of Mairéad and Séamus. Being a great admirer of folklore and ballads, he recognized the story of the young lovers, and realized "The Briar and the Rose" was the origination for a ballad better known to him as "Barbara Allen's Cruelty."

In 1765 Percy published his collection of old heroic ballads, songs, and other pieces of our earlier poets together with some few of later date, in three volumes, entitled *Reliques of Ancient English Poetry*. Among the poems published was "Barbara Allen's Cruelty."

After Percy's death in 1811, his diaries were discovered. In his diary for the years dated 1759–1761, he recounted the tale of "The Briar and the Rose," including research he did while in Ireland and a visit he made to a small churchyard where he witnessed the markers of Mairéad Ní Mhorain and Séamus O'Lionáird.

While it is clear Percy mingled the Irish tale with the more commonly known English ballad in his published version of "Barbara Allen's Cruelty," he did not include the end of "The Briar and the Rose":

"They buried her in the old church yard,
Séamus's grave was nye her
From Séamus's grave there grew a red rose
From Mairéad's grave a briar

They grew and grew up the old church wall
Till they could growe no higher
They lapped and tyed in a true love knot
The rose wrapped 'round the briar"

It wasn't until after Percy's diaries were found, and Child put together his collection of ballads in the 1800s, that "The Ballad of Barbara Allen" (Child Ballad #84) included the above verses.

But there is more to the story than Percy or Child ever knew . . .

PROLOGUE

Ireland, April 1827

The driver hauled on the reins with all his might. A horse shrieked. The team reared and plunged, and the girl fell to the road, a mere breath from being trampled.

Jarred brutally from his thoughts, the man inside the carriage lunged forward and shouted, "What the devil," just before he hit the floor with a thud. Gaining his feet with a low growl, he flung the coach door open. "Flaugherty!"

"Twas a girl, Lord Castlereagh," the coachman called back. "Ran right in front of me, she did."

The formidable, dark man stormed out, throwing his arms into the air as his boots hit the rain-dampened dirt. "You incompetent oaf! You cannot run these peasants down!"

"My lord, I did not run 'er over," he said in his own defense, pointing a gloved finger toward the forest. "There she goes, wi' nary a scratch on her."

His steely gaze snapped around to follow the driver's direction. At that very moment a woman with hair as black as midnight fled into the grove. A gasp escaped his parted lips.

"Lord Castlereagh, are you all right? You look as though you have seen a ghost."

CHAPTER ONE

Dahlingham Castle, May 1827

"*Katherine.*" Devan exhaled a long, drawn out sigh and turned the page of his book, but the text ran together in jumbled discord until at last, in defeat, he folded the cover.

More than two weeks in London, and another three in Ireland at Dahlingham, and no relief to be found. Every day Devan, Marquess of Castlereagh, forced himself to get out of bed and get dressed. Every day he sat at his table and partook of his meals and drank his port. Each day he buried himself in inane activities, hoping to somehow liberate himself from the memory of the savage fire that broke out the night of the ball at Dakshire, before he could whisk Katherine off to Gretna Green.

Without ceasing, the sound of Katherine's anguished pleas for him to save her haunted his mind day and night. He'd been unable to reach her, and at last fell unconscious from the suffocating smoke until someone pulled him from the flames, not hearing her cries.

Nothing could free him of the reality that he had failed her.

Throwing his book to the table with a growl, he rose and paced the library floor, feeling caged and restless.

What a damnable cruelty was this life—to find love at last, and in the space of the same heartbeat, lose it forever.

A sudden glimpse of one of the servants working in the garden made him halt before the window. His frown deepened into a scowl. What an easy life it was for people *like her*—spending her days amidst the roses, with not a care in the world.

While he spent his days trying to recall what it felt like to breathe.

The injustice of it tore at his heart, and Devan might have turned away from the sight of the servant then, had there not been something strangely entrancing about her that bound his gaze. He continued to watch as she trimmed the foliage and plucked each carefully selected blossom, placing it gently into the basket slung over her arm.

So this was the woman who made up the vases of fresh flowers scattered throughout Dahlingham since his return. He recalled Mrs. Captain mentioning her in passing one day; a beggar found on the lawn, near death, with seemingly no recollection of her past.

The Marquess of Castlereagh congratulated himself on his magnanimity. It wasn't every Englishman who would take in such a person; a homeless Irish peasant who was perhaps more than a little touched in the head, and give her shelter. He knew plenty of others who would have locked her away in an asylum and been done with her.

He had to admit her arrangements were exceptionally beautiful; odd mixtures of garden flowers and wild flowers and a single red rose in each. Her background may have been impoverished, but she had a particular eye for beauty. The arrangements were one of the few things that brightened the ancient and dismal interior of Dahlingham. He made a mental note to praise the woman's work to the housekeeper.

Just then she finished her undertaking and made her way from the gardens. A sudden gust of wind caught her cap. Still clinging to her basket of flowers, she grasped frantically in a desperate bid to seize it, but to no avail. Lifted by the breeze, the cap flew into the air. A mane of ebony curls fell loose and framed a complexion of ivory as she lifted her face toward him.

Katherine!

The cap took a fast dive. She raced toward it, but the light wind captured it again, sending it tumbling hither and yon across the ground. She took up the chase again, at last overcoming the unruly cap and putting an abrupt end to its rebellion with a firm stomp of her shoe. Kneeling, she clutched the cap securely within her fingers, then vanished through the servants' entrance.

Running his hands harshly over his face, Devan fought to regain his wit. With his very own ears he'd heard Katherine's agonized cries as a fiery beam fell between them, stealing her from his grasp. And though he fought to make his way to her side, he fell unconscious in the thick, strangulating smoke. When he came to, there was naught he could do save watch, helpless, as Dakshire was consumed in flames.

But still, his heart thrashed madly, and a glimmer of hope sparked deep inside.

"Mrs. Captain. *Mrs. Captain!* Come here at once!" he bellowed, his impatient voice reverberating throughout the corridors of Dahlingham.

In less than a trice, the housekeeper entered the library, holding the hem of her dress and white apron from the floor, huffing and puffing as a result of the mad dash made at his command. "Yes, my lord?" she wheezed with a quick curtsy.

"Bring me the woman."

"What woman, my lord?"

"The woman you took in during my absence!" he snarled.

"But, Lord Castlereagh, her chores are not finished for the day."

Devan spun to face the housekeeper, at last tearing his attention away from the gardens. "Mrs. Captain," he bit out, his teeth clenched, his voice uncompromising, "she works for *me*, does she not?"

She nodded nervously.

"*I* do not care about her chores. At this moment *I* wish to meet this woman who has been living under *my* roof. Have I made myself perfectly clear?"

Humbled, and quite thoroughly reminded of her position, Mrs. Captain dipped hastily again. "Yes, my lord."

The housekeeper hurried from the library, and Devan returned his stare to the empty garden below, where the apparition first emerged, and stole a shaky breath.

Once he could inspect her closely, he was certain the woman would not resemble Katherine in the slightest. There was only one Lady Katherine, and she was lost to him for eternity. This servant could be little more than a shabby imitation.

Hearing a scuffle and whispers in the corridor outside the library, he shifted his attention to the doorway just in time to see a young woman stumble into the room. He squinted dubiously at the maid, who quickly regained her balance and stood at attention in her colorless uniform of gray and white, her hair tucked fully inside the white cap once more, hands clasped together tensely in front of her and gaze cast to the floor.

The sight of the woman bound his stare as he walked slowly along the shelves of books to his favorite gold velvet armchair. He lowered himself into the chair, leaned his head against one hand, and grappled his chin with the other while contemplating the woman. The gray dress she wore was too large, and made her appear a child playing dress-up. The oversized cap covered her hair and shadowed her features.

Beneath his intense gaze, she shifted her weight nervously from one foot to the other, awaiting his command.

"Remove your hat."

Warily, her hand rose to pull the cover from her head. Little by little, black waves began to tumble across her shoulders, until every curl was at last completely freed from the confines of the cap. Vividly reminded of the hair he had entwined his fingers through just moments before the fire, Devan shut his eyes and stole a moment to savor the memory.

"Stand before me," he instructed.

She moved apprehensively around the chaise to the center of the library floor.

Rising from his chair in silence, Devan folded his hands behind him and circled the woman until at last he paused in front of her. "Look at me," he ordered, unable to prevent the gripping urgency he felt from seeping into his voice.

She lifted her head. Long black lashes fluttered to reveal eyes of deep lavender-blue that locked upon his and refused to release him. There were no other eyes in the world like those he now stared into!

Forcing his raging heart to slow, Devan pushed back the sudden urge to take the woman in his arms. He drew a deep breath. "What is your name?"

The seconds dragged like eternities. Her gaze fell away, and in a voice little more than a whisper she said, "I d-don't know me given name, me lord, but 'tis Raven I be called."

The lilt of her Irish brogue was like a dagger being thrust into his heart, then twisted. And it proved what he had, in reality, already known. Spinning on his heel, he returned to

17

stare out the window, refusing to look further into those haunting eyes. "Miss, uh, Raven, you are dismissed."

He listened to the soft patter of her feet as she made her way quickly across the library, and it was not until he heard the door close fast behind her that he let go the breath he'd held since confronting the face of his beloved Katherine.

Surely, this was fate's punishment; flaunting this . . . this *Raven* in front of him, a constant reminder. *Fate be damned!* She was a servant, nothing more.

It occurred to him that he could send her away immediately and be done with her. But that seemed a rather severe conclusion. It wasn't her fault she bore the features of the one who possessed his heart, even in death. And what would happen to her if he turned her out? Would she, too, perish, and would he have to bear that guilt as well?

There were servants who had been at Dahlingham for years whom he'd never seen, and he would simply make certain this woman did not cross his path again. He would speak with Mrs. Captain as soon as possible to see to the matter for him.

"Tourish!" Devan barked for his butler.

Within moments the effeminate Tourish entered the room with a low bow and click of his heels. Devan rolled his eyes, too tired and distraught to comment on the irritating mannerisms of the little man. "I will have my supper in the library."

His meal proved utterly tasteless, and Devan pushed it aside after only a few bites. A thorough soaking in brandy sounded far more appealing, so he poured the amber drink, and fell back into his armchair.

Draining his glass, a familiar numbness wafted over him. *The less felt, the better.* Another three or four drinks should be enough to quell the melancholy, possibly even put him into a deep sleep that would last the entire night—something he had yet to achieve since the fire.

Rising, he refilled the crystal chalice. In one great gulp, he threw that drink down. His body lost some of its tension. He filled his glass for the third time. Drink in hand, he went to the window and pushed back the green velvet draperies shut earlier to block the annoying glare of the setting sun.

A nearly full moon radiated a soft glow to the gardens below.

The gardens . . .

The *girl*.

Another swallow of brandy. Leaning against the pane, he stared down at the very place he'd first seen her gathering flowers.

Raven.

As if responding to his silent wish, she suddenly emerged from the shadows, dressed in no more than a night rail. Just where did the little chit think she was going at this time of night, dressed *that* way? Meeting her peasant lover, no doubt.

Besieged by a discomforting possessiveness, he set his glass aside and stormed from the library, intent on following the woman, and perhaps finding the reason he needed to let her go without contrition. After all, a servant of Dahlingham could not be permitted to carry on with villagers like a common harlot!

Out into the gardens he stomped, determined to find them and remove her from the grounds that very evening.

"Let her lover be the one to look into those imposter eyes," he muttered, just as he was about to step onto the walk that led to the lake.

But before his boot hit the cinders, he heard splashing.

Halting in place, Devan peered through the darkness. In the distance he saw her, the gentle radiance of the moon shimmering over her nakedness. And she was *alone*.

Crouching low, he stole from the shelter of the roses and down the cinder path, at last taking cover behind a tall oak where he could secretly witness the woman who played like a child, diving in and out of the water, splashing, singing, and laughing.

Fascinating.

The coolness of the night air and the sight of Raven's glistening body brought back his brandy-dulled senses. Her every movement was deliberate, graceful, unlike the frightened waif of earlier in the evening, who could scarcely step without tripping. Drawn into her frolic, he watched her massage the soap through her long, dark tresses. Then, arching her back, she revealed her full breasts to the moon as she immersed her head into the water, then rose, only to dive again beneath the surface, rendering him helpless to do anything but watch, entranced by the scene being played out before him.

Too soon, she stepped from the pool, and slipped back into her night rail. Then, twisting the water from her hair, she pushed the disheveled tresses into place.

Devan ducked low as she approached, and stopped breathing when she suddenly halted only a few paces beyond him.

Though her glance did not shift in his direction, her breath fluttered, body tensed. "Surely me lord can find more amusing entertainment than the bathing of his servitress in the loch," Raven admonished coolly. Then, with a haughty lift of her chin, she marched away.

It was not until she was well within the boundaries of the Dahlingham walls that he rolled over onto his back, brought his hands behind his head and allowed a grin to ease across his face. Gazing at the stars above, at last he surrendered to roaring laughter.

That night, for the first time, Devan's dreams were not filled with scenes of the fire nor the sound of Katherine's cries. Instead, it was Raven who called out to him, from beneath the hood of a black wool cloak, sitting astride a tall white mare in the mist-shrouded meadows of Dahlingham. He could not see her face, and she spoke in the native tongue. But he was certain it was she, and just as certain it was he she beckoned.

Through the forest he fought to clear a path, branches and brambles tearing furiously at his clothes and flesh. But try as he might, he could not make his way to her, for the end of the wood was always just one step beyond him, and the meadow from whence she called further still.

Waking from the nightmare, his shirt soaked with sweat, Devan struggled for enough air to fill his lungs. He reminded himself that it was only a dream, but it felt so real and left him with a discomforting sense of helplessness.

Rising from his bed, he paced the chamber, hands balled into fists of frustration and his jaw set. He could find no logical explanation to the vision, nor the way it had made him feel—vulnerable, shaken.

At that moment, had he known which of the dozen or more chambers of the first floor she occupied, he'd have sought her out. But what would he say?

There was something about the woman, more than her resemblance to Katherine. Precisely what he did not know. But there was no question he would not rest easy until he discovered what it was about her that fueled his dreams and tore at his heart.

CHAPTER TWO

"Rogue!" Raven hissed, scraping the bar of soap across Lord Castlereagh's shirt. She immersed the shirt into the iron tub with such force the soapy water splashed out and drenched her from head to toe. Drawing her sleeve across her wet cheeks, it occurred to her that she could forego the rinsing altogether and watch him scratch his way through till the next laundering.

"*Ha.* Deserves worse, the villain!" Her smirk faded quickly. Mrs. Captain would have her head for such a crime. She would care not that he'd sneaked up upon her without announcement while she bathed, without even so much as an apology.

But Raven cared. Though she may be a mere servant in the arrogant marquess's household, it did not give him the right to take such liberties, and she vowed to flog him with his own wet shirt if he ever thought to try it a second time.

With a sharp flick of her wrist, she dipped the soapy shirt in the rinse water but twice, just enough to remove the lather from the surface of the material, but not enough to take it from the fibers.

"At least one will give him a fitting rash." The thought of the itching marquess brought with it a wry and vengeful grin.

"Raven! Come quick!"

At Collette's alarmed shout, she turned to see the wild-eyed maid, arms flailing in the air as she raced across the lawn. Meeting her halfway, Raven took her by the shoulders. "God Almighty, Collette! Calm yerself. What be the matter with ye?"

"Maime wants to see you right away. She's in a frenzy and spittin' out commands all over the house and she's havin' your chamber cleared out!" Her blue-gray eyes were wide, frantic, and her trembling hands clung to Raven's dress. "What have you done?"

Mrs. Captain could not possibly have seen the half-hearted rinsing she'd given the marquess's shirt, and there was nothing else she could bring to mind that might raise the old housekeeper's ire. "On my life, I can't think of anything."

"Best you go and see if there isn't some way to make amends, even if the deed is not of your doing. A far cry better it is than living as a pauper in Dublin."

Raven rushed off, prepared to face whatever Mrs. Captain had to throw her way. There was no question the housekeeper had taken a strong dislike to her from the day she awoke at Dahlingham. It was only Collette's insistence that prevented the old woman from casting her into the street. But no matter how hard she labored or how great the care she took to perform each task perfectly, she could not win the woman's favor. More than ever she wished she could remember her clan, if she had one. Then she could run away from Mrs. Captain and the wretched Marquess of Castlereagh. But in truth, she had nowhere to go, and by the time she approached the door to her chamber, Raven was determined to throw herself upon Mrs. Captain's mercy, if indeed she had any.

"Mrs. Captain, I—" she began with her first foot inside the doorway, but was abruptly cut off.

"No time for your talk, girl!" the housekeeper said firmly while she threw the linens from Raven's bed into a pile on the stone floor. "Change out of that filthy dress and get yourself into a fresh one."

An irrevocable tear trickled down Raven's cheek. "Please don't turn me out, Mrs. Captain."

The woman spun and faced Raven fiercely, her eyes slits and her hands set firmly on her wide hips. "*Turn you out?* Oh, *nooo,* my dear! I'll not be turning you out today!"

"Th—then why have ye emptied me chamber?" she asked with a piteous sniffle.

"It seems you made quite the impression on Lord Castlereagh three days past in the library. Precisely *what* took place between the two of you?"

" 'Twas little more than his lordship askin' me name, ma'am, and I said no more than that."

The old woman glared incredulously. "You mean to say you spoke naught but your name, and that alone is the reason he moves you upstairs?"

Raven blinked, unable to trust her own ears. "Movin' me?"

Staring sternly down her long nose, brows knotted, Mrs. Captain pursed her lips tightly together. "Lord Castlereagh has ordered that you and what little you possess be moved to the third floor immediately."

Stunned, she drew her sleeve slowly across her face, drying the streaks left by her tears. "I'm to be an upstairs maid?"

"*Ha!* You little fool. The maids who work upstairs sleep in the attic. You are being given a third floor suite, which means you won't be working for your keep." And then with a rueful sneer, she added under her breath, "At least not as a maid."

24

The realization of the insinuation suddenly set in. Now it was insult that stung her eyes, and Raven stubbornly crossed her arms and matched Mrs. Captain's glare. "Ye can tell his lordship that I'll *not* be workin' on me back!"

Shoving a clean gray dress into Raven's hands, the old woman shook a fat finger in her face. "You'll not be putting my position in jeopardy, is what you'll not be doing. You shall, however, change that dress and you may quibble with him yourself, once I've escorted you upstairs."

Only the once, when she was called before Lord Castlereagh in the library, had Raven visited the ground floor of Dahlingham Castle. Even then she had not actually seen much, for Mrs. Captain had dragged her quickly up the stairs, straight down the corridor, and pushed her harshly into the library. This time, Mrs. Captain escorted her to the drawing room, demanded she sit, and left her alone to face the man who evidently intended to force her into a life of iniquity.

Well, she would have no part of it! She may have no money or clan, and she may have temporarily misplaced her memory, but she was not about to let him use her as his . . .

Raven shuddered.

Her gaze scanned the drawing room. Never had she witnessed such grandeur—at least not that she recalled. Yet there seemed an unmistakable familiarity to it all.

Waxed and polished wood floors covered with thick wool woven carpets were a drastic contrast to the bare stone floors of the servants' quarters she'd occupied these last weeks. Burnished marble made up the face and mantle of the fireplace, while brilliantly shining brass gleamed from the doorknobs, candlesticks, and lamps. Above her, hundreds of resplendent crystals in the chandelier sparkled with tiny dancing rainbows, as rays of sunlight streamed through the Cimmerian velvet draperies of the long windows. The tables and trim were polished mahogany, and the chaise and chairs were covered in gold and deep wine-colored velvets.

Such a room was more regal than anything her imagination might have conjured, and under different circumstances, it would have been a welcome change from the bleak, sparsely furnished servants' chamber. But now it was a place to be feared.

Her gaze rose to the large, intimidating portraits lining the walls. Those who once roamed Dahlingham, with their solemn faces and ancient eyes, seemed to scrutinize her unrelentingly, and threaten to call out to the current lord of the manor if she attempted to escape her elegant prison.

Lord Castlereagh took a seat across from her, in the largest of all the chairs in the drawing room, startling Raven, who had been so engrossed in the scowling ancestors that she had not heard his entrance. She fisted her hands nervously in her lap to prevent them from wringing while he contemplated her in silence, appearing nothing less than a vile wolf, anticipating the taste of the lamb he was about to slay.

Even more frightening than the prospect of becoming his prey was the unexpected flush that prickled her skin when she shifted her stare and at last met his fathomless black gaze.

She'd scarcely looked at him that day in the library, and had only sensed his presence and then caught his shadowed form out of the corner of her eye that night by the lake. But now, to gaze at him . . . thick onyx waves that fell in disarray across his forehead until his fingers harshly pushed them to the side, deep golden tanned skin that sharply contrasted the stark white of his shirt, and dark mysterious eyes, relentless, glinting dangerously as they drifted lower, boldly caressing each time they paused over her body. And even though she knew the man intended her nothing but harm, she found herself suppressing the strangest urge to . . . *sigh.*

Raven reminded herself that she despised him.

In the library, she'd stared mostly at his boots, and had not realized just how very tall he truly was. His black trousers hugged well-muscled thighs, and his wide shoulders looked as though they could carry the world upon them. Three buttons of his starched shirt had been carelessly left undone, revealing a chest lightly sprayed with black. Large hands gripped the arms of his chair loosely, and, she thought, despite their size and probable strength, they would be gentle when they touched her.

Shaking herself quickly free of such errant and perilous thoughts, she took a deep breath to quell her racing heart. Then came a healthy dose of disgust—*with herself.* For to feel such things for this man was worse than anything he could possibly do to her.

"As I am certain you have been told," he began, his voice commanding, yet soft, "I have ordered you moved from the servants' quarters into your own suite."

Startled again when he spoke, she swallowed hard, scooted taller in her chair, and shifted her eyes to study the intricate design of the carpet, rather than the marquess, who now had her thoroughly unsettled.

Lord Castlereagh exhaled with a sigh. "I despise gray, and have therefore provided you several dresses, which will be suitable enough attire until I can have more made. You will take your meals with me, and spend your evenings with me."

Raven forgot all about the oriental carpet as his words

snapped her attention fully back to him.

He cleared his throat and dragged his hand roughly over his hair. "Anything you need you are to inform Mrs. Captain, and she will see it is granted you. Have you anything to say?"

Though she'd prayed her intuition would be proven wrong, she now knew, without question, that her worst suspicions were true. He intended to make her his whore! Unbidden tears welled until his solemn face was a blur, her chest tightened painfully, and Raven struggled to catch her breath. Biting down hard on her trembling lower lip, she focused on that pain, rather than that tearing at her insides.

"Aye, me lord." Stealing a moment, she looked away and steadied her voice. She could not permit him to see her alarm, lest he realize the extent of her fear and use it to his own advantage. At last, when she was confident she could look to him with the same calm control he exhibited, she met his gaze squarely. "I have much to say on the matter."

He nodded.

"I am not in need of yer generosities, Lord Castlereagh."

He cocked a brow, seemingly taken back, but remained silent.

Gathering her courage, she rose boldly and marched to stand in front of him, sporting her best imitation of an austere Mrs. Captain, placing her hands on her hips and looking him dead in the eye. "I will walk meself out of yer house naked, without a single farthing in me hand, and sleep in the streets of Dublin with the rats before I become yer mistress!"

He brought his hand up to mask his expression, then shifted in his chair, all the while meeting her glare. "So . . . am I to understand you do not wish to be my, uh, *mistress?*"

She held her ground solidly. "Aye, me lord."

"And precisely what would you propose I do with you, if you are not to be my . . ." A beguiled expression danced within his eyes as he let the word fall lightly into the air. *"Mistress?"*

Raven had not expected to have a choice of positions. Pondering his question for but a moment, her arms dropped to her sides. "If it please me lord, I would prefer to go back to me laundry and garden and me chamber below."

Leaping all at once from his chair, he towered over her. "It does not please me!" he thundered.

She felt as though she was on the brink of the scene she'd envisioned only a short while earlier, and as she stared into that black, ominous gaze, the lamb knew beyond doubt that the wolf could devour her were it his desire, and there wasn't a solitary thing she could do to prevent it.

Refusing to back down, Raven swallowed her fear and proudly lifted her chin. "I may not be a fine London lady, me lord, and ye may not think I be worth more than the life ye be intendin' fer me, but I will not be allowin' ye to take the only thing in the world that belongs to me!"

His expression retained its hard lines, but his tone softened. "And just what might that be, pray tell?"

"Why, me lord," she answered thoughtfully, her words now hushed to little more than a whisper, " 'tis me *self*."

The way her quivering lower lip protruded into a pout when she spoke . . . the flickering of those long sooty eyelashes above the large round eyes the shade of the violets she placed in the vases . . . the child-like naiveté about her, mixed with a passionate spirit and unerring pride. It all brought Devan to the brink of tenderness toward the woman. But before his contemplation got the better of him, he shielded himself against her. He was not supposed to *feel* anything, nor would he permit himself to *feel*.

Perhaps a fitting lesson in deference was in order? Before the thought fully registered, he found himself pulling her tightly against him. *"I* am lord of this manor, and I claim ownership of anything or *anyone* within these walls. If it be my will to take you as my courtesan, then you will suffer my pleasure, and suffer it *gladly."*

"Lord Castlereagh, *please,"* she choked on the tears that now streamed freely down her porcelain cheeks.

Fear had replaced the fierce pride in her eyes. Her breasts rose and fell rapidly against his chest. Desire stirred. Her lips had tempted him too long, and Devan suddenly found his mouth pressed to hers.

Flattening her palms against his chest, she pushed hard against him in a valiant effort to emancipate herself from his arms. He held her closer, while pulling the cap from her head and freeing the raven tresses that had been hidden from him.

Drawing her nearer still, he grasped her hair within one hand and drew her head back, his tongue urging her lips to part. The struggle ended, her body resigned itself to his possession, and she opened to his kisses with a passion he had not expected.

It would have been easy to indulge in the ecstasy the encounter promised—that everything within him now longed for. But he summoned his control, pushed her away, and stormed across the room.

"If I wanted you as my mistress," he ground out, facing the wall so she could not witness his turmoil, "I would take you here and now. But *that* is not what I want from you." He reached over and rang the bell.

"Th-then what?" she asked, disbelief thick in her tone.

Mrs. Captain scurried into the drawing room. "My lord?"

Devan did not alter his gaze from the wall. "Mrs. Captain, you will accompany our guest to her suite now."

"Yes, my lord."

"You will allow her a choice of servants. She is to be bathed and served her supper within her chamber this evening, but I expect her dressed and ready to partake at my table first thing in the morning."

"Yes, my lord."

"And you will instantly make it known to my entire staff that from this moment on, this young woman is to be referred to only as *Miss* Raven. She is to be treated with the utmost respect and allowed whatever she desires."

"B-but, Lord Castlereagh!" the older woman stammered.

At last he turned on her, his face grim. "Am I speaking French, Mrs. Captain? Or are we of an understanding?"

The housekeeper nodded with a curtsy. "Come, *Miss* Raven."

The new title seemed as bitter as poison to Mrs. Captain's tongue, and as apparently displeased as the young woman was to be stolen from her life as a servant, the satisfaction that hinted upon her kiss-swollen lips did not go unnoticed by him. He stood motionless, watching as the housekeeper and Raven disappeared from the drawing room. Then, with a sigh, he threw himself into his chair.

What would he do with her now?

It seemed as though forever passed before darkness settled over Ireland. Ever since she quit his drawing room, Devan had tried to focus his thoughts on anything but the woman who now occupied the suite of chambers next to his, but to no avail.

He made his way up the winding staircase, intent on

31

seeking the salvation of slumber. Pausing before her door, it occurred to him that the maids had left her chamber some time ago. By now she was bathed and all traces of the servants' quarters had been replaced by the sweet scent of the rose water he had supplied to her room, and her flannel night rail replaced by the gossamer gown Tourish had found in his mother's trunk in the attic.

Envisioning Raven alone in her chamber, he recalled what it felt like to hold her in his arms and her passionate response to his kiss.

Hastening down the corridor, he threw open the door to his suite, closed it fast behind him and ignored the door adjoining her rooms to his as he threw himself onto his bed. Of course he would not visit Raven this night nor any other night. Her sole purpose and use to him was to put an end, or at least a reason, to the peculiar dreams he'd had since their first encounter. *Nothing more.* The last thing he needed—or wanted—was an entanglement with the seductive Irish hellcat.

Sleep was elusive, and so he simply stared into the flame of the candle on the table beside his bed, contemplating the mystery of Raven. The key, he decided, would be to uncover her past. Though he'd spent the better part of his childhood in Ireland, he was convinced now he had never truly known her, for Raven was not the sort of woman a man forgot. Yet every time he gazed into her eyes, he felt as though he'd somehow always known her.

Could this feeling of familiarity, the strange dreams, and even the desire that still stirred within him be merely the result of her uncanny resemblance to Katherine? *No,* he thought, pushing back the sudden vision of Katherine, as she appeared that night at Dakshire, and with it, the familiar dull ache. Though it would certainly be a simple enough explanation, there was nothing simple about what he felt toward Raven, and these feelings were for her alone.

All at once he heard the creak of a door. Leaping to his feet, he flung open his door and peered down the corridor, catching but a glimpse of Raven, fully dressed, a shawl draped loosely over her shoulders, before she disappeared down the stairs.

His first instinct was to bellow a command forceful enough to bring her to a dead halt. But he quickly decided against it and held back a few moments before following her out the servants' doorway.

As he stepped outside, he caught sight of her silhouette moving hurriedly into the stables. But just as he approached, a great, shadowed form bounded through the gate. Devan dove out of its path, for had he not, his own steed would have run him down.

Racing into the stable, Devan caught hold of the first horse he came to and hoisted himself on to his back, praying that after all the years of sitting in an English riding saddle, he could stay atop the beast without one. Grasping the mane for dear life, he jabbed his boot heels firmly into his mount's sides. The horse reared, almost unseating him, and then leaped to the chase.

They raced along the road that led to Dublin, the chill of the night air piercing his skin and stinging his eyes. What did Dublin at this hour hold for the woman who claimed no family nor memory to speak of?

At length the answer came, as the sound of fiddles and pipes rose through the night and Raven turned the red toward the pier. Knowing now her destination, Devan guided the blood into the shelter of the trees, then made the rest of his journey on foot.

The music grew louder. A great fire threw an orange and

red glow about the harbor. Devan stepped back into the shadows, lurking just beyond the light. At the far side of the circle stood Raven in a dress of sky blue muslin that seemed out of place amidst the drab tones of the garments worn by the peasantry. Her long sable curls were invisible against the night, except when she happened to move, just so, and the locks reflected the hues of the fire.

Raven did not dance with the others, but a smile eased across her lips and a particular gleam sparkled in her eyes as the storytelling began; the folklore of the Irish he'd heard from the servants as a child. When the tales of faeries and magic were over, the dancing began again. But the music, for Devan, was the sweetness of Raven's laughter that rose quite beautifully to his ears.

He watched uneasily as one of the men approached her, and felt a particular satisfaction when she turned him away. Apparently, he was not the first who'd failed to win her favor, for his friends received him back into their circle with laughter and jeers. And Devan listened as each, in turn, related his moment of rejection by the lovely *Mairéad*.

CHAPTER THREE

Raven lay upon her feather mattress, peeking from behind the sheer gauze of her canopy, out the window as morning sneaked over the hills beneath the pink and orange sky, while sparrows and nightingales sang praises to her glorious appearance.

She'd awakened long before the songbirds or the sun, jolted from a restless slumber by the sound of *his* door. Certain he would come for her, she slipped a brass candlestick beneath the dusty rose satin coverlet, prepared to render him unconscious and bloody the moment he touched her. But all that came was the quiet thud of his door closing again, and, to her great relief, not another sound was heard until the maids began their pre-dawn bustle through the corridors.

Letting go the gauze curtain, Raven yawned and stretched her arms over her head. Suddenly, the remembrance of a dream flashed.

The dreams had haunted her ever since the day she first opened her eyes at Dahlingham. In the beginning, they'd been hazy, merely images—roses and a woman with hair of fiery red.

Last night she'd dreamed of the quay by the sea. The woman from every dream was there, in the midst of a small assemblage of town folk, who danced and sang around a great fire. And the blaze-tressed woman with the emerald green eyes was at last given a name—*Mairéad.*

Raven, at one time, had hoped this woman was somehow the link to her past, for she felt everything the flame-haired woman felt, whether joy or sorrow, as intensely as though the feelings were her own. But after so many weeks of visions, she'd come to doubt they were little more than her mind, blank as it was, creating something to fill it.

A soft knock at the door pulled Raven from her thoughts. She reached for the candlestick that still lay beneath the sheets. "Who is it?"

"It is I, Collette."

Thrusting aside the white gauze curtain, she slid from her bed and rushed to unlock her chamber door. "Come in! Come in!" she whispered, throwing her arms around the maid's neck. Then, peering down the corridor, she yanked her inside and secured the door fast behind them. "Oh, it feels like forever since last I saw ye!" She hugged Collette again, but felt her stiffen. "What be the matter with ye? Are ye ill, love?" Raven's brow furrowed and she placed the back of her hand to Collette's forehead to check for fever.

Looking timidly to the floor, the maid shifted her stance. "Maime says you requested my service."

"So now *mo chara* can't look me in the eye? Or return me embrace?"

"It would not be proper, Miss Raven," she reasoned softly.

"Ach! *Miss* Raven, 'tis it?"

Collette nodded.

"So he moves me into this grand chamber," she said, flipping her hand dramatically through the air, "and now ye be thinkin' I be too high and mighty fer the likes of ye?"

Another nod.

Raven mulled the situation over. This would not do. She

would not lose the only friend she had in the world over such nonsense. "Collette?"

"Yes, ma'am?"

"Look at me."

The woman slowly lifted her head until she stood eye to eye with her new mistress.

"I order ye," she commanded, tapping her foot and shaking her finger in the maid's direction, "to call me by the name ye gave me when we are alone. In this room, regardless of what his lordship says, I am not *miss* nor *ma'am*, do ye understand?"

"Yes, Mi—*Raven*," Collette grinned.

"And ye will be speakin' freely to me when we be alone. I did not have ye brought up here so ye could shun me. Now greet me the way ye been greetin' me every morn since we met, or it's back to the scullery wi' ye!"

The two hugged and fell, laughing uncontrollably, onto the bed like children, until at last they lay flat on their backs, gasping for air.

"Is it bad here?" Collette asked, her expression suddenly staid.

"What would ye be meanin'? 'Tis a far cry from the space I had below, to be sure."

Collette propped herself up on her elbow and stared down. "No . . . I mean . . . with *him*."

At that, Raven sat up as well. "I haven't seen hide nor hair of him since yer maime brought me in here." Her brows knitted together, and she scraped her teeth across her lower lip as she pondered her circumstance herself. Then she confided, "He says 'tis not mistressin' he'd be wantin' of me."

"So he hasn't *touched* you?"

Judging by Collette's stunned expression, she gathered

the whole household was under the impression that the marquess had ruined her by now.

"Nay, and he won't be, I tell ye." Retrieving the candlestick from beneath the covers, she waved it in front of Collette with a giggle.

"Lord, girl, then what is he bringing you up here for?"

"I don't know. But he says I can have whatever I be desirin' and 'tis sure 'twill be time away from him. Should be no time till I be back workin' alongside ye."

Just then the heavy thud of footfalls sounded in the corridor, and Raven tensed when they paused in front of her door. Both she and Collette sat silent, anxiously glancing from each other to the door and then back, until finally they heard him continue on his way.

"It is time to get you dressed. My orders are that you are to be at his table, and we're going to have to hurry you along so he won't be put in a mood for the waiting." Collette moved quickly across the floor. "Here," she exclaimed triumphantly, pulling a dress of light chintz adorned with dainty blue flowers from the wardrobe. "It will be a grand appearance you will make, Raven."

Collette made an absolute production out of the dressing, first helping her into the shift, then holding the dress while Raven stepped into it, and at last the stockings and slippers. Then she sat Raven down, took up the brush, and smoothed the unruly ringlets into soft waves that fell loosely over her shoulders and down her back. With an expert rounding of her wrist she had the long tresses pulled up at the sides, and quickly secured her artistry with two combs. As a final touch, she brought down a few carefully selected curls to frame Raven's face.

"Well," she prompted with a pleased sigh, "have a look at yourself."

Rising from the dressing chair, Raven walked to the mirror. She was even more a stranger to herself now than she had been the first time she had gazed into a mirror after awakening at Dahlingham. "Ah, Collette, 'tis a miracle ye worked on me," she breathed, turning to the side to study her reflection.

The white chintz, unlike the gray uniform dresses she'd worn until that day, fit snugly to her body, revealing a graceful, womanly figure, and the low scoop of the neckline, trimmed in delicate white lace, though reasonably modest, revealed the slight swell of her bosom.

"If ever I saw anyone who looked like they should be a grand lady, it's you, Raven," Collette said wistfully, making a final adjustment.

"I was beginning to wonder if you were coming," Lord Castlereagh grumbled, as he ran his finger beneath his collar and looked up when she entered the dining room.

"Forgive me, me lord." Raven took the chair Tourish held for her at the opposite end of the long mahogany table. "I won't be late again."

"See that you are not." Turning to the butler he nodded, and Tourish disappeared through the doorway that led to the kitchen. Devan cleared his throat. "May I inquire as to your night? Did you sleep well?"

" 'Twas a long night, me lord, and sleep was scarce."

"Was it now? And why might that be, Miss Raven?"

Headsley entered the room with his silver tray. Holding up one finger, Lord Castlereagh indicated the conversation was to cease momentarily. The footman placed an elegant china plate of eggs and sausages with warm toast and jam, then tea before each of them, before standing at attention against the wall.

"Is the food satisfactory?"

Raven stared at her plate in wide-eyed awe. "Aye, me lord, 'tis much more to me tastes than lumpy gruel," she admitted, wrinkling her nose at the thought of the thick white stuff she'd eaten every morning until this.

He laughed out loud at the face she made and rubbed his chin. "Now, back to your restless night. I am certain I heard you leave your chamber. Did you walk the grounds?"

"Nay, I did not leave me room at all last night. Must be ye was dreamin'," she said, spreading strawberry jam thickly over the toast. She bit into her bread and chewed self-consciously while he eyed her.

"Then what could possibly have been responsible for your lack of sleep?"

Putting the toast back to her plate, she lowered her gaze and said quietly, "I dare say 'twas ye, me lord."

"Oh!" he roared, breaking into a fit of scratching down the sleeve of his shirt, from his shoulder to his wrist. "So it is *I* who am to blame? How so?"

Dropping her fork to her plate, she folded her hands in her lap, where their nervous wringing was concealed beneath the table. "Do ye really want me to be answerin' that?" she asked, glancing apprehensively at the footman.

Indicating Headsley, the marquess waved his hand into the air dismissively. Once the servant quit the room, Devan returned his attention to her. "Do tell."

"Well . . ."

"Yes?"

"Ye still have not told me why ye've brought me up. Ye won't let me work fer me keep. Me lord, 'tis no sense ye be makin'. I be sore afraid ye may be losin' yer wit, and 'twas thinkin' ye might be a-changin' yer mind and thinkin' ye can take me as yer mistress after all."

Lord Castlereagh's left brow arched mischievously. "So . . ." The very devil's grin danced across his fine mouth and danger flickered in his dark gaze. "If I had come to your room last night, what would you have done?"

With such a forthright question put before her, her response came equally blunt. "Why, me lord, I'd have killed ye."

The odd marquess burst into roaring laughter. "Miss Raven, rest assured, your virtue is safe within my house. I will not knock upon your chamber door . . ." His laughter ceased, and he placed his elbows on the table, leaned in her direction, and then, in a hushed voice added, "Unless, of course, you invite me."

His bold gaze and the glimmer in his eyes made her cheeks flare hotly. Then his vile grin grew even more so when he recognized her discomfort.

Her throat constricted and caught her breath, making a reply nearly impossible. But she refused to let him gain the edge. It was time to know, once and for all, her purpose. "Then, if 'tis not me favors ye be wishin', 'tis truly a kindness ye pay me, and it makes less sense than the other. Ye owe me nothin'."

The marquess brushed his mouth carelessly with his white linen napkin, then threw it atop his empty plate and leaned back in his chair. "You come to Dahlingham on the verge of death. You do not recall so much as your name. For me to take you in as a servant, I am placing my own reputation in peril. For all I know, you are the daughter of an earl or the wife of a nobleman, and it is my responsibility to see that you are treated as such until we can find your people."

"And ye be expectin' nothin' else?"

"On my honor . . . except that if you remember anything—*anything at all* of your past—I am to be the first one you confide in. Are we in agreement?"

"Yes, me lord. That much I can do fer ye."

Lord Castlereagh smiled. But the smile faded when he gritted his teeth and scratched furiously across his chest.

Realizing the marquess now wore the shirt that had been hung to dry without a thorough rinsing, she asked innocently, "Is somethin' troubling ye, me lord?"

His gaze locked on hers and he studied her intently. "Nothing a change in attire won't cure, I suspect," he answered, raising a suspicious brow.

Clearing her throat, she masked her grin with her hand.

"Or might I suffer the same affliction regardless of which shirt I choose?"

"Lord Castlereagh?"

"Do you suppose it is possible that someone thought to make all my shirts unwearable?" he asked, narrowing his eyes.

"Why, Lord Castlereagh, I couldn't say. Though I believe no one would . . ." She gritted her teeth in an effort to refrain from laughing out loud as he was thrown into another fit of scratching around his collar and then down his arm. Forcing her countenance to remain straight, she met his stare squarely. "Surely no one could be so heartless, me lord."

"Surely," he muttered, taking to his feet all at once. He then hastily excused himself from the table, leaving her alone in the dining room to finish her meal. No sooner had she taken her last bite from her plate, Mrs. Captain bustled into the room, looking substantially less haughty than Raven had ever witnessed her.

"Miss Raven, the marquess has instructed me to take you to the library for your lessons while he is away."

"Lessons?" she asked, rising from her seat.

"It appears he is having some difficulty understanding that mucky brogue of yours, and he has left it up to me to tame it."

Laughing, she shook her head in astonishment. "First he dresses me like a lady, and now he thinks he can teach me to speak like one. 'Tis a grand thought he be havin', but I don't think I can be speakin' the way he and ye be speakin', Mrs. Captain."

The woman rolled her eyes with a loud sigh, and then taking Raven swiftly by the arm, led her from the dining room.

The entire morning was spent in the great library. The first thing the housekeeper did was hand her *Hamlet*. To Mrs. Captain's apparent delight, Raven could not only read, but read well. She was instructed to recite the entire first act aloud, while Mrs. Captain corrected her inflection as she went along.

In all the time she'd lived at Dahlingham, it never occurred to her to attempt to mimic the precise English some of the servants were so adept at. But she soon found the pronunciation was not all that difficult to master, although she had to concentrate on each word she spoke or she would inevitably slip back into the unschooled Irish brogue.

When their afternoon fare was brought in, Mrs. Captain evidently thought the break in the lessons the perfect opportunity to satisfy her curiosity. "Miss Raven, may I be so forward as to ask . . . ?"

"Yes, Mrs. Captain, ye—*you* may ask," she replied, minding each syllable.

The older woman gave a slight nod and an acknowledging smile for Raven's accomplishment. "I am not quite sure how to broach such a delicate subject." The dilemma appeared to cause the housekeeper a great deal of chagrin, apparent by the thousand expressions that twisted her face as she tried to find words appropriate.

"What you want to know is whether Lord Castlereagh had his way with me?" Raven offered candidly.

"W-well, uh, yes, f-frankly," she sputtered.

"He did *not*." She wanted to chuckle at the shocked countenance that came as a result of her confession, but thought better of it, and went on to explain. "He says he cannot keep me as a servant until he knows who my people are, and that he wants no more of me than to help me regain my memory."

"Is that so? *Hmmm* . . ." she hummed thoughtfully, resting her elbows on top of her abundant bosom while tapping her finger gingerly to the side of her nose. "May I offer a bit of advice?"

"I welcome your advice."

"I practically raised Devan Castlereagh from the cradle, and I love him as I would my own son. I can still picture him playing around my feet while I tended to the business of his father, when he was lord of this manor. But love him or not, the simple truth is, *men lie*. It may well be that he intends to aid you in recovering your past, but you must remain cautious. I have not noticed even a hint of vanity in you, my dear, but you must realize you possess a natural beauty that was apparent even beneath the uniform and the dirt of your duties. Now he has you clothed in fine dresses, bathed in the scent of flowers, and your hair unveiled. I dare say you might be more than a man with even the most honorable of intentions can resist."

She filled her teacup once more and took a calming sip. "It is my speculation that whatever tragedy befell you also

44

befell your family. I'm sorry to say, it is doubtful you will ever find them, even if you do regain your memory, and even more doubtful that you were born or married into a family of means. *However,*" she stressed, as she popped a biscuit into her mouth, "you have been given something that I have never seen granted a common Dubliner, and that is the opportunity to make something of yourself in society."

"What are you saying, Mrs. Captain?" Raven asked, unsure whether it was the muffling caused by the mouthful of sweets, or some hidden meaning in the housekeeper's words. Either way, she wasn't following the drift of the conversation.

"You have the looks, and it seems you are taking to the speech better than I would have expected. With my instruction, you shall be ready to stand on your own against any lady in London at the ball."

"The ball?"

"Yes, my dear, and some of the most eligible young lords and dukes of England will be in attendance. This is your opportunity to escape the slums you probably came from and make a life for yourself. But you must act the part, and never give the marquess any notion that he could spoil it for you. You must keep your distance from him, or risk losing any hope you may have of winning the heart of any other gentleman."

"I still do not follow."

"You test my patience, girl." In exasperation, she wiped the crumbs from the corner of her mouth. "Must I come right out and say it? Oh, I suppose I must!" Mrs. Captain sighed, and rushed on. "Lord Castlereagh has a certain reputation and it is safe to say, being that he is almost thirty and has not shown any sign yet of a willingness to enter into a contract of marriage, that what is said about him is true. It is rumored that many a young woman has lost her maidenhead to the dashing Marquess of Castlereagh, and if you are not careful, you may just be next."

Raven gasped and then giggled at the housekeeper's forthright choice of words.

"A born lady can get past that little . . . *inconvenience*, for she has her father's title and sizable dowry to make up for anything else she may lack. But you, my dear, have naught to offer a young man but the reward of your virtue. So do not allow him to ruin your chances with the others who are much more apt to marry you. You brought my daughter up a station in life, child, but if you were to fall out of the marquess's good graces, she would be forced to return to her previous position. I will turn you into the finest lady Dublin has ever seen. Even the English ladies who attend the ball at Dahlingham will have nothing over you by the time I'm done and you may very well win yourself a title. Of course, I am certain you would see that Collette goes with you."

Gradually, understanding set in. "Ah, so you will teach me to be a real lady, and in kind, should I happen to marry well, I am to take my dearest friend in the world along."

"That is correct. And the ball is the perfect opportunity."

Raven lifted her teacup to Mrs. Captain with a bargaining smile. It was ludicrous to think the old woman's scheme could work, but less than twenty-four hours earlier she had been washing Lord Castlereagh's shirts, and Mrs. Captain was her most feared opponent. My, how things could change in the space of a day! At this rate, anything was possible.

"Well then, my good woman, it is time we resumed our lessons," Raven quipped in her best impersonation of an English accent, bringing a light-hearted snort from her tutor.

CHAPTER FOUR

Devan peered up from his book when Raven appeared at the entrance of the drawing room.

"Mr. Tourish said you wished to see me?"

"Indeed." Standing, he swept his arm out. "Come in. I was beginning to wonder if you would ever emerge."

"And I, Lord Castlereagh, had begun to wonder the same," she replied, walking toward him. "Mrs. Captain had supper served in the library."

"So I understand. Do sit down." He motioned toward the chaise.

She smiled—the sort of smile that seemed to brighten the room as though a host of lamps had been lit at once, he thought as she moved past him.

"It appears your lessons are going well, Miss Raven. I am impressed by your ability to have taken to them so quickly," he said, noting the precise English in her cadence, then regaining his seat in the chair after Raven took her place on the chaise.

"Thank you, my lord."

Closing his book, he eased back, striking a more casual pose. "All is well, I assume?"

He watched her intently, mesmerized by her every movement. There was a particular grace about her that one would not expect from a commoner. The way she held her head, chin up, shoulders squared, she appeared nothing less than regal.

He'd not seen her since the morning in the dining room, and throughout the day he'd caught his thoughts drifting from the task at hand to her. Mostly, he found himself attempting to make sense of her ride into Dublin the night before. Why had she denied it?

"My lord, I have most enjoyed Mrs. Captain's tutoring. Though . . ."

"Though?"

She grinned sheepishly. "I must say the experience has left me rather spent."

Laughing aloud, he threw his book to the table beside him. "Our Mrs. Captain can be a somewhat intense woman, especially when carrying out my orders. She takes her role quite seriously." Stroking his chin thoughtfully, he added, "I will see to it that your time with Mrs. Captain is broken up by other less . . . *um* . . . *taxing* activities."

"I look forward to it, my lord."

There was so much he longed to ask—so many questions to be answered. But tonight he did not wish to challenge her. He was in no mood to indulge in the shouting that had taken place when last they occupied this room together, and he had to admit he rather enjoyed this easy conversation between them, so he decided to keep it that way—light, casual.

"Tell me, Miss Raven, what do you think of Dahlingham?"

"Your estate is quite lovely."

"And you have acquired a friendship of sorts with Collette?" he asked, crossing his legs and propping his elbow on the arm of the chair.

"Ah, sweet Collette. She is the kindest, warmest person I have come to know."

"She is a wonderful young woman, and I am quite

thankful to have both she and her mother."

"My lord," she ventured hesitantly, her eyes shifting from his as she nervously shook the wrinkles from her skirt, "if it would not be too much to ask . . ."

"You may ask anything," he urged, gaining his feet and walking to the liquor cupboard. He poured another glass of brandy. "Please, continue."

"It's just that I feel guilty that I should be wearing such beautiful new dresses like those you have given me, while Collette is left to wear the same old gray dresses she always has. And considering your distaste for the color—"

"Done!"

"Lord Castlereagh?"

Making his way back to his armchair, he grinned. "I shall arrange for dresses to be delivered for Collette at the same time the rest of your wardrobe is brought. Does that fare well?"

"Oh, it does!" she exclaimed, clasping her hands together.

"And if there is anything else that Collette is in need of, you have only to ask." Devan sipped his brandy. "What of you? Is there anything more you need to make your stay at Dahlingham more comfortable?"

"Oh, no! 'Tis nothin I be—" She brought her hand to her mouth and blushed, realizing her slip of tongue. "There is nothing I am in need of at this time, Lord Castlereagh. You have been far too generous as it is. I do not know how I shall ever repay you."

"Nonsense. It shall be payment enough if I am able to return you to your family safely. By chance . . ." He sat forward, resting his elbows on his knees, "Has anything come to you? Any memory at all?"

"There have been none," she said, rising and moving quickly across the room where she pretended to contemplate the portraits that lined the wall. "I fear I may only disappoint you."

How could she not fall short of his expectations? What if she were never to remember anything? Certainly he would grow tired of having a *guest* under foot at every turn, and eventually, he would long to cast her into the streets where she more than likely belonged.

Raven heard the sound of the glass being set to the table where his forgotten book rested. "How could you possibly disappoint me?" he queried softly, walking nearer.

The hair on the back of her neck tingled as the marquess approached. As he drew closer, she was filled with an overwhelming desire to flee.

His hand fell upon her shoulder. "Raven," he murmured.

She drew in a swift breath and spun to face him. "Lord Castlereagh, please."

"What is it?"

"I—I do not know." The words caught in her throat. She stared into the black, endless depths of his eyes that threatened to steal her soul. She backed away from his scorching touch.

"Raven . . ." He took her hand, far too tenderly, and cradled it within his. "You shall not disappoint me, I assure you."

"But there is nothing in this head of mine, save strange visions of people that are unfamiliar in every respect, and in the weeks I have resided at Dahlingham, not a solitary memory has occurred. I may be condemned to never regain my life, Lord Castlereagh, whatever it may have been."

With her confession, the warmth in his eyes quickly vanished, replaced by something far cooler. "That will not be the circumstance, Raven, for you *must* recollect from whence you came, who you are. You must, and you *will.*

Believe it as strongly as I believe it," he stated firmly, leaving her to feel that, somehow, he had more to lose than she if she did not remember.

Dropping her hand, he spun on his heel and made his way to the bottle of brandy, where he filled a new glass. Raven stood silent, helplessly transfixed on the marquess, his very presence somehow hypnotic—eerily so.

Then, without warning, he faced her. His countenance transformed, his expression now hard and set, his lips drawn tight into a dark scowl. Apprehension pulsed in time to the frantic beating of her heart. A little voice inside cried out to her to run, as far and as fast as her legs would carry her, but it was as though her feet were chained, and she could not move.

"Miss Raven," his dry, blunt tone cut through her like a dull sword, "it is said the Irish meet at the harbor after nightfall and dance and sing. Perhaps this is where you might find your people? You are welcome to take my horse."

"M—my lord, 'tis not the hour for a woman alone to travel the distance into Dublin for any reason." Raven straightened her back and lifted her chin.

Devan grinned, drank the rest of the brandy remaining in his glass. "Of course, you are correct, Miss Raven. No *lady* should travel alone in the darkness and consort with ale-filled farmers around a fire." He drew his hand through his hair and fell back into his chair. Then reaching for his book, he opened it, and at last removed his aggravated glare, placing his concentration on the pages within his hand. Without so much as another glance in her direction, he abruptly concluded their conversation. "You have no reason to stand there gawking. Be gone."

For the space of several heartbeats, Raven stood staring

at the man, unable to fathom what she'd done to deserve such a stern dismissal. Then she told herself she shouldn't care one way or the other.

She swung around, prepared to quit the room, but paused, drawing a deep breath, realizing that, though it was beyond reason, she did care.

Devan heard the rustle of her skirts, and the soft sound of her feet scurrying from the drawing room, then up the staircase. He fought the temptation to run after her and demand an explanation for her ride into Dublin the previous night, just as he had fought the lure to take her in his arms and kiss away her tears only moments before.

Brandy in hand, he remained in his chair until he'd finished every drop in the bottle, unable to comprehend a solitary word on the page, his thoughts consumed by Raven.

A soft rap at her window startled her from her dozing. Mairéad squinted in the darkness and made out a shadowed figure behind the shutters. The smile spread quickly across her face. "Séamus!" she whispered, leaping from her straw mattress, bounding toward the window and flinging the shutters open excitedly. "I was about to give up all hope of seein' ye tonight!"

He reached in and pulled her toward him, kissing her passionately. "Never doubt me, my love. Are you ready?"

"Is sea!" she exclaimed quietly, taking his hand and climbing through the open window and out onto the ground.

Already the white mare stood waiting next to his steed, ready to carry her away into the night with Séamus. Her horse snorted excitedly when she saw Mairéad.

"We should be hurrying, ye know. 'Tis late already."

"I know," he said, adjusting the cap atop his silken chestnut hair. "Dah was ramblin' on about the ball again. I had no

choice but to listen until he finally retired."

Hurt swept through her usually merry eyes. "When are ye goin' to tell him, Séamus?"

Drawing her into his embrace, he held her tight. "Look at me, Mairéad," he implored softly, gently cupping her chin in his hand and guiding her eyes to his. "As soon as this ball is over, I will tell my father everything. But you know I have been ex-pected to marry Áine from the time we were children, and would have, had fate not brought you to me. Just a while longer. Then, when the time is right, even if I must give up everything, the whole world shall know of my love for you." Séamus took hold of her shoulders and held her out where he was able to regard her clearly. "Dah has enough on his mind right now, and this may well be the last Ó Lionáird ball for years to come. Please . . . be patient, love. Our time will come. You have my word."

Mairéad's lower lip trembled and she fell into his arms again, snuggling against his chest. " 'Táim sorry if 'tis selfish o' me, Séamus. But me heart is fearful that the longer we wait, the better the chance of fate steppin' in and tearin' us apart."

He kissed the top of her head, nuzzled his face in the warmth of her fiery mane. News of his plans to wed this girl from Dublin, a commoner with no dowry, no family of name, would most as-suredly send his father into one of his rages. His entire life, from his London education to his father's training him to maintain the family estates, had all been to ready Séamus for his inheri-tance. An Ó Lionáird and Ó Seachnasaigh union would bring the two wealthiest clans in all of Ireland together, thus securing a future for his heirs that even the English king would envy.

But what good was any of it without Mairéad? Her fragile beauty, the mass of delicate flame curls that framed her perfect features, the eyes greener than the greens of Eire that captured his soul, and her passionate spirit. He knew, no matter what the cost, he could not live without her.

"There is nothing under the heavens that could ever tear me away from you. I am yours for all eternity."

With a forced smile, she gazed into his reassuring blue eyes. *"I shall hold ye to that vow Séamus Ó Lionáird. And if ye break yer vow, I shall place a curse upon yer head that the faeries themselves would covet."*

Séamus pecked her cheek playfully. *"And what would that be, oh, sorceress?"*

She became solemn again and backed out of his grasp. The ice suddenly evident in her eyes let him know she had not spoken in jest. There was no question in his mind that she would curse him or bargain with the faeries to do the deed. She had given her heart to him, and had waited the better part of a year for him to disavow the arrangement with Áine, forced to be his secret, their love cloaked in the night, hidden in the shadows of the pier.

Séamus vowed to himself that one day he would make up for all she had suffered on his account. One day he would walk with her arm in arm, through the streets of Dublin, so all would know she was his lady.

"I have been practicing that jig you taught me," he said at last, tenderly lifting a tear from her cheek with the pad of his thumb.

She sniffled and he saw a hint of a smile twitch her pouty lips. *"Ye have?"*

"Aye. No more tears?"

She nodded.

"Tonight we dance, Mairéad." He placed his hands around her waist and lifted her atop her horse . . .

CHAPTER FIVE

After three days of being cooped up inside the stone walls of Dahlingham, Raven was near madness. So when Tourish interrupted Mrs. Captain's lessons and informed her the Marquess of Castlereagh had requested her presence on the lawn, she leaped at the chance to get out, even if it meant spending time in the company of the brooding marquess.

As they approached, Lord Castlereagh and another man stood talking. Crossing her fingers behind her back, Raven made a wish that her host was in a better temperament than he had been the last two days.

"Miss Raven, my lord."

The marquess whirled around and greeted her with a jaunty smile. She quickly told herself she'd only imagined that her heart had skipped a beat, and that she was imagining the caress of his full and brazen gaze. But her cheeks flamed, just the same.

"Raven!" Hurrying to her side, he lifted her hand while bowing, and brought it to his mouth, lingering a moment before rising. "Victor."

The other man joined them, dressed in a red and gold riding habit and polished black riding boots. Sweeping his black cap from his sandy head of unruly curls, he bent into a deep, exaggerated bow. "Miss Raven, I have heard so much about you!" He straightened and smiled broadly. "I am the Duke of Brookshire, one of Castlereagh's oldest friends. It appears the one thing he failed to mention was just how beautiful his guest truly is."

"Enough, Brookshire," Lord Castlereagh snapped, wrapping his hand possessively around Raven's and leading her toward the chairs. Then, facing her, the tension eased from his countenance and the smile returned. "Shall we take tea?"

Uncertain what to make of the marquess's odd behavior, Raven warily lowered herself slowly into the chair he'd indicated for her without a word. All at once, the duke scooted into the seat beside her. Slanting Brookshire a cool glare, Devan grudgingly took the only chair that remained on the other side of the duke.

"So, Miss Raven," the duke ventured, absently taking his cup from Tourish, "I must admit to being quite fascinated by your tale. You truly cannot recall anything from before the time you came to Dahlingham?"

She squirmed in her seat, resenting the fact that Devan seemed to have made her something of a conversation piece. "Yes, Your Grace," she replied. Then, determined to change the topic from herself, rather than give the bored peers anything more to gossip about, she put on her new dialect, articulating each word to perfection. "You are an accomplished horseman, I take it, Your Grace?"

Brookshire leaned closer, nodding his head eagerly. "Indeed, Miss Raven. And you? Do you ride?"

The realization that she had just brought the subject back to herself hit her with the weight of a stone. "Honestly, I do not know," she conceded with a sigh.

"My, my, Miss Raven. Are you certain you do not know?"

Raven's gaze rose and collided with the marquess's, stunned by the accusation evident in his taunting voice. "I do not."

"I would have wagered half my holdings that you

knew how to ride," he countered.

She smiled nervously at the duke and then shot a glower back to Devan. "It would have been a lost wager, my lord, so be grateful the opportunity did not present itself."

His expression remained smug, as though enjoying a secret she and the duke did not share. "I could have sworn I saw you riding."

"You are mistaken," she said softly, fighting to retain the curse that troubled her tongue. "What I did before my misfortune, I do not know. But I am clear that I have never been in your stable, let alone ridden a horse, in all the time I have been at Dahlingham."

"Well," interjected Brookshire, before Castlereagh could say more, "when you're prepared to learn, I would be honored to teach you."

"Thank you, Your Grace." Raven flashed a grateful smile at the duke for his gallant rescue, earning her a discreet wink in return.

Without a word, the Marquess of Castlereagh lifted himself from his chair, and marched angrily toward the house.

"Do not mind him," Brookshire declared cheerfully. "He's been strange ever since returning from London. Temperamental, he is. But who can blame him, with the woman dying and all?"

"Woman?"

"He did not tell you?"

Raven shook her head, and as the marquess disappeared inside Dahlingham, she turned to face the duke.

"It is my understanding he had finally found the woman he wanted to marry. It was one of those love at first sight sort of things—met her the very night she died. Bloke wouldn't tell me any more than that, except . . ."

"What?"

"Except that you could be her *twin*. He said the first time he laid eyes on you, he could have sworn you were her ghost. Are you?" he teased, leaning closer with a gentle nudge.

"Of course not. I may have lost me—*my* memory, but I am positive I am not a ghost!" she laughed.

"Splendid! Would be damn terrible for me to be falling in love with an apparition!"

Raven giggled behind her hand.

Gently laying hold of her wrist, he brought her hand away from her face. "Do not hide your beautiful smile."

The Duke of Brookshire's slate colored eyes were as merry as his laughter. Such a contrast he was to the Marquess of Castlereagh. He entertained Raven with humorous stories about his adventures with Devan, and for a while, managed to make the intense marquess seem a trifle more human.

Perhaps his foul moods were the result of the death of the woman in London, rather than her own inadequacies. But still, there had been no reason to humiliate her so in front of Brookshire, and when Tourish returned, announcing dinner, Raven jumped at the opportunity to invite the duke to stay on. His good nature and agreeable conversation would surely make the time in the marquess's presence pass more pleasantly, and she welcomed the diversion.

Brookshire accepted the invitation readily, but the glower on Lord Castlereagh's face when Victor accompanied Raven to the dining room was a clear sign he was not even half as pleased with the Duke's acceptance. Another excuse to be surly, she was certain.

Throughout dinner, the duke's interest in her was apparent, with his not-so-very-subtle flirtations and rapt attentions. Could he be the man Mrs. Captain had spoken of? The one whose affection she could win, thereby securing herself, and Collette, a future?

Each compliment Brookshire paid her brought something resembling a grunt from Lord Castlereagh, and each smile in her direction, a sneer of sorts. If she continued to irritate her benefactor at every turn, as it seemed she did, she would soon find herself back in the servants' quarters or worse, and lost would be any hope whatsoever.

Brookshire's glance darted back and forth between Raven and the marquess. As though deciding it was time to lighten the mood and ease the tension in the room, he spoke up. "Did my friend tell you the story of old Arlington Coushite?"

"Not now," the marquess cautioned, his voice rising.

"Ah, come now, Castlereagh, it's the talk of the isle. Has probably spread to London as well!"

He turned again to Raven, and although she did not wish to further anger Lord Castlereagh, she gave Brookshire her attention, finding his story far more appealing than the other man's sullen countenance.

"Have you had the opportunity to make Lord Coushite's acquaintance?" he asked.

She shook her head.

"Wise of our Castlereagh. Old Arlington is well known for his excesses, Miss Raven. One night, a few months back, he'd had a bit too much of the spirits, and Castlereagh here had him in debt more than a thousand pounds."

"Brookshire!"

Without bothering to see the ominous frown that accompanied his name, the duke went on. "The sly old coot looked to Castlereagh, and slurred, 'One more hand. If you win, you get all that I own in Ireland. If I win, I owe you nothing, and you escort my daughter to your ball,' " Victor garbled, holding his glass in the air, in obvious imitation of Lord Coushite.

59

Devan's fist slammed down on the table. "Brookshire!"

The duke, so caught up in his own storytelling, did not bother to so much as glance at the man at the head of the table, and so did not see the menace in his eyes.

Determined the tale had to be told, he raised a quieting hand in Devan's direction. "Let me finish! Now, Lady Priscilla, Coushite's lovely daughter, has had her eye on Castlereagh for years. So we all know she put her father up to it. Coushite had the luck of the draw, and wound up with three queens! Probably had them up his sleeve, but not a one of us could prove it. Now, it's true, it would have been better to win Coushite's land, but Lady Priscilla will surely find a way to make the loss a little easier to swallow. She always does, doesn't she Castlereagh?"

Finally, the duke looked to the marquess, who stood abruptly, knocking his chair to the floor in the process. "*Enough,* Brookshire!"

The grin faded and Victor's face flamed. "But Castlereagh. . ."

"One more word out of you, Brookshire, and I swear, by God, friend or no friend, I will bloody you!"

The rest of the meal was eaten in silence, and it was evident, when the duke bid them farewell before dessert could be served, it was because he did not wish to tempt fate and incur the wrath of the Marquess of Castlereagh for tarrying any further beyond his welcome.

Dreading the idea of being alone with him, Raven let out a long, dramatic yawn. "Oh, dear, I am *so* tired. If you don't mind, I will retire to my chamber for the evening."

"I *do* mind," he retorted, rising from his seat. "I will be in the drawing room. I expect you to join me." He then left the room, giving her no opportunity to think up a more convincing excuse.

★ ★ ★ ★ ★

"Be seated," he grumbled when she entered the drawing room and took her place on the chaise opposite his armchair. "I see you have managed to take to all aspects of your lessons with Mrs. Captain quite effortlessly."

"I try, my lord."

"Yes, it appears you do." His dry voice was condescending, and she felt like a child who fell short of the expectations of an overbearing father. He walked to the cupboard and poured his brandy. "Would you care for a drink?"

"I would not."

Lord Castlereagh returned to his seat, leaned back, and sipped his brandy, studying her as if she were a curious riddle he could not decipher. She chose to acknowledge the stares of the portraits, which looked somewhat ghastly above the flicker of the lamps, but less intimidating by far than the dark countenance he wore. An eternity passed before he broke the silence.

"Are you finding your situation here . . . agreeable?"

Agreeable? That was not quite the phrase Raven would have used to describe her feelings regarding her present situation or her host. And he was certainly aware of her discomfiture, for he'd gone out of his way to make her feel it.

Inhaling deeply, she wondered again if he resented her resemblance to the lady in London, but decided that it was more likely he was merely a cruel and heartless man who took great satisfaction in her unease.

If only she could make a wish and disappear into thin air. She could not remember being born, so perhaps *not being* at all would not be such a great loss. But there was another part of her that wanted to lash out and curse him in every breath. The latter took control of her tongue before she could stop it.

61

"You're a mean one, you are!" she hissed.

"Why would you say that, Miss Raven?" he pushed boldly, leaning forward in the chair.

"I say it, for 'tis the truth. I did naught but happen upon yer stoop in me delirium. And believe me, had I me wits about me at the time, I'd a-found me a warmer stoop, to be sure!" Blinded by anger, Raven did not notice the gradual return of her brogue, and at that point could not have stopped herself, even had she wanted to. "But God rot yer soul, 'tisn't enough fer ye I work meself to the bone, doin' yer laundry and tendin' to yer garden." Raven soared to her feet and shook her finger vehemently at the marquess. "*Nay!* Ye decide I be brought up here, without ever consultin' me! Ye put me in yer fancy clothes," she continued, with a flip of her hand along her skirt, "and tell me to speak like ye, then ye set me down at every opportunity!"

Silently, she damned her trembling voice and the tears that came with her rage, and then damned the marquess, for he appeared utterly unmoved by her tirade. Turning, she stormed toward the doorway. Then she paused abruptly, spun on her heel and faced him once more.

Breathing deeply, she steadied her voice, this time careful to mind each word, every syllable. "You know I have nowhere to go, and it surely gives you great pleasure. Now, you have a choice, which is more than allotted me at any time since my misfortune of stumbling onto the hallowed grounds of Dahlingham. I am going to my chamber. You may either forcibly cast me into the street or you may allow me to remain for the night. If you decide to let me stay, then come morn, you may either cast me into the street, or you may keep to your bargain and I will keep to mine. The choice is yours."

In a violent swish of skirts, Raven left Devan, mouth

agape and speechless, and marched up the stairs to her bed-chamber.

The devil take her . . .

Devan emptied his glass. Pushing himself to his feet, he intended to go after her, shake the truth from her, get the answers she *owed* him. But the notion barely formed before he fell back into his chair with a helpless groan.

As if dreaming of her at night were not enough, she'd begun to invade his every waking thought as well. Brookshire's unexpected arrival that afternoon had provided Devan the excuse he'd needed to summon her to him to satisfy his need to look into her eyes, hear her voice. Brookshire's obvious interest in her had sparked his anger. But it was her blushes and smiles for Victor that nearly drove him to the brink.

Why? He had no cause to feel such flaming possessive-ness. Yet the flirtations between she and the duke had him reacting as though he were a spurned lover.

He'd managed to convince himself he felt nothing but anger for her deception and lies. And he'd ordered her to the drawing room, determined to at last have it out with Raven, demand the truth once and for all. But she'd turned on him fiercely, her wrath sparking in her eyes, trembling upon her lips. Suddenly Devan's anger was replaced by an undeniable desire to take her in his arms and finish what he'd started in that same room three days prior.

It was only the certainty that she'd have kept good on her promise to kill him that prevented him from acting on the longing that raged through him.

It made no sense, this gripping desire. Leaning his head back with a growl, Devan forced himself to remember his reason for bringing the woman close, and it was *not* to sat-isfy his lust.

He had to keep his head, focus on his purpose. *Get answers.*

Apparently there would be no easy answers with that one. If he pushed her, he harbored no doubt she would leave Dahlingham, just as she'd vowed. And that was one thing he would not allow.

He'd hoped the new clothes and lifestyle he'd handed her would bring about a gratitude that would render her co-operative. He almost laughed at the absurdity of the notion.

Mere dresses and trinkets would not be enough for a woman like Raven. She was going to force him into playing the role of the charming marquess, as well. *The old saying about flies and honey,* he thought.

Damn! What a constant contradiction she was; the face of an angel, the body of Aphrodite, and the tongue of a drunken Irishman . . .

Bloody hell! He'd never met anyone so infuriating . . . so seductive . . . so . . .

His jaw tensed as he slammed his fist down on the arm of his chair.

A nagging little voice told him the woman would be his end yet.

CHAPTER SIX

The sun blinked suddenly over the eastern horizon, filling Raven's room with light that beamed through the half opened draperies and stung her tired eyes, still bloodshot and burning from the salty tears shed during the night.

She'd practically dared the marquess to throw her out into the street. Worse yet, she'd let her anger get the better of her and lost control of her emotions and her tongue like a mere child.

She'd made a dreadful mistake. While he was impossible and stubborn and arrogant to the extreme, by the light of day it seemed a more tolerable choice than homelessness. But after the way she had lashed out at him in her pain and fury, she was certain there would be no alternative open to her now. Indeed, the Marquess of Castlereagh would surely have her escorted—none too gently—out his door the moment she stepped foot outside the haven of her chamber.

The door fell open with a quiet squeak of the hinges. Unwilling to face the inevitable, she closed her eyes tight and feigned sleep.

"Raven, are you awake?"

Bolting upright, she pushed the dusty rose satin and lace comforter to the side and peered through the canopy curtain. "Close the door! Quickly, Collette!"

With a skeptical glance, Collette pushed the door shut behind her. "What has you so unstrung, Raven?" she asked, moving to the wardrobe where she began shifting through the dresses.

"I did something appalling last night."

"So you told me."

"I fear he will ask me to leave Dahlingham. Oh, whatever shall I do?" Indulging in self-pity, Raven threw herself face down into her pillow and sobbed woefully.

Laughing lightly, Collette drew the curtain aside and sat next to her, stroking her disheveled tresses.

Astonished that she would make light of such a dire predicament, Raven met Collette's amused gaze. "Why would you be about laughin' when me very life is in peril, woman?"

"Aren't you being just a wee bit dramatic, dear?"

Raven scowled. "Under the circumstances, I don't think so."

"Well, I do. Now stop your weeping. Lord Castlereagh is already waiting for you in the dining room."

"I knew it! He's going to turn me out." She threw herself into her pillow once more.

Rolling her eyes, Collette sighed. "I overheard him telling Maime there were a dozen dresses being delivered for you, in the most fashionable designs, made of the finest cloths, and she was to see that every one suited you. I may be wrong, but I doubt he would dress you up to set you out."

Raising her head, Raven sniffled and wiped the tears from her face with her sleeve. "Are you certain he was talking about me?"

"Who else?"

"He did not seem angry?"

"Not in the least. But if you keep him waiting much longer, that may change," she teased, rising and taking full control of the situation.

66

★ ★ ★ ★ ★

The marquess stood the moment Raven entered the room, greeting her with a short bow and strained politeness. "Good morning, Miss Raven." He waited for Tourish to seat her before taking his chair once more.

"And to you, Lord Castlereagh," she responded timidly.

Devan stared at the woman across the table, whose lavender eyes drew him in and threatened to drown him in their mystery. Her glance darted away from his forthright gaze, and she pretended a sudden interest in the plate that was placed in front of her. Still, he could only stare, finding her remarkable to behold, in ways indescribable, resurrecting flashes of feelings and a desire like none he'd ever experienced before, save that one night at Dakshire.

Splendor of God, this was different than the night at Dakshire. What he'd felt for Katherine was an overwhelming urgency to make her his and his alone. With Raven there was a deep, nagging sensation that she was a part of his past that could not be put behind him, as well as a part of a future he could not avoid.

Against his will, this woman, with her every movement, every uttered word, was quickly wearing down the walls he needed to survive her.

Startled out of his thoughts by the clank of his plate against the table, Devan decided to be done with this unsettling situation once and for all. "Miss Raven, I would like to—" He paused self-consciously, tasting his tea. "*Ahem.* I would like to *apologize* for my . . . behavior yesterday," he offered.

At last her eyes moved to the disconcerting gaze of the man at the other end of the table. He seemed quite uneasy, clearly unaccustomed to making atonements and not at all enjoying this one. For a moment she almost pitied him.

But then thought better of it.

Still, if he was willing to put forth the effort, she would do the same. "No, my lord, it is I who should apologize. I . . ."

"Yes?"

"I should not have spoken so boldly."

"I acted inappropriately?"

"You are the lord of Dahlingham, and I am—"

"You are *what?*" He leaned forward, as if lessening the distance between them to only eleven feet, instead of twelve, might better his ability to hear.

Was he trying to be conversational or badgering her? The latter, of course, she surmised. "I honestly do not know what I am, Lord Castlereagh!" she exclaimed at last, in pure exasperation. "Would you be so kind as to clarify that for me?"

A dazzling grin emerged from the threat of a grimace. "You are my guest, Miss Raven. And as such, I expect you to feel free to express yourself, although your full-fledged outbursts are truly not necessary." The marquess leaned back in his chair, taking the opportunity to observe her reaction.

Raven pushed the food around her plate with her fork, then set it aside and challenged his stare. He hadn't honestly believed she intended to let the conversation end with such a comment, without first pleading her own defense, and it was merely a matter of waiting out the long seconds while she chose her words.

"My lord, while I agree wholeheartedly that I quite possibly overreacted to your mood of last eve, I must also confess that I find your constant set downs offensive and insulting. I may have lost my memory, but that does not make me oblivious to the fact that you hold me in little regard." Raven sat up taller, gaining steady confidence with each word, her eyes resting squarely on his. "If I am to continue to be your *guest,* as you say, then I expect to be treated with the same respect you would afford any other you would invite into your home. If this is too much to ask, then pray return me to the servants' quarters, that I may earn my keep and trouble you no further."

He rubbed his hand thoughtfully over his chin and contemplated the unexpected candor she displayed, finding it both daunting and stimulating at the same time, just like everything else about the blasted woman.

"Raven," he began, choosing his words as scrupulously as she had chosen hers, "I will agree to be more mindful of what I say—for I assure you I do hold you in the highest regard—if you will temper that tongue of yours. I dare say a bit of restraint on both our parts may pave the way for an understanding, if you will, and quite possibly, even pleasant conversation now and again."

Satisfied, she exhaled slowly, then brought the delicate china teacup daintily to her lips, sipping her hot tea just as Mrs. Captain had taught her. "I believe your terms are fair, Lord Castlereagh," she said at last, with a slight nod of her head.

The corners of his mouth drew up into a grin, taking the shadows from his dark eyes, and bringing in response a smile that tumbled unbidden upon her lips. There was something about the way his face softened at times, losing all traces of the tension that usually set his jaw firmly and furrowed his brow, that touched her somewhere deep inside and made her heart flutter.

Devan was utterly beautiful when he smiled and allowed the light into his eyes, something he did far too rarely. Usually his expression was grim, his eyes clouded with a combination of what she believed could only be sadness and an anger at the world, for nothing less could possibly make one so disagreeable. Had he always been this way? Or was this a new aspect to the man, caused by the loss of the woman he loved in London?

Again, it occurred to Raven that it might be she alone who brought about this brooding, quite possibly something about her he simply found impossible to tolerate. She was stunned at just how heavy the thought made her heart, and even more so by the rush of conflicting emotions Devan Castlereagh seemed to bring about in her, all within the space of an instant.

"Is there anything else you wish to say on the matter?"

Brought abruptly back from her private moment, she sipped her tea again in an effort to clear her thoughts. Then, setting the cup in its saucer, she replied quietly, "No, my lord."

"Very well." With a brisk swipe of the linen napkin across his mouth, he rose. "I have a day's worth of affairs to see to, but I look forward to supper and your delightful company. Good day." He practically flew from the room, and within moments she heard the distant echoing thud of the library door as he locked himself within.

Raven didn't have the stomach for her breakfast that morning, and rather than sit there idly and allow the disturbing thoughts of the marquess to grow even more so, she sought out Mrs. Captain. If Devan desired a lady of her, she would oblige him.

Mrs. Captain was already waiting impatiently for Raven in her chamber, along with a pile of dresses laid out upon the bed. As Raven entered, the woman quit her frantic pacing and the mutterings she'd been quite intent on only moments earlier.

"It is already well past eight o'clock," she clucked fretfully, taking her by the arm and leading her brusquely into the room. "We have a busy day ahead of us if we are to have you in any way fit for the ball. You only have a few months' time, and a miracle is in order as it is, so if you will be so kind as to be prepared to begin your lessons no later than eight o'clock each morning, it will increase our chance for success."

Raven could only nod before Mrs. Captain continued.

"The seamstress had these dresses delivered, and she assures me they are the style for the Season," Mrs. Captain remarked, holding up a damask rose dress, trimmed in the most beautiful pale green, for inspection.

"Oh, it is lovely!"

"A bit daring, as well," she indicated the low cut of the neckline with a disapproving wag of her finger. "But who am I to argue? It certainly won't hinder your chances of catching the eye of the gentlemen who frequent Dahlingham during his lordship's stays," she conceded with a particular gleam in her eye. "I have taken the liberty of sending word to London to a dressmaker there, who creates the finest gowns worn by the gentry, that she is to send an original, unmatched in its elegance, just for the occasion of the ball. It is to be here in time that Mrs. O'Dooley may make any necessary alterations. Now, we are to try on each of these dresses this morning, and I will take care to nip and tuck wherever needed, and there will not be a soul who will speculate they were not custom tailored just for you."

As each dress was stepped into and paraded in front of Mrs. Captain, and then pinned to Raven's exact proportions, she found herself wondering more of what the Marquess of Castlereagh would think, than of how she might be viewed in the eyes of the *haute ton*.

While she was certain Mrs. Captain's speculations as to the danger of involvement with Lord Castlereagh were altogether justified, she could not help but imagine what might await her in his arms.

She pressed her hand softly to her lips and recalled the feel of his kisses that afternoon in the drawing room, and how, against her own resolution, she'd shamelessly wished him to have his way with her right there. The same flood of emotion swept through her body as she remembered the firmness of his chest against her hands, while she made only half-hearted attempts to push him away. A fluttering sigh came as she recalled the heat of his breath as it stole her own. Her skin prickled hot and blushed crimson at the very thought of what might have happened if only . . .

But reality was, she'd given in to his demanding kisses, and still he'd pushed her away, seemingly repulsed.

"For pity sake, child, pay attention!" Mrs. Captain scolded harshly, yanking at the skirt of her dress to bring her back to the task at hand.

Raven threw back her shoulders and stood tall for the housekeeper. Shortly after the last hem was pinned in place, Headsley brought a tray of light fare and tea to the chamber. Mrs. Captain proceeded to rattle on regarding various aspects of etiquette while they ate, and Raven found herself in a constant struggle to pay heed to her lessons rather than her wicked notions of the marquess.

Undeniably, Devan Castlereagh was not the man she should focus her attentions upon, for he would surely only bring her grief. So when Collette appeared in the doorway, announcing the advent of the Duke of Brookshire, Raven was glad a diversion had finally arrived.

"Your Grace!" Raven exclaimed, sweeping into the entranceway where the duke, sporting another exquisite riding ensemble of black and gold, waited.

He met her halfway, bent low to take her hand and lifted it gently to his mouth. "Good day to you, Miss Raven. You are beautiful," Brookshire drawled, rising. "I hope I am not interrupting anything?"

"Nothing at all."

Her violet eyes fairly danced and a flattering pinking graced her silken cheeks, rendering Victor weak-kneed.

"Well, my dear," he said, regaining himself, "would you consider a walk out of doors? I have come with a mission that I feel must be carried out." He held his arm out to her.

"I would quite enjoy a walk," she replied, looping her arm through the crook of his, quite curious as to this *mission*.

They strolled out into the drive, where the duke's tan thoroughbred stood tied to the post, next to another horse, somewhat smaller, and dappled gray. The horses whinnied and pranced in place, eager to be released from their ropes.

"What do you think, Miss Raven?"

"I think they are handsome, truly, your Grace. But I am puzzled as to why you have saddled two, when surely one mount is enough for any man."

Stroking the long, sleek neck of the gray, he chuckled. "This is not my mount, dear girl. I brought him along so that you may ride with me."

"B-but, Your Grace, I already told you I do not know how to ride," she stammered, backing away from the sudden threat the beast presented.

"And I told you I would be too happy to teach you. So what say you? You're not going to send me away without at least giving it a try, are you?" he asked, cocking his head to one side, his mock frown barely masking a sheepish grin.

Warily, she reached out her hand and slid it down the gray's nose, and he answered with a snort and a gentle nuzzle, telling her she had nothing to fear from him.

"I do not care to be confined to the indoors for the whole of the day," she said, glancing to Victor and then back to the horse, "which is precisely what Mrs. Captain has in store for me if I were to let you leave. I shall return the favor of your rescue by humoring you in this activity you seem determined for me to engage in. So lead on Victor, Duke of Brookshire, before I lose my courage."

CHAPTER SEVEN

"Splendid, Miss Raven. Splendid!" complimented the duke, holding fast to the reins as he led the horse across the lawn by the bridle at a near crawl.

Raven sat in the tooled and polished English riding saddle while the gray moved smoothly beneath her weight. Sitting so high off the ground, with nothing to hold her in place but her own balance and the steed's good nature, was at first quite frightening. But soon she settled comfortably into the saddle and allowed her body to move with the gray's rhythm, loosening her white-knuckled grip on the reins. Now she longed for more.

"Brookshire, this pace is enough to lull me to sleep," she complained, barely containing her yawn.

"I will not be responsible for breaking your lovely neck, my dear. One step at a time."

She flashed the duke a pretty smile, "As long as it's a quicker step, Your Grace."

Brookshire shook his head with a crooked grin. Plainly, he experienced quite a bit of difficulty refusing her anything, and she intended to take full advantage of his predicament if it meant feeling the full power of the beast at her command.

Oh, she had *felt* Mairéad's mare as if it were her own, carrying her at defiant speed through the streets of Dublin. She felt the wind through her hair, and the long strides of the mare's powerful legs. She tasted the freedom that such power under her control offered, even if only in her dreams, and with the gray came the promise of experiencing the thrill of that freedom again.

"Very well. I will step up the pace, but there will be no running whatsoever until you have mastered the basics of the walk, canter, and gallop first."

Raven bit back another plea.

For more than an hour Brookshire led her over the grounds and he reluctantly walked the gray faster each time she threatened to pout. The idea of poking the horse in the ribs to bring about an *accidental* run occurred to Raven, but she decided it might be wiser to bide her time, or risk losing her good natured instructor.

"My dear, you've done well for your first day." He brought the horse to a smooth halt near the gardens.

She began to protest, but he cut her off with a wag of his finger.

"I will call on you tomorrow, and you may ride again then," he said firmly, helping her down from the saddle. "That is, if it is agreeable to you."

"Do you swear?" she asked as he set her to her feet.

Briefly, their eyes locked and he was unable to answer with more than a nervous clearing of his throat, while his usually fair face reddened. For all his boasting, he seemed uncharacteristically awkward and boyish at that moment, and Raven giggled.

Brookshire slowly withdrew his hands from about her waist with a frown, and suddenly began laughing along with her to mask his embarrassment. "Yes, I give you my word, Miss Raven."

"Please say you'll stay for tea on the lawn?"

He bent near her ear. "Will it keep you from Mrs. Captain's feared lessons?"

She nodded.

"Then I would be most happy to oblige."

"Brookshire!" a voice boomed, causing them both to start and the tea to splash from the duke's cup. "What the devil are you doing here?"

The Marquess of Castlereagh strode fleetly toward them, followed close behind by a tall, thin miss in a gray spring linen cape, who could scarcely keep up with his long gait.

A flash of recognition sparked in Brookshire's eyes as the woman approached. He rose and nodded briefly in her direction. "Lady Priscilla. What could have possibly brought you to the isle when it's the height of the London Season?"

Priscilla rushed to Brookshire, untying the bow that bound her cape, and then shrugging it from her shoulders, handed it to the marquess while offering the duke an obviously well-practiced smile. "Why, Victor, darling, I could ask the same of you. The Season was quite the bore. And when I heard Devan had left, well, I hardly had cause to stay on." She eyed Raven with a speculative glance. "You've a friend, Victor?"

"I have come to call upon Miss Raven."

"Come to *call?* She lives here?" Priscilla turned to Devan, her pale complexion seeming quite colorless against the soft cream satin of her afternoon dress, except for the bright pink blotches on her cheeks. Though she continued to glare at Raven, Priscilla spoke as though she wasn't even present. "Is this the homeless urchin your housekeeper took in? What is *she* doing having tea with the duke when she should be minding her place and meriting her keep with the work of a maid? You shall punish her severely, I would think."

Raven wished to scream at the top of her lungs. Was

there no one in Ireland who did not know of her situation?

"On the contrary, Priscilla. Miss Raven is not a maid, but my guest."

The fair-haired woman stepped back from the marquess in apparent disgust. "Surely you jest, Devan! What would society think? And you, Victor, coming to *call* upon her?"

"I don't give a swine's—" he stole a fast look at Raven and cleared his throat. "*Back end,* whether I have society's approval. Miss Raven is my guest, and she will be treated as such, until we locate her family and she can be returned to her home."

"I'm certain she will render some sort of payment for her keep," Priscilla said dryly, putting her arm possessively through Lord Castlereagh's. "I hope you will have the decency to be discreet, Devan." She led him around to the empty chairs across from the two occupied by Raven and Brookshire.

Discreet? "What are you implying?" Raven asked, her voice trembling with anger.

Priscilla ignored her.

Inching forward, she was about to give Priscilla a fitting piece of her mind, but Brookshire leaned close. "Do not allow her the satisfaction, my dear," he whispered into her ear, before regarding the marquess. "I say, old man, what plans are in the making for your little affair?"

"If it is my ball you are referring to, the plans are made and the invitations are being printed as we speak."

"Jolly good show, Castlereagh! I am looking forward to it, as always," he teased, lifting the teacup and slurping unbecomingly. Victor's fair face sparkled with mischief as he placed his cup back to the small white iron table. "And you, Priscilla, I imagine are quite looking forward to this year's ball?"

It did not escape Raven's notice that the pale witch practically leaned into Lord Castlereagh's lap, her mouth stretched into a false and biting smile. "Why of course, Victor. How could I be anything less than thrilling with anticipation when I shall be on the arm of the most distinguished and handsome man in attendance? I see this as just the beginning for Devan and me. Do you not feel the same, Devan?" she purred like a cat with a belly full of mouse, sending a twisted and satisfied smirk in Raven's direction.

Raven studied the little group that surrounded her, intently eyeing each man and then Priscilla. How odd an assemblage it was; Priscilla seemed to be wringing herself wrong side out to acquire the attentions of the marquess, Devan appeared quite uncomfortable with her clinging, and Brookshire took a great deal of delight in the whole situation. As for Raven, she felt entirely out of place.

Even though Devan did not seem at ease in the lady's company, he was not inclined to quiet her consistent gushing, either. On the other hand, he was neither doting nor overly agreeable, and she found herself feeling rather pleased.

"Oh, fair Lady Priscilla," Brookshire chirped, interrupting Raven's speculations and leaning forward, winking a twinkling eye at the lady, "I dare say I see nothing but surprises ahead for you where the dashing Marquess of Castlereagh is concerned."

What was Brookshire implying? That Lord Castlereagh had intentions concerning Priscilla? Raven's heart dropped clear to her toes.

"And Miss Raven," continued the duke, "I see naught but a life fitting of a lady as grand as yourself, and happiness beyond your wildest desires." A warm grin spread across Brookshire's face, and for the first time there was no bantering in his tone. Staring straight into her eyes, he raised the delicate bone china teacup in toast. "Here is to your complete happiness, Miss Raven," he said quietly, "for there is none I know who deserves it more than you."

Priscilla noticeably stiffened with Brookshire's words. "Really, Victor. The way you coddle these Irish! You would think she had royal blood, the way you pour over her. It is hardly fair the way you two men are setting her up, when," and suddenly the blonde head turned sharply to face Raven, sheer ice shooting from cold blue eyes, "she'll *never* be anything more than she is right now—a peasant playing dress up."

Indignant tears swelled in Raven's eyes, and Devan's chest tightened around his heart, her pain becoming his own. He reached out to her, but before he could counter Priscilla's viciousness, Raven stood and fled the lawn for the protection of the Dahlingham walls.

Following Raven with his gaze, he longed to run after her. He turned sharply on Priscilla, who confronted him with a tight smile. She apparently thought herself the victor in this game she'd been so intent on, but he was determined she would not harbor the satisfaction of a win long.

Devan pushed her off his arm. "That was uncalled for and callous!"

"Oh, Devan, I spoke nothing save the truth. And someone had to say it, lest she begin thinking she was one of *us*."

Gaining his feet, he paced in between the chairs. Then, halting in front of her, he fixed his heated glare on Priscilla. "Who is to say she is not one of us? For all we know, she could be the blood of society higher than ourselves."

Brookshire leaned back in his chair, crossed his legs and rubbed his chin thoughtfully, a jesting grin bearing itself once more. "And if not blood of society, who is to say she will not surprise us all and marry into it?"

Devan's scowl grew darker as he faced the duke. "Precisely what is that supposed to mean?"

The duke shrugged dismissively and his mouth curled sheepishly, bringing an irritated grunt from his friend.

Priscilla gasped, horrified. "Surely you cannot be serious, Victor! It is almost illegal, and most certainly a crime, even though not punishable with a prison sentence, for a man of English title to marry an Irish commoner." Dramatically, she fanned away the great stress and dismay of the entire circumstance. "The next thing you will be telling me is that she is to attend your ball, Devan, and that you shall escort her, Victor!"

Halting his pacing once more, Devan smiled. "By God, if she resides at Dahlingham until then, the fact is she *will* be attending the ball. If that is too much for you to bear, then perhaps it is best *you* do not attend."

Priscilla went ghostly white.

Brookshire stifled the desire to let loose in uncontrolled laughter that threatened to break free at any moment.

"You are impossible, Devan. But if it is your wish to indulge her with this fantasy, so be it," she conceded, her thin lips a mere line of bitter reconciliation across her pale face.

"I'm glad you can see your way clear to allow me to invite whom I please to my own ball. Now, by coming to Dahlingham unannounced, you really did interrupt some business that demands my attention. You are welcome to sit here with Brookshire, but I must take care of more pressing concerns."

The devil! Victor thought. He would not be left alone with Priscilla, by Heaven, and be forced to bear the brunt of the rantings that were visibly fuming inside her. "I really must be leaving, Castlereagh! Things to do myself, you know!" The duke stood and extended an arm to Priscilla. "May I escort you to your carriage?"

Without another word, she stormed right past Brookshire's invitation, toward the drive. Devan, too, raced past him, headed for the doorway of Dahlingham.

Crossing his arms over his chest, and with a shake of his head, Victor grinned. "Ah, my friend. It appears you are in quite the predicament over the lovely Irish miss," he observed out loud to no one. As the light of his newfound understanding twinkled in his eyes, Victor wondered if Castlereagh was aware of the situation himself.

CHAPTER EIGHT

In the library, Devan gnawed incessantly at the tip of his quill, finding concentration on the ledgers before him quite impossible. In an attempt to lessen the nagging, dull pounding in his head, the result of polishing off a bottle of brandy the night before, he rubbed his temples and sighed. Last night, even the liquor had not freed him of the disturbing and constant presence of the woman in his thoughts, and today, not even this headache that made deliberation over facts and figures unrealizable could lessen the image of her in his mind.

Another day wasted. Nothing further could be accomplished, and his solicitor would simply have to wait for the records.

Rising, Devan walked to the bookshelves that spread from one end of the room to the other. His father had had a particular fondness for books, and the abundance of leather-bound volumes in his library was more than most men could read in a lifetime. In the hope of finding something to snare his interest, he scrutinized the titles, in search of a story of daring and adventure. At last he pulled *The Shipwreck* down from one of the upper shelves, and threw himself into his well-worn reading chair.

He'd barely finished the second page when he heard a woman's distant laughter through the open window. Clearing his throat loudly to drown out the sound of her voice, he again probed the pages in earnest. Once more, Raven's musical laughter tickled his ears. Devan slammed the cover closed, flung the book to the end table beside his chair, and flew to the window.

"Brookshire, you son of a—" he started at the sight of the duke leading the gray by the reins across the grounds, with Raven in the saddle. A scowl distorted his features as he observed the pair, who seemed quite at ease with each other after the last three weeks.

He told himself it was for the best. Let Brookshire occupy her time. For his part, Devan had more important matters to attend to than playing caretaker to a child.

But she was not really a child. A child did not stir a man to such heights as her every movement or uttered word stirred him. The diversion of a child's attention upon another did not bring about such recurrent possessiveness, as did the mere notion of Raven's interest in Brookshire.

No, he did not care for this circumstance in the slightest, he admitted to himself at last, leaning his head against the window. Shielding his eyes to block the glare of the sun, he continued watching as Brookshire made a complete ass of himself in his effort to induce her laughter. And Raven urged him on with each flirtatious tilt of her head or bat of her wide, seductive eyes.

Wild schemes to interrupt their games and remove the duke from Dahlingham post haste whirled through his mind. But no strategy he concocted seemed discreet enough to employ at the moment. Pressing his nose against the window, his frustration fogged the glass. "The woman means nothing to me save the key to these blasted dreams," he told himself out loud. *"Nothing . . ."* he said again in an effort to convince himself.

A woman such as Raven was not only damned infuriating,

but most likely more complication than pleasure. Even so, there was something about her that reached deep inside and embraced his heart, brought forth a tenderness, a covetousness, and a desire to protect her from whatever horrific fate had befallen her in her past, and the uncertainty of her future.

Too many conflicting feelings, too much emotion to grapple with. And no rhyme nor reason to put to it. But still, Devan could not tear himself away from the window. He watched as Brookshire loosed the reins and she capably ran the horse into the western meadows. A lump formed in his throat as the wind unbound her hair and it fell freely into the breeze.

All at once she reined the gray around to face Dahlingham. Her gaze rose to the window and there she and the mount stood in the meadow, just like the vision in his dreams. And Devan could swear he heard the whisper of her soul calling out to his, yearning for the deliverance she sought from him each night.

Yanking the draperies shut, he forced the image from his mind. He paced the library, raking his fingers through his hair, and attempted to make sense of a situation that made none. Throwing himself into his chair, he picked up the book, but no matter how he tried over the course of the next agonizing hour, he could not will his mind to absorb a solitary word.

At length he heard them below the window, as the duke finally made his farewell.

Sheer determination anchored Devan in the chair. But his resolve gradually waned, need overwhelming reason, and at last he rushed to the window, telling himself he only wished to catch a glimpse of her without Brookshire at her side.

His gaze frantically roamed the grounds below, until finally resting on the gardens, where Raven drifted among the flowers.

Raven knelt to untangle the roses that wound themselves around the trestle in tumultuous knots. She'd been away from them little more than three weeks, and what a mess they'd become! Had no one taken her place in the gardens? Prying them free of the snarls, she carefully arranged the roses so that each blossom had its own space in which to grow, in which to reach for the sunlight and drink in the nourishing Ireland mist.

Leaning to touch her nose to one of the buds and breathe in its essence, a tear slipped to her cheek.

What was it about the roses that made her heart ache so? It occurred each time she visited them, this irrepressible sorrow mingled with every other emotion her heart could muster. And still, no matter the pain, she could not stay long away from them, whether it was a glance to the gardens from her chamber, or inhaling their fragrance carried on the breeze, or even stealing away for a few moments to gaze upon them and touch their silken petals. It was as though the roses beckoned and she could only obey.

"It appears they have not fared well without your attention."

His tone was startlingly tender, and Raven froze as the rose slipped from her fingers. "The roses are stronger than their delicate appearance, and will flourish regardless of the tempests they must endure," she answered at last, gathering herself to her feet. Spinning to face him, she found him merely a breath away.

"Like you?" He reached out, gently brushing the tear from her cheek, seemingly disturbed by its presence there. "What is it that makes you weep in the midst of such splendor?"

Unable to look into those endless black eyes that threatened to draw her in and never release her, she turned away. "I—I was not weeping, my lord," she lied.

"Do you miss the gardens, Raven? Do you miss the time you spent tending the roses?"

Facing him once more, she nodded.

"And I miss the arrangements you made." The heated intensity of his gaze washed over her, and he stepped closer. "If you like, you may see to the gardens, on the condition that you will also see to it that every room in Dahlingham is filled, every day, with your bouquets. I will appoint a servant to assist you."

"If it pleases my lord," she could barely whisper.

A long, uneasy silence passed between them, his stare penetrating, unnerving. Raven quickly looked away and ducked around him, scurrying deeper into the grove.

"Wait! Where are you going?" Devan called out after her, hurrying to catch up. "Did I say something to offend you?"

"I am not offended by you, my lord."

"Then what is it?" Gripping her firmly by the shoulders, he angled her toward him.

How could she explain what she did not understand herself? How could she tell him all that she felt, or how his very presence brought her to the brink of absolute love and hate and hope and fear, all at the same time, without any rhyme or reason whatsoever? Of course she could not, for he would surely believe her as impaired as she believed herself at that moment.

Raven shrugged out of his grasp. "It is nothing."

"Then you won't mind if I join you for a walk."

She might have objected given half an opportunity. But he gave her none as he took her hand, lopped it through his arm, and guided her down the path.

"I spent a great deal of time out here, myself, as a boy," he began. "I found it enormously peaceful compared to the constant uproar my father kept Dahlingham in in those days. Well," he amended, "the uproar that accompanied him *when* he was here. The gardens were the only place I could find quiet enough to think my own thoughts."

"Your parents were very social?"

"My father, yes. From what I was told, my mother was quite the beauty, but she died soon after my birth."

In his eyes, Raven thought she saw the reflection of a lost little boy at the mention of his mother, and it tugged at her heart. "I am sorry."

With a sigh, he attempted to mask his sorrow. "I would have liked to have known my mother, but Mrs. Captain was as good a nurturer as one could ask for. And Collette as bothersome as any blood related little sister."

"Your father never married again?"

A dark cloud descended over his countenance, and his hand swept roughly through his hair. "My father found comfort in quantity, rather than quality. No lady ever lasted in his life longer than a few visits. It was only with Mrs. Captain and Collette that I ever felt part of a family." The muscles in his jaw became rigid and an edge of bitterness crept into his voice. "When I was ten, my father put an end to even that, declaring I was too old for a governess, and it was high time I learned the family business."

"You were raised in Ireland?" Raven looked up into his eyes, for the first time unguarded, and their warmth enveloped her.

His smile returned and spread lazily across his face when she wrapped her arm further through his. "There was little room in Father's life for a small child, so I was left in Mrs.

Captain's care during the part of the year he stayed in London. He even went so far as to bring an English tutor over here for my education, rather than have me tag along or interfere with his carousing. It wasn't until I was almost grown—seventeen—that he allowed me to accompany him to England for the Season, and even then I was sent back to Ireland for the rest of the year, once his heir had made an appropriate appearance before his peers."

"Is your father in London now?"

"My father joined my mother three years ago. For all I can say against him, I honestly believe he loved my mother to the end of his life, and is a far happier man dead than alive. You see, he was never happy after her death—no matter how much wealth he acquired, how much respect he commanded, or how many women adored him."

Or how much his son needed him, she thought. Raven now understood what Mrs. Captain referred to that day in the library, when she said she raised the marquess from the cradle and loved him as if he were her own son. She was the only mother he had ever known, and apparently the only source of affection.

"Enough of me. My life is really quite dull." He led her to the wrought iron bench that sat in the very center of all of the blossoming grandeur, and motioned for her to sit next to him. "Let us talk of you."

"Little more than a month's worth of recollection does not make for very interesting conversation, my lord." She gave him a faint smile and fidgeted, wringing her hands, which did not escape his notice.

"Did I ever tell you I am an expert palm reader?" He took her hand gently within his own and flipped it over so her palm faced upward. "No, no. Of course I didn't! It's a gift I do not boast of to many." The tip of his finger traced a trail across her palm, sending delicious shivers through her as he pretended to study the lines etched in the skin.

Did he think she did not recognize an attempt at a swindling when confronted with it? She pulled back. "You do not!"

Holding fast, still marking a path in her palm, he chuckled. "I *do*. Hold still and allow me to concentrate," he insisted, his feather soft touch sending waves of warmth from his fingers through her body. "*Hmmm* . . . let me see. You were born in Ireland."

His attempt to sound authentic brought unguarded laughter from Raven.

"But," he continued, ignoring her disbelief, "in reality, you are a princess who has been hidden away for her own safety . . ."

If he insisted on this game, Raven decided she would play along. "Why must I be hidden?"

"Because your homeland has been in a state of revolution, and in order for the rightful heir to the throne of . . . of . . ." Devan's brows knitted together and he chewed at his bottom lip as he delved deep into his own imagination, something he had not used for years, not since he was a boy, teasing Collette about the dragons that lived under her bed or the *cry baby faeries* that preyed upon little girls who cried too much, and who would make her face freeze eternally in a sorrowful expression if she did not cease her whining. "*Somethingorotherdom!* Yes, Somethingorotherdom to reclaim the throne, you have been tucked away in the far off country of Ireland to wait until it is safe for you to return."

"So, at last we know my true identity! I am a princess. Pray tell, oh great seer, why it is I cannot remember any of this grand life I was born to?"

"Ah," he said, his finger now following a new line,

bringing a quivering breath from Raven, "it seems you were entrusted to . . . *faeries*. It is the faeries of Ireland who have raised you since the day you were born, and they have cast a magical spell upon you, so that you have no memory of them, and cannot tell a soul which part of the forests they dwell in."

"B-but why don't they—" She steeled herself against the disconcerting effect of his touch. "Certainly they could simply take me back to the forest with them rather than cast such a merciless spell upon me?"

He grinned wickedly, rather enjoying the effect he was having on her, deeming it sweet revenge for all the torture he'd endured at her hand these last weeks. "Indeed they cannot," he replied without a hint of jest in his inflection, "for you have grown too large for their tiny faerie cottages, and your beauty is so radiant that it would illuminate even the darkest part of the wood, and they fear your light would enable their enemies to seek them out."

Suddenly her expression grew staid and she stole her gaze away from him, casting it to the dirt at her feet. "What if I never remember?" she whispered, her long lashes glistening again with tears.

"Do not weep, Raven. It was a game meant to cheer you. Surely there must be something that has come back to you by now, and in time, it will be more."

"There is nothing in my mind, save my time at Dahlingham. *Nothing.* Even my dreams are of someone else's life!"

"How can you be certain it is not your own past you dream of?"

"Because it is not I who walks in my dreams, but another woman, and it is *her* life."

Perhaps it was compassion that guided Devan at that

moment he cupped her chin in his hand and directed her eyes back to his. And as he regarded her, this young woman who now seemed to have lost all hope, his heart ached for her.

A tear finally broke free and trickled a delicate path down her cheek. Without words, he reached behind the bench and plucked a single rose, a bud more beautiful than all the rest, and held it up to her. She inhaled it deeply, seemingly soothed by its fragrance. He glided the silken petals of the rose softly over her cheek, removing all traces of her sorrow.

Calmed by the delicate brush against her skin, Raven closed her eyes. His lips, warm and achingly tender, pressed to hers.

Laying her hand softly against his cheek, she felt the downy bristles of an afternoon beard. The fingers of her other hand pushed into the silken waves of his hair. And her lips parted. His kiss deepened. His arms embraced her. And Raven wept, desperate for the intimacy and the comfort of him.

Gradually, her eyes fluttered open, needing to drink in his affection and burn this moment into her memory for a lifetime. But it was not the wavy black hair of the marquess she ran her fingers through, but the dark auburn waves of the man in her dreams. And it was not Devan's gypsy eyes that gazed back, but the warm blue eyes of Séamus Ó Lionáird!

Raven pushed him away and stumbled to her feet. Hoping to chase the frightening apparition back into her dreams, she blinked, but Séamus rose from the bench and lunged toward her.

"Stand down!" she cried, turning and darting through the gardens for the safety of Dahlingham.

CHAPTER NINE

"Devan . . . mo stór . . ."

"Where are you?"

"Here, mo ghrá."

The sea winds whipped about wildly. A storm was nigh. The trees bowed and swayed and the winds all but drowned out her beckoning voice.

Where was she? Clouds covered the moon and stars. So dark. Yet he ran with all his might toward the faint sound of her calling.

Breathless, he cried out to her. "I cannot find you!"

Her voice seemed to come from just beyond the wood. He rushed headlong through the thick trees. Branches and brambles tore at his shirt and trousers and ripped at his flesh until blood, sticky and wet, trickled from his wounds. But no matter the pain, he could not turn back. She needed him, and he would fight the hounds of hell to get to her.

A distant bolt of lightning filled the night with a flash of light, and there, far out in the meadows, he saw her. He ran harder. Faster. The muscles in his legs cramped and sweat stung his eyes. Suddenly the skies burst wide open and rain poured to the earth, as the end of the forest grew closer. Faster and faster he raced, only the goal of the meadow keeping him to his feet.

Every night he ran through these woods. Every night he tried to save her. And every night he failed. For as soon as he reached the end of the trees and tried to fight his way into the meadows, *she would be far away again, and the forest stretched out long before him once more.*

He had been here before, many times. But this time, just short of the edge of grasses, he came to an abrupt halt. Falling to his knees, exhausted, Devan held his arms outstretched to the silhouetted figure on the horse.

"You must come to me," he begged, his voice broken, desperate.

"The way is too dark, my love."

He held his arms out further, his heart pounding furiously. "I implore you."

Slowly, the white mare stepped forward, until at last they were merely an arm's length beyond him.

"I can come no further."

"You can. You must. Believe in me."

The rain fell and thunder rolled in the distance. He held his breath, praying she would dismount and put an end to this nightmare once and for all.

"Come to me," he pleaded.

Hesitantly, she slipped from the mare's back. She walked pensively but a few steps, and then stopped just out of reach.

"You have only to take my hand," he begged, standing, extending his arm to her. "Take my hand."

She lifted her trembling hand until it came to rest softly within his. Holding fast, Devan drew her to him, wrapped her in his embrace. The storm ceased, the clouds gave way to the stars and moon, and the wood disappeared.

"It is over," he whispered.

Raven bent her head slightly, and pulled the hood of her black cloak until a mane of blazing tresses rained over her shoulders. A stranger's gaze met his. "Nay, 'tis not over yet, Séamus."

Bolting upright in his bed, Devan gasped. He flung himself to his feet, ran to the window, thrust it open and leaned straight into the wind. As he peered out into the night, he half expected to see the woman in his dreams.

Rubbing the sleep harshly from his eyes, he inhaled deeply to clear his head and slow the frantic thud against the walls of his chest.

Hell's teeth, who was she? *Raven.* Of that he was certain. No, she did not resemble Raven, but she was Raven nonetheless. But what did it all mean?

The summer breeze cooled his heated skin and dried the sweat from his brow.

Of all the dreams that plagued him since the moment Raven entered his life, this had been by far the most bizarre. The most frightening. And it had shaken him to the very core of his soul.

Slipping quickly into his silk night jacket, he stole silently from the confines of his chamber. He would spend the remainder of the night in the library, he thought. Find something to take his mind off the dream, off Raven.

Then he came upon Raven's door. Something compelled him to try the knob. It turned. The door fell open.

There were no sounds save her soft, rhythmic breathing. Stepping lightly through the doorway, he entered her chamber. She stirred as the door clicked shut. He remained motionless until her breathing resumed its slow, peaceful pattern.

Drawing closer, he marveled at the sight of the woman who lay sleeping, bathed in soft moonlight through the veil of translucent gauze that curtained her bed. Pushing the curtain aside, he peered down upon her. How content she now appeared in her slumber. Draped across the satin pillow, her hair glistened. Her ivory skin contrasted the ebony of her hair, and her lips, slightly parted, were the deepest shade of pink.

Devan leaned against the high bedpost, entranced by the sight before him. Who was this mysterious young woman? And why, of all places in Ireland, had she ended up at Dahlingham? And how had she become such a constant part of his very existence? Thoughts of Raven filled his every waking moment, whether it be frustration or wonder. And even his dreams did not serve to free him of her, for in his dreams she tore at his heart, consumed him, just as she did by the light of day.

Weeks had passed since they'd sat together in the gardens. Raven had fled and locked herself inside her chamber for two days, refusing even Collette's attempts to draw her out of her seclusion. At last, upon Devan's repeated requests, she made an appearance at his table on the morning of the third day.

He'd made a point of begging her pardon for his brazenness. Though he had done no more than kiss her, in a moment of compassion turned weakness, he reasoned. Certainly something so harmless should not offend her so, and had she not returned his kiss? Regardless, it was evident now she wanted as little to do with him as possible, whether alone or in the presence of a chaperone. So he kept his distance during the day, leaving her to her lessons with Mrs. Captain and her dalliances in the gardens, watching her in secret.

Brookshire made a habit of visiting Dahlingham daily, leaving no doubt in Devan's mind as to his intentions. And Devan told himself it was better this way, even though the very sight of the two of them together made his heart twist painfully.

After all this time, he was still no closer to solving the mystery of the dreams than he had been that first night Raven had come to him, pleading her deliverance. And now, after that night's vision, he was more confused than ever.

Devan breathed a heavy sigh. There had to be a way to get to the bottom of the meaning of the dreams that plagued him night after night. And the nightmares that tormented Raven as well.

Oh, yes, her slumber was as restless and fitful as his. He'd heard her cry out in her sleep each night, her past, whatever it was, drawing her back.

What was it that terrified her so?

She'd promised to reveal any memories that came to her. Surely, there had to be something by now—a name, a face, something to confess. But never once had she come to him.

Nor did she ever mention her trips into Dublin. They'd only been sporadic in the beginning, but of late, she left Dahlingham almost nightly. He knew when her nightmares began, for he would hear her soft weeping through the walls. And it would not be long until he heard the sound of her door creaking open and her footfalls in the corridor.

Every night he followed, and every night she visited the harbor. From the shadows he watched as *Mairéad*—as the Irish referred to her—stood, radiant against the glow of the fire, while the peasantry sang and danced around her, as though she had not a care in the world beyond the moment.

It had occurred to him that Raven seemed oddly detached from everyone there, almost as though she was there only for something else. He witnessed her rejection of more than one young and eager suitor, and found no apparent closeness with any of the women. So what was it that drew her into their company?

Leaning closer, he contemplated Raven. The hint of a smile flickered upon her lips. He breathed in the scent of roses that lingered around her and reached out, the desire to feel the satin of her skin against his hand overwhelming. But just before his fingers met her cheek, Devan recoiled.

Turning away reluctantly, he walked to the door. He glanced over his shoulder one last time. At that moment, Devan decided he'd waited long enough for the truth. After the disturbing dream he'd had that very night, he would not be put off longer. The next journey she made into Dublin, he would follow. And once she had surrounded herself with the music and the people—when she could not dare deny anything—he would make his presence known.

Then he would get the answers he sought.

"Castlereagh!"

Peering up from his papers at the sound of his name, Devan grimaced when Brookshire strolled into the library.

"She's not in here, Victor," he said flatly, returning his attention to the ledgers in front of him.

"She? Oh, you mean Miss Raven."

"*Ahem,* yes, whatever."

"It's just as well, for I came to see you on a private matter." The duke threw himself onto the chaise and stretched his legs out the full length of it, folding his arms casually behind his head.

"Is that so?"

"Ah, you sound put off."

Dropping his quill to the desktop, Devan eased back into his chair, crossed his arms and eyed Victor dubiously. "Not at all."

"Are you certain? Perhaps I have spent too much time in the young lady's company of late?"

"Why would I care whose company you occupied?"

"You tell me."

"I haven't time for your riddles, Victor," the marquess

growled, picking up his quill, splattering ink as he began an agitated drumming on the desktop.

Brookshire leaped to his feet and bounded to the desk. Halting directly across from Devan, he rested his hands on the edge and leaned forward. "Is there a reason you're avoiding the question?"

Uneasy beneath the duke's scrutiny, Devan threw back his chair, rose abruptly and moved to the window, where he looked out over the gardens, finding them substantially less offensive than Brookshire at the moment.

"What question might that be?" he asked at last.

"Do my visits with Raven trouble you?"

"Of course not," Devan lied, even though the very sound of Brookshire speaking her name set his blood ablaze. "If she chooses to entertain your attentions, that is entirely her affair and none of mine, even if you are a rogue of the worst kind." Then, rounding, he faced the duke head on, eyes narrowed, glinting black. "But none of your games with this one. Do you understand?"

"No games, Castlereagh, on my honor," Brookshire hastily replied.

Devan's mouth became a hard line. "We both know you have none. *Honor,* that is."

The duke's hand rose to his chest in mock pain. "I have been a bit of a cad at times, haven't I?" He didn't bother awaiting a response. "Trust that I have no intention of causing Raven a moment of grief."

"Then call as you please."

"May I take that to mean you do not mind if I escort her to the ball?"

Devan's jaw clenched and he fisted his hands until his knuckles went white. Of course he minded! But he could hardly say as much, since he'd be escorting Priscilla. Damn the wager, and damn Coushite for baiting him into it! Then Devan damned himself for being too thick-witted to see through Coushite's ploy before the bastard got the better of him.

But did any of it matter? Raven obviously preferred Brookshire, and Devan could not afford the indulgence of speculating what might be if things were different. He then reminded himself in no uncertain terms that she was merely a catalyst to the meaning of the dreams. *Nothing more.*

"Castlereagh?"

Ripped from his thoughts by the persistent duke, Devan stiffly took his chair. "Do as you will," he muttered, shifting his aggravated gaze back to the ledgers.

CHAPTER TEN

That night, when he'd heard Raven leave her chamber, Devan had counted slowly down from one hundred, giving her a good head start. By the time he arrived at the harbor, she already stood among the others while the music filled the air.

The Irish whooped and shouted, dancing wildly around the fire. Even centuries of oppression could not quell this spirit, their courage, he marveled. Devan Castlereagh lifted his chin, reminding himself of the proud Irish blood that flowed in his veins.

Then his shoulders slumped. To the Irish, the Marquess of Castlereagh was an Englishman. And as such, he knew the moment he walked into their midst and to Raven, their protection of her would be fierce.

Thinking back to earlier in the evening, he recalled the vision of himself in the mirror; a pair of muddy brown trousers, simple cambric shirt, black boots intentionally dirtied that afternoon in the stable, and an Irishman's cap upon his head. Studying the people gathered around the fire, he let go a shaky breath, confident once more he blended in.

Cautiously he eased his way into the crowd, Raven his objective.

A hearty slap on the back jolted him from his concentration. "*Dia dhuit!* Good evenin' to ye, man!" came the voice attached to the hand that struck him. "I haven't seen ye before. Visitin' are ye? Or have ye come to fair Dublin-towne to stay?"

Devan gulped. He hadn't planned to carry on a conversation with anyone this night but Raven, and he hadn't thought to practice the brogue he'd been so adept at as a child. " 'Tis passin' through, I be," he mimicked, trying hard to mask his British inflection.

Another harsh hit and a pint of ale offered. "*Ach.* 'Pears ye got ye a wee bit of an Ulster accent, it does!" the stout man exclaimed with a jolly laugh. "If Ida heard ye talk before I asked, I woulda known!"

Forcing a smile, Devan nodded and took a long drink from his pint.

"Ye are welcome to stay as long as ye like, me man. Enjoy Dublin while ye be here!"

He kept the jug to his lips and smiled. Fortunately, his new Irish friend found the festivities that went on around them of greater interest, allowing Devan's attention to drift back to Raven.

Her gaze roamed restlessly, and he found it peculiar the way she seemed to stare beyond the people, as though *searching* . . . But for what?

Perhaps the more appropriate question was *for whom?* He swallowed the bitter taste of jealousy that rose in his throat.

The Irishman next to him acknowledged the direction of Devan's stare. " 'Tis a right pretty lass, she be."

"Aye," he sighed.

"Wandered in not much more than a full moon back." The man handed Devan another pint, and continued. "Says her name's *Mairéad.* Never sees her boot at night. Never dances, not much fer talk. Strange one, she is."

"Aye," he responded again. *Strange, indeed.*

Suddenly Raven's wandering gaze paused and rested squarely on Devan. Certain she would bolt, he prepared himself to charge after her, determined he would not let another opportunity pass, nor live through another night haunted and tormented by the incessant dreams. But to his amazement, her expression lit up, and a shy smile eased itself slowly over her lips.

"Looky there, man!" his Irish acquaintance exclaimed in his ear. "She likes ye! Not a one of us ever got a smile like that from her. Go on, introduce yerself!"

Still stunned by the unexpected warmth in her smile, Devan shook his head. As he made his way through the circle of people toward Raven, his mind raced with a thousand justifications as to why he'd come to the harbor. But every one sounded as lame as it truly was. By the time he reached her, he'd prepared himself to admit the truth, take her quietly aside and demand *she* admit the truth as to why she, too, had come into Dublin.

" 'Twas about to give up all hope of seein' ye tonight," she whispered, when he approached.

He stumbled a step back. "Y—you expected me?"

Had she known he followed her all along?

"Aren't ye even about askin' me to dance?"

Dance?

" 'Tis a sad thing to be lettin' the music waste," she said, wrapping her fingers around his hand.

There was something about the gleam in her eyes, and the way her full, pink lips curled at the corners into the most beautiful smile he'd ever witnessed, that rendered him helpless to refuse. Bending low into a formal bow, he lifted her hand to his mouth, then rose. "Would you care to dance, my lady?"

Lifting the hem of her skirt, Raven dipped into a curtsey.

"Why, me lord, I would be honored," she replied, stepping into his waiting arms.

Surrounded by the sounds of Ireland—the pipes and fiddles, the sea crashing against the cliffside, and the moaning wind that sang of eternities—he carried her as though they'd danced together all their lives.

Who was this woman? Surely not the fiery wench who blistered his ears and scorched his soul at every turn.

His jaw tensed. *More questions.*

Then Raven pulled out of his embrace as she whirled round and round. The questions suddenly forgotten, Devan drew her back to him, holding her closer than before, their bodies almost touching, moving as one.

His heart thundered, and Devan was acutely aware at that moment that he was a man holding the object of his desire. He tried to let go, reminded himself of his purpose. But then he felt the light pressure of her bosom against his chest. His brazen stare drifted lower to the soft ivory swell of her breasts that threatened to break free of the confines of the material of the rose damask dress she wore. The consequences of his thoughts were almost painful.

Her lips, like a dewy summer rose, needing but a kiss to bring them to bloom, reminded him of the kiss they'd shared in the gardens. Before the temptation of tasting her again overwhelmed him, Devan shifted his gaze to her eyes of the deepest lavender that drew him in completely. Realizing then that it would do him no good to fight her, he allowed himself to drown in her eyes and breathed for the first time since he took her in his arms.

Raven's cheeks flushed rosy as she lifted herself to him, and her words fluttered softly against his ear. "I believe ye will be havin' all of Dublin talkin', sir, the way ye be holdin' me."

Shimmering sable curls were caught up into the summer breeze and tickled his face when they turned in time to the music. Craving her nearness, Devan wrapped his arm further around Raven, bringing her closer, until the warmth of her body pressed against his. "Say the word and I shall release you."

"Let them talk, *mo ghrá*. 'Tis long I have waited fer ye," she murmured, "and I'm not about lettin' ye go."

Never had such an overwhelming fullness settled in Devan's heart, as it did now. It had been Raven who fled into the wood that first day upon his return to Ireland. He'd thought her merely a figment of his imagination—or a specter—until she appeared in his gardens, and then stood before him in the library. Somehow, then and there, she had become the very reason for his existence.

But Devan had not understood it until this very moment.

He'd brought her up from the ground floor three days later, convinced doing so would give meaning to the dreams. But had it been something more he'd desired of her?

Impassioned and assertive, she'd stood before him in the drawing room. He'd kissed her, and then denied the attraction. But over the weeks she'd been at Dahlingham, no matter how many times he disavowed his longing, he could not stay away. He yearned to touch her, protect her, know the secrets of her heart.

Everything about Raven was so damned perplexing; one moment she made it clear she despised and loathed him, and the next, she responded to his kisses.

Confused by his own conflicting emotions, Devan had reasoned that it was her resemblance to Katherine that stirred him. But now it was only Raven reflected in his eyes, in all her earthy splendor and unrefined glory, more a mystery to him than ever.

Devan Castlereagh was a broken man, left utterly power-
less in the wake of that unbridled spirit. And he knew then
that nothing would ever be the same.

His mind flitted to the dreams, but only briefly, convinced now they meant nothing beyond a foretelling of his
destiny. And the dream of the red-haired woman the night
before had been merely the result of unfulfilled desire
sending him to the brink of madness.

Gradually the music faded and the storytelling began.
Entwining her fingers possessively through his, Raven led
him out of the glaring light of the brilliant fire, into the veil
of shadows. Concealed by darkness, it took all the strength
within him not to pull her into his arms once more and
claim the lips that fairly pleaded for his kiss. He slowed his
agitated breathing and blew out his frustration, employing
caution lest he break the spell that seemed to be cast upon
them.

All at once she halted her step and faced him, breaking
the silence. "Why did it take ye so long to come to me?"

So long? "I did not know that's what you desired of me."

Her eyes searched his, unyielding. "How could ye not
know? Did ye not hear me heart callin' yers?"

"I did," he admitted. "Every night I heard you calling
out to me in my dreams."

"Then why did ye not come to me until now?"

Was he losing his mind? Was it not she who had proclaimed her intention of killing him if ever he came near
her? Did she not put up the walls and obstacles herself, including the Duke of Brookshire? *Blast!* He had never met a
more contradictory female in all his life!

"You—"

Raven brought his hand slowly to her mouth, and lightly

brushed his palm with her lips, putting an abrupt end to Devan's objection.

"Do ye doubt me now?" she asked, her long lashes flitting lazily, as she brought his hand to her bosom, securing it there with her own hand. "Can ye not feel the beating of me heart?"

"I do," he breathed, the words a hoarse whisper.

Still guiding his hand, she drew it lower.

Devan swallowed hard, his fingers pushed gently into the rounded swell of her breast. She moaned softly when his thumb traced the taut outline of her nipple beneath the fabric.

Unable to resist the temptation any longer, he pulled her into his embrace and brushed his mouth to hers. He ran his tongue lightly over the seam of her lips until they parted. He brought her tighter to him, her thigh firmly pressed to the heated aching in his loins.

Raven yielded to his possession with a husky sound that came from deep in her throat. Her kisses became hungry, ardent. Her body quivered, her fingers, trembling, hot, ran over the cambric, loosening the laces until the shirt fell open and her hands found his flesh.

The sweetness of the taste of her upon his tongue, and the feel of her body arching against him, urged him further. He lifted her skirt, grasped her thigh, and raising it to his hip, he stroked her slowly, his kiss deepening, her soft moans more insistent.

Then, all at once, she pushed him back, gasped for the breath he'd stolen with his kiss, her eyes wild, frightened. " 'Tis not the time."

Willing his racing pulse to slow, Devan reluctantly released her. Gradually regaining his wit, he nodded.

Raven shook out her skirt, then hastily pushed her hair

back from about her face. "I trust ye will not speak of this?"

"Of course not," he finally replied, still dazed.

"I must go."

Before he could halt her, Raven was beyond his reach. He watched as she mounted the red and sped off into the night.

Devan lay in his bed, and for the first time in his life that he could recall, he wished he was not alone there.

No matter how tight he closed his eyes, or how many sheep he counted, sleep eluded him. And no matter how he attempted to force Raven from his thoughts, he could still smell her . . . taste her . . . *feel her.*

With an aggravated groan, it occurred to him that he'd only succeeded in trading one hell for another, far more torturous. It also occurred to Devan that there were many other delectable women who would provide him endless pleasure and none of the grief. *Why, of all women, Raven?*

Because in Raven he'd finally met his match.

And with the dawn came his willing surrender to his destiny.

God, how empty his arms felt. Suddenly, all he could think of was holding her again.

But Devan had a full day ahead of him. First, he would send word to Coushite, and invite him and his daughter for dinner. Then, with Raven present, he would inform them both that, despite the wager, he would not be escorting Priscilla to the ball. Arlington would be just as happy with crates of sherry. And Priscilla, being that she was blessed in beauty, if not depth, would certainly have plenty of invitations to choose from, perhaps even old Brookshire, since he would not be attending the ball with Raven on his arm, contrary to their conversation the afternoon prior.

As for Raven, she would be his. In every way.

Then, like a blow to the gut, it struck Devan that Raven might well already be married. What if she regained her memory, only to discover she already had a husband?

To hell with him!

Devan would do whatever it took to make her fall so madly in love with him that leaving him, even for a husband, would be impossible. He would shower her with diamonds and trinkets, and a wardrobe grander than any in London.

London. Of course! Devan would whisk her away to London, to Winterbourne, right after the ball, far from the menace of any claim any man might attempt to make on her.

CHAPTER ELEVEN

"Good morning!" Devan exclaimed, seemingly about to burst with good cheer while holding her chair for her.

Warily Raven returned his smile, but kept her eyes on the chair as she lowered herself into it, half expecting him to pull it right out from beneath her. "And to you, Lord Castlereagh."

He guided her chair closer to the table and smiled down at her.

"You seem in high spirits this morning," she noted, as he walked to the opposite end of the long table.

"I am! It is a glorious day, do you not agree?" he asked, taking his own chair.

The sun was shining and the birds were singing, so she could hardly argue the point. "I suppose."

"And you slept well?"

"Surprisingly so, my lord."

"And did you dream sweetly?"

"*Aye.*" The hint of a dream remembered flickered in her amethyst eyes, bringing with it an unconscious grin to her lovely lips, before she recovered herself. "I mean, yes, as a matter of fact I did."

Relieved that she seemed to recall the night with the same fondness as he, Devan finally allowed himself to exhale.

"You?"

"Pardon?"

"Did you sleep well, Lord Castlereagh?"

"I confess I did not sleep a wink. But my dreams were the sweetest I have known."

She contemplated his last comment while spreading her napkin over her skirt. "It is odd that you are able to dream without slumber."

"I had the memory of a certain lady's kiss, and visions more beautiful than any dream, for I embraced an angel last night."

"Lord Castlereagh!" she scolded, her wistful expression suddenly distorted by apparent disgust.

Oaf! he chastised himself, raking his fingers through his hair. He had sworn he would not speak of what had occurred between them, and with Tourish and Mrs. Captain possibly within earshot, he had done just that. "I apologize. It is simply that my heart is so full, I think it might burst. Say you forgive me. On my honor, I shall mind my tongue."

"I should hope so, if for no other reason than to protect the reputation of the woman you speak of."

Desiring privacy, Devan dismissed Headsley as soon as the food was brought in.

"Tell me what you have planned for the day?" he asked, wanting to know every thought that filled her bewitching mind.

"I have no plans, my lord. I expect I shall have my lessons, as usual. Then I will fill the vases with fresh flowers, as usual. And after that, I suppose I shall spend the remainder of my day with Collette. *As usual,*" she sighed.

"Lovely! But may I ask a favor of you?"

"You may, of course."

"Promise you will meet me at the stables this afternoon at precisely two o'clock—not a minute later."

Nodding dully, Raven sighed again. "You have my word."

"Well and good!" He rose from his chair, without so much as touching his food. "There are pressing matters that will occupy my attentions this morning and into the afternoon. But do not forget—you have given me your oath that you will meet me at two o'clock."

Without further explanation, the marquess as much as ran from the dining room and out the doors of Dahlingham.

Just like the rogue! To flaunt his midnight escapades— probably with the ever popular Lady Priscilla. And then to make demands of her time still! Having quite lost her appetite, Raven pushed her plate aside.

There would be no lessons today, she decided. If he wanted a lady, let Priscilla fill the role. Nor would there be any fresh flowers in the vases. His *angel* could replace the now wilted and browning bouquets. Raven had no intention of stealing the life from the roses merely to lend beauty to Dahlingham for Priscilla's pleasure.

Oh, her time at Dahlingham had been almost unbearable. Ever since he kissed her in the gardens, she could not look into his eyes without Séamus Ó Lionáird gazing back. So Raven had done her best to avoid Lord Castlereagh, occupying her afternoons with Brookshire after her morning lessons with Mrs. Captain, and the rest of the day with Collette until supper.

The marquess allowed Raven her distance, only commanding her presence in the dining room for the first and last meals, and in the library each evening. His summons to the library would be brought to her by Tourish or one of the other servants. She would find him sitting in an old, worn chair, book in hand, or at his desk, shifting through papers. After a polite greeting, there was the inevitable question: "Is there anything you wish to discuss, Raven?"

Of course what he wanted to know was whether she had

remembered anything from her past, and since not once had she a miraculous recollection of any kind, she would simply shake her head.

There was never a dismissal. No further dialogue between them. He simply went back to his book or ledgers, and Raven would go to the shelves, select a book of her own, and take her seat in the chair by the marble fireplace.

It was then, in the library, that Raven stole glances, watching him as he read or worked at his desk. Then it was only Devan, until he inevitably would look up and meet her gaze, and then, before her eyes, Séamus Ó Lionáird would appear. As soon as the terrifying transformation took place, she looked away, but Raven could feel his stare, dark and intense, as though he sought to pry every secret from her soul. The end of the evening would be signaled by his sudden and silent departure from the library.

Last night something had changed. Her dreams began as they did every other night, at the quay by the sea. But this time, she was not the observer. She stood in the circle around the great fire. And for the first time, she dreamed of Devan. He came to her in her dream. And in her dream she'd felt the fluttering of her heart when their gazes met, danced to the music in his arms, tasted his heated kisses and, for the first time, knew the rapture of his touch.

It had all felt so real, that when she awoke, Raven reached out for him, only to find she was alone in her bed.

She had been truthful when she told the marquess her dreams had been sweet. But it had been a lie when she told him she slept well, for after awakening in the middle of the night, she dared not sleep again for fear of slipping back into that beautiful dream, only to lose him all over again with morning's light.

The warmth of his greeting as she'd entered the dining

room caught her off guard, and Raven had looked into his eyes without thinking. And it seemed then that all the misery of the past weeks was suddenly behind her, for it was the marquess who stood there smiling, holding her chair.

Oh, how her heart had danced to hear the affection in his voice, and to at last be able to meet his gaze. But her joy was short lived, for he soon made it clear that it was a midnight visit from Lady Priscilla that had brought about his good humor!

What sort of woman was it that would steal into Dahlingham in the middle of the night?

Raven recalled the day she met Priscilla and how she'd thrown herself at Devan. She remembered Brookshire's offhanded comments regarding the lady. Mrs. Captain was under the impression the marquess enjoyed the company of such women fleetingly, but it appeared Priscilla had him thoroughly smitten and lovesick as a boy.

Rising from the table, Raven dabbed the mist from her eyes.

Worse than Lord Castlereagh's apparent affection for Lady Priscilla was the fact that she even cared. How was it she could be so enraptured with a man who treated her barely civilly? Whose only concern was that she remember her past so he could return her to her family and be done with her?

No use crying over something that she'd never even had the right to hope for, she thought, swiping away another tear. Lord Castlereagh was a nobleman, wealthy, powerful, and with a physical beauty any woman would covet. Certainly he would never choose someone like her, a woman with no dowry, no name, and not even a past to call her own.

As Raven climbed the winding staircase, she thought of Brookshire. Though he was a duke, had he not visited

Dahlingham almost every day since they'd met, proving his interest, regardless of her station? And did he not go out of his way to compliment her and indulge her every whim?

Walking the long corridor toward her chamber, Raven reminded herself a woman could surely do worse.

The door to her chamber was open, and Mrs. Captain and Collette stood together, shifting through the wardrobe.

"Mrs. Captain?"

"Do you realize what time it is?" she queried, her expression stern as she faced Raven.

"Mrs. Captain, I am in sore need of a day with no lessons or fittings."

"But—"

Collette put her hand to her mother's arm, abruptly ending her protest.

Mrs. Captain looked from Raven to Collette and back again. "I suppose one day will not put us too far behind schedule."

"Thank you."

"Do not thank me just yet, my dear," she muttered, straightening one of the dresses before moving away from the wardrobe. "I will exact what you should have done today on the morrow. Twice the work."

"Yes, ma'am."

"As long as we are clear on that issue, a day away from these lessons may be precisely what I need so that I can catch up on my other work."

"You do not look well," Collette observed when her mother quit the room.

Raven shrugged. "All is well."

And why shouldn't all be well? The Duke of Brookshire would inevitably call on her this day, and, she was most positive, due to the subtle hints offered, an invitation to the ball was forthcoming. No, he was not Devan Castlereagh, but he might well be the man who would spirit her away from Dahlingham and rescue her from the torment she was certain to endure if Lady Priscilla were to become the new marchioness.

Collette tried the entire morning and into the afternoon to lighten her mood, while Raven sat on the bed and sulked. She tried to laugh at the silly stories, and feigned interest in the good-natured gossip, but her thoughts wandered back to Devan, again and again.

"You haven't heard a word I've said," Collette noted.

"Of course I have," she lied. Fortunately, the clock chimed at that moment, and Raven took Collette's hand. "Let us take tea."

"Very well. I will walk you to the dining room."

"Did you not hear me? I said let *us* take tea." Raven slid off the bed, brushed out the wrinkles in her skirt. "Today you shall sit with me."

"Oh, no!" Collette objected, pulling her hand free. "I cannot sit at the marquess's table! It's unheard of!"

Raven's eyes narrowed and defiance rang sharply in her tone. "Do not argue."

"But what will Lord Castlereagh say?" Collette practically squealed as Raven dragged her down the staircase and into the dining room.

Acknowledging the footman, Raven requested tea and some of Mrs. Captain's biscuits. Headsley held out her chair, and then left the room to fill her request.

"The marquess will not return until precisely two o'clock," she said when they were alone.

Nervously, Collette glanced around her before sitting next to Raven. "How do you know?"

116

"He told me as much this morning."

"But even if he were to return this very moment—"

The maid came up out of the chair, but Raven caught her arm and pulled her down again. "If he dared say a word, it would give me the excuse I need to leave Dahlingham once and for all," she insisted, drumming her nails steadily on the table.

"And just why would you want to be leavin' now? You have free run of the house and grounds, and don't have to lift a finger. Makes no sense, the mood you're in today, if you don't mind me saying."

Headsley entered the room stiffly with tea and a tiered tray of scones and sweets.

"It is not your duty, dear Collette, to worry about the marquess. Your duty is to me, and since it is I who has ordered you to keep me company, it is I who shall take full responsibility. All you need do is have your fill of all that is placed before you."

"He will not approve."

"*He* said I could do whatever I please, and that is precisely what I am doing."

Headsley snorted and then regained his statuesque composure and quit the room quickly.

"But I don't think he meant—"

"He's so preoccupied with Priscilla, I sincerely doubt he would give a second thought to anyone sitting at his table. In fact, I should invite the entire staff to indulge in tea and sweets!"

"Why do you ramble on so? And what does Priscilla have to do with this?"

Scowling, Raven poured the heavy cream into her tea and stirred. "Apparently she paid the marquess a visit in the night."

"No! *Lady* Priscilla?"

"The very same."

"He told you that?"

"Aye," Raven sighed, sipping and then placing the cup in its saucer. "And if she mollifies him this night, perhaps you shall dine with me on the morrow."

A sudden light went on behind Collette's blue-gray eyes. "Sweet Mary, you're jealous!"

"I am not!" Raven shot back defensively.

"It's written all over your face, it is!" she laughed hysterically.

"You have a truly perverse sense of the humorous!" Her cheeks pinkened and her eyes burned with tears.

Collette's giggling ceased abruptly. Patting her hand, she tried to soothe Raven. "I apologize. I didn't realize—oh, please don't cry because of me!"

" 'Tis not you," she wept.

"Him?"

" 'Tis not even him."

"Then what?"

"My heart's folly. And there's nothing I can do about it."

"Why not?"

"How could I ever compare to Lady Priscilla?"

"Gads, girl, you don't want to compare to her. She's naught but a wicked harpy, more cunning than a serpent!"

Raven sniffled, suddenly more interested in what Collette could offer than her own woes. "What do you mean?"

"Ah, she's had her sights on the Marquess of Castlereagh for years. And you would not believe how shameless her attempts at snaring him have been. And as though it's not enough that we must suffer her, her fat, smelly, wretch of a drunken father often accompanies her to Dahlingham, and spends his time swimming in sherry and trying to get his lecherous old hands up the skirt of any maid that passes him."

"Apparently Priscilla's attempts have not been futile."

"I swear to you I have never seen even a hint that his lordship has any interest in Priscilla. What gives you the impression she came to Dahlingham last night?"

"He as much as said so."

"He *told* you about it?"

"*Aye!* Says he, 'I embraced an angel last night.'"

Collette's eyes grew wide and her jaw dropped. "He *didn't!*" she gasped, inching closer to hear the whole sordid story.

"He certainly did!" Raven confirmed with a quick nod of her head. "Then goes on to say he dreamed of her without sleeping. Now just *what* is that supposed to mean?"

"It sounds indecent if you ask me."

"That is precisely what I thought, Collette."

"But how do you know it was she he spoke of?"

"Because the Duke of Brookshire told me Lord Castlereagh lost a wager with Lord Coushite, and payment to be rendered was escorting Lady Priscilla to his ball."

"This is the first I've heard of it."

"He did not deny it."

"Oh, my."

"Victor apparently thought the entire situation wildly funny, and Devan not only defended the lady, but was prepared to thrash Brookshire over the jest he made."

"You don't say!"

"I *do!*"

Collette snickered, covering her face with both hands. "If everything you say is true, it seems Priscilla has already more than earned an invitation to the ball."

Unadulterated revolt curled Raven's lip. "Ach!"

Their conversation was interrupted when Tourish swayed into the dining room. "The De-uke of Brookshire, to see Miss Raven," he drawled.

Both women rose as Victor stepped into the room, hat tucked beneath his arm, tipping his head to Raven, and then the maid.

"Good day, Victor."

"Miss Raven. And Collette."

Spying her opportunity, Collette greeted the duke with a quick nod, then hurried from the dining room.

Grimacing, Raven reminded herself to reprimand Collette the moment the duke departed. Then, she forced her countenance to brighten and faced Victor.

"What has you so unstrung, Victor," Raven asked, contemplating him as they walked across the lawn.

He scratched his head, the nervousness of his expressions easing away with a grin. "I have come with something very important to request of you." He slowed his pace and took her arm.

"You know you may always ask me anything."

"That is what I had hoped."

Scraping his teeth over his lip, his jaw set again and tension creased his brow. This was certainly not the jocular Victor she'd come to know, and somehow, without his clever grin and with the mischief missing from his gray eyes, he was dreadfully . . . *average.*

All at once he dug his heels into the grass and halted, turning her to him. "As you know, Miss Raven, the ball at Dahlingham takes place in less than two months' time."

"Of course."

"I wondered if . . . if . . ."

"*Yes?*"

"Would you do me the honor of allowing me to be your escort?" he blurted all at once.

At last! Raven feigned surprise, fanning herself dramatically with her hand. "Oh, Your Grace! It is I who would be honored."

Her acceptance seemed to relieve him, and that familiar grin was suddenly back in place on the duke's face. "I thank you, lady." Taking up their walk again, he casually noted, "Lady Priscilla has sent off to London for her dress."

Raven attempted to sound disinterested. "Oh?"

"Seems she thinks a proposal is inevitable, and is planning a winter wedding."

The thousand responses that came to mind were more bitter than anything that might have rolled off Mrs. Captain's sharp tongue, but she kept her tone sweet. "Perhaps the lady knows something we do not, Your Grace."

He laughed heartily. "Castlereagh always has been a tad unpredictable. Has he mentioned anything to you?"

"You must understand, the marquess and I do not share the sort of acquaintance that would warrant confidences. He is my benefactor, nothing more."

"I see. Walk with me to my carriage?"

"You've only just arrived. Must you leave so soon?" She had hoped he would stay at least until Devan's return so that she might flaunt her invitation and the duke's interest. Not that Devan would care, but playing tit-for-tat would certainly make *her* feel better.

"I'm afraid I must or risk a tenant uprising. Too lenient I have been, I tell you," he chuckled. "But they've demanded my attention this day—my tenants—no doubt to request less toll for the land they use. I suppose I must show the

Irish some charity every now and again."

The carelessness of the duke's comment cut through Raven like a blade. "Your Grace," she said, mindful of each word, lest she lose her escort to the ball, "it should not be forgotten that I may well be the daughter of one of your tenants, or, at the very least the daughter of some tenant farmer in Eire. And, whatever they ask of you, I hardly think it is a charity you cannot justify, considering the land from which you reap your fortune once belonged to the men who now work it."

Brookshire took her hand and touched it to his lips. "I highly doubt you come from peasant lineage, my dear, for there is nothing common about you. My use of the word *charity* was bad form. Forgive me?"

She smiled and removed her hand from his gloved grasp with a flick of her wrist. "I forgive you, Victor."

"And with your clemency, I shall take my leave, lest I place my muddied boot in my mouth again. Good day, Miss Raven."

CHAPTER TWELVE

Removing her shoes and then her stockings, Raven slipped her feet into the cool blue water, then leaned back, closed her eyes, and lifted her face to the warm kiss of the June sun.

It had been an eternity since last she'd roamed the grounds without escort, and just as long since she'd bathed in the waters there, or walked along the running brook that led from the lake toward the meadow. Though she did not miss the duties, she envied the servants, and missed the liberties she'd once had in what now seemed like another lifetime.

Another lifetime.

Her hollow laughter echoed around her. How many lifetimes was any one person to have?

What had life been before Dahlingham? Had she been a peasant as everyone assumed? Or could it be she'd been a lady? If she were truly a lady, would Devan think of her differently?

The dream came back vividly. In her mind she could hear the haunting harmonies of the pipe and harp. She could smell the fragrant sea, and see the faces of the people as they danced around her. And she could feel the warmth of Devan's body as he pressed her to him. Remembering his lusty kisses, she licked her lips, and recalled the desire that swept through her, enveloped her, made her weak.

Why had this dream not been cloaked in the veil of illusion? Why had it felt so . . . *real?*

Raven pushed back a sigh.

Then it occurred to her that she could lucidly recall every detail of her dreams, yet not a single detail of her past. She was no closer to discovering who she was or where she had come from than she was the day she first awoke in the small chamber on the first floor of Dahlingham.

Was she doomed to never know the truth? The thought terrified her.

The distant thunder of horses' hooves sounded from the main road.

Forgetting her stockings and shoes, she rose from the bank, and headed up the hill toward the stables, her skirt rustling about her ankles, and her hair whipping about her face as she walked into the wind.

Just as she came to the peak of the hill, she saw the marquess's carriage round the bend. Squinting in the bright sunlight, Raven made out the figure of Devan sitting atop the red. Then the breeze blew a cloud across the sun, the glare ceased. It was not the red that carried the marquess, but a tall *white* horse.

A stunned gasp escaped her parted lips. *Mairéad's horse,* as sure as if it had stepped straight out of her dreams.

The Marquess of Castlereagh caught sight of Raven and waved his arm wildly about in the air as he reined the horse to his right and raced it toward her. "Raven!" he called out, bringing the horse to a halt. Leaping from the saddle, he kept hold of the reins. "Right on time."

Her head began to spin; her breathing came too fast, too shallow.

"How do you like her?" he asked.

How could he have known about Mairéad's mare?

He wrapped her hand in his, the pad of this thumb running lightly over her fingers. "Raven?"

His touch gradually brought her back to him. "Sh-she is a fine horse, m-my lord," she managed to sputter at last.

"Here," he said, pushing the reins into her hand, "she belongs to you now."

Raven stepped back, away from the beast, raising her hands in front of her like a shield. "N-no. I could not possibly accept such a gift."

"Nonsense," he said, thrusting the leather toward her once more. "You have been riding with Brookshire long enough. It's time you had your own mount."

The mare shifted her weight toward Raven, as though sensing her new mistress. Slowly, hesitantly, Raven reached out her hand and took the reins.

"Go on," the marquess urged, taking the red's lead from Flaugherty and hoisting himself on to his back. "Mount up."

Her gaze darted to the horse, then Devan, and then to the mare again.

"Unless you do not believe you are equal to the task," he taunted, amusement filling his eyes and his mouth curling into a rakish grin.

Hang the dreams! She'd become more than capable of any mount with Brookshire's instruction. Lifting her left foot into the stirrup, Raven swung her right leg over the mare's back and straddled her, then slanted a saucy glance at the marquess. "My ability to handle this creature is not in question, my lord. Perhaps you should ask yourself if you and that hack of yours can keep up?"

With a firm heel into the mare's side, the horse bounded forward with a high-pitched whinny and headed back down the hill, racing beyond the lake and headed for the wood. Raven drank in the thrill of the speed, marveling at the strength she felt move beneath her. Short runs had been all the overprotective Brookshire had allowed, and she'd never felt quite secure enough on the gray to let the horse take rein. But on the mare's back, she felt as though they'd ridden together ten thousand rides.

In her mind, she saw herself atop the white horse, in far off fields, the cumbersome skirt replaced by boy's breeches and boots. For a brief moment, she wondered if there had been a time before Dahlingham that she had ridden. Then she realized it was not a vision of the past, but of the future. She would ride every day, and the boots and breeches would surely make for an easier ride!

Leaning forward, Raven urged the horse faster with another sharp nudge to the ribs. Then, dropping the reins, she held fast to the white mane. Together they raced the wind at defiant speed. Tears blinded her eyes, and she closed them, at last relinquishing all control, as the horse vaulted into the shelter of trees. The mare followed a course of her own, leaping fallen branches, dodging trees that stood in her path, her hoof beats solid and steady on the hard dirt floor of the forest.

Ahead, light broke through the dense shadows of leaves and branches. Devan called to the red, pushing him hard to fight the thick underbrush and catch the mare and her rider. He gave another stern heel, determined to close the distance between them, just as the white horse soared into the grassy, sunlit meadow with a triumphant bray.

All at once, the mare spun around and reared, wild and untamed. Raven and the white horse confronted him now, just as they had in his dreams. Hauling on the reins, he brought the red to a jolting halt, just short of the edge of the wood.

Raven's breathless laughter wafted to him on the breeze,

beckoning him. Flipping the leather, he commanded the red forward a few steps into the grass and let go a relieved sigh when he felt the warmth of the sun upon his face. Pushing his boot into the red's side, he made his way to Raven.

He came up beside her, both he and the red out of breath and rather humbled after having been left so thoroughly in the wake of Raven and her mare. "This horse . . ." He paused to catch his breath. "She suits you?"

"Oh, she does!" she exclaimed, her cheeks still flushed from the exhilaration of the ride.

Pushing his windblown hair from his eyes, Devan's grin emerged. "I am glad." He swung his right leg over the red's back and dropped to the ground. Looking up into her eyes that sparkled like amethyst crystals in the afternoon sun, he held out his hand. "I fear your pace too exhausting for me and my *hack*. Would you care to join me for a leisurely walk?"

Nodding, Raven accepted his hand, as he put his other around her waist and lifted her from her saddle. Her body slid along his as he set her to her feet, and when she turned to him, their gazes locked.

It was a dreadfully precarious position Devan now found himself in, so close her fragrance filled his senses. Her body trembled against his with her every quivering breath, her eyes were wide, expectant, and her fair lips parted slightly. God, his desire for her in that moment was beyond bearing, and without thought, he inclined his head and brushed his mouth to hers. But before he could kiss her fully, she broke the kiss, ducked her head and moved around him.

"The mare is truly handsome, Lord Castlereagh," she called back, flipping her black tresses over her shoulder as she walked further into the meadow. "I thank you."

Devan chuckled, momentarily lost in the sway of her

hips. Loosening his cravat, he regained himself, struggle that it was when one considered the beauty possessed by the woman, and went after her.

After leaving Raven that morning, he'd ridden straight to Baron Coushite's estate just north of Dublin and issued his invitation for he and Priscilla to attend supper at Dahlingham that evening. There was part of Devan that longed to be done with Coushite and his daughter once and for all, and he'd been tempted to simply set forth his intentions then and there. But he knew Priscilla, and once she had her mind set on something—as she had her mind set on becoming the next Marchioness of Castlereagh—nothing he said would be enough to sway her. No, with Priscilla, it would take much more aggressive tactics. So, as much as he wished it could be otherwise, he would have to bring the woman into his home, allow her to witness his affection for Raven. Then, not only would he gently explain that he could not be her escort to the Dahlingham ball, but he would issue his proposal to Raven.

As he caught up to her in the meadow, Devan shuddered. He was not the sort of man who took pleasure in another's pain, even someone as callous as Priscilla. And it was an unfortunate thing that it would take such drastic measures to convince her once and for all of his affection and intentions where Raven was concerned. But better to set matters straight now—entirely—than allow her to harbor any further delusions.

Pulling Raven's arm through his, Devan gazed down into her eyes. When she smiled up at him, he knew then, regardless of the difficulties he faced tonight, all would be well. For when all was said and done, Priscilla would find another peer on whom to bestow her attentions, and he and Raven would begin their life together.

The penetrating heat of his dark eyes enveloped her, and his touch, as he wound her arm around his, sent a tingle through her body.

What had gotten into him? For that matter, what had come over her? When confronted by his smoldering gaze, she had longed to kiss him the way she had kissed him in her dream, and she would have, had he not leaned to kiss her first. But then something made her pull back—fear, perhaps, that he'd acted only on impulse, whereas she craved his kiss as she did life's breath. Or could it be that she feared her kiss would transform him once more?

Warily, she smiled up into his eyes, and when there was no sign of Séamus, she breathed a quiet sigh, and fell easily into his rhythm as they strolled, allowing herself the indulgence of holding his arm a little tighter and walking just a bit closer.

"Raven . . ." Her name tumbled musically from his lips causing her pulse to flutter. "May I ask a favor of you?"

"Of course."

"All things considered, it would honor me for you to use my Christian name. Devan," he insisted.

"*Devan,*" she said, tasting it.

"Ah, very good." He took his eyes from her and looked straight ahead as they came upon an ancient oak that stood taller than any tree she'd ever seen. Slipping his arm from hers, he shrugged off his coat and laid it upon the ground. "Let us sit a while beneath this beautiful blue sky." He waited until she was seated, and then came down beside her, stretching his long form out casually, while reaching into his waistcoat. "While in Dublin, I found something that reminded me of you."

"Of *me?*"

When his hand reappeared, he held it fisted. "Your

eyes," he said, unclenching his fingers.

A delicate golden lace necklace wound itself around his fingers, and at the end, a glittering tear-shaped amethyst, set in the midst of tiny pearls.

"Did I ever tell you how beautiful your eyes are?" he asked, guiding his hands beneath her hair to clasp the necklace around her neck.

Speechless, she could only shake her head.

Pushing her hair back over her shoulders, his fine mouth curled at the corners as he admired the ribbon of gold and amethyst. "In comparison, the jewel pales, for it has not the light of your eyes."

"Lord Castlereagh—"

"Devan, remember?" Taking her hand in his, he raised it to his mouth. "As I am certain you are aware, there is to be a ball at Dahlingham."

"Mrs. Captain has told me and—" She stopped just short of confiding Brookshire's invitation. How she'd anticipated flaunting it before him only a short while earlier. But somehow, now, the thought was not so very appealing.

"And?"

She shook her head. "It is certain to be a grand event."

"Grand, indeed," he smiled. "It is a tradition that dates back more than two centuries. Truth be told, I am not so fond of such pomp and extravagance, though I have kept this tradition since becoming marquess. However, this year, for the first time I recall, I find myself looking forward to the event with great anticipation."

"What is it that is different this year, my lord?" she asked, even as her heart sank. Priscilla would be on his arm, and no doubt warm his bed after. She glanced away from him, now finding the glimmer in his eyes detestable.

"You, Raven."

Stunned, her eyes rose to his once more. "M-*me?*"

The rich, merry sound of his laughter swathed her in its warmth. "Do not tell me that astounds you?"

"Frankly, my lord—"

"*Devan.* I understand Mrs. Captain has taken the liberty of having your gown made in London?"

"So she has said."

"I have told her to spare no expense," he said, taking her shoulders gently in his hands. "You are to have whatever you desire in the way of adornments—emeralds, rubies, diamonds. Anything. You have merely to ask and it shall be granted."

She pressed the amethyst lightly between her thumb and finger, still stunned by the extravagant gifts he'd bestowed upon her. "Devan, this . . . and the mare . . . you have already given me too much."

"I want to give you everything your heart desires, Raven."

As if reading her heart, the marquess leaned closer and pressed his lips to hers, his arm encircling her, and his hand splaying across her back to hold her to him. But this time Raven had no fear—not of Séamus, not of losing herself, for she had to admit to herself that she loved him. Had somehow always loved him.

Raven gave in to the gentle force of his mouth and melted into the warm haven of his arms. In a sensuous, lustful dance, his tongue met hers, his kiss deepening, becoming more urgent. She heard herself moan softly, as the sweet, heavy ache of yearning settled deep inside her.

Longing to touch him, she ran her hands over the contoured muscles of his chest beneath his white linen shirt. His heat surged from her hands through her body, and then became a flame when he broke the kiss and his tongue leisurely trailed a hot path to the hollow of her neck where her pulse raced madly.

His eyes blackened with hunger when they again met hers. "And I want *you,* Raven," he said huskily, his mouth capturing hers once more in a kiss that rivaled his passionate gaze.

The world began to spin around her in glorious madness. He wanted *her.* She might have thought it another dream, but the truth was in the way he touched her, the fire in his eyes when he looked at her, his kisses.

"There was a time I thought myself destined to be alone for the rest of my days," he murmured in her ear, his breath hot and feathery, his tongue flicking at her earlobe. "But last night . . ."

Raven stiffened, the moment shattered. "Last night?"

"Last night I realized that no man is truly complete unless joined to the woman he loves." Putting his finger beneath her chin, he brought her gaze to his. "I long to be complete. Do you understand what I'm saying?"

The walls of her chest constricted, crushing her heart. She was no lackwit. Of course she understood! A lump formed in her throat and her eyes welled with tears.

Smiling, he pulled a kerchief from his waistcoat and dabbed lightly at her eyes. A few moments before he'd not been so certain Raven would take well to his intention of making her his wife. But such emotion as that now displayed in those lavender-blue eyes . . . now he was most assured she would be agreeable to his proposal. "Which leads me to another matter. While in Dublin, I took the liberty of selecting a dress of amethyst to complement the jewel and your eyes. You are to wear it this evening for supper, for I have invited Arlington and his daughter in order to make an important announcement."

Wiping at her eyes with a sniffle, she pulled abruptly from his arms and leaped to her feet. In wide-eyed wonder, he watched, speechless, as Raven turned, ran to her mare, mounted, and raced from the meadow. Rising, he started to go after her as she disappeared into the trees.

Then a smile eased over his countenance. If nothing else, Devan, Marquess of Castlereagh, was an enlightened and modern man, a man of great insight. And it was this keen understanding of the female nature that assured him that at a time such as this—when a woman's heart was so utterly filled with joy—that she feared coming apart in his presence and merely needed time alone.

Lowering himself to the ground, his grin broadened, and Devan leaned back against the great oak with a satisfied sigh, certain life could get no better.

CHAPTER THIRTEEN

From the streets of Dublin the music rose, and the breeze carried it to the outskirts of town. Mairéad hastily laced her shoes, then ran to the door.

From the kitchen, her mother's voice halted her just as she lifted the latch. "And just where is it ye think ye be going, daughter?"

"Mam, can ye not hear the pipes?"

Her mother rounded the corner, carrying a ladle. Folding her arms in front of her, she smiled. "Aye, daughter, I hear the pipes loud and clear. I expect ye will be home before the sun goes down?"

"Not a moment past," she assured, skipping to her mother and pecking her cheek.

"Don't be in such a hurry, Mairéad."

Mairéad stopped just short of the doorway and turned again to her mother.

" 'Tisn't much, but I want ye to take this." From the pocket of her apron, the woman pulled three coins.

"Oh, Mam, I can't. 'Tis all ye have."

" 'Tis not all, and not often ye get a chance to spend a day like this, now is it?" She gently pushed the coins into Mairéad's palm and closed her fingers around them.

"Yer a saint, ye know." Mairéad threw her arms around her mother's neck, squeezing tight. "I love ye, Maime."

"And I love ye."

Stepping back, Mairéad frowned. "Are ye sure ye won't be about comin' along? The day will do ye good."

"Nil, daughter. 'Tis not me way. Run along and have a day o' it, and tell me all about it when ye return."

It was not her mother's way. Festivals, in her mother's eyes, were frivolous, and her mother's way was working her fingers to the bone, tending the sick and poor of Dublin. Today, while Mairéad danced in the streets, her mother would take soup and fresh bread to the McCollums, the whole lot of them down with the fever.

The day would come when her mother would never have to work again, she vowed to herself while kissing her mother's cheek one last time before racing out the door. She would be a fine lady with a house full of servants to do for her. Séamus had sworn it.

Little by little the music grew louder as Mairéad approached the center of town. Crowds gathered, and the smell of sweets and meats filled the air.

A hint of a pout formed on her lips. She would not see Séamus today, but only a few weeks remained until the ball, and then she and Séamus would be together. Forever.

The smile returned, as did the carefree step as she tripped lightly down the street, searching the merry faces for Sionáinn. She giggled out loud at the comical masked jesters who juggled apples, and stopped to watch some dancers.

Again she felt a pang deep inside. How she longed to share days like this with Séamus, to have him walk beside her, stealing kisses when nobody was looking, holding hands, laughing together.

Not much longer, she reminded herself, scanning the crowd once more for Sionáinn. It wasn't like her friend to be late, especially for something as important as the festival.

A round of raucous laughter behind her made Mairéad spin around, just in time to see a mass of short red curls come flying through the doorway of the Lochwood Tavern. The young man attached to the bouncing curls stumbled into the street and slid, belly down in the dirt, nearly at her feet, bringing a roar from the men who now stood in the doorway watching.

He scrambled to his feet, his stance at the ready. Swiping his unruly hair from his eyes, he balled his fists, and it was then Mairéad realized the scrapper was naught but a boy.

"I'll take all t'ree of ye on!" he declared, raising his fists with great bravado, flexing the tight, sinewy muscles of his arm.

Three of the onlookers stepped away from the others and moved toward the boy. For a moment, Mairéad thought she was about to witness the lad's death, for his boldness and determination alone would not be enough to best these three who were men grown, and were each better than twice the boy's size. The largest of the men raised a hand to his companions, halting their step. He continued on alone, until he stood less than an arm's length from the boy.

He rubbed his chin thoughtfully, then ruffled the boy's curls with a brotherly affection. "What are ye, fookin' daft, Quin?" he asked quietly.

The younger only glared in response.

"Ye know Dah will take the strap to ye if he hears ye was in the tavern, and would do worse to us for allowin' it."

Quin's arms fell limp at his side and his shoulders slumped. "Dah doesn't have to know, Kel."

"Ah, but those bastards Sean and Paddy," he said with a wink and a discreet nod of his head toward the other two brothers, "would tell the tale on ye, sure as the world."

"Bastards," Quin agreed with a pout.

"Now, give me one good one for the lads to see before leavin'."

Mairéad only had a moment to wonder Kel's meaning before Quin drew back his arm with a grin and gave his brother a blow to the gut that would have sent a less formidable man reeling. "I don't think I'm about wantin' to drink me ale with the likes of ye anyway!" he shouted, loud enough for all to hear.

Kel grimaced and clutched his stomach for good measure. "Good, lad," he laughed under his breath. "Now off with ye!"

Quin mouthed his silent gratitude that his older brother had spared him his dignity, then turned and fled toward the festival.

Noticing Mairéad for the first time, Kel just shrugged with a smile, and then put on his best pained expression before facing the others. "Wait 'til I get me hands round 'is scrawny little neck!" he growled, meeting up with his brothers.

Mairéad watched as the three, and all who had stood watching in the doorway, disappeared inside. She'd been so absorbed in the brotherly battle that she didn't even hear the chorus of fiddles strike up a spirited jig inside the Lochwood Tavern, nor did she notice the sudden rush of people beckoned by it, until it was too late. All at once, she was knocked harshly from her feet and to the dust in the road. Half-dazed, she stood slowly, brushing the dust from the lovely new cream-colored dress her mother had made especially for this day as she straightened. Turning, she was confronted by the last person she'd expected to encounter—Séamus Ó Lionáird.

A beautiful, silvery-blonde haired woman stood beside him, clinging to his arm. Their stares locked. The woman sneered.

Áine.

Her heart began to thud like the hooves of a thousand horses racing through her chest. She glanced back to Séamus and opened her mouth, but the sight of the two of them together, arm in arm, rendered her speechless. Apparently, the sight of Mairéad left Séamus the same.

The uneasy silence was broken by Áine. "Look, Séamus. This beggar is mute as well as clumsy."

Mairéad's stare darted back to Áine.

"I'll have your apology," she demanded.

She looked helplessly to Séamus. He remained silent. Though her gaze remained fixed on him, her words were directed pointedly to Áine. *"And just why would I be about apologisin' to the likes of ye? 'Twas ye who ran me down, and 'tis ye alone who ought to be makin' amends."*

Áine, too, faced Séamus. *"She cannot speak to me in such a manner. Are you not going to say anything, Séamus?"*

At last finding his voice, he took her arm. *"It is a misunderstanding, I am certain. I do not believe the girl meant any harm."*

The girl? *His cool indifference sliced through Mairéad like a blade.*

Gritting her teeth, she turned to Áine, in much the same way Quin had faced off against Kel. *"Ye waged this battle, and 'twill be me pleasure to end it, Áine!"*

At the mention of her name, she stared hard at Mairéad. "Who are you?"

Mairéad advanced, intent on introducing herself in a manner Áine would be hard-pressed to forget, but Séamus cut between them, pushing Áine to the side.

"Young woman, for your own sake, it would be best to walk away. Now," *he stressed.*

She glared at him defiantly, her eyes burning with anger and humiliation, and her heart aching as though it would break in two. Mairéad envisioned herself lunging at him with a banshee's scream, and exacting an injury that would rival the pain his defense of Áine had inflicted upon her. Before she could enact her vengeance, someone grabbed her from behind, pulling her back.

"No, Mairéad," Sionáinn whispered, drawing her into her arms. "Don't let her win."

"Raven, it is time."

Her eyes blinked open, and Raven was startled to still be

sitting in the tub, with Collette looking down on her.

"Gads, girl, you have been in there for more than an hour. You must be freezing!"

"I am," she confessed, grasping the soap with stiff fingers, and working up a quick lather over her arms and legs, and then her face. Finally, she plunged fully beneath the icy water before coming up for air with a body-wracking shudder.

"Is it late?" she asked, her teeth chattering behind bluish lips, as she stepped out of the tub and hastily ran the coarse towel over her skin.

"It is after five o'clock already. We've not much time." Handing her a robe, she waited until Raven was seated, then began smoothing the ratted curls of Raven's dark tresses.

Gazing at her reflection in the mirror, she contemplated the face that stared back at her with a frown. Oh, why must she have these feelings for the impossible Marquess of Castlereagh? They led to nothing but torment and heart-break for her. But no matter how irritating, or how seem-ingly mean spirited, her feelings for him grew stronger each day. It made no sense at all—longing for the attentions of a rake, and finding nothing desirous in a man who twisted himself in knots trying to capture her attention.

Then and there she decided there was no choice left to her but to cast all the charm she could muster upon Brookshire, for he seemed to be her only escape from Dahlingham before any wedding between Devan and Priscilla took place, which she was now certain would tran-spire with the announcement that was to come this evening.

Still, she found it odd that Devan would bestow such grand gifts upon her—the mare, the necklace and the lovely lavender brocade dress—on the eve of his announcement to wed Priscilla. Then, like the broadside of a sword, his inten-tions struck her. Devan's gifts, his kisses—it had all been

his not-so-very-subtle way of letting her know that he expected her to stay on as his . . . *mistress!*

She closed her eyes tight, pushing back the tears that
threatened to fall with the realization, vowing then and
there she would never weep for Devan Castlereagh again.

Worse fates could befall her, possibly already had befallen her, than a marriage of convenience. Such a union
was all she could ever hope for with Brookshire, for her love
for him would always be much as she would expect her love
for a brother to feel, if she had one. But in return for the
promise of escape from the inevitable agony she would
know were she to remain at Dahlingham, Raven would be a
good wife to Victor and give him his heir. Then, since apparently men of title commonly took mistresses, perhaps
Victor would find his own. If he didn't come up with the
notion himself, she'd suggest it—hand pick one if need be—
so her duties as a wife would not be so necessary, for it
would most certainly muddle their friendship.

Checking herself over in the mirror, she pouted, feeling
rather sorry for herself at that moment. The vision of her future was hardly a romantic one. But it would be comfortable
and secure, she reminded herself, and it would put an end to
any illusions she might harbor where Devan was concerned.

Her sigh echoed the hopelessness she felt inside. Any
time now, Lord Coushite and his daughter would arrive for
dinner. Then, in the fashion Mrs. Captain would expect,
Raven would greet them. And when Devan made his announcement, she determined, drawing a ragged breath, she
would hold her head high, and never let anyone know her
heart was breaking in the bargain.

By the time Raven entered the drawing room, Lord
Coushite, every bit as horrid as Collette described, stood

talking with Devan in the center of the room, while Priscilla stood on his left.

Devan's gaze fixed on hers the moment she stepped through the doorway. "Miss Raven!" he exclaimed. "Come here, please. I would like to introduce you to our company."

Priscilla slipped her arm possessively through his, an unmistakably fraudulent smile straining her thin mouth as she leaned her flaxen head shamelessly against Devan's shoulder. Her pale eyes of cool blue fairly scoffed at Raven, while her fine features seemed to disappear in the colorlessness of her complexion and hair. Her dress, a putrid shade of yellow-gold satin, fit tightly to her slender frame, with a neckline cut scandalously low, revealing much of her small bosom, which had apparently been pushed as high as manageable.

Had the moment not been quite so heart wrenching, she might have laughed at the woman's failed attempt to appear blessed. But pallid and unendowed or not, she was still somehow quite beautiful, in a deceptively fragile way, and it was she Devan carried on his arm as he met Raven halfway.

"Miss Raven, I would like you to meet Arlington, Lord Coushite, and, of course, you have already had the pleasure of meeting his daughter, Lady Priscilla."

Pleasure? There were many ways she would have described her last encounter with Priscilla, but *pleasurable* was not among them.

Lord Coushite grabbed Raven's hand and brought it up against his salt and pepper whiskered mouth. The man was truly repulsive, but she feigned a smile, and then, freed of his grip, she employed a discreet swipe against his cuff to remove the sticky sherry residue he'd left on the top of her hand.

"Why, Devan, I had no idea the Irish could look so remarkable dressed up!"

Devan's eyes darkened and he shot a scowl in Coushite's direction. "Arl—" he began, before Lady Priscilla cut him off.

"Father is correct. If I did not know better, I might actually mistake her for a London servant," she sniped, clinging tighter to his arm.

Indignation burned her eyes, and suddenly all she could think of was fleeing.

But before she could turn away, Devan's fingers wrapped possessively around her hand. "Miss Raven, you are the very image of loveliness this evening." Stepping out of Priscilla's hold, he bowed and brushed her wrist with his lips before rising.

There was something about the way he looked at her then—something tender, something infinite. Her cheeks prickled with a heated blush and he grinned.

"Oh, Devan," Priscilla sneered, pushing her way through, forcing his hand to part with Raven's, breaking the magic. "A glass of wine?" She took him again by the arm and led him away.

"*Ahem,* I'll have another sherry, as well," Coushite exclaimed, hurrying behind them, leaving Raven standing alone in the center of the room.

Lady Priscilla was determined to slight her at every opportunity, and the thought of enduring an entire evening with her might have been unbearable had all thoughts of Priscilla not dissipated with the marquess's summons.

"Please, join us," he beckoned, pouring a glass of wine and holding it out to her.

Walking across the room, she took the glass from his hand, their fingers meeting for just a moment, sending a shiver of warmth through her.

He motioned for her to sit on the chaise, and Raven could have sworn he moved to sit next to her. But before it became a full realization, Priscilla shoved her way in between them and placed herself strategically so he had nowhere to sit except at the furthest end of the chaise, away from Raven. When Priscilla shot an insolent smile of satisfaction in her direction, Raven bowed her head, knowing it had merely been the imaginings of her heart.

"Raven." Priscilla made it sound obscene. "Such a silly name must be a dreadful burden."

Devan came gallantly to her defense. "I, for one, am fond of it."

"But that couldn't possibly be your *real* name, could it?" she asked, ignoring him. "Certainly even the Irish do not name their children after birds."

"Birds," Lord Coushite sniggered, slurping his sherry.

Priscilla was treading dangerously close to the edge, and Raven was inclined to push her over. The woman had won Devan's heart, and of that Raven had no control, although it was difficult to fathom how he could have ever referred to such an odious female as an *angel.* Her endurance having reached its limit, Raven stood, her hands clenching into white-knuckled fists.

At that very moment, Tourish entered the room, unwittingly saving Priscilla. "Dinner is served, my lord," he drawled.

"Ladies, Arlington," Devan said tensely, clearly recognizing the fire in Raven's eyes, "shall we go to the dining room?"

The blonde vixen threw a tight-lipped sneer in Raven's direction. "I would love to! And of course, you will sit next to me, won't you, Devan, darling?"

★ ★ ★ ★ ★

On this night, the servants were out in full force. Six footmen stood in attendance around the table, with Tourish's impeccable eye overseeing the whole affair. The best bone china and Venetian crystal were laid out, with a fresh arrangement of flowers in the center of the table, and tall golden candles lined from end to end.

Rather than risk a chair placed next to Priscilla or her father, Raven did not wait to be shown to her seat, but sat in her usual chair at the far and of the table, opposite the marquess. Supper had not yet been fully laid out when the familiar—and *welcome*—boom of Victor's voice permeated the corridor leading into the dining room.

"Castlereagh!"

An ally.

Brookshire's entrance was not without his usual flair, and he tossed her a wink and a smile.

"I saw Arlington's carriage, and assumed you'd be occupied, so I took the liberty of letting myself in," he explained, placing a hearty slap on Devan's shoulder before rounding the table to stand next to Raven. "Hope you don't mind, old man."

"Why would I?" the marquess growled sarcastically. "Do have a chair."

Victor bowed, a devilish light twinkling in his eyes. "Miss Raven, you are the picture of perfection this evening!"

"Why, thank you, Your Grace. And you are looking rather dapper yourself."

"Ah, as kind as you are beautiful." He lifted her hand to his lips.

Priscilla's face paled to a sickly grayish-white. "Victor?"

He angled around to face the woman, as though he'd only just realized she occupied the same room. "Lady Priscilla, greetings," he offered with a distinct edge to his tone. Then he nodded stiffly to Lord Coushite, "And to you, Arlington."

Devan cleared his throat, bringing all eyes from an apparently speechless Priscilla to him. "I am curious, Brookshire, does your visit have a purpose," he asked, his brows slanting into an ill-humored frown, "or have you simply come to beg another meal?"

Victor fell into his chair, his grin broadening. "I most assuredly have a purpose, Castlereagh." There was no small amount of sarcasm lacing his words, and Raven braced herself for whatever mischief he was about. "When I met up with you on the road to Dublin this afternoon, you said that choice mare was a gift for our lovely Miss Raven. So actually, my visit was merely to see how the beast had gone over." As soon as his glass was filled, he sipped his wine. "Of course, I also remembered you mentioning that our good friend Arlington and his handsome daughter would be calling, and I could not bring myself to pass up the opportunity to dine with such entertaining company."

"I dare say *our* Miss Raven took rather well to the animal," he said, eyeing the duke suspiciously.

Priscilla seemed to find her voice at that precise moment, in the form of a high-pitched squeal. "You actually purchased a horse for her?"

"He did," Victor answered for Devan. "A blood. And a damn fine one, to boot!" A wide, almost taunting, grin spread across his animated face.

Whatever his game, Raven thought, he was enjoying it immensely.

Priscilla's piercing glare landed on Raven, her rage simmering just below the calm veneer. "How like Devan, to indulge you in whatever you ask of him. And how like . . . *your kind.*"

"Pardon?" Raven asked, dropping her fork to her plate with a clank.

"You really must learn not to solicit gifts, otherwise your peasant upbringing will become all too apparent. In fact, some may even speculate that you are little more than a practiced swindler, using your wiles and charms to take advantage of unsuspecting men of title."

Devan crumpled his napkin within his fist. "What are you—" But Raven raised her hand, cutting him off.

Out of respect for Devan, she'd held her tongue with every belittling comment that spewed forth from Priscilla's venomous mouth. But the look of sympathy in his eyes, and the chilling triumph in hers, was more than Raven could bear, and she was not about to let this last degradation pass.

Suddenly, Brookshire's hand reached under the table and firmly pressed to her knee, preventing her from standing. Raven tossed the duke a frown.

Shaking his head discreetly, he leaned toward her and whispered, "Keep smiling, fair Raven. Do not allow her this win."

Victor was right, she realized. Priscilla had baited her all evening, and no doubt a scene was precisely what she hoped to accomplish. And the last thing Raven wished to give her was the satisfaction by making a spectacle of herself.

Taking a deep breath, she squared her shoulders, and trained her most innocent smile upon Priscilla. "We could not be more in agreement, Priscilla. A lady of quality would never ask for a gift, and I assure you, I did not ask."

"Why else would he see fit to bestow such an extravagant benefaction?"

"I truly have no notion as to the why of it." Raven's gaze shifted to the marquess, her grin growing wry. "Perhaps he could enlighten us both?"

Priscilla faced Devan as well, awaiting his explanation.

Shrugging, he simply said, "Raven is an accomplished rider, and I felt she should have her own mount."

For a moment, Priscilla seemed incapable of comprehending, and then her features drew into a dark scowl. She nudged Arlington.

The old man choked on his mouthful of pheasant. "*Ahem,* Castlereagh . . ." He glanced to his daughter while swiping at the grease trickling from the corner of his mouth, then looked uneasily back to Devan. "It may not be the appropriate time—"

"Has that ever stopped you before, Arlington?" he asked dryly, sensing the conspiracy.

"Oh!" he bit out, taking a long slurp of his sherry. "Rare form, Castlereagh! But as I was saying, there is a matter I must take up with you."

"And what would that be?"

"Well . . . I . . . *um* . . ." Coushite's reservations were becoming more apparent, and he stumbled over the words.

"Oh, for Heaven's sake, Father, spit it out," she seethed in annoyance.

"There have been, *um,* rumors, if you will—"

Priscilla's patience bottomed out. "What Father is trying to say, Devan, is it seems your little Irish pet has been stealing away in the night when you are asleep, and carousing with a band of peasants."

"That is a lie!" Raven took to her feet swiftly, the intense anger that had been building inside now blazing in her eyes.

Brookshire only leaned back in his chair, knowing things had progressed to a point where there was no preventing the inevitable. And, all things considered, he thought it time.

Disregarding Raven's outburst, she continued. "One of

Father's tenants came across her a week past in the market with your housekeeper, and said he recognized her then, but couldn't quite put his finger on just where he might have seen her before. Then, last night, he saw her again, this time in the company of a man he could only describe as dark and sinister. Apparently, the two seemed rather well acquainted, even though this man was no one Father's tenant had seen in Dublin before. And your Raven was acting quite the little slut."

Raven stood there, too stunned to form the words that would exonerate her of Priscilla's lies and accusations.

"It pains me to be the one to tell you this, but you have been deceived, Devan. I think it fair to assume this woman never lost her memory. In fact, I am most certain she and this man have taken advantage of your generosity for a purpose. But now that you know the truth, you can do away with her, before she robs you blind—or worse."

Lord Coushite slurred his concurrence. "*Ahem*. Yes, robs you blind."

The room became deathly silent. Then Devan's rumbling laughter rang out, but just as quickly trailed off when he gazed into Raven's eyes. Tears glistened on her lashes, and he noted the slightest trembling of her chin. She'd mistaken the intent of his laughter, but before he could explain, she turned from him and fled.

His glare fell on Priscilla, who now sat looking quite smug.

Devan opened his mouth to admit the *dark and sinister* man was himself, but decided she was not worth the effort of an explanation. Muttering a curse, he pushed back his chair, rose, and stormed from the dining room after Raven.

"Well, I never!" Priscilla shrieked.

Brookshire smirked and scratched his chin. "No, I am

certain you have not, Priscilla. But that is entirely beside the point, now isn't it?"

"What do you mean, Victor?" she pouted.

"I say, in your hurry to shame the girl and assail her character, you have effectively concluded this little party. Not quite the end you had plotted, is it?"

At that moment, Tourish entered with a designing nod to Brookshire. "Lord Coushite, I have taken the liberty of having your coach readied."

"B-but we have not even had our after-dinner port," objected Coushite.

"And I must speak to Devan."

Shaking his head at Priscilla, Brookshire took her by the arm and helped her to her feet. "It is best you do not press the issue. But I'll personally see to it the marquess does what is proper, and I assure you, everything shall work out as it should."

"Oh, Victor, do you promise?" she whined as he guided her down the corridor.

"On my honor, Priscilla."

"I knew I could count on you, Victor."

"Ah, yes, thank you," sputtered Lord Coushite, allowing Headsley to help him with his overcoat, at the same time as he was being escorted out the door.

Victor leaned toward Tourish as the two watched Coushite and his daughter step up into the carriage. "How did you manage to get the carriage and their wraps so quickly, old boy?"

The butler tossed him a conspiratorial grin. "I have had them ready all along, Your Grace."

"Ah, good show, Tourish."

CHAPTER FOURTEEN

"Raven, please open the door."

"I have nothing to say to you!" she shouted from inside her chamber.

He pounded his fist against the door, louder than before. "Open this instant, I say!"

Suddenly the door opened a mere crack, and Collette peeked out. "I do believe you should allow her some privacy. She is quite upset at the moment. Could this not wait until the morn?"

"I have something I must tell her."

"She is quite aware of the purpose of this night's gathering," she whispered, "and if I may say, Lord Castlereagh, I do not think she is up to hearing any of your declarations. Have you no heart?" she whispered.

"But—"

"Be on your way and do not press the issue further."

The door shut firmly. Devan leaned against the wall and slid to the floor, letting his head fall hopelessly into his hands.

Priscilla had been true to form the entire evening. But he'd held his tongue, resisted the urge to put her in her place, reasoning his forthcoming announcement would be a harsh enough medicine.

Had all things progressed as planned, after dinner, he'd have broken the news to Coushite and his ill-tempered daughter that he would be unable to escort Priscilla to the ball. Then he would have gotten down on bended knee and proposed to Raven, and when she accepted, he'd intended to announce they would wed as soon the banns could be posted.

That announcement, in itself, would have been quite enough to throw Priscilla into a frenzy of wailing and tears, for Raven would have won the very thing Priscilla coveted most—a place in society as the marchioness.

To hell with Priscilla and her besotted father.

Then he cursed himself for not seeing soon enough where the evening was headed. This was *not* the end he'd envisioned for this night.

More than two hours later, Collette slipped from Raven's chamber and into the corridor. She offered not a solitary word that he might vindicate himself against. Only a bladed glare, before she spun and stormed away.

He glanced to Raven's door and wondered if it would be a better thing to put off this moment. But time had a ghastly way of stealing love from his grasp.

Rising, he took a deep breath. Taking hold of the doorknob, he turned until the latch let go and the door fell open. As he crossed the threshold, the sound of Raven's quiet weeping came to him.

Summoning his resolve, he closed the door behind him, then made his way slowly through the chamber and knelt beside her bed. Glistening teardrops veiled her lashes. But Raven was asleep.

Gently, he brushed back a stray lock of hair from her face.

Her eyes fluttered, then gradually opened. Raising her head, she squinted into the darkness, then drew a sharp breath and pulled back, as though scalded by his touch. "Ye should not be here," she whispered, moving quickly to the other side of the bed and sliding from beneath the quilt.

"I had to see you . . . to explain—" He walked toward her, reached out his hand. When she recoiled, his arm fell limply to his side. "This cannot wait until the morrow."

Raven covered herself hastily with her robe. "What could ye say that I'd wish to hear?" she asked, throwing back her shoulders and meeting his gaze squarely, the pain in her eyes more than he could bear. "How could ye let her assail me that way?"

He came a step closer, but she pointed an accusing finger, forcing him back a stride. "If you only knew how I longed to take you in my arms and tell her everything."

"Do ye not understand how it tears me apart when I see her on yer arm? And ye did not defend me against her."

Tenderly, he traced the trail of an offending teardrop with the pad of his thumb, causing her to draw in a sharp breath. "I know I do not deserve your forgiveness. Yet I seek it, just the same, and pray you can find it in your heart to grant it."

"I've loved ye far too long, and ye just keep breakin' me heart," she sobbed.

The breath caught in his throat. She *loved* him. Devan pulled her into his arms.

She fought his embrace. "Let me go."

His arms gently enfolded her to him, and he held on, until at last, unable to fight any longer, she gave into his possession and wept against his chest. Cradling her closer, he stroked her hair and kissed the top of Raven's head. "*Shhh,*" he soothed. "No more tears."

"Make me yers," she pleaded, clenching his shirt within her hands. "Give me your vow for all eternity."

"If it be your wish, we shall wed immediately."

At last she lifted her eyes and met his gaze, new misery marking her cheeks. " 'Tis not a marriage before man I ask," she whispered, her fingers sliding over his chest and slipping beneath the lace of his collar.

"Then what?"

"The joining of our souls, this night, and for all time."

Devan might have thought he misunderstood, until her fingers drifted to the buttons of his shirt, and the heat of her lips against his bare chest branded his skin.

"Now, love," she murmured, her kisses falling like hot silk down the muscled line of his stomach. Then, straightening, she stood eye to eye with him once more. "And then, even *eternity* can't sever us, one from another." Raven's arms slipped around his neck. Closing her eyes, she brought him down to her, and touched his mouth with hers. Feathery soft, her lips quivered as they brushed his a second time.

Taking her by the shoulders, he held her away from him and gazed into her eyes. For the first time, he saw himself reflected in dark lavender. He drank in the fragile beauty of each delicate feature.

An ebony strand of curls dropped to shield her face when she looked away. Devan moved it aside, cupped her chin in his hand and brought her gaze back to his. She peered up to him through long, dark lashes, her eyes posing one thousand questions, and whispering ten thousand vows to his heart.

More emotion than he'd felt in the whole of his life swept through him, and in that moment, he realized he was, for the first time he could recall, truly fulfilled.

"I love you, *Raven*."

The sound of her name brought Raven from her dreams, to find Devan embracing her in a way most intimate. The rapid beating of her heart and the quickness of her breathing echoed inside her head.

A startled gasp was all she could manage when he cupped her cheek within his warm, tender hand. The pad of his thumb smoothed over the curve of her lips. "There is nothing in life I desire more than to make love to you," he murmured, his words a flickering sigh against her mouth. "But a moment more in your presence, and I will not have the strength to walk away. If it is your will, send me away now, before it is too late for us both."

This is a dream, she told herself, a chill passing through her. Another bittersweet dream, just as it had been a dream the night before when he'd danced with her at the pier. She struggled to awaken, knowing too well the sheer heartbreak of living out in her dreams a life that could never truly belong to her.

Inclining his head, he brushed her hair with a whispered acceptance of what he'd heard in her silence. A half-smile formed amidst the shadows that danced across his face, then his fingers slowly released her, his arms dropped to his sides, and he turned toward the door.

Raven fell back against the wall with the full force of the realization that he was not a figment of her imagination. Indeed, he was as real as she, and all the love she felt for him.

The caress of his calloused hands had been gentle and his words, a selfless denial of the hoarse desire in his voice. And his eyes, reflecting so tender an emotion in their dark depths that she could almost believe it was . . . *love.*

Did it matter how they had reached this moment in time, when to love him, and be loved by him—if only for this night—was all the love she needed to live out the rest of her days?

"Stay."

Her breathy whisper brought Devan around on his heel, and in one stride, he reached out his arms and gathered her to him. In the next moment, he was kissing her, her lips parting of their own volition, an invitation that required no words. There was no lingering hesitancy as there had been when she'd kissed him before, for her lips yielded beneath his, her tongue meeting his. She pressed her supple young body to him, and her head fell back to allow him a taste of the delicate skin of her neck.

He kissed where her heart pulsed in the hollow of her throat, while tugging the robe over her shoulders and down her arms. With his fingers, he traced the pebbled outline of her nipples through the soft pink gossamer gown, and then his mouth followed, pleasuring her with gentle nips, until her hands fisted in his hair and he heard the first sweet moan of desire from somewhere deep in her throat.

His passionate kisses had sent Raven's world reeling, and a tight knot of longing settled heavily in her belly when his mouth claimed her breast, and his hands rode down over the swell of her hips.

Raven brought his kiss back to her lips, but Devan broke the kiss and stared into her eyes with a raw hunger that stole her breath. "From this moment, you are *mine*, Raven." He gathered the pink gossamer within his hands and began to draw the night rail up. "Mine to have," he said, placing a tender kiss to one eye and then the other. His lips then lightly touched each cheek, while he smoothed a hand over the flat planes of her stomach and through her silky curls. "And mine to hold." Devan's mouth came down over hers, just as his palm cupped the soft folds hidden beneath the curls.

One finger slipped into her, stroked her, to the same slow, sensuous rhythm his tongue stroked hers. Her body answered with a need to draw him deeper inside her and she arched against him.

"And mine," he breathed huskily, falling to one knee before her, "to worship."

Lifting her leg, he brought her foot to rest on his knee, and he kissed first the inside of one thigh, and then the other. His next kiss was the most reverent of kisses, and the most merciless. Raven sucked in a sharp breath, stunned, braced her back against the wall, and in the same moment she entwined her fingers into his silken black waves, drawing him closer, as desire became a torturous physical ache.

Then Devan proceeded to soothe that ache with his heated, branding kisses and masterful hands, worshipping her in ways she never dreamed possible. An agonizingly sweet surge of pleasure shuddered through her, over and over. She cried out softly, and just as her legs gave way, Devan rose and caught her to him.

Sweeping her up into his arms, he carried her to the bed and gently set her to her feet. He drew the pink gossamer gown up over her head and cast it aside. Though the light in the chamber was but translucent streams of moonlight, his brazen gaze roamed over her nakedness like a hungry wolf. Her arms came up to cover herself in a sudden burst of shyness.

Devan grinned. "It is a bit late for modesty, my lady," he said, bringing her arms to her sides.

He eased her down to the feather mattress and gazed upon her—naked, beautiful, the soft glow of the moon caressing every supple curve. No woman had ever been so exquisite, he thought, running his finger slowly over the bow of her lips before kissing her once more. Nor had any woman ever brought so much emotion—ecstasy and pain combined—to his heart. Kicking off his shoes, he came down beside her and nuzzled his face into the curtain of damp curls strewn across the satin pillow. Inhaling her sweet fragrance, he tasted her skin once more.

It occurred to him that, until that moment, his heart had never been so fully awakened. Never had he wanted any woman so much as he wanted Raven now, nor had he ever loved any woman so deeply—not even Katherine.

Tenderly, his fingers traced the line of her jaw, then drew a teasing path downward. His tongue flicked across her heated skin, tasting the salty dew, lingering delicious torment upon one nipple and then the other, until Raven fairly mewled in pleasure.

She'd never dreamed the touch of a man . . . No, not just any man. Only Devan's feathery touch could spark such tortuous waves of shameless desire.

He chuckled when a whimper of need escaped her, and with a flaming blush she realized he had been watching her every reaction to his ministrations, and delighting in them wickedly. He continued his agonizingly slow torment, his gaze holding hers, as he coaxed her thighs apart and slid one finger into her. New sensations rippled through Raven as he stroked, in and out, until she shivered with raw longing. Her hips arched to him, forcing him deeper. Her hand curled around his neck and brought his mouth to hers. His thumb found her tender gem, while his finger thrust in a sensuous rhythm, until the force of the blinding light that exploded deep within her brought her to him and then sent her plummeting in a hazy blur of bliss, that left her full, but somehow still unfulfilled.

When Raven opened her eyes, Devan hovered over her, smiling. Gradually, she regained her wit and smiled back, while reaching up and fisting the material of his shirt within her hands and bringing him down to her.

"And what of your modesty, my lord?" she asked teasingly, relieving him quickly of the garment.

"I have none," he replied seriously, as she ran the palms of her hands over his chest. He hadn't believed the fire inside him could rage any hotter, but then her fingertips encircled his sensitive nipples. His fingers fumbled clumsily as he hurriedly worked loose the buttons of his trousers, but at last, they were shed, and he came down to her, cradled between her thighs, the searing heat of her body pressed beneath him. "Touch me, Raven," he breathed into her ear, guiding her hand between them.

Her trembling fingers caressed his swelling manhood, timidly at first, and then exploring the hard length of him with a gentle curiosity. He pushed himself into her hand and claimed her lips with a guttural moan, but the risk of spending himself too soon made him pull away.

Gripping her wrists like silken shackles, he held them securely to the pillow above her head.

"Devan . . ." His name fell as a plea from her lips in a husky whisper. He gazed into violet eyes, hooded by a yearning as strong as his own. Raven's body arched, pressing the moist heat of her womanhood to him.

Instinct was to sheath himself within her, but Devan bit off a deep breath and held back.

One had only to gaze upon her to know, without question, a beauty such as Raven's would have been the most sought after in all of Ireland, by commoner and aristocrat alike. But even if she had been another man's lover before tragedy befell her, anything she might have known regarding the relations between a man and a woman were more than likely lost to her.

Her responses seemed instinctive, untutored, proving

her naïve. Her blushes, as she stared into his eyes, proved her an innocent.

He could not allow the lust that raged through him to take control, and loose itself in violent passion, lest he hurt or frighten her. Steeling himself, he freed her wrists. His hands covered her breasts, kneaded gently, while he suckled teasingly on a nipple. Her throaty sigh of pleasure alone was enough to drive him to madness. Her arms drew him to her, while her body rose again to meet his. Beneath him, Devan felt her, quivering and breathless, her heart racing against his chest.

There was nothing or no one then, save Devan. His musky scent enveloped her—man and sweat, heady, masculine. He pressed firmly against her, and somehow, then, Raven knew what was to come. And she welcomed it—prayed for an end to this glorious assault of her body and senses.

"Fill me," she implored him in a ragged whisper.

He slipped one hand beneath the crook of her knee, raised it and held her thigh firmly within his hand. Her searching mouth claimed his kiss in a sensual, lustful dance of tongues and lips. He moved deliberately, tantalizing her with each thrust that fell just shy of its mark.

"Now," she commanded, and again, Raven raised her hips, longing to slake her need, yearning to be consumed, and at last, flesh penetrated flesh.

With a harsh groan of surrender, Devan let his weight fall and buried himself deep within her.

The pain was sharp, searing. He held still, allowing her body to adjust to his size, and gazed down at her with a look of such tenderness that tears blurred her eyes. She blinked, and a tear fell to her cheek. Devan kissed it away and withdrew, leaving her with an emptiness far more painful.

The need to become one with him became stronger,

more urgent. "Love me," she pleaded.

Wrapping his arms around her, he pressed his mouth to hers. She rose to him again, and he pushed slowly into her, until their bodies melded together in rapture, one at last.

My God, you are beautiful to behold, he thought, his chin propped upon his hand, staring down in the dim light at the sleeping woman beside him. Twisting a lock around his finger, he marveled at its silkiness.

There had never been another man, he thought with a grin. He had been her first, and by God, he would be the last! There was no time to waste. He would not give Priscilla, or Brookshire, or even fate the opportunity to foil his happiness this time.

Lowering his head, he nuzzled his face into Raven's hair. She stirred just a bit, her legs entwining around his. Desire gripped him, but he fought it. He would leave her to her peaceful slumber, even if there would be none for him. Breathing her in, he was content to spend the rest of the night gazing upon an angel. They had a lifetime ahead of them to make love.

A tender hand caressed his cheek without warning. Her eyes flickered open slowly, and in her smile, sweet affection.

"Oh, you are awake?" he asked, lightly brushing his fingertips over her hand.

"*Is sea.* I need no longer dream, when every dream has come true."

"And mine." He wrapped her possessively in his arms. "So, how many children shall we have?"

Raven raised up from the pillow. "Children?"

"You do want children?"

"Aye, I want a house full of babes scamperin' 'neath me apron."

Pushing the hair away from her face, he chuckled. "You may have as many babies as you like, but you will not wear an apron. There are plenty of servants at Dahlingham— more than enough to leave you time to spend playing with your children, for that is what children need." He sighed and let go some of the tension that came with the thought. *His* children would never want for anything, least of all their parents' attention and devotion.

Raven's finger softly outlined the furrow in his brow, then glided down the length of his nose to his lips, effectively silencing him. She rose up, touched his mouth with her own, biting tantalizingly at his lower lip.

"Ah," he sighed, "I would advise against teasing me, my lady, unless you are prepared to be ravished."

"I expect nothing less," she murmured against his lips, resting her head back against the pillow, drawing him down with her.

He was not about to argue with the little temptress.

CHAPTER FIFTEEN

"I love you," he whispered, just as she was beginning to doze.

With a yawn, Raven nestled her head against his chest as her eyes slowly fluttered shut. "And I . . ." she breathed, her words faint and trailing off, "I love ye, Séamus."

His mind was suddenly filled with the vision of the flame-tressed woman in the meadow. "Raven!" He shook her gently. "Wake up."

Startled, her eyes opened wide. The Marquess of Castlereagh stared down upon her—she who lay in his arms shamelessly uncovered. Her cheeks colored violently and she concealed her nakedness with the sheet, while moving quickly to the edge of the bed away from him. When he reached out to her, she slid from the mattress to her feet, winding the sheet around her body.

"I am sorry," she murmured, throwing an embarrassed glance to the floor.

"You apologize? For what?" He climbed across the bed and came to his feet. He brought her to him. "There is no need of it," he offered. "You were dreaming. Weren't you?"

She wriggled from his grasp. "You should not still be here."

"Nonsense. We've hours before any of the servants are up and about." Reaching for his trousers, he stepped into them, and then handed her her robe.

"Turn around, if you please."

A throaty laugh escaped him. "It is a little late, don't you think?" he asked, facing the wall.

Blast! She had been rather uninhibited if memory served her. She could have died right then and there. What must he think of such careless and reckless behavior on her part? The one thing she knew for certain was he would never let her live this night down. *Cad.*

"May I look now?"

Raven finished securing the robe. "You may."

"Now that that is settled . . ." Devan sat down on the bed and patted a place beside him.

She turned away, unable to look into his eyes, certain he was surely about to put her in her place once and for all.

His whiskers made a dull scratching noise as he rubbed his unshaven cheek. He sighed with a shake of his head. "Raven, you said something peculiar just before I woke you."

She spun around quickly and faced him once more, terrified. What had she said in her sleep?

"Séamus."

"M-my lord?"

"You called me *Séamus.*"

Panic clutched her and made her stomach twist. "You must have heard wrong." She tried to prevent her fear from seeping into her tone. "I-I know no one by that name."

Of course it was a lie. Séamus was the man who walked with Mairéad in her dreams—and the man she'd half expected to see when she'd opened her eyes, only to be confronted by the marquess, as the recollection of having taken him into her bed came rushing back.

Raven moved to the window and stared out at the tranquil night sky, still avoiding his prying gaze. Suddenly, from behind, his arms enfolded her against him. Pushing the curtain of her hair aside, he placed soft, warm kisses to her neck, rendering her able to do naught but close her eyes and give in to his possession.

"I may have misunderstood," he allowed, his hands roving lightly over the satin robe. He laughed with delight as he felt the pebbling of her nipples. "Woman, I dare say you are more than I can resist."

Slowly, his hands slid lower, masterful as they slipped beneath her robe and sought out the place that ached for his touch. And to her great sorrow she realized her only desire was to fall into his arms and give herself over to him completely.

Breaking free, she angled around to face him. "Devan . . ." His name fell into the air, barely a breathless whisper on her lips. She summoned her strength, braced herself. "Devan," she said with full authority this time, *"no."*

His arms fell limply to his side. "Raven?"

"We *must* come to an understanding."

"What is so urgent that we must reach this understanding at this very moment?" he sighed, his features drawing into a child-like pout.

"What took place between us this night," she began, walking around him and into the center of the room, "must never happen again."

Devan paled, as though her words were a physical blow.

"I admit, my lord, that I am to blame. You were honorable, and set to quit my chamber, and it was I who halted you." God help her, she had wanted him to stay. She had acted on her heart—a heart that loved him madly, a heart willing to sacrifice itself to know, just once, what it felt like to be loved by him in return. But now, she had to reason with her head, lest she lose her heart forever.

Standing tall, she squared her shoulders and prepared to

deliver the words, but they lodged in her throat and became a cry she could scarcely suppress. But it had to be done, now, while she could still bid her heart to deny its most sacred desire.

"I know it is much to ask, but I seek your favor."

"You seek my *favor?*" His eyes left the rumpled sheets where they had laid, bodies entwined, only a short time before. The wounded countenance he wore did not suit a man of his strength and stature, and she almost took back her conviction before dealing it.

"Hear me out, and I believe, once you have had time to consider it, you shall see it is truly best for both of us."

His eyes narrowed skeptically. "Do proceed."

"Though I did not remain at your table long enough to hear your declaration, trust that I knew what it was to be. And I must say, knowing your intentions makes it most improper for me to remain under your roof, especially after . . ." Her glance darted to the bed.

"Improper? How can you—"

She raised her hand quickly, preventing his interruption. With a great sigh of resignation, he leaned back against the wall and crossed his arms over his chest and nodded for her to continue.

"Victor." She walked to Devan and took his hand.

"What has Victor to do with any of this?"

Leading him to the bed, she pulled him down to sit beside her on the edge of the mattress. "I have thought this over at length, and with your help, I believe Victor is the key to freeing us both of this muddled acquaintance."

"*The duke?*"

"As you are aware, Brookshire has called on me quite regularly of late. And upon his most recent visit, he asked to act as my escort to the ball."

165

"*Ahem.* Is that so?"

"It is. And I feel confident in saying it is within my power to obtain an even greater offering from the duke."

"What are you saying? *Marriage?* To *Victor?*"

She nodded. "And with your assistance, I believe it could take place soon." She leaned closer, whispering as though they were discussing a secret strategy against France, rather than conspiring to lure Brookshire into a proposal.

He might have roared with laughter at her scheming if it hadn't cut so deep. "Have you been smitten by the good duke, lady?" he bit out.

Shoulders drooping suddenly, Raven frowned. "If you are asking if I am in love with Victor, I am not. I do, however, consider him a dear friend and care a great deal for him."

"What sort of marriage will that make for my friend?" Devan appeared to make light of the plan, for she detected more than a hint of cynicism in his curt tone. "And what sort of man am I that I would lead him into a loveless marriage?"

" 'Twould not be loveless! I will be a suitable wife and run his household. He would have the love of our children, and my love as his friend. I dare say it is more love than many among your society."

"But what of *passion,* woman? Is the poor wretch doomed to live without it?"

Casting her sight beyond the marquess, she inhaled a deep breath and held it a long moment before answering with a sigh. "I will permit him the freedom to find *that* wherever he chooses."

"Ah," Devan chuckled, "so you will allow him a mistress?"

She nodded.

"And your husband will never feel your . . . *abandon . . .*"

he drew the word out as if he was tasting it, "as *I* have?" He peered at her with a sly sideways glance, while a perverse grin stretched across his mouth.

"Oh, you are impossible!" she hissed, rising to her feet, storming to the other side of the room, her skin prickling hot with humiliation.

"You are correct, I am impossible. Suffice it to say you caught me off guard, but I apologize. Now, pray divulge all, that I might aid you in this little contrivance."

"There is really nothing more to tell you, Lord Castlereagh. I will do my part, and if you would be so kind as to give the duke some gentle prodding of your own, I think it is only a matter of time before I trouble you no more."

"Agreed."

"*Agreed?*" His assent seemed far too easy to obtain, quite out of character for the marquess. And it wounded deep.

"Absolutely. It is time to put an end to all of this. Now, I must be on my way. It wouldn't do for anyone to witness me slipping from your chamber at this hour—at least not if you have designs on old Brookshire, that is." He stormed past her to the door.

The words of Mrs. Captain echoed in her ears. She may well have ruined all chances for herself with the duke, for she'd allowed the one thing Mrs. Captain warned her against.

"Devan?" she ventured warily, knowing she was pressing her fortune to the extreme. But at that particular moment, she did not see any other choice.

Halting in his tracks, he flung a withering scowl her way. "Is there something more you wish to ask of me?"

"Your oath. That you shall not speak of this—*um*—this . . ."

"Do you ask that I not confide to Brookshire that you

freely gave me the passion that he will never know?" A smirk twisted his lips as he turned the knob and opened the door. "I assure you my silence."

The door shut firmly behind him, and she was alone. *Too alone.*

All at once chilled, she wrapped her robe tightly around her shoulders and fell into the chair. Tears welled as she recalled the tenderness of his touch, his words of sweet affection and the emotion in his eyes.

Had she not known better, she might have thought he loved her. But had he loved her, he would have refused to help her win over the duke. It had been love on her part, but merely a moment of pleasure for the marquess. He'd taken of Raven what he'd wanted, and now he would marry Priscilla. Her hand rose to her chest, and she felt the breaking of her own heart.

Raven attempted to convince herself she'd done the right thing, ending it before the affair could go any further. For, she was most positive, to lie with him again would be to lose herself to him completely, and thus she would have no choice but to be his mistress forever. And to possess less than his very soul would be unbearable.

"Raven!" Collette stood in the doorway, with a look of utter confusion sketched upon her face.

Swiping her sleeve across her cheek to dry her tears, she tried to mask her sadness with a smile. "What are you doing here so early, Collette? It is certainly not your duty to be awake at this hour just because I am."

"What have you done?"

Raven swallowed hard and directed her attention to the window at the other side of the room.

The woman rounded the chair and knelt in front of Raven, placing her hands on her knees. "I saw him leave your chamber, and I see the story written in your eyes."

"I will not deny it. I do not know what I have done, Collette," she succumbed to weeping once more and flung herself into the arms that awaited her.

"There, there, Raven. It is not the end of the world," she soothed. "What is important is what follows."

Straightening, she peered down sternly at Collette. "Absolutely nothing is to follow, except that I intend to be far from Dahlingham before Lady Priscilla moves in."

"You mean he's still going to wed her? After . . . ?"

"Of course he is! What happened between us was a mistake. But he did consent to aid me in obtaining a proposal from Brookshire so that we may put an end to this misery once and for all."

"The *duke?* But you do not love him."

"Ach! What is love besides a means to heartbreak? 'Tis better to marry a man with whom I am friends, than to wed one who does not even love me that much. It will work out splendidly, you'll see," she sniffled. "And I will be taking you with me, my dear friend, for it is only you that I could not live a day without."

CHAPTER SIXTEEN

Devan slammed one fist against his desk and let his head fall hopelessly into his other hand. What in the hell had last night been to her?

The fact that she had never been with another man proved she was not in the habit of giving herself casually. But what else could it be considered, if not casual, when she asked him to help her obtain a proffer from his best friend, while the sheets they'd shared were still warm?

Did she really believe he could follow through with such a hideous pact? Did she truly think he would give up his claim on her that easily?

By her own admission, she'd known he'd intended to propose to her, and still, made it clear it was not him she desired, but Brookshire. And he'd sarcastically made the promise she'd requested—hurt, angry, and too proud to fall to his knees and beg.

What choice did he have now, but to help her win a proposal of marriage from the duke, if that's what she truly desired?

None of this made sense.

He'd felt her hesitation, and had been willing to walk away. But *she* had stopped him from quitting the room.

Devan closed his eyes, and the image of her upon the bed came back to him. Again, in his mind, he saw the reflection of love in her eyes. He felt her quivering responses to his every touch. He heard the whispered endearments, as her body arched to meet his, and they found release together from the passion that consumed them both.

His hand came to his chest, and again he felt the tears that had fallen from her eyes when she'd snuggled against him, as he cradled her in his arms before she was lost to peaceful, contented slumber.

The Marquess of Castlereagh, in his little more than thirty years, had known more women's favors than he cared to admit. Yet none of them had ever touched him as completely as Raven. Nor had any ever felt as much for him. And he knew she felt everything as deeply as he—even if she would not admit it now.

Why this bit about marrying Brookshire? She professed to feel little more than friendship for the man. So why would she thrust him away in order to marry a man she did not love?

Devan chewed his lip, tried to put logic to a situation without reason. But no flash of brilliance presented itself.

Always more questions with this one! A grin twitched at his solemn countenance, but the scowl returned quickly.

How could he keep his word to Raven, yet not lose her in the bargain? In frustration he drew his hand through his hair and clamped the tip of his quill between his teeth. His fingers began to drum steadily on the top of his desk, faster and faster as he struggled for a solution.

At last it came.

He would keep his promise to Raven, for he was honor bound. But before Brookshire fell into this farce, Devan would convince her she could not deny her heart and follow through with her plan to wed the duke.

Something deep inside told him his very life depended on it.

★ ★ ★ ★ ★

"Raven!"

The marquess's long stride brought him quickly toward them. Raven sat on the lawn with Brookshire, her stare fixed upon Devan. There was an odd lilt to his voice and glint in his eye, making her wonder what dreadful scene was about to occur. She tensed, her teeth set in apprehension.

"Victor!" He moved swiftly beyond her to shake the hand of the duke and slap him—rather harshly she thought—on the back.

Brookshire choked from the unexpected blow, but Devan's grin seemed to prohibit the duke from thinking it anything other than a well-meant gesture. Somehow, Raven thought otherwise.

"C-Castlereagh!" he sputtered. "I was under the impression you were tending to the duties of your lands today."

Devan sat next to Brookshire, across from Raven, and leaned back in his chair, stretching his long form out casually. "All work and no entertainment makes for a dreary life, old man," he laughed heartily, his voice dripping heavily with the *beau monde* tone Brookshire often sported.

Although with not quite as much exuberance, the duke laughed, too. "So this is where you come for entertainment? I think if amusement is what you seek, you shall be gravely disappointed, friend."

"Oh, I think not, *friend*."

She winced at the bitterness in Devan's voice, and a particular heat prickled her cheeks when he focused his bold gaze on her.

"I find the two of you *most* amusing." Devan sat up a little straighter in his seat, and leaned toward Brookshire, though his gaze never left Raven. "I mean that in the best of ways, of course."

"Of course, Castlereagh."

"What have the two of you been chatting about on this beautiful summer day?"

When Raven said nothing, Brookshire piped up. "It seems our Miss Raven has no passion today."

Of all the misbegotten words to use! She felt her cheeks color violently when she realized Devan caught the use of the word as well, for his grin broadened vilely.

"Oh, I am most certain Miss Raven is entirely *passionate*." He drew the word out, slow and painfully.

"Not for riding, it seems," Victor responded, seemingly oblivious.

Raven let herself breathe again, relieved. But it was not to last long.

"Oh. Riding. Yes, of course." Devan cleared his throat. *"Riding."* He cast a sideways glance in her direction, and she believed she saw the hint of a smirk flash in his eyes.

Damn him. He'd given her his word. And he may not be disclosing the truth in words, but if he were to continue in this manner, Victor would most assuredly catch his not-so-subtle drift.

"I have not lost my passion for the ride, Your Grace."

"No," Devan murmured, "I can attest to that."

Her jaw dropped and Raven nearly expired right there on the lawn. Darting her glance to the duke, he smiled, completely unaware—or so she hoped.

"I-I would simply rather sit in the gentle breeze and enjoy the pleasant company I've been so fortunate to receive," she said, forcing herself to flash a flirtatious smile toward Brookshire. "Is a lady not permitted to sit idly once in a while without cause?"

Lavender fire shot from her eyes, a silent warning to Devan. He knew good and well sitting atop a horse would

173

be most impossible. How she loathed him for trying to force an explanation from her!

"Most assuredly. In fact, most ladies of breeding prefer to sit than engage in any activity that might dishevel their appearance or rumple their skirts. I was just under the impression that . . ." Devan grappled his chin roughly, eyeing her from head to toe in the most indiscreet gaze he could muster, that brought a somewhat amusing blush to her cheeks and then to her bosom and wherever his eyes roamed. "Oh, never mind. It is truly of no importance what I think. Brookshire," he said, facing the duke, "I wish to speak to you in private."

"I promised our lady a carriage ride into Dublin."

Devan put his arm around the duke's shoulders and drew him close. "Listen, *friend,* what I have to say will not take long, but needs to be discussed immediately. I promise I will not steal you away from Raven long."

With a questioning expression, Brookshire sought her approval.

Though the marquess had given her his vow, she wondered now if he intended to disclose the whole sordid truth to Victor. But to protest would serve only to raise the duke's suspicions, so she had little choice other than to trust Devan to keep his word.

"Run along, Your Grace. I will meet you in the drive," she insisted, feeling much like she was leading herself to the slaughter by doing so.

"Lead on, Castlereagh," Victor sighed, throwing Raven a wink and a grin as he stood. "I am quite looking forward to spending the afternoon with the lady and do not wish to be long away from her."

Watching their backs nervously, she chewed fretfully on her lower lip as the two men disappeared into Dahlingham.

She prayed Devan would remain honorable in this matter to the end, and that Victor would take to the prospect of marriage.

"What is it that is so important that you had to drag me out of the company of a beautiful lady?" Brookshire asked impatiently.

Devan motioned to the chaise.

Victor sat, crossed his legs and stretched his right arm along the back of the chaise, his gaze focused intently on Devan as he crossed the drawing room to pour two glasses of brandy. "You seem rather unstrung today, Castlereagh. What is it?"

Devan handed him his glass and then settled into his armchair. Taking a long drink from his chalice, he sighed. This was one conversation he did not wish to engage in. But he seemed to have little choice in the matter. Suppressing a frustrated groan, he compelled the words to come. "It concerns Raven."

"Lovely woman, Miss Raven." The duke's face positively lit up when he spoke her name.

Damn you, Brookshire, Devan thought, *you don't have to make this more difficult than it already is.* Needing to pace off some of his aggravation, Devan stood and moved to the fireplace, where he remained with his back toward the duke, pretending to rearrange some of the items on the mantle.

"Brookshire, it does not appear Raven has had any return of her memory whatsoever."

"Pity."

"And she cannot remain merely a guest at Dahlingham. It isn't proper."

"I would have to agree with you there, old man. Rumors will surely abound throughout London that the rakehell

175

Marquess of Castlereagh has taken an Irish mistress, should she remain sleeping in the chamber next to yours without a husband. You know how the matrons love to gossip. And I must confess, I've often wondered myself if that's been the case," he chuckled.

Turning on his heel, he confronted the duke. "The idea of taking her as my mistress has *never* crossed my mind, Brookshire!" he snapped. "Do not imply that I would ever put her in such a position."

The duke sipped at his drink, carefully noting the emotion that flickered over Castlereagh's face. Obviously he intended to marry the girl, so the sorrow that clouded his dark eyes seemed out of place. "I was not implying you had actually done such a thing. But I have seen the way you look at her, and I dare say it is clear you not only admire her beauty, but you long to possess it." There, he'd paved the way for his friend to make his announcement.

Swallowing the rest of his brandy in one large gulp, Devan moved to pour himself another. He needed something to dull the aching in his heart if he were to follow through with this hellish promise. The second drink he downed straight, and while waiting for the burning in his gut to pass, poured a third.

"I wish only the best for her," Devan said, careful to monitor his tone, as he turned to face the duke once more. "However, even if I was so inclined to possess that hellion of a woman, as you seem to believe, there can be no delusion by either us that she would sooner hang me than wed me."

His heart twisted when Brookshire laughed out loud. "Yes, it does appear that you bring out the ire in her, more often than not."

"For God's sake, Brookshire, would you let me finish?"

He stormed back to the mantle where he did not have to look into the eyes of the man who would most assuredly revel in the knowledge he was about to impart.

"Certainly. Go on."

"She is in need of a husband—someone who will care for her and look out for her best interests. Raven has expressed her fondness for you."

"*Me?*"

"Yes, *you,* Victor!" He summoned the courage to face Brookshire, but oddly, rather than the elation he anticipated, the duke seemed quite befuddled.

"I—I had no idea," he stuttered.

"Now that you do, pray tell, what do you intend to do about it?"

"Do? *Blast,* man, what do you expect me to do?" Victor exclaimed, repositioning himself to the edge of the chaise. His brow was creased and his mouth pursed nervously. "God's blood, Castlereagh! I was not expecting this. I need another drink."

Brookshire rose and walked quickly to the liquor cabinet. Devan watched with interest the way the news of Raven's fondness seemed to throw him off balance, the way his hand shook as he poured the liquor into his glass. He'd been nearly certain the duke had grand designs on Raven; the way he courted her, indulged her, and presented himself as her champion at every opportunity. Was it possible he had not forsaken his vow of eternal bachelorhood after all?

Of course it wasn't! He'd witnessed Brookshire's conquests. Hell, never once in all the years they'd been friends had the duke's attentions toward one woman ever lasted beyond a few visits, in which he charmed her as only Victor could charm a woman. But once he'd achieved the captivation of her body, he was gone, only returning for her favors during periods a new bounty had not presented herself.

But Raven was obviously different, for Victor had gone out of his way to place her on a pedestal. There apparently had been no conquest, of that Devan could personally testify, for it had been he who had taken her virtue. In fact, from the manner in which Raven spoke of the duke, it was safe to assume that not even a kiss had passed between the two of them.

"You have accomplished what you set out to."

"What do you mean by that?" Victor swallowed a mouthful of his drink.

Devan planted himself squarely in front of the duke and pointed an accusing finger mere inches from his face. "You know damn well what I mean! You have wooed her, taken her side, come to her rescue—you've made me look the jackass in front of her. Asking my blessing in your courting was merely a formality, for you'd already planned to possess the beauty you accuse me of desiring."

The duke soared to his feet. Although nowhere near as tall, Brookshire seemed not about to let Devan Castlereagh accuse him of doing anything intentional to bring about Raven's fancy without a fight.

In his scurrilous mood, the marquess balled his fists eagerly, welcoming the opportunity. "Please, Victor. Throw the first blow."

Suddenly, the muscles in his face relaxed, a broad grin replaced the scowl, and Brookshire began to roar. He took Devan's face between his palms and pulled him down to plant a sloppy kiss on his cheek.

Jerking away, he wiped his face harshly with his sleeve. "W-what the h-hell was that?" he stammered.

Victor grinned. "I love you, man! I would never strike you, even if I thought for a moment I could win." He lowered himself back to the chaise and leaned back, polishing off his drink. "Castlereagh, while I'm surprised she has confided in you this *fondness,* I will most certainly do my best to see to it that she is happy and loved for the rest of her life. I give you my oath."

Devan's shoulders slumped and his fists let go. *Damn Brookshire to the bowels of hell!* He'd *needed* to hit him—needed to make him feel a portion of the pain he felt, himself. Although a broken jaw would have been nothing compared to the anguish that tormented his soul.

"See that you do not hurt her, Victor, for I give you *my* solemn oath that I will kill you if you do. Now be gone with you and leave me to myself."

CHAPTER SEVENTEEN

Brookshire stared at his friend, who, with his back to him, stood at the liquor cabinet again. He shook his head in wonder and quit the drawing room.

So, Miss Raven had a *fondness* for him. He chuckled. *My dear Miss Raven, even if I believed you, which I do not,* he thought to himself, *a cad such as myself is hardly worthy.*

He stepped into the outdoors just as she rounded the hedges and walked toward the drive. Truly a beauty to behold, he counted himself as a lucky man that she should think highly enough of him to proclaim such a thing to the marquess. However, her greeting smile reflected not nearly the love as that which shone from her eyes whenever her gaze fell upon Castlereagh. The fire of passion in her eyes betrayed the abhorrence she seemed to wish him to believe she felt.

"Shall we set off for Dublin?" he asked, taking her hand, bringing it softly to his lips as he bowed before her.

Castlereagh had been as transparent as glass in the drawing room. He was entirely enraptured by this lovely creature. It was not merely her beauty, though. No, he was in *love*. But the dumb ox of a man was too damn stubborn to admit it. *Hell, they both were.* Now he was caught in the middle.

Troublesome place to be, the *middle*.

She nodded her head with a brief curtsey and something

of a forlorn smile. Brookshire extended an arm, and led her to the carriage, where he helped her up, and followed her in. Then he thumped the ceiling of the carriage and the driver called to the team.

"Did you and the marquess settle all matters between you?" she asked pensively, dreading the answer.

"Why yes," he gleamed, "as a matter of fact, we did."

Apparently, he did not intend to elaborate, and the suspense was distressing. She tried again. "Nothing too serious, I hope?"

"Absolutely nothing we could not handle, my dear."

"Oh," she sighed, the hint of a pout curling the corners of her mouth. She attempted to mask her disappointment, then suddenly, Raven found herself relieved the marquess had not kept his promise, for there were other things he might have divulged as well.

She did not require Devan's assistance. Victor was fond of her, and she him. It was merely a matter of expanding their friendship and bringing him closer.

"Is there anything special you wish to do or see in Dublin today, Miss Raven?"

Willing a sweet smile she shook her head. "With you as my companion, Victor, anything we do or see is certain to be special."

"What do you know of Dublin?"

"All I recall of Dublin is what I saw the day Mrs. Captain escorted me to town." She dared not confide the visions she'd had of Dublin in her dreams.

"And that would have been?"

"Only the main streets on the road from Dahlingham, and the interior of the dressmaker's shop."

"Nothing more?"

"It was a trip made for the singular purpose of increasing

a wardrobe already quite extensive."

"Oh, but a fine lady needs an enormous wardrobe and lots of trinkets and baubles to make it complete. Do not discount the importance of your gowns and jewels," he laughed.

"I've plenty of gowns, to be sure, Your Grace. And I have a magnificent array of gloves and hats and slippers."

"No jewels? No gold, or rubies, or emeralds, or diamonds, lady?" he asked, taking her gloved hand and inspecting it for signs of rings beneath the fabric.

Raven reached to touch the amethyst draped around her neck.

He feigned shock. "Do not tell me that is the only ornament in your possession. 'Tis beautiful, but goodness! You must have more! Trinkets galore to adorn that sleek neck and these delicate fingers."

"Brookshire!" She withdrew her hand abruptly from his and shooed him away.

"Trust me, Miss Raven. One day you shall wear a treasure chest worth of gold. But there shall be one special band of gold, worn upon this finger," he said, indicating the third finger of her left hand, "that will be more precious to you than all the rest put together."

Could it be that Devan had actually spoken to Brookshire? Were his words a subtle hint that he'd taken well to the possibilities Devan presented? Joy filled her, but then abruptly dissipated when she remembered that it would not be Devan who would present her with that perfect and precious band of gold. No, if it were Victor who placed the ring upon her finger, it would only be a symbol of vows taken, not of love.

Tears clouded her eyes, and she turned away, hiding them from Brookshire. She must continue to remind herself of the danger of loving Devan, and the escape Victor represented.

"Why, Miss Raven! Do not weep. I promise, when that day comes, you will be the happiest woman on God's green earth. Now cheer up." He lifted her chin and looked into her eyes. "I always keep my word."

It was just after dusk when they arrived back at Dahlingham. Lifting her from the carriage, Victor swung her around and set her to her feet upon the stone walk. Then, bowing, he tipped his hat.

"I had a lovely day, Brookshire."

"It has been my honor, truly."

He moved a step closer, so that she thought he was about to kiss her. Closing her eyes, she puckered her lips. But instead of his lips meeting hers, Victor gripped her hand firmly and shook! Then, with a turn on his heel, he was back in the carriage and gone.

Raven stared after him until the carriage was out of sight. Oh, very well, she sulked, shuffling her foot to kick a stone from the walk back into the drive. I did not wish to kiss you anyway.

An entire day wasted, she thought, turning toward the door. She'd been quite under the impression Devan had kept to their bargain, and the duke had taken well to the prospect, but his refusal of her willingness to allow him a kiss said something wholly different.

Raven stomped up the steps and walked inside. The house was entirely dark, save a dim flicker from a lamp Collette had left alight. Rounding the corner into the drawing room, she drew a breath to snuff out the flame, but all at once her blood ran cold and the hair tingled on the back of her neck.

"Where are you, Devan?" Raven called out into the darkness, placing her hands defiantly on her hips.

His resounding laughter echoed throughout the room. She increased the wick so the lamp's glow softly fell on every corner of the room, and then spun to face him, eyes narrowed. The rumbling trail of his voice gradually faded. Raven walked to stand before his chair. "And just why, pray tell, are you sitting here in the dark?"

"I've been anxiously awaiting your homecoming. At this late hour, one might assume all went well?"

Absolutely nothing had been accomplished by her outing that day, but she would hardly confide that to Devan. "As a matter of fact, I found Brookshire's company most agreeable."

"Come. Rest a while, Raven." Reaching out, Devan grasped her wrist and pulled her down onto his lap. She struggled to get up, but his fingers wrapped around her wrist tighter. "You must be dreadfully weary after such a long day chasing the prize duke."

Her free hand bolted upward and rounded swiftly, but he caught her arm mid-air.

"Do not stoop to defending yourself physically. It is a behavior manifestly unbecoming in a lady. You *are* a lady, are you not?"

"Victor went quite out of his way to show me just how very much *he* believes I am," she hissed, lifting her chin.

Devan flinched and Raven looked away.

"What did the two of you do on your little excursion?" he asked dryly, pulling her closer, forcing her to face him.

"*That*, my lord, is none of your concern. Now loose me before I have no choice but to wipe that smirk from your face." Her skin prickled angrily when he laughed.

"Oh, but it is my concern. As long as you remain within

the walls of Dahlingham, you are my charge and I must see to it that you are not taken unfair advantage of by a womanizer such as Brookshire."

"You are besotted!" she exclaimed bitterly, smelling the brandy on his breath.

"While I may have had my fair share of spirits tonight, my dear, I am most assuredly *not* in my cups. Now, do confess; with what amusements did he fill your day?"

Refusing to play this twisted game he seemed so intent on, she once more attempted to break free, but somehow her struggle ended with her straddling his legs in a most unladylike fashion. His left arm moved about her waist, anchoring her to him, while his right hand entwined itself in hers.

"Then let me guess. Shall I?"

"You're insufferable!"

"*Hmmm . . .*" He ignored her statement effectively. "What did our friend do that caused you to return so late? Was it this?" he asked curtly, his hand gently brushing her cheek.

The moment he touched her so tenderly, her breath caught and her heart began to race madly. Oh, why did he torment her this way?

"Or was it this?" He slowly ran his hand down her neck, and his finger trailed a hot, teasing path over her dress and dipped into the fold of her cleavage.

"My lord, please!"

"I must know, Raven. I will not release you until you have told me *everything*." His fingers ran beneath the material, skimming lightly over her breast.

A soft moan came from deep in her throat, followed by a sob. "Devan, I beg you—"

She felt the buttons of her dress let go, one by one, until

her breasts were freed from the confines of the fabric. Her breath fluttered when his thumb made slow circles around one nipple, and before she could ward him off, his tongue flicked lightly over the other, igniting an unwanted flame of desire. Beneath her, she felt his desire, hard and uncompromising.

"Did he marvel at the silkiness of your ivory skin, Raven?" he rasped into her ear, sending delicious shivers down her spine.

Under such circumstances, it was all she could do to maintain a shred of wit. "H-he did not, my lord."

Inclining his head, he drew a nipple fully into his mouth. Her body tingled, and the flame flared and coiled through her. With a resigned whimper, her hands threaded through the black silk of his hair, and, against her will, she arched into his embrace.

Groaning lustfully, Devan began to move beneath her, straining against her heavy aching. His mouth came up to capture her parted lips in a searing kiss. Their tongues met and dueled passionately, the taste of the brandy sweet.

His hand worked its way beneath her dress, slowly over her stocking to her knee, and then found its way to the top of her thigh. Her hips thrust forth unconsciously when his finger pushed lightly into the soft flesh, and he brought her closer.

"And did he cause your heart to race so, dear Raven?" he whispered between kisses, placing a tender kiss to her heart, while his fingers continued their torturous stroking.

"Nay," she murmured, tears stinging her eyes. "Only you."

Raven pushed him away from her. He grabbed her by her waist, but she made no attempt to take flight. Instead, she opened his satin burgundy robe, exposing his chest to her hungry mouth, showering his skin with soft, scorching kisses, and then her tongue flitted teasingly up his neck, and when it found his lips, she kissed him once more.

He suddenly broke the kiss, leaving her breathless. "Tell me you love me, Raven," he commanded.

"I . . . *cannot.*"

Slipping his hands up the back of her dress and into her hair, he tugged and pulled at the pins, until her hair fell loose, across her shoulders and down her back. Then he kissed her, long and slow, weakening what little will she still retained.

"Speak my name and tell me you love me." His mouth covered hers again, drawing her breath into him. Another murmured sound of rapture escaped him as he raked his hands longingly through her mane of ebony curls.

A tear slipped from her eyes onto his cheek. Taking his face tenderly within her hands, she breathed his name in a tattered whisper against his lips. "Devan."

"Say it," he urged.

Her confession fell as softly and bittersweet as her tears. "H-how can I not love you, when you are the very essence of my heart?"

Lifting her into his arms, he stood and gazed deeply into her eyes. "Then surrender your heart to me fully, Raven."

She laid her hand lovingly to the side of his face, relinquishing the last of her resolve with a tender brush of her lips to his. "Unto you, my lord, I yield my heart and all that I am."

CHAPTER EIGHTEEN

Raven wrapped the satin burgundy robe around her, and bent her head down to inhale the fragrance of it. *Devan.* His scent was all over her, sprinkled in her hair, blanketing her skin.

Closing her eyes, she turned her face to the open window where she stood. How masterful he had been during their lovemaking. Such tenderness was there in his touch, in his eyes. She had never known such rapture as that when at last he came into her and her name fell from his lips like a whispered prayer.

Gazing at the sleeping man who lay naked and beautiful, the sheets coiled loosely around his long, muscular legs, she stepped slowly toward the bed and sat down.

A wisp of shimmering black fell across his forehead. Careful not to awaken him, she gently brushed the hair away from his face. Devan smiled sweetly in his slumber and she lightly followed the contours of his cheek, then ran her hand along his strong, defined jaw. The lure of his sensuous lips, full and dark, curled slightly at the corners, was irresistible, and she traced their outline with her finger. Without thinking, she brushed his mouth with hers.

Suddenly, he reached around her waist and pulled her down to him, until her body molded quite perfectly to his. "Sleep, Raven," he murmured, holding her close. Soon, his breathing resumed its slow, restful pattern.

Running her hand over his arm, she snuggled closer and breathed him in again. He enveloped and comforted her, and lying beside him, cradled protectively in his arms, felt more right than any feeling she had ever known.

She would never have this contentment with Victor, she thought. Nor would she ever feel this desire. Her wistful smile turned down into a frown. Raven could scarcely stand for the duke to kiss her hand, let alone contemplate his kiss upon the most intimate places of her body.

How could she ever walk away from the man who now lay beside her—the man who filled her heart and body with more emotion than she ever dreamed possible?

Raven wiggled closer, pulling Devan's arm tighter around her and entwined her fingers through his. She felt every twitch of his body and the movement of his chest against her back as he breathed. She felt the beating of his heart, and hers skipped a beat to match its rhythm.

Would it really be so horrible to be this man's mistress? she wondered.

What if Priscilla were sent to live at his estate in London? Then she could remain in Ireland, where Devan spent most of his time. They could spend every night as they had the last two, and every day as well. On those occasions when he went to England, she could pretend he was merely away on business—pretend there was no wife awaiting him in London.

And to the devil with what the servants, or even Collette, thought of her for being his mistress! Wasn't her happiness to be valued more than their opinions of her?

But what of her opinion of herself?

Could she settle for anything less from Devan than the whole of his body and heart—*his very soul?* Her love for him was too great to accept less, for she would begin to resent every moment he spent with his wife, and every instance she had to hide her love for the man. She would become demanding, placing more and more stipulations upon his time. And he would begin to resent her, for after all, she would be merely his mistress, not his wife.

Raven's tears fell to the satin pillow beneath her head, and her body trembled with sorrow.

Brookshire was her last, best hope of eluding the life part of her longed for, which was also the life that would be the death of her if she did not escape it before she was in too deep—if she was not in over her heart already.

Mindful not to stir him, Raven slid from beneath Devan's arm and from the bed. Quickly she picked up the soft pink dress she'd worn the day before. She slipped the satin robe from her shoulders, but the musky scent of him wafted fleetly to her. Shrugging the robe back into place, she tied it securely, and then tiptoed quietly from his suite into her own, where she locked the door and wept for the love she had to abandon.

Slipping out the rear entrance, Raven headed for the gardens that were concealed by the mist of a new morning. Kneeling, she plucked a rose, mindful of the thorns, and gazed at its delicate petals, folded tightly into a perfect crimson bud. The soft glow of the early sun gently kissed the dew sprinkled flower, but today, not even the roses seemed to be able to comfort her.

Sleep had eluded Raven since leaving Devan's side, and ten thousand tears had fallen before dawn peeked over the horizon.

Whatever her life had been before the day she awoke at Dahlingham, it had to be better than this life in which she was bound to the torment of loving a man she could never truly possess for the rest of her days.

Bringing the rose close, she inhaled. Her eyes fluttered shut. The fragrance brought a vision: a churchyard, barren of beauty, save for a single scarlet rose that climbed the church wall, coiled and entwined within a briar.

A great and inexplicable woe clutched at her heart.

Fierce winds blew, swirling the dust across the lifeless graveyard that surrounded a little stone chapel. The scene in her mind purely colorless, save for the deep blood red of the rose and the briar that grew around it.

Warm lips touched the side of her neck, startling her out of the vision.

"Good morning," an agonizingly welcome voice whispered into her ear.

Her heart accelerated madly when he wrapped his arms around her and nuzzled his face into her tresses.

"*Mmm,*" he growled, pulling her body against him.

Forcing herself from his spell, she twisted out of his arms. "Devan, it would not do to give the servants a show."

"Nonsense. We are buried too deeply in these gardens." He embraced her once more, nipped lightly at her ear, making her quiver from head to toe.

She took his hands and moved them from about her, and walked away, down the path, deeper into the gardens.

Catching up to her, he smiled down at Raven, his dark eyes seizing her, like a knight capturing a coveted bounty.

How she filled his heart! It was, at last, time to put an end to this damnable waiting once and for all. Time to ask for her hand. He prayed God she would accept. She had to. She was his fate and he would not live another day without her.

"It is time we talked, Raven."

Leading him to the white iron bench in the center of the

191

gardens, she sat down. "I agree," she said, motioning for him to sit next to her.

"I never slept more soundly than I did with you by my side." Grinning, he put his arm around her shoulders and brought her to him.

"And I did not sleep at all last night," she said, sliding further down the bench and out of his arms.

Taking her hand, he brought it to his lips. "Whatever it is that troubles you, my darling—"

"Devan, please!" She jerked her hand away as if blistered. "Do not make this more difficult than it already is."

Confused, he stared into her eyes, searching for some explanation for her behavior, but all he saw mirrored there was sadness, and a glimmer of determination.

She put a little more distance between them, then inhaled deeply and met his gaze. "I have never known such pain as that which my heart knows now . . ." Her voice faded off, and she wiped the tears from her eyes with the back of her hand.

Drawing on all the strength within him, he fought to keep from bringing her to him once more to protect her from whatever it was that brought her such grief.

"But I must do what is best for both of us," she continued. "This has all been a dreadful . . . *mistake.*"

"*What?*"

A raised finger placed gently to his lips cut him off. "Please, let me finish. I . . ." She blinked, and another teardrop broke free. "I shall go through with my plan to wed Victor, if he will have me. And if he will not, I will have no choice but to leave Dahlingham."

The searing edge to her words pierced like a sword through his heart, and the break in his voice betrayed his anguish. "You cannot mean this."

"I have never meant anything more."

"But *why?* Why Victor, and why must you ever leave Dahlingham?"

A slight smile of resignation was all she could manage. "*Why* matters not. Only that this is what must be."

"You do not want Brookshire. You've admitted it. More than once!" he shouted, gaining his feet and storming away from her.

How, in the name of all that was holy, could she still intend to do this?

"You are mistaken, Devan," she said calmly.

He spun to face her.

She raised her gaze to his. "What I said was that my love for him is but the love for a dear friend. Though you should not underestimate the extent to which I *want* him for my husband, and how quickly I wish for our marriage to take place, if it is to be."

"And what, pray tell, am I to do once you have married Brookshire?"

"You shall carry on, Devan. Your life will be full and happy, long after I am gone."

"Mark my words, Raven," he growled, lunging to his knees and gathering her into his embrace, "you will not marry Victor!"

Only hours before, she had accepted his kisses willingly. But when his mouth met hers, her lips were closed tightly against him. Her body stiffened in his arms.

"Why do you forsake me?"

"It is only myself I have forsaken," she wept, tugging free from him and standing. "Let it be, I implore you!" she cried, before turning and leaving him alone in the gardens.

Stunned to stillness, he collapsed against the iron bench. The woman he'd made love to only the night before loved him. She had whispered it in rapture, murmured it in his arms. And he'd felt it, with his body and his heart.

That woman could never have spoken such torturous words, nor could she even consider spending the rest of her life with anyone else, let alone the duke.

Tears pricked Devan's eyes. He held his breath and forced them back, knowing if even one fell, they would never end.

He reached for the rose that lay in the dust—the very rose she'd been admiring when first he found her in the gardens. A thorn pierced his finger, and a drop of blood colored the dirt crimson.

Shaking the pain from his finger, he carefully picked up the rose with the unwounded hand. Inspecting it, he saw traces of her tears.

Devan put the rose to his lips and tasted the salty mist on the petals, then closed his eyes and let go his agony.

"Oh, what have you done now, Raven?"

Raven fell into Collette's waiting arms and broke down. "I've put an end to this misery, Collette," she sobbed. "It is the right choice, but my heart is broken because of it."

"Lord Castlereagh?"

"Yes."

Collette took Raven's face gently in her hands and brought it away from her shoulder so she could look into her eyes. "You were with him again?"

Raven nodded with a sniffle and a swipe of her sleeve across her cheek.

"And you are in love with him." It was not a question, but an observation.

"I-I told him it had to end—that I would soon be leaving Dahlingham."

"But why would you leave Dahlingham, and why . . . ? Lord, Raven! None of this makes any sense at all."

Shrugging away from Collette, she walked to the other side of the room. "Nothing makes sense anymore. Not that anything I can remember ever did, mind you." She almost laughed at her own sarcasm, then quickly grew serious again, with a sagging of her shoulders and drawn brow. "But I'm more confused than ever now."

"What did he have to say?"

"It matters not," she sighed. "What does matter is what he didn't say, and he never said he would not marry Priscilla. I cannot be his mistress, nor live under the same roof with her."

Collette sat down on the bed and patted the space next to her for Raven. "Are you absolutely certain he intends to wed Priscilla?"

Throwing herself dramatically face down on the bed, she pouted. "Aye."

"And how is it you'd be knowing it for certain? Did he ever come straight out and say so?"

"He didn't have to. Is it not enough that he held that dinner to make the announcement? Is it not enough that when I sought his help in gaining Brookshire's affections, so I could be gone from this wretched estate before his marriage took place, he agreed?"

"I don't know anymore, Raven. After you left with the duke last afternoon, the marquess seemed quite beside himself."

"How so?" Raven raised her head from her arms.

"Well, first he paced the drawing room. Then he barked out orders left and right, and not a servant among us could please him. He must have asked me a thousand times when you might return. And the later it became, the fouler his disposition grew, until at last not a solitary one of us could stand him and we all sneaked off to our rooms at the first opportunity."

"Oh," Raven sighed. "Is that all?"

"What do you mean *all?*"

"That means nothing. If you ask me, his state is tempestuous more often than not."

Collette laughed and came down beside Raven on the bed, nudging her with a shoulder. "You really are blind to it, aren't you?"

"To what?"

"I have known him all my life. He really is very amiable, and truth be told, it wasn't until he met you that he's had such extremes. I think he feels more for you than you have given him credit for."

"You are simply—" Raven put her hand to her friend's cheek, but didn't feel any sign of fever. She shrugged and shook her head. "Wistful and romantic is what you are. But I assure you, he feels little for me save some kind of duty or ownership—or both. If he loved me, he would have told me how he feels."

Collette rose from the bed and walked toward the door, but before making her exit she spun around, staring Raven square in the eye. "As you have him?"

Before Raven could argue, Collette was gone. But she stood anyway, challenging the door, her fists clenched and tears streaming from her eyes. "You are wrong, Collette!" she shouted. "Wrong, I tell you!"

She had told him, only the night before.

CHAPTER NINETEEN

Not so much as a knock sounded before the chamber door swung open and Brookshire appeared. "Good day, Castlereagh!" the duke thundered, brushing off the front of his brown waistcoat of imaginary dust.

Devan let his fist fall to the table, once again inconvenienced by one of Victor's interruptions. "Your timing is impeccable, as always. To what do I owe the honor of this *unannounced* calling?"

Coming down beside him with a bounce on the mattress, Brookshire draped his arm around Devan's shoulders. "Have you forgotten, man? It is derby day in Dublin! We haven't missed a year since we were children. Tell me you have not forgotten our standing date to mingle with the common folk and drink ale until we burst."

"As a matter of fact, I had," Devan snapped.

"But what of the wenches and fair maidens? Certainly you have not forgotten them!"

The duke's perpetual good cheer was nauseating, and Devan took to his feet and moved to the other side of the chamber in order to escape it. "That, as well, Victor. I hardly have the time to chase skirts throughout the town. I'm not a boy anymore, even if you fancy yourself as such."

He leaped to Devan's side. "Is there something you are not confiding to me?" he asked dubiously. "What could possibly distract you from such entertaining pursuits, old man? Could it be a lady?"

Devan bit his tongue and pretended not to hear the last question posed. "Be on your way, Victor. I am certain you will manage your philandering quite nicely on your own."

Victor roared. "On my own? Oh, I think not. Miss Raven has graciously agreed to accompany me this afternoon."

Devan confronted Brookshire with a cold glare. "Miss Raven has agreed to accompany you . . ." he repeated. "She hasn't been well of late. I should think it would do her no good to spend the day in the sun."

"She appeared quite fit mere minutes ago." He shrugged his shoulders dismissively. "In fact, she looks rather magnificent in every way. She awaits in the sitting room for me to return with news of your acceptance of my invitation." Brookshire nudged Devan in the ribs and leaned closer. "I must say, she didn't appear too keen on the notion. I could only assume she looked forward to the two of us spending the day together *alone*." He grinned wickedly and resumed his boisterous stance. "However, I was firm in my explanation that the race is an unbreakable tradition for you and me, that we shall honor until we are too gray and fat, and confined to our old-age beds, to do otherwise. Besides, I've got one hundred gold pieces to give away, and thought you might wish to match my purse. What say you?"

Pushing Brookshire hastily toward the door, Devan said, "On second thought, that sounds like a stupendous plan, Victor. You may inform Miss Raven that I shall accompany you, and will join you momentarily."

"Good show!" he exclaimed, as the marquess pushed him straight into the corridor, before slamming the door.

So, Raven wanted time alone with Victor.

Over his dead body.

For more than three weeks not a moment had passed

that she'd left herself unaccompanied by either the duke or her maid, keeping as much distance between herself and Devan as possible. On those few occasions when she wasn't gallivanting across the countryside with Brookshire or strolling over the grounds with Collette, she locked herself away inside her chamber, with the excuse of a bad stomach or an affliction of the head.

Yes, she'd managed to steer clear of him in one way or another—but not today! A hundred pound purse was a small price to pay for the bittersweet joy that would be his when she had no choice but to spend an entire afternoon and evening in his company, he thought with a crooked, satisfied smirk.

Blast Devan Castlereagh for dashing my plans! Raven thought bitterly, as she tuned out the clamorous conversation of the two men riding along beside her. The one to her right ignored her, while the one on her left held her beneath his impregnable glare, refusing to relinquish her. Collette rode to the right of Brookshire, mesmerized by the conversations taking place between the two men, and Raven would have had to yell to carry on any kind of dialogue with her.

Why did he always see fit to make her life difficult? He knew damned well her intentions where Victor was concerned, and rather than busying himself tending to the needs of Priscilla, he insisted on interfering in her life.

Even without Devan's interference, persuading Victor was truly going to be a task. On one hand, Devan made the duke out to be quite the womanizer. And the duke, for his part, had made more than a few comments of his own that would lead one to believe he was precisely as the marquess described. But on the other hand, Brookshire had lavished her with gifts and his attentions, but still, had not even so much as kissed her cheek, or held her in his arms. If anything, he had become more distant, more formal in the last weeks.

Strange creatures, men. How was a woman ever to understand them, when apparently they did not know where they stood themselves?

Adjusting her Lavinia straw hat, and smoothing the soft yellow Jaconet muslin of her skirt, Raven gripped the reins of her mare with her leather-gloved hands. Come hell, high water, or Devan Castlereagh, Raven was determined to make the duke see the mutual benefits of a union.

The road into Dublin was a rough one today. The rains that had blown in from the sea the night before had softened the dirt, and the heat of the summer sun had hardened it, grooved and pitted by carriage wheels and horses' hooves. At a turtle's pace they made their way into Dublin, and Raven was more than ready to stretch her legs and dismount when Brookshire led their horses beneath some trees on the outskirts of Phoenix Park.

Leaping to the ground, Devan held his hand up to her.

"Miss Raven?" Brookshire presented his hand, cutting Devan off.

A simple choice, she thought, accepting Victor's offer. Devan scowled, an expression he wore more and more often these days. A twisted grin graced her lips as it occurred to Raven that the lack of good humor the marquess sported these days was most likely on account of Lady Priscilla's prolonged absence. *Let the devil suffer!*

"Why, Miss Raven, it does my heart good to see you smile," Victor commented, folding her hand around his arm. "She is exquisite when she smiles, is she not, Castlereagh?"

Raven turned her attention to the marquess, who now assisted Collette out of her saddle. Something akin to a grunt escaped him, in response to the question put forth by the duke.

"Thank you, Your Grace."

When Devan shot a glare in her direction, she simply smiled broader and slipped her arm further through Brookshire's, batting her eyes coyly for the duke.

The foursome walked into the center of Dublin. Now it was Victor and Raven who carried on the conversation, while Devan kept to himself and Collette followed close behind. Music rose from the streets, as did the smells of baked goods and the sounds of merry children laughing. How familiar it all seemed.

"I could certainly use a pint of ale. Miss Raven, would you like some lemon punch?" Victor asked, bringing her back to him.

Raven nodded.

"And Collette?" he asked with a wink to the maid.

Collette smiled bashfully. "Please."

"Very well, two lemon punches for the ladies, and two pints for Castlereagh and I it is." He released Raven's arm and walked into the pub.

Collette leaned closer to Raven and whispered, "It seems you've managed to put Lord Castlereagh in a mood."

"Nay, Collette, 'twas not I that put that man in a mood. He was *born* in a mood and never grew out of it!"

They giggled, drawing the attention of the marquess, but only for a moment before he turned his back to them again, folding his arms over his chest in obvious annoyance, which only made them laugh all the more.

"Trust 'tis you who makes him scowl. Perhaps it is your affection for the duke that offends him?"

"Nonsense!" Raven hissed. "Devan Castlereagh is not in a position to take offense at anything I do, least of all my time spent with Victor."

"I haven't seen a trace of Lady Prissy, nor heard a word uttered about her."

"Do not fear, Collette. I am most positive the lady will honor us with her presence soon—after all, the ball is now only a moon away."

Collette pondered the circumstances for a moment before inching closer to Raven. "That means you have as long to give up this notion of marrying a man you do not love, and to win the heart of the one that you do."

"Bite your tongue!" The warning in Raven's eyes was as severe as the tone of her voice. She sighed. "I'm sorry for snapping, Collette." She took the maid's hand and pressed it to her cheek. "I know you mean well, but please trust that I know best in this matter."

Just then Brookshire came bounding toward them, his hands full. "Ladies! Castlereagh! I'm back!"

Raven hurried to meet him. "Let me help you," she offered, taking two of the mugs from his hands, and passing one on to Collette. "Thank you." She sipped the cold lemon punch. "You truly spoil me," she smiled flirtatiously, ignoring the dramatic rolling of Collette's eyes and the indistinguishable mutterings from the marquess.

"You deserve to be indulged, my dear."

"Are we here merely to stand about, sip our drinks, and spout flattery?" Devan asked impatiently.

"Of course not!" Brookshire exclaimed, raising his pint. "We have a race to run! Here, Castlereagh," he said, finishing his in one great gulp and releasing a satisfied sigh, "I got them, now you can return the empty cups. The ladies and I will meet you at the starting line."

"You know, Miss Raven," the duke said, taking her by the arm, "when Castlereagh and I were boys, this race exceeded anything in England. It was the one time of year the people of Dublin could forget their woes and the oppression they have suffered. Here, all stood on equal ground, tenant and lord alike, and the streets were filled to the brim with merry-making and music and jolly laughter."

"As they are now."

"Not quite. The last few years have been exceedingly difficult for the Irish. Lately, some of the Irish aristocracy seem harder on their own people than the English. Many an Irish family has been unable to pay his toll, and has been driven from his home, so that their wealthier clansmen could take it over, and add it to their already abundant holdings."

"It is a shame they have forgotten the ties."

"Indeed." Victor put her arm through his, bringing her closer. "The desire for gold and land tends to make a man callous and do that which he knows in his heart is wrong. Mind you, it's not just the Irish aristocracy—the English have done more than their share to drive the Irish from their homes. But you would think the Irish would have more compassion for the plight of their brethren. And let's not forget the potato blight a few years past," added Brookshire. "It has made holding onto their land and feeding their families even more difficult. But no one can accuse the marquess of injustice toward his clansmen."

"*He's* Irish?"

"Oh, yes. Better than half Irish, he is! He didn't tell you?"

"He speaks very little of his family."

"His mother's family owned Dahlingham and the Castlereagh title. His father was an Englishman by birth, and Earl in his own right. The two of them met during the Season in London when they were quite young. The earl and Lady

Grace were married less than a year, and she in the last months of her confinement, when the former Lord Castlereagh, Liam Ó Lionáird, died of the fever."

Suddenly, Raven's heart thrashed against her chest. "D-did you say *Ó*—" she had to force the syllables to come. *"Ó Lionáird?"*

CHAPTER TWENTY

"Yes. Liam Ó Lionáird was Lady Grace's brother, and the only male heir to Dahlingham. Since their parents were also deceased, Devan's father, the Earl of Duran, and his young bride returned to Ireland. It was not long after that she, too, died, in childbirth. Sad, I tell you," Victor sighed, shaking his head woefully, "but then, if you listen to the tales told, that family was plagued with misfortune as far back as any can recall. Now there's not a single member of the clan remaining, save Castlereagh. Miss Raven? Are you all right?"

"I-I'm fine," she lied, turning away so he would not see the paleness of her complexion.

She steadied her nerves and forced herself to breathe. It was ludicrous to even suspect that the *Ó Lionáird* in her dreams—*Séamus*—could be any relation to Devan, for, as Brookshire said, the marquess was the last known member of his family. But still, her skin prickled and her stomach twisted.

They are just dreams, she told herself. And then she told herself again, just to be certain she understood.

"You know, Miss Raven, Castlereagh really is a good chap. Treats his tenants better than any other land owner I know, Irish or English."

"It truly is a beautiful day, is it not?" Raven asked, facing Victor with a smile, while adjusting her straw hat just a bit to block the glare of the sun.

He grinned and nodded, but he did not permit her attempt to change the topic. "He's become something of a legend, and it makes it damned difficult for the rest of us when his tenants boast to ours."

"Hmmm," she mumbled, feigning interest, then threw the snickering Collette a grimace.

"Would you believe he's not charged his tenants a single pence since he became marquess? And if that isn't enough, he's been known to loan them money as well, without interest. Actually, none on the island save old Coushite and myself will have anything to do with him on account of it."

This was certainly an unexpected revelation. Somehow the marquess was not one easily pictured as the charitable sort, and for a moment she felt the wall she'd built around her heart concerning Devan begin to crumble just a little.

Raven finished tucking the last bit of her dress inside the saddlebag. Then she handed her hat to Collette, twisted her hair into a braid, and pinned it tightly to her head. She replaced the Lavinia straw hat with another of leather, with a wide brim to shadow her features and fully cover her hair.

"Well," she asked, "how do I look?"

Collette laughed and fastened the saddlebag once she'd gotten the last item fully inside. "You're still beautiful, Raven. Those trousers don't change that."

Raven looked down at the clothes she wore, borrowed from the stable boy at Dahlingham, who, believing it a grand ruse, had been all too happy to bring the saddlebag of clothes and meet them just before the race. It was just as she'd imagined; the freedom the trousers allowed, and the boots, broken in and soft, were like Heaven to her feet. She checked to be certain the hat she now wore was secure, and clapped her hands together, quite pleased with herself.

"It is not beautiful I wish to be today, Collette. Do you think I'll pass for a boy?"

"Keep your head down, and," she added, fumbling with Raven's shirt, "don't keep this tucked in so tight, or those bosoms will give you away for sure, bound or not!"

Raven laughed and gave Collette a light tap. "Stop now! Be serious!"

"Are you certain you wish to do this?" she asked as they stepped from the alleyway and into the street. "It really is a madman's race."

"I think I do." She peered nervously around at all the brawny men and their horses that were accustomed to the rough terrain that lay ahead of them. She held the mare's reins tighter.

With a kiss to her cheek, Collette whispered, "Then good luck to you. You have my prayers."

Lifting her left foot into the stirrup, she dropped her weight squarely into the saddle and nodded a farewell to her maid. As the mare wended her way slowly to the starting line, Raven caught a glimpse of Devan in the distance, upon the red that pranced about excitedly, surrounded by a group of other riders on unstrung thoroughbreds.

The marquess appeared somehow different then. Was it the way in which the early afternoon sun danced across his bronze features? Or was it a new aspect to the man, provided by Brookshire's revelations that day?

Shaking herself free of the spell the sight of him had put her under, she focused on the more pressing matters she needed to contend with, like marking her place in the starting line.

Weaving through the other riders, Raven chose her spot, as far away from the marquess as possible.

She hadn't a notion as to what the course that lay ahead

of her might be, only knowing it would be marked by occasional white flags for guidance. Her place in the line was perhaps one of the worst, but the mare's speed would make up for that disadvantage.

Peering back down the line, she tried to find Devan amidst the others, but could not make him out. With a sigh she brought her attention back to the mare. She could not be concerned with the marquess. She had a derby to win, after all. And a handsome purse.

Another rider pulled along side her. Raven kept her head down, looking neither to the left nor to the right. She would merely keep to herself, not encourage any conversation from anyone.

"*Bloody hell!* What the devil are you doing?"

The rogue!

She kept her head down and did not respond.

"Raven!"

"Are you trying to spoil this for me?" she hissed.

"This trek is by far more treacherous than the riding you and your horse are accustomed to. I'll not have you breaking your neck senselessly."

"And I'll not have you telling me what I may or may not do with my own neck, Lord Castlereagh." Her voice was firm as she continued to stare straight ahead.

"You do not see the folly in this? And these . . . these . . . men's garments!" he growled, waving his hand at her clothing.

"You are making a spectacle of yourself, Devan."

"And you're not?"

"I shall go wholly unnoticed if you will be so kind as to keep your voice down."

"Very well, be stubborn." He leaned close, peeking under the brim of her hat.

She averted her eyes, and side stepped the mare slightly to the right, away from him.

"You look flushed, Raven," he said, grinning up at her. "Did the good duke say something to bring this about? I suppose he's in on this with you?"

"He did not, and he is not, Lord Castlereagh."

He chuckled. "*Devan,* remember?"

"I remember, *Lord Castlereagh,*" she snapped.

"Oh, Raven, Raven, when are you going to admit your scheme is utter foolishness?"

"I have no scheme."

"You do not consider your intention to lure the duke into marriage a scheme?"

"I will admit no such thing! Why, Victor and I grow closer every day. He is such a gentleman, unlike some men I know, and I have, of late, found myself quite drawn to him," she asserted, hoping to put an end to his prying.

He laughed, cutting her to the quick. "Now *that* would surprise me, my dear. Especially when it appears the only time you can bring yourself to hold his arm or stand close to him is when you are aware that I am watching. Strange, but I seem to recall a lady who is quite generous with her affection, and I haven't seen the vaguest hint of it with Brookshire—nothing like what you gave to me anyway."

"You are deplorable!"

"*I* am honest!"

"You are a loathsome wretch if you believe for one moment I feel anything but contempt for you," she spat.

"And you are a wicked wench if you would give to any other man what you gave to me."

Though she wished to scream, she could only allow her exasperation to remain a harsh whisper, as the other contestants were beginning to line up next to them. *"Wretch!"*

Devan grinned viciously. *"Wench!"* Then the grin faded. "Please, give up this foolish notion of racing."

Raven straightened herself in her saddle, her gaze fixed on the trek ahead. "I will not."

"Very well. Let your mule-ish pride get the best of you."

All at once he was gone. Out of the corner of her eye she saw him turn into the center of the line.

There was a call for the riders' attention, and a moment later the crack of a gunshot in the air. Raven jammed her boots into the mare's sides and the horse bounded forward with a great leap into a wild run.

Devan had not intended to run the race for anything but a bit of entertainment. He'd teased Raven about the flush to her cheeks, but he knew it was not Brookshire or even himself that had been responsible for it, rather a return of the fever that had kept her confined the last few days. Now he would have to try to keep up with the mare in order to see to Raven's safety.

He dug his heels into the red's ribs, and tried desperately to catch up with the white beast she rode, already well ahead.

Why had he ever gotten her that horse? A woman with her temperament belonged in a carriage or upon an aged, swayback nag, for to have control of a mount with such strength and speed obviously took away her reason.

He leaned forward, his head low by the red's. "Faster, old boy!" he yelled, pushing the steed onward.

The wind whipped furiously at his eyes and Devan's vision blurred. With the sleeve of his white shirt, he wiped the tears away, and squinted, trying to make out Raven and the mare up ahead, amidst the other riders. At last he spotted her, ahead of the pack, with only one other rider close on her heels.

He urged his horse forward, loosening the reins.

They were almost outside Dublin now, headed out into the country, where the hills were steep and landscape treacherous. What if the fever were to get the best of her while racing at this speed? Surely, she'd fall from her saddle and be trampled before he could ever reach her.

Then Devan saw the other rider move up alongside her, and in an instant, the man pulled the reins sharply to the right, forcing his charger hard into the mare. The mare stumbled and his horse moved ahead.

"Damn!" the marquess gritted out between his teeth, kicking the red pointedly again.

He'd obviously intended to push Raven out of the race. Little did he know it would only serve to anger his opponent, make her more determined. He had to reach her, get between them.

Little by little Devan's horse gained ground. But the mare caught the black horse that had nearly fallen her, and again they were side by side. This time she seemed to be far enough to the man's right to preclude another collision, until the black was maneuvered closer and cut her off, just as Raven was about to overtake him.

Devan could feel every straining muscle of the red, as they closed in. The beast was not a racer by nature, and his coat was drenched in sweat and his mouth foamed from the exertion required of such speed.

"Just a little farther, boy. Just . . . a little . . . farther."

At that moment the red moved in between the mare and the black monster that threatened her every step. The man attempted to push the red out of the way, as he'd done to Raven's horse, but Devan was ready for him and quickly sidestepped the encounter.

Raven didn't even appear to notice Devan's intervention, and she bent her body over the mare's neck and took the lead.

The man focused on her again. Out came his whip, and he savagely beat the black. The horse shrieked in pain and lunged forward.

Ahead, a hill appeared with a rocky climb, that would challenge even the most skilled horseman, and if this lunatic continued this way, they'd all three meet their doom. Devan pushed the red and inched his way toward the black horse until at last they were almost nose and nose.

Still, Raven's eyes never veered once to the side. She purposely challenged the madman with her every movement, risking her life. Not only was he determined to save her from her own reckless ways, but he had half a mind to turn her over his knee once he caught her, and teach her a fitting lesson.

Suddenly the mare and the black flew half a length in front of Devan, and the man, apparently realizing his opportunity, decided it was time to do them both in. Devan barely got out of the way as the man attempted to ram the red with his black mount. He caught his breath, and then saw no other direction than to move to the man's left, and attack from his blind side while the man, thinking he'd pushed him out of the running, went after Raven.

Fortunately, Raven was not as oblivious as he'd thought, for she sensed the man's plan of attack, and jumped the mare further to the right.

The wind caught her hat and pulled it from her head. The man brought his whip up high, unmistakably ready to take advantage of the newfound physical upper hand.

Raven's gaze rose, and Devan saw the fear in her eyes. He charged the man, grasping frantically for the raised whip, just as Raven countered with a sharp leap to her left, setting the black off balance.

Three horses collided. Devan and the man fell from their

saddles as he struggled to steal the whip away.

"Let go, damn you!" Devan shouted, ripping the brown leather weapon from the man's clenched fists.

The man stumbled quickly to gain his feet, and Devan, taking him harshly by the collar of his shirt, assisted him.

"It was none of your concern!" he bellowed.

"Oh, but it is," Devan growled, raising the whip. "You do not play fair. And if you do not wish to die today, you will run as far outside of Dublin as your cowardly legs can carry you."

The man's eyes darted from Devan to Raven and back again, as he clearly ascertained the situation. Devan towered a solid head and shoulders above him, and even a man of modest intellect would know he could not win a conflict against a man of Devan's stature and fury.

"Be gone *now*, before I lose my good humor and beat you to a pulp!" the marquess declared hostilely, waving the whip in the air, ready to strike.

Cursing under his breath, the man mounted his horse and took off.

Devan spun around to Raven. The impact of the clash had knocked her from her saddle as well, and she sat on the hard ground, her head between her knees.

He ran to her and gently lifted her to her feet. "Are you hurt?"

Tears threatened to fall from her eyes when they met his. "No," she answered with a pout, jerking her arm from his grasp. "I'm not hurt."

"All you can think about is this blasted race!"

"I could have won it if you hadn't interfered," she argued flatly, standing.

"No, you'd have been beaten or killed."

"And I supposed I am to be beholden to you?" she countered, before storming away as a string of horses flew around them.

Then, all at once, Raven dropped to her knees. At her side in an instant, Devan lifted her upright once more. Her complexion had washed from pale to a pasty shade of yellow, and he held her tightly against him to keep her steady on her feet.

"Raven," he said softly, brushing her fevered brow tenderly while leading her out of the path of the other riders, "I will take you home."

Slowly her eyes focused on him, and this time, she was too weak to even attempt an argument.

"I saw what happened!" Brookshire exclaimed, racing up to them on his steed, then dismounting. "What in the hell were you trying to prove with this stunt, Miss Raven?"

Oh, why did these two men think they had the right to scold her like a naughty child?

"That I could win the race." If only her stomach wasn't twisting so, she'd have given Victor and Devan both a fitting piece of her mind!

He took hold of the mare. "And what in the name of God Almighty was that imbecile trying to do? Kill the two of you? What did he do to you, Miss Raven?"

"I'm not hurt, Victor."

"I sent him on his way. But it seems all this excitement has been a little too much for her. Will you please take this," Devan said, pulling a velvet purse from his waistcoat, "and divide it up among the contestants that did not place in the derby?"

"You are not returning to Dublin?"

"I think it best to get Miss Raven back to Dahlingham and into Mrs. Captain's care."

214

"Shouldn't that be my duty?" Victor objected, making a move to take Raven's arm.

Devan quickly blocked the duke's hand with a glare as hard as stone. "You have done quite enough with your constant gallivanting all over Ireland with her. *I* will take her home to Dahlingham, where she *belongs*."

The Duke of Brookshire did not protest further.

CHAPTER TWENTY-ONE

"Truly, I am fine," Raven asserted as she was hoisted to the back of her horse, quite against her will.

"Enough argument, do you hear?" Devan's voice was firm, as was his handling of her as he sat her squarely in the saddle.

She took a deep, unsteady breath, the abrupt motion obviously making her stomach churn.

"You don't have a single good excuse to stay here, Raven, and I'll be bloody damned if I'm going to allow you to expire just to spite me."

Resignation reflected in her eyes as she let out a quiet sigh, and her complexion took on a mild green tinge. The marquess chuckled to himself.

"You win this time. But rest assured it is only because I'm too drained of strength to waste what little I have in childish sparring."

Still holding the mare's reins, he climbed into his own saddle. "Well and good it is! Now enjoy the ride. We'll be back at Dahlingham soon."

"I am not an invalid. I am quite capable of handling my mare."

"If it will quiet you, fine. Take the reins." With a frustrated growl he slung the leather in her direction. Anything to keep her from getting so angry that she collapsed again, he thought.

The marquess gently patted the red's neck. The old boy had run the race of his lifetime, and the tender touch of his master let him know he'd performed well. The red answered with a grateful whinny and took off at a leisurely trot.

Many long minutes stretched out as they rode without conversation. Occasionally, he peered back at her, to make certain she was steady. The first time, she ignored him. The second time, she shifted her gaze quickly to the trees, pretending not to have been watching him. The third time, Raven stuck her tongue out at Devan.

"Ah-ho!" he exclaimed. "I see we are feeling a mite more sprightly, and quite capable of some *childish sparring*."

"On the contrary." Raven brought the mare up to trot side by side with the red. "It is simply that *you* bring out the worst in me."

"Now, now. I dare say I brought out the best in you. Over and over again, if I recall correctly." He grinned wickedly, and noticed the sudden tinge of bright pink that replaced the sickly coloring to her cheeks. "Ah, you, too, recall, I see."

Her eyes narrowed and her nostrils flared. "Why do you take such delight in reminding me of the gravest mistake of my life, Devan?"

"It is not a mistake I remind you of, sweetheart. The only mistake you are making is continuing with this charade of wishing to marry Brookshire. *That* is the erratum."

"It is none of your affair," she said, lifting her chin defiantly and directing her attention to the road ahead.

"I take exception to that."

"*You* would."

"After all that has passed between us, Raven, how can you say your happiness is none of my concern? You will not be happy wed to the duke. Mark my words."

"Think what you will. I intend to be deliriously happy. Ecstatic even. In fact, nothing that I can think of at this instant would make me happier than marrying Victor before sun up tomorrow and moving to London immediately so that I never have to lay eyes on you again."

"My London estate is quite close to Victor's. You would still see me. *Often.* I may even decide to move to London once and for all."

"I will move to Scotland."

"I have an estate there, as well," he lied. "And Germany and France and, heavens, I have so many homes I've forgotten the lands in which all of them lay."

"I would move to hell, if it would get me away from you."

"I'm certain there is a place reserved for me there, also," he mumbled under his breath.

"As am I," she countered, not missing an opportunity.

His teasing tone became suddenly serious. "Raven," he said softly, "it is not me you run from. It is only that I remind you of the truth in your heart."

With that she turned on him fiercely. "Let us get one thing perfectly clear. *You,*" she pointed an accusing finger, "will never know what lies in my heart, truth or otherwise. Because I will *never* allow you that close to my heart again."

"Then I have been there."

Her countenance turned from anger to confusion. "Been where?"

"In your heart."

"Oh, you're infuriating!" she scowled.

He chuckled.

"Wretch."

"Wench." His laughing voice rose into the wind and echoed around them.

They turned the sharp bend in the road, and just past the thicket and tall trees was an open mead. Encamped there, a coterie of travelers, who had not been there earlier in the day when they'd made the journey into Dublin.

Wagons and horses and a few stray dogs surrounded a small group. People in ragged clothing, of colors that had once been bright but were now dull with age and wear. Some gathered around a fire, while others banded together in little groups, setting up the camp.

Raven slowed her horse. "Tinkers." A smile formed as the word fell from her lips.

"*Gypsies*. Keep your gaze on the road ahead."

"They are harmless."

An old woman hobbled toward them, raising her gnarled walking stick into the air and grousing in the Irish.

"I think she wants us to leave," Devan said anxiously, "and I think it wise, before the whole lot of them descends upon us."

Raven put her hand out, preventing him from moving forward. "Wait. She only says that she has been waiting for us. Perhaps they are in need of assistance."

"Perhaps they are cannibals, in need of a hearty supper."

Rolling her eyes, she sighed. "Be courageous, Lord Castlereagh. Surely an aged female is no threat to a strapping young lord such as yourself."

"Oh, yes," he grinned, *"strapping."*

As the woman approached, Devan felt the curious stares of the entire camp upon them. A lump rose in his throat. He'd seen the Tinkers from a distance before, and had overheard the servants speak of their wisdom and mystical ways. But never had he been so near. Swallowing hard, he forced back his awe and fear.

He was no small boy, and he did not believe the nonsense

regarding Minceirs of second sight, or faeries, or any of the other Celtic mythology. And that's all it was—*mythology.*

"Can we help you, good woman?" he spoke up bravely.

"I have been searchin' for ye these last weeks."

"And just how would you know me?"

In silence, she stared solemnly back and forth between he and Raven.

"Madam, why have you been searching for *me?*"

The old woman mumbled again in the Irish, shooting an assessing glance at Devan while doing so.

"What did she say?"

Raven giggled. "She said her name is Úna and that you talk too much."

"How dare—"

"Shhh!" Raven admonished, making him feel like a scolded child.

He crossed his arms, pouted and pretended to have no interest in their conversation.

"Excuse the marquess," she addressed the ancient Minceir. "He sometimes forgets etiquette. It is one of his *least* annoying qualities."

"Is sea!" the old woman exclaimed with trembling laughter in her raspy voice.

Raven smiled down at the Tinker woman. Eyes, black as coal, and a dark, weathered face, marked by many years of living. From beneath a peasant's scarf, straggles of coarse gray hair fell, catching the breeze to flit gently about her face. Simple black faded cloth made up her dress, and a red shawl draped itself across her shoulders. Frail, yet somehow sturdy, hands held the walking stick, which she tapped lightly upon the toe of one of the brown leather men's boots she wore.

"Do you need help, ma'am?"

THE BRIAR AND THE ROSE

Úna happily corrected her. "Nay, child, I've come to offer it."

Devan laughed. "Oh, *really?*"

Raven poked him in the ribs. Hard. He gasped, then groaned. She smirked. Then focused her attentions back on Úna. "I do not understand. How can you possibly help me?"

"I know from whence ye came, girl."

This peaked Devan's curiosity, but only for a moment before he realized there was no plausible way Úna could possibly know Raven. She may have been a commoner, but it was beyond doubtful that she had ever shared a life with these people. Raven was obviously somewhat educated and gently bred, even if of peasant lineage. The graceful way she moved, the way she held her head, regal and self-assured, left little question that Raven was not a traveler.

"You do?" Raven leaned down, closer, her eyes filled with questions.

"The woman is mad."

"*A thóin!*" the Tinker spat directly at the marquess.

"What did she say? "

"She said you are an *ass*. Now would you quiet yourself? *Please?*"

"Very well, I could use some amusement."

"The lad does not understand, girl. 'Tis not his time. But heed me words and ye shall."

"Understand what?" Raven leaned ever closer.

"Ye be ridin' upon the horse of Fionne ag'in. 'Tis a sign."

"Who is Fionne?" asked Devan anxiously.

Raven sighed impatiently. "Ancient Fenian warrior chief. *Shhh!*" She again turned to Úna. "A sign?"

She smiled with the girl's knowledge. "Last I saw ye, ye rode the same mare."

221

"When did you see me last? Do you know who I am?"

"*Is sea,* I know ye well, for I knew ye then, child." Úna lightly touched Raven's hand and closed her eyes.

"Knew me when?"

"Ages have passed since last I seen ye, and 'tis long I have waited fer ye to return from *Tír Na n-Óg, Mairéad Ní Mhorain.*"

Raven gasped and backed quickly away from the woman, her face paling.

"What did she say?" Devan recognized *Mairéad,* but had no understanding of the Minceir's meaning.

This time Raven did not answer, clearly left speechless by the words of the old woman.

"*Tá tú ag iompar clainne.*"

Raven quickly gathered the reins. "You *never* knew me, woman!" she hissed. "And you know me not now!"

Before Devan could stop her, she kicked the mare and flew like light toward Dahlingham.

The marquess glanced back at the Tinker. A tear ran down her leathery, wrinkled cheek. "I shall pray fer ye, girl," she whispered.

"What did you say to her?" Devan demanded.

"Ye shall learn soon enough, lad. Now go to her."

The old woman inched around and began to limp away from him. No time to shake the meaning from a senile Tinker. He raced off to find Raven.

Raven left the mare outside the front entrance of Dahlingham and ran straight to her chamber, where she threw herself upon the bed and wept.

Tá tú ag iompar clainne . . .

The fates would not play such a cruel prank on her. Or wouldn't they? It seemed fate found no greater pleasure than turning her life upside down.

And Úna had touched her, and spoken those words—*Tá tú ag iompar clainne . . .*

She buried her face in the satin pillow and wept. And prayed. And her heart broke.

"Raven! Open this door this very instant!" came Lord Castlereagh's booming command.

She held the pillow tightly around her head to muffle her weeping.

The knob jiggled and turned, but did not permit him entrance. She breathed a sigh of relief.

Another knock, loud and demanding. "What did that insane woman say to you? Open the door, Raven. Talk to me!" he shouted while continuing to knock, as though intending to break the door down.

She cringed, held her tongue, until the only sound from the corridor was the deafening silence. Then, at last, she heard his footsteps, slow, dull thuds, as they walked away.

The shock of the Minceir woman's words gradually eased, as did her tears.

Devan was right. The old woman had to be deranged, for she also thought Raven had come from *Tír Na n-Óg*—the *Western Isle!*

Everyone knew the only way one could visit the Western Isle was to die first. And one of the few things Raven knew with all certainty was that she was not dead. *A heart cannot feel such pain in death.*

Yes, Úna was no more than a crazed old woman. The horse of Fionne! Raven laughed softly. *Tír Na n-Óg!* Just the ravings of madness. A *child,* indeed! There would be no *clainne.*

CHAPTER TWENTY-TWO

Raven slipped cautiously from her chamber into the corridor.

Hours had passed since the last sound of footsteps or chatter of the maids. She had lain awake in the darkness ever since awakening from strange and frightening dreams. But the memory of the dream had eventually begun to fade as the complaints of her empty stomach grew stronger, and now her only thought was stifling her immense hunger.

The previous two weeks had found her with a constant ailment of the stomach, and oft was the occasion she managed little more than a bite or two before it all came back up. The only good to come from such a dreadful bout with illness had been the excuse it provided to confine herself to her chamber, away from the marquess's questions and prying glances.

Her slippered feet moved quickly and lightly down the staircase. The clock chimed two. There were still several hours before the servants would awaken. Time enough to prepare herself a feast and steal it back to her room, where she would savor every bite.

Turning the corner, she crossed the dining room and made her way down to the kitchen. She raised her candle high. At first glance, it appeared the servants had effectively polished off anything that might have been left from supper, but then, in the soft glow of the candlelight, she saw a half loaf of bread that had been overlooked near the ovens.

The very thought of the taste of warm toasted bread,

laden with sweet cream butter and luscious gooseberry jam made her stomach feel all the emptier.

She fanned the dimming fire, then cut the remainder of the loaf, placing five thick slices into a pan, and set the pan on the rack.

While the bread warmed, Raven gathered the butter and jam, then waited. The time that passed seemed eternal as the smell of hot bread filled the kitchen, while she anticipated the feast soon to be hers.

At last, she could wait no longer and grabbed the pan from the fire. Her hands trembled as she picked up the first piece. Bringing it to her nose, she inhaled, then took the knife and spread the butter on thick, until it melted into the hot bread. Next came a heaping portion of gooseberry preserves, sticky and sweet. She pushed it over the butter and they blended together.

Raven put the first piece of toast on a plate, and reached for the second. But her hunger got the better of her and she gave in to the temptation, and took an enormous bite out of the first slice. And then another, and another, until her mouth was full.

What heaven!

Closing her eyes, she savored the creamy butter and sugary preserves that melted in her mouth, and moaned in the sheer delight of it all.

"Am I interrupting?"

Raven stopped chewing. And moaning.

Blast! She hadn't even heard him enter.

Keeping her back to him, Raven tried desperately to swallow, a task made vastly difficult by the disgusting amount of bread stuffed in her cheeks.

"Thinking of me, were you?"

Turning on her heel, she faced him, glaring, forgetting

225

entirely about the mouthful of bread and jam.

His insolent brow raised, he sported a jeering grin, and her temper flared.

Of all the swaggering arrogance. "You are truly—" she mumbled, at last swallowing the last of the bread.

Devan moved closer, backing her into the table, halting when less than a breath separated them. "Truly . . . ?"

"Am I to have no privacy?"

"This is the kitchen, Raven. Not the place to go if one desires privacy."

"What are you doing wandering around at this time of night?"

"I might ask you the same. You have a bit of gooseberry on your chin, my love," he declared softly, holding her chin and gently lifting the preserves from her skin with the finger of his other hand.

His eyes roamed boldly over her, and she felt the heat of his body, lightly pressed to hers. His scent overwhelmed her senses, bringing back memories of a tender nuzzling into the fold of his neck when she breathed that scent in, willingly, fully. Nearly forgotten desire surged through her, and Raven found herself breathless in anticipation of his touch.

He brought his finger to his mouth and licked the preserves from his finger. Then, without warning, his lips came down to rest delicately upon hers. Her lips parted, and she tasted the gooseberry again, ever sweeter when mingled with the taste of him.

Devan reached behind her, pressed his body against hers. His heart beat strong against her bosom, and the longing in her own heart made her breath quicken.

Staring lustfully into her eyes, she thought he was about to kiss her again, however, it was not his lips that came to her mouth, but a second slice of the bread, that he'd topped with butter and jam.

"It does me good to see your appetite has returned," he whispered.

The gentle radiance of the candlelight reflected in his dark, shadowed eyes, drawing her deeply into them. Timidly, she opened her mouth and bit into the corner of the bread. Watching her chew, he smiled, and then offered her another bite.

The moments that followed were nothing short of sweet agony. His warm breath fluttered against her cheek. Their bodies were so close, they were no longer two separate people, but part of the same body.

His hands slid down her arms, to her thighs. He lifted her to the table, wrapped her legs around his waist and drew her nearer still.

"Devan—" She gave a half-hearted attempt at pushing him away.

"I've missed you, Raven."

And she had missed him, these long, lonely days locked up within the confines of her chamber. But he was dangerous, for his nearness, without fail, reminded her of her love for him. A love that was the very essence of her. A love all-consuming. *And a fantasy.*

It would be so easy to give in—give herself to him, and take what she longed for. But to do so would only serve to break her heart again. And that, after all the torment she'd endured as a result of her love for the Marquess of Castlereagh, would be impossible to bear.

"Admit you have missed me."

"I—" How could she, even if was the truth etched eternally upon her heart? She had missed him. She'd ached for his touch. Yearned for his kisses. Dreamed of his voice speaking her name.

But to admit such things to him would surely leave her at his mercy, and he had none.

Devan brought her face back to his and captured her lips once more. Her body responded against her will, as visions of him making love to her right there in the kitchen filled her mind.

"I cannot," she gasped, turning her face away.

"You must."

"It is wrong. Can you not see how wrong this is?"

Devan released her from his grasp and stormed across the floor, raking his hand through his hair, his chest heaving in evident exasperation. And then, halting his furious pacing, he spun back around to face her, his expression bordering somewhere between heartbreak and anger. "No, by God, I do not see! The only wrong I see occurring is that you refuse to admit the truth." His eyes grew wild and his jaw tightened. "Is this some kind of game you play? The passion in your kiss belies your protest."

Raven followed him across the kitchen, her hands planted firmly to her hips, as she prepared to . . .

She paused, stepped back. How she longed to run her fingers tenderly across his furrowed brow and take the pain from his voice, his eyes. How she wished she could give him what he asked of her, but it was too late to even contemplate such things, for there was so much more at stake now than her pride.

"Devan. I need your most sacred promise."

"Anything!" he exclaimed, falling to one knee, taking her hands within his own. "I will promise you *anything*."

Tears threatened to fall as she gazed into his pleading eyes. Summoning all her strength, she held them back. "If you care for me at all, you must let me go."

"But—"

Placing a finger to his lips, she quieted him. "You are correct, my lord. 'Tis a perilous game the two of us have engaged in. But it is time we think of everyone concerned. I think it best if, for the remainder of my time here, we do not allow ourselves to be alone in the same room. I will always think of you as my most generous benefactor in the hour of my greatest need, but nothing more. And you must never again think of me as anything more than a guest, who shall leave at first opportunity. Your word, Devan."

"I cannot give it."

"Very well." Raven nodded dully, cupped his cheek with her hand. Blinking back the tears, she swallowed the pain of the moment. "I shall leave Dahlingham at dawn. Perhaps it is for the best."

The marquess rose from his knee and took her by the shoulders. "Where will you go?"

"It is not important." Of course, she had no idea where she would go, but one moment longer at Dahlingham, without Devan's oath, and there was no question she would never be able to leave.

Angrily, he turned his back to her. "I give you my word."

"Your word?"

"I swear by all that is holy, I shall keep my distance for the duration of your stay at Dahlingham."

An offer of his own death sentence could not have struck him as soundly as the words that fell from his lips, like a sword through his heart. But the promise was easier made than it would be to watch her leave.

"Return to your chamber. *Now,* Raven." His voice was barren of emotion, as drained as his soul at that moment.

He heard the rustling of her gown and slippers across the floor. She paused momentarily in the doorway, before finally turning and rushing away.

CHAPTER TWENTY-THREE

The young man sat, leaning against the huge and ancient oak tree, far into the meadows where the hills surrounded him, and he could write in peace. A gentle breeze lifted his long rusty waves, and moved them lightly. He chewed on the tip of his quill, contemplating his writings in the leather-bound journal he held in his lap. A smile of sweet recollection flitted across his mouth, and an apparent urgency struck him as he quickly dipped his quill and began scribbling again.

She is like Heaven. Everything about her brings about a violent pounding in my heart, and I do not know if it is solely this great love I harbor for the lady, or if it is my love, mixed with my admiration of her spirit, as well as my frustration.

By all that's holy, I love her! If only I could go to my father this instant and disclaim this damnable marriage he's sworn me to.

The ball is close at hand. That very eve, as soon as the final guest has departed, I shall disavow this arrangement. And I shall marry my love the very next day.

Oh, how my heart is filled with her. It is emotion such as mine that has caused many a man to lay down his life for the love of a woman, either on the battlefield or in a duel to the death. And after having tasted the sweetness of her kisses, and felt the satin of her skin beneath me, her body one with mine, I know I would sooner give my life than let her go.

"*Séamus!*"
It was a woman's voice that beckoned, but not the woman he wrote of, for a frown suddenly replaced the contented smile upon his lips.
He hurried to scrawl a few more words in the journal.

I pray for the days before the ball to pass quickly, for each moment without Mairéad in my arms is an eternity.

Quickly, Séamus sprinkled sand from his pouch, blew, closed the journal, and replaced the cork to the inkbottle. Then, as he heard the woman approaching, he hastened to replace the book into an iron box, which he then placed into a hole in the ground, and covered it with a rock . . .

Devan's eyes flew open. He raced from the bed to look out his window, half expecting to see the young man of his dreams, still sitting far out in the meadow. He inhaled deeply, and attempted to shake the sleep from his weary mind.

"It was only a dream," he spoke out loud, reassuring himself. He sat back down on the bed, rested his elbows upon his knees, and held his muddled head between his hands, attempting to make sense of this new dream.

Séamus . . .

Who was he? And why should he dream of him? *Séamus* was the name the cloaked Raven of his dreams had called him, and it was the very name Raven had whispered as she drifted off to sleep in his arms.

Mairéad . . .

It was what the Irish at the harbor called Raven, and it was the name the Tinker woman had used.

Hell and rot! Nothing made sense anymore. The only thing he knew with certainty was that Raven was at the bottom of this nightly torment he endured.

But how? Why?

Damn!

Rising, he began to pace. If he wasn't mad already, these dreams would no doubt do the trick. And if not the nights filled with dreams, the days standing at a distance, helplessly watching Raven with Brookshire, were bound to send him over the brink.

Devan grabbed for a pair of trousers and stepped into them. A walk would do him good; calm his nerves, and perhaps bring reason to light. The night air would cool him, ease his agitation, and clear his head of anything having to do with Raven.

It was a full moon that shone down, casting a soft glow to the world below. Only an occasional cloud, carried across the night by the rising sea winds, managed to darken the land, but only for a moment before the moon, in all her glory, pushed the intruder aside and reclaimed her reign in the sky. Like a million tiny jewels, the stars twinkled, each vying for her attention.

Devan inhaled deeply. The summer air was warm, but cooler still than the stale air of the manor. The fragrances that surrounded him invigorated, took the remaining sleep from his eyes, sharpened his senses.

In frustration, he raked both hands through his hair and down over his face. Stretching his long arms into the air, Devan faced the increasing wind, defying it, challenging it.

The breeze cooled his sweat-covered body. Closing his eyes, he filled his lungs again.

The brief contentment was shattered when the scent of the roses rose above all other fragrances of the night.

Raven.

"No!" he shouted, lunging into a sprint across the lawn.

No more, by God! He had to put an end to this turmoil that bound him. There must be something etched deep within the cobwebs of his memories that he had forgotten—something that he only remembered in these wretched dreams.

Running beyond the lake toward the meadows, he raced through the wood, briars piercing his tender skin and tearing at his trousers. The sticks and stones he tore over bloodied the soles of Devan's feet. But he did not notice the pain, for all he could see was the edge of the wood, just as he'd seen it ten thousand times in his dreams.

Halting dead in his tracks, his chest heaved and muscles strained, damp and glistening in the moonlight. Light-headed, he bent down to catch his breath, gasping for precious air. Then slowly, ever so cautiously, Devan lifted his gaze to the meadow. He ran his hand harshly over his face, wiping away the salty drops that blurred his vision. A long, relieved sigh escaped his parted lips. There was no sign of the cloaked Raven with the red tresses.

Then, in the far eastern meadow, he saw it—the enormous old oak, which stood tall and formidable against the night sky. The tree he'd sat beneath with Raven when he presented her with the amethyst necklace. The tree in his dream!

Drawing a deep breath, he launched into another run, new strength surging through him. At length he halted beneath the long, gnarled branches of the tree and looked Heavenward. The wind kicked up, shook the leaves, and brought the dew sprinkling down upon him.

He'd seen this tree before, many times, he thought. Was it so odd that it should appear in his dreams?

"You are not aging well, Castlereagh," he gasped, spent. A laugh rumbled inside and then slipped out.

Dropping to the ground, he rested at the foot of the massive trunk, and stared toward Dahlingham. It was no use, he decided. He could no sooner free himself of Raven than he could escape his own heart.

Leaning back against the oak, he closed his eyes, weary of fighting the memories. And so he let them come, until, consumed by them, he drifted back into dreams.

Awakened from dozing by the cool sprinkling of rain against his heated skin, Devan remained, eyes closed, soothed by the light wind and rain.

A hint of roses. Lips, warm and wet, caressed his mouth. For a moment, he thought he'd succumbed to his dreams once more, until he reached out blindly, and his hands met with silken tresses.

He opened his eyes, and there, on her knees before him, was Raven, meeting his gaze fully, smiling.

Pushing himself straight, he could do naught but stare at the vision of her, drenched to the skin, rain-soaked waves hanging loose about her shoulders, and linen dress clinging to every curve.

"What's the matter?" she asked, startled by his sudden jerk away from her.

Devan blinked, unable to trust his own eyes. "I . . . was not expecting you."

"And why not? 'Twas ye that summoned me here."

In the last month, she'd made a point of keeping her distance, and barely two words had passed between them since the night she forced his vow in the kitchen, let alone an invitation to meet him. Hell, he hadn't even known *he* would be there.

Something was different. Not just the hair and wet clothing. Nor the features, illuminated eerily by the pale moon that shone down from above them. It was something else. Something more profound. But precisely what Devan could not place his finger on.

Then he decided it did not really matter. All that mattered was that she was there, beside him, kissing him. And nothing beyond that meant anything.

Warily, Devan reached out his hand and tenderly cupped her cheek. She leaned her head into his hand.

Without a second thought, he brought her into his arms. "You do not know how I've longed to hold you," he whispered as she came down beside him and nestled into his embrace.

Her fingers lightly traced the lines of his face, as if memorizing each feature. "And I you."

Drifting gradually downward, her feathery caress scorched his skin wherever it roamed. He suppressed a groan. Then her fingers made little circles in the coarse hair of his chest, while she bent her head and her kiss lingered upon one nipple and then the other.

He squirmed, summoned his control, and forced the vision of laying her down beneath that oak from his mind.

Raven slid her nail teasingly down the center of his stomach and dipped it into his navel with a grin.

Twitching, he chuckled. "Enough."

"Ye don't like it?" she asked, gazing up with mock innocence.

Devan grimaced. "I believe I like it too much."

"And this?" Suddenly, she leaned over and her tongue replaced his finger in his navel.

Devan grabbed her by the hair and brought her face to his, so close, her laughter fluttered softly against his lips. "I can think of nothing more in life I'd rather do right now than make love to you." He kissed her forehead affectionately. "But we must talk."

"Of what?"

The dark skies began to ease away, as the sun prepared to climb the horizon.

He gazed deeply into her eyes, searching for something there to give him hope that she'd forgotten all about her designs on Brookshire once and for all. But the lavender seemed glazed, clouded, strangely distant, and he could read nothing there.

Usually so expressive and animated, even at times when lost in thought or trying to disguise her emotions, now her expression was odd—almost detached, as it had been those many nights he'd watched her in secret at the pier in Dublin.

"Us," he answered at last, bringing her back into his arms. "It feels as though a lifetime has passed since we last spoke to each other."

"It has been long." She wound her fingers through his and sighed. "Are ye still writin' in that book of yers?"

"Book?"

"The one ye brought back with ye from London towne. Don't tease me," she laughed. "Ye know good and well which book I be talkin' about. Yer journal, Séamus!"

Séamus. He recoiled and his arm fell away from her. "M–my journal?" he stammered.

"The one ye keep under yon rock?" She pointed to a rock, just to his right.

Could she have possibly had the same dream as he?

He would settle this once and for all. "You dreamed it.

There is nothing under that rock," he pronounced matter-of-factly.

Gaining his feet quickly, he squatted before the large, heavy rock, took it between both hands, and heaved it from its resting place in the grasses.

"There!" he proclaimed triumphantly, motioning to the place in the meadow where the rock had been. *"Nothing!"*

Raven leaned over, reached out, and brought forth a small iron box. "There!" she grinned. Then she looked Heavenward. "Ach! The sun is comin' up, and Mam will have me head if she finds me gone."

"Who?" he asked, mesmerized by the iron-tooled box.

She set the box at his feet, then stood on her toes and pecked his cheek lightly. And without any further explanation, she took off across the meadow.

Devan turned to watch her chase the dawn, and just as his stare fixed upon her, the rising sun captured her tresses, painted them fiery red, and they blew in the wind, as though untouched by the rains.

He blinked hard and rubbed his eyes, and the rain-soaked ebony locks returned to the fleeing woman.

Devan did not bother to seek Raven out to demand explanations. For now, she could sleep, and he would deal with her later.

He held the iron box tightly in his hands as he made his way up the staircase and past a stunned Collette.

How could he have possibly known about this box, that it would appear as a prop in his dreams?

Had Raven, too, dreamed of the leather-bound journal—and Séamus?

What was this bond they shared?

Hurrying down the corridor, he entered his chamber,

and shut the door fast behind. He sat and placed the box on the mattress in front of him. For a long time he stared, apprehensive of what he might find inside.

Slowly he pushed the latch to the right. The lock, pitted with rust from damp ground that had harbored it, wouldn't budge.

How long had the box been buried?

Rising, he moved to his chest of drawers, and withdrew a small knife. He dropped to his knees beside his bed and carefully poked the tip of the knife into the lock, until he heard a click. Wedging the blade beneath the lid, he pushed down, and at last it gave way.

Devan held his breath and told himself the box could not possibly contain a book and the writings of a man named Séamus. It had been merely a coincidence that the box had been in the very spot where it had been hidden in the dream. That was all. *Coincidence.*

He shut his eyes tight. Prayed to find none of the items of his vision and inhaled a long breath. Flinging the chest open, his heart stopped cold and the breath was ripped from his lungs. Panic overcame him, his hands tingled, then went numb. His heart thrashed until it felt as though it would burst through his breast. Within the box, a perfectly preserved reddish-brown leather book, a small corked jar of black ink, and a quill.

With trembling hands, Devan lifted the book from the box, slowly opened the cover and read the inscription.

Séamus Ó Lionáird, 1626

Ó Lionáird . . . Lady Grace Castlereagh, his mother, had been an Ó Lionáird. But who was *Séamus Ó Lionáird?* The marquess turned the page.

15 May 1626

Having returned to my homeland after an extended stay in London for my education, I find I have no one with whom I can share my thoughts. Dah is much preoccupied with the workings of his land and he and Dermot are planning a marriage within the year between Áine and myself.

Áine is pleasant to behold, but I find her lacking in other qualities and fear my life shall be rather empty once we are wed. However, it is the least I can do for Dah, for the future of Dahlingham shall be secured with a joining of Ireland's two wealthiest and most powerful clans.

I find it odd—Ó Lionáird and Ó Seachnasaigh were by no means clans of great importance until the English overcame Eire in days gone by. Strange how loyalty to one's sworn enemy can make one rich. For this, of course, I cannot condemn my father, for it was his ancestors who first befriended the English when they realized the potential rise to power such allegiance held for them. And in those days, it was a matter of survival, for a nation so small as Eire could never have stood against the Normans and their massive armies.

The past is in the past, and that has been determined. It seems my future has been determined for me as well, and I pray I have misjudged Áine, and this union will hold some love for me once I come to know her heart.

Devan pondered the writings. There was nothing special in them save a trivial history lesson, and the sadness of a young man destined to marry a woman he did not love. But what of this *Mairéad?* Who was she and how did she fit into all this? Perhaps she was not written of in the diary at all, and he had mingled Raven within his dreams.

He parted the pages and read on . . .

CHAPTER TWENTY-FOUR

Devan threw Séamus's journal to the nightstand in a fit of fury. Rather than giving him any clues as to what meaning the dreams held, it was merely a journal of a lonely young man who was being forced into an arranged marriage. After reading nearly a third of the large volume of writings of Séamus Ó Lionáird, he was convinced, once again, that finding the journal had been a coincidence—some knowledge of his past that he had merely forgotten.

But how would Raven have known of his ancestors or the journal, when she did not even know her own identity?

He grabbed a shirt from his wardrobe, and eased it over his wounded flesh where the briars had torn and gashed the night before.

Half the morning wasted reading an ancient journal, he thought as he hurriedly traded his shredded trousers for a new pair, and then pulled his boots over his feet, too preoccupied to notice the cuts and bruises.

Damn this insidious waking in the middle of the night, and damn Raven's midnight outings! Devan mumbled a string of foul curses as he tripped down the corridor and then the staircase, over another night's rest lost.

"Mrs. Captain!" he bellowed, throwing himself around the corner of the library. But the housekeeper was not there. Devan stormed into the drawing room. "Mrs. Captain!" But she was not there, either. "Thunder of God, Mrs. Captain!"

he roared, his arms flailing into the air as he made his way into the dining room.

"What sort of behavior is this?" Suddenly Mrs. Captain appeared from the service area, hands firmly set to her hips and her gray eyes on fire. "I may be naught but the house-keeper of Dahlingham, and you may be the marquess, Devan Castlereagh, but you'll not be cursing me without cause."

Devan came to a halt, his face softened with the flash of a scolded child's expression taking the place of his glower.

"That's better," she sniffed haughtily. "Now what is it that has you in such a state?"

Minding his tone, he asked, "Where is she, Mrs. Captain?"

"Where is *whom?*"

"Raven. I must speak to her at once."

"It sounds urgent," she noted, regaining the servant's posture and condition she was usually so careful to maintain.

It had only been a handful of times since the marquess reached manhood that she had admonished him. Every now and again he needed a stout reminder not to take her for granted. After all, she had been the closest woman on earth to him most of his life, and knew him better than all others. And when she did so, he could almost feel her yanking his ear to pull him back into line. On another occasion, Devan might have had to suppress a chuckle, but there was no tendency toward gayety at present.

"Of the gravest importance. I've no time to explain, Mrs. Captain. If you will just point me in the appropriate direction, I will be eternally grateful."

Raven lifted the rose into the bright late morning sun and studied the silken petals. What meaning had the roses to her dreams? During the last month her dreams had become more bizarre—dreams of sorrow and death. Yet even in these nightmares, the crimson roses and their fragrance were always present.

Every night she prayed that sleep would not come, but no matter how she tried to avoid letting her eyes fall closed, ultimately she would fall into visions. And then she would awaken, weeping and panicked.

The night she returned from the race in Dublin, she dreamed of Mairéad's visit with a young Minceir named Úna, who spoke the same words as the aged Úna had spoken to her; *Tá tú ag iompar clainne.*

On another night Mairéad was beckoned to the deathbed of Séamus by his manservant, but she refused to go. The dream played again every night, until at last Mairéad went to him. He pleaded for her forgiveness, but she refused him. And night after night, Séamus cried out to her, but her heart was stone, and night after night, she abandoned him.

It was the very night before, in the most distressing of all her visions, that Mairéad followed the lifeless body of Séamus Ó Lionáird to a small graveyard. Just as the wooden box was about to be lowered into the ground, Mairéad flung herself upon it.

"Lay down, lay down your corpse of clay, that I may look upon him," she cried.

There were those who refused her, but one man stepped forth—a man she knew somehow to be Séamus's father, though he'd never appeared in any of the dreams before. As he stared into Mairéad's eyes, Raven felt her own soul exposed to him. He bid the coffin be opened.

The more Mairéad gazed into the still face of her beloved, the greater her agony, until she fell to the ground in sorrow. *"Sweet Séamus died for me today. I'll die for him on the morrow,"* she whispered.

At last, Mairéad was pulled away, but not before placing

242

a scarlet rose upon Séamus's bosom. Then the coffin was nailed shut and lowered into the hole that had been dug beside the church. Even when the last mourner left the churchyard, Mairéad remained, watching over the grave.

When Raven awoke, she searched in the darkness for the mound of dirt Séamus lay beneath, before regaining herself fully from that place which lies between one's most sacred heart and the light.

Then, drifting back into slumber, she dreamed again of Séamus, but this time he was not in the graveyard, but alive and sitting beneath a great oak. Mairéad went to him and he held her. When she awoke from this dream, she'd found herself lying in the garden, drenched from the morning rains, surrounded by the roses, and there she had remained.

A shudder wracked her body. How had she come to the gardens? The dreams had become far too real, and she felt herself losing the battle for her sanity.

"Raven."

She turned to see the marquess standing over her with a determined, scrutinizing gaze. He stepped back, apparently unprepared for what must be, in her estimation, a ghastly appearance. Of course she looked horrid; she'd slept in the gardens, her hair was surely a mass of knots and tangles, and her dress, still damp and rumpled. But there would be no explanation, for a confrontation was not something she cared to take part in that particular morning.

Averting her eyes, she dropped into a brief curtsy. "If it pleases my lord, I am not feeling so well and prefer to return to my chamber at the moment." The rose dropped from her hand as she moved past him.

He caught her by the arm before she could make her escape. "It does not please me," Devan insisted, his fingers digging into her flesh, "and I shall not allow you to put me off any longer."

"But—"

"I want answers, Raven."

"You are hurting me!" she cried sharply, yanking her arm free.

"Just answer me this—how did you know about the journal?"

"Journal?"

"Another game, Raven?" he asked, the glint of accusation in his black eyes.

"I-I know nothing about a journal, my lord," she said uneasily beneath his dangerous glare. Was it not enough that her life was spinning beyond her control? Why now, of all times, did the marquess feel compelled to confront her with these nonsensical riddles?

"I beg to differ, for it was you who revealed it to me this very morning."

Spinning on her heel, Raven stomped off. "You must have been dreaming!" she called back angrily, having had all she could bear of this bizarre scene. But then she froze in place as the dream suddenly unfolded, and she recalled Mairéad speaking of a journal and then pulling an iron box from the ground.

The blood drained from her face and she felt as though the world was being pulled from beneath her feet.

Devan took hold of her arm to steady her. "Raven," he said, his voice lowered and more controlled, "you must tell me how you knew of the journal that was buried beneath the oak in the meadow."

"I-I know n-nothing," she lied. Or was it a lie, when all she knew was what she'd dreamed?

"Nothing?" he shouted, taking her by the shoulders an-

grily. "We shall see!" And with that, he took hold of her hand and dragged her out of the gardens.

She struggled to pull away from him, but his grip was too tight. He stormed through the back entrance of Dahlingham, Raven tripping alongside him, barely able to keep up with his fast and furious pace. The marquess seemed a man possessed as he led her through the corridors, nearly running down several unsuspecting servants, oblivious to their existence at that instant.

"Where are you taking me?"

"We are going to get to the bottom of this once and for all."

No sooner had he spoken those words than he rounded the corner into the great room—a room that was locked to the world and forbidden to all but the occasional servant carrying a duster or a broom. It was a room Collette had said was used for only the most formal of events.

The room was darkened, but only for a few moments. Then Devan threw open the heavy cerise velvet draperies one by one, and the room was suddenly filled with the bright sunlight that shone through the tall windows.

Taking her hand again, he dragged her across the room. "Now," he hissed, drawing her attention to the portraits on the wall, "I want you to look carefully at these paintings. Look hard, Raven."

She suddenly felt threatened by him in a way she never had before, and terror rose inside her. "You make no sense, my lord. Why should I gaze into the eyes of your ancestors when there is nothing I know of them?"

"Do as I say, before I lose what little remains of my good humor." He pointed to a portrait of his grandfather. "Does this man look familiar?"

"Of course he doesn't."

Devan watched the expressions that played upon her face, searching for any sign of recognition as he pointed out each picture individually, stepping farther and farther back into time as they inched along the wall. At last, he spied the portrait of the young man in his dream the night before.

"And this man, Raven?"

Her eyelids fluttered upward and met the blue eyes of Séamus Ó Lionáird. Then Devan saw it—the sign he'd been waiting for. Clearly the portrait spoke to her in some way. Her complexion paled and her breathing quickened and her hand trembled violently within his.

"Well?"

"I–is this truly necessary?" she asked, turning away from the portrait.

Cupping her chin, he guided her gaze back to Séamus. "Tell me what you see when you look at this painting—have you ever seen this man before?" *Has he appeared in your dreams as well, Raven?*

Yes, I have seen him, for he is the very man that visits me each night in my dreams!

This was most certainly impossible, that Séamus Ó Lionáird would be an ascendant of the marquess! It was acceptable to believe at one time that Séamus was connected to her past. More recently, that he and Mairéad were merely figments of her vivid imagination. But it was truly beyond reason that a man long dead could walk so lifelike within her slumber, and bring about such tumultuous emotion, when she could not possibly have known him.

"Please, my lord, loose me now and let me quit this room and its ghosts," she pleaded.

"Raven . . ." His voice had softened, a hint of desperation in his tone, matching the desperation in his dark eyes. "This very man I dreamed of last night. And I dreamed of a leather bound book where he wrote his deepest thoughts."

"You've seen this portrait hundreds of times in your life. Surely, it is not so uncommon."

"But I awoke from that vision, and went out of doors to clear it from my head. And it is then you came to me, and you, also, spoke of the journal and pointed to a rock it lay hidden beneath. How shall we explain that?"

Raven's heart raced madly. She felt as though she was sinking into a deep, dark hole with no hope of salvation. Pieces of what she had lived in her slumber began to slip back to her. "And did I kiss your lips, and did you hold me in your arms, my lord?" Her faint voice faltered and truth clouded her eyes.

"Yes."

"And the rain fell softly upon us . . ."

"Yes."

"And I—I asked if you had been writing in the book you brought back with you from London . . ."

"*Yes!*"

"*No!*"

Taking her gently by the shoulders, he angled her to face him. "You called me Séamus that night in your chamber as you drifted off to sleep."

"Lord Castlereagh—you had a dream. And it appears I, too, have had similar dreams. But it cannot be explained, nor do I have the inclination to indulge in this conversation any longer. It was a *dream*—nothing more!" she wept, twisting herself free from his clutches.

Raven ran from the great room, and went straight to her chamber, where she locked the door against Devan Castlereagh and Séamus Ó Lionáird.

CHAPTER TWENTY-FIVE

Devan stared at the ceiling above him, watching the flickering shadows cast there by the flame of the candle on his nightstand. Each breath of the night caused the shadowy images to dance wildly together, and then, as the breeze died down, the forms upon the ceiling seemed to bow to each other as the flame was drawn back toward the open window and then stood upright again.

The frustration and pain of it all ground tormentingly at his insides. If he could but bellow at the top of his voice, and curse his own heart, perhaps he would at last find peace. No, it would take more than a childish bout of shouting. Only death could serve to cease this wretched agony. But he would not make it that easy on Raven. He would live a long life and plague her till the end!

He stood and gazed out at the stars that twinkled above the hills. There was always *hope,* he thought, and no matter how many times she would deny him, he was not ready to give up the fight for her heart or the hope that he would win it.

Nor would he give up on the dreams and the meaning they held for both him and Raven.

He had not seen her since that morning, when she locked herself within her chamber, and even Collette could not gain entrance from her. There had to be a significance to the fantasies of the night they shared, but it was not *logical* they should share such visions.

Grasping the sill, Devan leaned his face far out the window and straight into the wind. Roses drifted up to him, and the sound of horse's hooves echoed in the night.

Squinting, he saw the gleam of the mare's white coat aglow in the pale moonlight, and astride the horse was Raven. He rubbed his eyes and opened them again, but the vision persisted. The ghostly mare danced around in circles, raised up on her hind legs and pawed at the sky. Just below the window the dance ended, and all at once, Raven drew rein and peered out from under the hood of her cloak straight into his eyes.

For a long moment, neither of them moved. Something tugged fretfully at Devan's heart.

"Enough, woman," he growled, his eyes never wavering from hers. "Either you are a witch or the devil himself—or you are the mirror of my immortal soul. But I intend to end this hold you have upon me once and for all, by God!"

With that, he fled his chamber and raced down the staircase and out onto the lawn. Raven still stared up to his window, seemingly not realizing he was no longer there. Cautiously he stole across the grounds, until at last he stood beside her.

"Raven."

Her gaze remained fixed. " 'Tis yer ghost come to haunt me," she whispered, still gazing toward the window.

"Whose ghost?" he demanded.

Without answer, she turned the horse and nearly knocked Devan to the ground as she sped by him.

Not this time! he thought. He ran. He ran with all his might, until he reached the stables. Appearing to have been expecting his master, the red stood at the open gate and nodded his fine head with an urgent snort.

Devan hoisted himself onto the steed's back and gave a sharp kick to his sides. "Do not let her get away, old friend," he muttered, jerking the horse's mane fast in the direction Raven had gone.

The red must have felt his master's urgency, for he flew as he never had, and for the first time, Devan felt he could outrun the mare, even without the aid of another rider to slow her. He pulled back so he did not overtake her.

It occurred to Devan that on a night so still she should have heard the second set of hooves hitting the hard ground, even if at a distance. But she never looked over her shoulder, and though traveling fast, it was not an attempt to outrun them.

Suddenly Raven strained the mare to a furious halt. He slowed the red, kept their distance.

The moon and the stars bathed her in a soft radiance, and she and the mare stood motionless in the middle of the road. Devan dared not breathe while he waited for her to make the first move.

At last, she dismounted and walked toward an old churchyard, set far back amidst the trees.

Sliding from the steed's back, Devan followed.

The winds shifted as Raven entered the churchyard. The dampness of the air pierced his body, and a wave of alarm gripped him. Drawing back pensively, he squatted at the gate and watched.

She wound her way through the tombstones, occasionally pausing to lovingly caress the names etched upon the stone with the tips of her fingers, as if she had known the person who lay beneath it. But the last corpse had been laid to rest in the abandoned cemetery nearly two hundred years ago, so she could not have known any who slept beneath that ground.

Working her way up to the small stone church, Raven stood in the center of the churchyard, long overgrown and run down.

Devan positioned himself to see better, for she was far from the gate now, and the clouds veiled the moon.

Kneeling, Raven appeared to make the sign of the cross. But for whom did she pray?

Chasing away his dread with a brisk run of his hands across his face and through his hair, he drew a ragged breath and slowly stole silently through the gate.

There was something dreadfully wrong with the scene he witnessed. More than the fact that Raven had left the house in the middle of the night to visit a deserted old graveyard. A small voice cried out to him to turn and leave that very instant, for tarrying longer could well be too long. Swallowing his fear, Devan pressed onward.

Mist rolled eerily across the stone landscape, and the sea breeze carried the faint sound of her sorrow to his ears from where she knelt near the church wall. Then she stood, running her hands along the wall, embracing a thorny briar. Her weeping, forlorn and bitter, tore at his heart until he thought it would break.

Setting his jaw, he balled his fists, unable to bear witness to any more. If she continued, she would surely shred her hands upon the briars, and since she seemed incapable of halting herself, it was up to him to do so.

He moved swiftly up from behind her, seized her wrists firmly within his hands, ceasing her frantic grasping. She stiffened. The briar fell from her fingers and Devan drew her back against him.

Then he saw it, just beyond her possession, entwined within the briar, a perfect crimson rose. With one hand still around her waist, holding her back, he reached up and plucked the rose. But she would not accept it.

"Who are ye?" her trembling voice whispered.

"You know who I am."

" 'Tis ye. At last," she sighed, her body collapsing against him. She ran her finger carefully along the petals of the rose. "And should I be afraid?"

"*Afraid?*" Devan brought her around to face him.

Black locks soaked from her tears, her hands bleeding from the thorns, she refused to meet his gaze.

"Of *me?*"

Slowly she raised her head until her eyes at last met his. " 'Tis all me own misdeeds that have brought this about, and me heart has broken ten thousand times because of it. I have prayed for both our souls, that God might see fit to take pity on us. And I have dreamed long of yer comin' to me."

"I am here."

"But what shall I make of it?" Her hand gently grazed his cheek. "That I can feel ye, against me own hand of mortal flesh, and I can feel yer arms around me? That I feel yer breath, warm and full of life, and," she laid her head against his chest and breathed in deeply, "I hear the beatin' of yer heart, as though ye were truly here, flesh and blood."

"I do not understand—"

"Nor do I." She smiled then—a crooked, wry smile—and gazed up into his eyes again. "It may well be that I am mad, or perhaps cursed. But I do not care what the cause is of yer bein' here on this night, for all that matters is that ye are here. Be ye angel or demon, ye are far more than I ever dared dream."

The wind shifted again, sending an icy chill straight through him. Whatever she spoke of with words soft and shaken, even if delusional, was very real to her. Emotion flowed from her lavender-blue eyes like an endless river of misery. Devan tenderly wiped the tears from her cheeks and brushed a tangled lock from her face. Now was not the time to try to make sense or seek answers. Her condition was obviously fragile.

Cautiously, for fear of frightening her and sending her frail mind beyond his grasp, he enfolded her to him. *"Shhh,"* he whispered.

Gradually Devan took to his knees, bringing her down with him, until at last they sat on the ground. Still embracing Raven, he gently rocked her back and forth and stroked her hair while she wept. In time she surrendered to sleep, cradled in his arms.

Comforted by her nearness, he leaned back against the wall of the church . . .

CHAPTER TWENTY-SIX

He heard the creak of the door. Séamus lifted his weary eyes to witness Mairéad's entrance—the woman with the fiery ringlets and emerald eyes who possessed his heart.

"You have come at last."

"Aye," she said flatly, "I've come. Yer servant would not leave me until I agreed to see ye."

He reached out for her hand. "Tell me you are here to stay, and shan't leave me again."

"I cannot promise ye that."

"Táim i léan, Mairéad. I'm very sick. I hear the death wind howling. No better," he gasped then, his voice pain-racked and failing. "No better . . . I never shall be, if I can't have you, Mairéad."

"I saw ye with Áine."

"She means nothing to me," he breathed heavily, each word a struggle to deliver.

"Ye held her in yer arms and danced with her. And the toast ye raised to her . . . Ye slighted me, Séamus Ó Lionáird, and I cannot forgive ye that."

"I shall die without you, I swear it. I am dying even now, Mairéad," he pleaded, breathing ever more difficult.

Mairéad leaned over his bed and let a tender kiss fall to his fevered brow. "Then so be it," she whispered, "for ye have as surely seen to my death already."

Without another word, she left his chamber. A tear that had fallen from her eyes streamed down his cheek, and at last Séamus surrendered to his sorrow.

"It is not over, Mairéad," he vowed in a long, drawn out breath, as the life slipped from his body.

Darkness surrounded him, and a frightening cold pierced his being. The four winds came together and blew straight through him.

Where was the light?

Séamus ran with all his might, along a strange and unlit path, but somehow, he knew each step before he took it.

There was some place he needed to be, and someone he had to see. But who was it?

Ahead, the faintest hint of light appeared. He paused, unsure of what lay ahead. But his heart told him the light would lead him where he needed to be.

Little by little, the darkness dissipated. Suddenly he was there, in the midst of a small assemblage, surrounded by mourners dressed in black, crying and moaning.

Who had died?

It was a dim and dreary day in Eire, and the sorrow cut through him as though it were his own.

A coffin.

Remembrance found his heart as a young woman flung herself, weeping, upon it. Warmth replaced the cold within him as her name fell from his lips. Mairéad. Séamus ran to her. "Why do you weep, my love?" he asked. "Who has passed on and left you behind?" He attempted to reach out to her, only inches away, but she was beyond his grasp.

The cover of the wooden box was raised then, and inside, a pallid, lifeless man. He peered closer and then lunged back, realizing the face he looked upon was his own!

He cried out. But no one heard him.

"Sweet Séamus died for me today," she whispered, her voice tattered by misery. "I'll die for him on the morrow."

"But I am not dead. I am here, Mairéad, beside you!"

She placed a crimson rose upon the bosom of the man in the box. Then two men took her by the arms and pulled her away. Séamus watched as they nailed the lid to the coffin, and slowly lowered the corpse into the ground.

And there he stood, until the last prayer was offered and the mourners left the graveside.

"I am alive!" he shouted.

The sound of muffled sobs drifted to him on the breeze. He spun around. Mairéad still sat against the church wall, rocking gently back and forth as her tears rained to the ground.

"Do not weep, Mairéad, for I am here," he pleaded. "Can you not hear me?"

"Séamus, me love, I hear ye. 'Tis the curse of the faeries, to be sure." A bitter laugh escaped her then. "I am losing me mind, and hearin' voices of the departed. But all is well, love. We shall come soon."

The blackness enveloped him once more, and the wind caught his cry.

Devan opened his eyes directly into the first light of dawn, rubbed them harshly, and yawned. Then, realizing all at once that he was not in his own bed he sat upright. The churchyard . . . *Raven!* He looked around frantically, but she was nowhere in sight.

How could he have fallen asleep? She was in no condition to be alone, and God only knew what might have happened to her in the last hours before the sunrise.

Rising to his feet, he stretched out the muscles in his shoulders, set and aching from the cold and damp ground. Deep crimson caught his gaze and fixed it upon the stone wall of the church. The night before he had picked the only rose from the tangled briar and given it to Raven. Yet overnight, another rose grew in its place.

His gaze followed the winding stem of the rose and the briar entwined around it, down the wall, until the two separated, one from the other. And then his eyes fell upon the two markers before him—the very markers Raven had knelt before—where the briar and the rose ended.

The red rose sprouted forth from the ground before a large marble stone. The inscription read:

Séamus Ó Lionáird
Died at three and twenty
13 September 1627

The briar grew near the second marker, merely a weathered cross, time-faded letters carved in the wood:

Mairéad Ní Mhorain
Beloved daughter

It was as though the rose and the briar grew from the hearts of Mairéad and Séamus, and over the centuries, had climbed the church wall, entwining themselves in a lovers' knot.

An uneasy sickness clawed at the pit of his stomach.

Not so very long ago, he would have sworn such things were impossible. But now the picture created by all the pieces of the puzzle of Raven indicated otherwise, as much as the logical side of him hated to admit it.

"Yer time has come, me lord," a quivering voice proclaimed from behind him.

Devan twisted toward the crackling rasp. *"You!"*

The old Minceir stood behind him, peering through hazy dark eyes. Her wrinkled mouth curved into a frown. " 'Tis not much time we be havin'. The doorway to the past has opened itself to ye, and ye must decide if ye shall pass through."

"I do not understand. Úna, pray tell me what this all means."

"Look into yer heart, man. 'Tis all there!"

"Raven—*Mairéad?*"

The woman nodded.

"But how is this possible?"

"A soul unfulfilled shall return to claim that which it must have for peace."

"And what is Mairéad—*Raven*—in need of? Whatever it is, I shall get it for her!"

Úna scowled and stared hard into his eyes. Then her frown slowly transformed itself into a clever, toothless grin. "Ye cannot get it for her, Lord Castlereagh. Ye must *give* it to her."

"You are speaking in riddles, dear lady, and I dare say I am not up to them this morning." He forced back his anger with a deep breath. "Can you not simply tell me what I must do to help her?"

"Tell me what ye believe ye know of yer Raven."

"If my dreams mean anything, and if this is true—that she is Mairéad—then she was in love with a man named Séamus Ó Lionáird, a man who happens to be a distant uncle of mine." He searched the dark eyes of the Tinker for a sign that he was on the correct path, but saw no hint of it. Devan released his mounting frustration in a tense sigh. "It seems this Séamus went to his grave over a broken heart, but I know not why. And what of Mairéad?"

" 'Twas I who found Mairéad sleeping upon the grave of

her Séamus, and two were buried 'neath yon cross that very day," Úna crackled, pointing to Mairéad's marker.

Devan looked over his shoulder, again at the graves. "*You* found her? Good woman, these markers were erected two hundred years ago!"

"*Is sea,* 'tis an old woman I am, me lord, and I have grown weary waiting to witness *mo chara* find her peace. I expect ye will see to it that I can rest soon."

Úna dug her cane into the ground and began to walk away from the marquess. In several hurried strides he was again beside her.

"You cannot leave yet, Úna," he pleaded. "You said two were buried beneath the cross. If Séamus lies beneath the stone, who lies with Mairéad beneath the cross?"

"The child."

"But—"

Her expression became guarded. "I can say no more. The rest is up to ye."

"I do not understand."

"Ye have the book, man," Úna creaked, annoyed with his persistence, her leathery knuckles whitening from her grip on her walking stick. "Use it to discover the truth that lies within yer heart—and hers."

Devan glanced back toward the graves of Mairéad and Séamus. With Raven's current state, there did not appear to be much time left to resolve this mystery. He turned again to Úna, intent on obtaining the key to unlock the answers, but she was nowhere in sight.

CHAPTER TWENTY-SEVEN

Raven brought her hands, aching and covered with dried blood, to her face.

Panic gripped her. What had happened in the night while she slept to cause such wounds?

Rushing to the washbasin, she thrust her hands into the icy water, over and over again, until the dark red disappeared. And when she pulled them from the basin, not even the slightest hint of a laceration remained.

Her stunned stare shifted to the mirror. How was it she'd awakened fully dressed? Her hair was matted as a wild woman's, and her cheeks smudged with dirt and the traces of tears. She'd left Dahlingham in the night, but had no memory of it.

Raven drew a red and yellow sycamore leaf from her tangled tresses, then closed her eyes and tried to recall her dreams. A vague remembrance of a thorny briar . . . and a rose. *Always the roses . . .*

She knew then, without question, that she was losing her mind. And Devan Castlereagh was the cause of it. What other explanation could there possibly be? It was his gardens that nurtured the red roses she dreamed of, and it was he who drove her heart to the brink of utter anguish.

Now, more than ever, she knew she had to leave Dahlingham and the Marquess of Castlereagh far behind, for it was this maddening love that filled her heart, that threatened to push her over the edge of sanity. And the only way she could end this torment and save herself was by putting as much distance between herself and the object of her pain as possible.

Slipping out of the tattered and dirty dress, she exchanged it for a clean one.

Tonight was the ball, she thought, running the boar bristle brush frantically through her matted hair. Brookshire would be her escort.

She had to forget the sorrow and strange and frightening occurrences of the previous two nights, and focus her attention fully to preparing herself for one final attempt at obtaining the proposal from the duke.

Raven had already tried everything she could think of to try where Victor was concerned. Except one thing—the *truth*. Suddenly, she knew what she must do.

Devan threw himself into the chair next to his bed, and snagged the journal of Séamus Ó Lionáird from his nightstand. He flipped the pages to the folded down corner where last he'd read. His eyes scanned the age-worn paper for any mention of Mairéad. At last, he found the first promising entry in the diary.

Úna offered little to guide him, other than her conviction that the book would provide him with the truth of Raven's heart—and his own. Whatever *that* meant.

Very well. He had the whole of the day to figure it out before the ball that evening.

Hours passed as he read, entranced by Séamus's story, and amazed by the kinship he felt with the man he'd never met but as a cipher in his dreams. When she made her appearance, Séamus's Mairéad was every bit the perplexing maid that Raven was, and little by little, the thought that the two were one and the same became less and less preposterous.

Devan shook his head, pitying poor Séamus in his quest to understand the spirited Mairéad—it seemed she was a hellion for eternity.

As he read on, the situations experienced by Séamus and Mairéad were almost identical to those situations Raven had placed herself in over the last months. Like Raven, Mairéad had waited for Séamus at the harbor, where they danced to the fiddles and pipes, keeping their love a secret.

After a confrontation between Áine and Mairéad at the Lochwood Tavern in Dublin, Séamus stole through Mairéad's window, pleading her forgiveness. The exchange between Séamus and Mairéad had been almost indistinguishable from the words between Devan and Raven that night that he'd entered her chamber to beg her forgiveness after Priscilla's accusations, right down to her request for the *joining of their souls for all time.*

The marquess shook his head in disbelief. It was as though Raven was acting out the life Mairéad once lived. What stunned him even more was the inexplicable similarities between his actions and those of Séamus.

Setting the diary in his lap, he leaned back and harshly rubbed his weary eyes. It was all beyond confusing, and went entirely against everything logical he'd ever known or been taught.

But then, Raven seemed to defy logical explanation as well.

Devan sighed and struck the arm of the chair with his fist. What was it that Raven needed in order to be at peace? He could not bring Séamus back—nor did he really wish to. Although, if it would save her from this torment she was enduring, he would most assuredly bargain with Lucifer himself on her behalf.

The morning before, in the great room, Raven had referred to her appearance at the oak as a *dream*. He remembered the odd expressions she wore at times—the thick brogue that seemed to appear again from out of nowhere. Was she dreaming of Mairéad's past and reenacting the past in her sleep?

If so, that would explain why she had no recollection of riding the horse into Dublin on those many occasions, as well as her indignant response when he as much as accused her of lying. Raven, just as she'd professed, had not ridden into Dublin—Mairéad had, just as she had two hundred years earlier.

It all began to make sense.

And that's what scared the hell out of him.

Closing his eyes, he let his head fall back and drew in a weary breath. The words of the old Minceir rang in his ears. *A soul unfulfilled shall return to claim that which it must have for peace.*

The only thing Mairéad could possibly need was to reconcile the love and loss of Séamus—and her guilt for withholding her forgiveness. But in order to achieve this end, then she also needed Séamus.

His thoughts whirled.

All Raven seemed to truly want was Brookshire. Becoming his wife was almost an obsession, defying all reason.

The blood drained from his face and his soul went cold. If Raven was Mairéad, and all she desired was the duke, then it was plausible that his friend, Victor, was Séamus.

But assisting Raven—*Mairéad*—in obtaining the love of Victor—*Séamus*—meant he, Devan, would have to bow out.

Every hope withered and died that moment. He realized then that the only way he could help Raven meant losing her forever.

Devan delved deep within his breaking heart, and knew

he loved her too much to do otherwise.

He parted the pages once more and forced himself to read on . . .

For days I have sought to make my atonement with Mairéad, but she will not hear me out.

The night of the Ó Lionáird Ball was to be the night I achieved my freedom. Instead, I am imprisoned by my own careless and reckless misdeeds.

Dah was in remarkably gay spirits, and no one would have known the burden he carried. The wine flowed freely the entire evening, and I must admit to finding a pleasant numbing in my bottomless glass, that made the night slightly more tolerable. Dah and Ó Seachnasaigh toasted each other on their accomplishment of the union they believed about to take place between Áine and myself. And Ó Seachnasaigh's unexpected public announcement of the betrothal I could hardly deny, there in the presence of my father's peers. By this time, I fear a fair amount of the fermented beverage ran through my veins, and I drank more for good measure.

A dance was called for in honor of the proclamation, and I had little choice but to lead Áine to the center of the ballroom. By that time, Mairéad had found her way inside the walls of Dahlingham, but by all that is holy, I swear, I did not know. From the shadows she watched as I took Áine in my arms. The waltz was eternal. Then another toast was raised. All I could think about was Mairéad and the end of this charade. I closed my eyes, and lifted my glass to her . . .

CHAPTER TWENTY-EIGHT

In all the time she had been at Dahlingham, Raven had never felt so nervous, so unsure of herself. She stood before the full-length glass and stared at her own reflection, but that woman could not be herself. After all of Mrs. Captain's meticulous coaching and planning, and all of Collette's primping, the transformation was remarkable.

Scrutinizing her own reflection, she barely recognized the image she beheld. "Milk," Raven muttered.

"Milk?"

"I've absolutely no color beyond that which a smart pinch can provide my cheeks." She ran her fingertips lightly over the cream complexion, absent of the pinkish blush of sun and wind kisses.

Raven's slender fingers then glided from her face, down her neck, and over the smooth rounded tops of her swollen breasts, unbound and pushed high. She marveled at the wholly feminine look and feel of them beneath her hands, as she lightly cupped them before pressing her palms over the soft emerald satin that fit as close as a second skin to her waist. She stared down at the skirt, and heard the rustle of lace against satin as it swept gracefully about her feet with even the slightest movement.

She stood mesmerized before the mirror, once again finding a stranger reflected there.

Turning first to the left, and then to the right, she at last turned to check the view from behind. Then, facing the mirror fully, she placed her hand gently to her belly.

"You know, it won't be long till that babe demands more room," Collette said softly.

Raven spun around to face Collette with a gasp. "H-how did you know?" Was there nothing at all that escaped this woman? She'd barely figured it out for herself!

Collette took Raven by the shoulders and led her to the bed and guided her down to the feather mattress. "You've had that glow that women get when there is life inside them, Raven. I knew there was a child to come of that night the first moment I laid eyes on you afterward. Your spells and the way you keep absent-mindedly touching your tummy only confirmed what I already knew."

"You must promise me," she said, taking Collette's hand, "you will not breathe a word of this to another living soul."

"I won't have to, Raven. It's going to be quite apparent to everyone soon enough."

"I intend to speak with Brookshire this evening. If fortune is on my side, by the time my condition is revealed, I will be in a position that no one will give the circumstance that brought it about a second thought," she stated matter-of-factly, rising and walking away from the judgment she knew would reveal itself in Collette's eyes. There was no need for Collette's judgment, for Raven had already judged herself harshly enough.

Collette's mouth flew open in utter shock. "You're going to ask him to marry you? And let him believe the child you carry belongs to him?"

Eyes flaring with indignation and cheeks aflame, Raven angrily turned on the woman who still sat on her bed. "Most certainly not! I care far too much for Victor to do such a thing." Inhaling deeply to settle her stomach and calm her raging nerves, she began again, with only the faintest hint of an edge to the sweetness she willed into her voice. "I fully plan on divulging the entire truth to him, except for the identity of the child's father. No one but you and I shall ever know that secret. Is that understood?"

Glaring, Collette crossly folded her arms over her chest. "Oh, I understand perfectly. But do not think for one moment that it does not pain me that you shall be not only denying the babe and his father, but you shall be denying your own happiness to boot."

"*Ach,* Collette! I have seen nothing from the marquess that would indicate that he feels anything for me at all. Is Lady Priscilla not still attending the ball this evening? As far as I can see, he fully intends to wed her, so it is just your imagination." She felt a hard lump lodge in her throat as she exhaled the words. "Besides, it is not I who matters anymore. I have a baby's happiness to consider, and I'll be damned if that wretched witch of a woman will come within an arm's length of my child!" Raven put the appalling thought out of her mind. Tonight she had much to accomplish if she was going to clean up the mess she'd gotten herself into, and she wasn't about to let Priscilla get in her way.

Recovering from the unexpected sound of Raven cursing, Collette conceded. "I can't say I blame you there, Raven. But the marquess—"

"My mind is made up, Collette, and there's no changing it. I know what I have to do. Now I simply have to do it," she proclaimed, strutting back in front of the mirror to reexamine herself.

Collette came up from behind and began to stroke the sable locks with the brush.

Gazing hard into the mirror, the sensation that there was

something familiar about that moment—as though she'd lived it once before—shook her. The dress she wore, the manner in which Collette pulled the sides of her hair up, just so, brought sounds and images to her mind, as well as a shiver of remembrance.

Shutting her eyes tight, she willed the images to come forth. She saw herself before a mirror. She heard a voice, but not Collette's. She struggled to make out the face of the woman whose voice echoed inside her head, but the voice was too distant and the woman was shrouded in shadows.

Chasing the images away, she stood taller, and pulled a few curls free to frame her face, while Collette finished brushing the waves that cascaded like delicate silk across her shoulders.

The duke's gray eyes lit up at the sight of Raven the moment she stepped in the room. "Miss Raven!" Victor took her hand, while bowing low, and put a kiss to it. "You are a vision of beauty the likes of which these eyes have never witnessed!"

Raven attempted to smile, despite her unease, and curtsied with a nod of her head. "Why, thank you, Your Grace." Even to herself, her voice sounded bland, without emotion, as she prepared her heart to cut all ties to Devan Castlereagh once and for all.

"Miss Raven, why the melancholy eyes?" Victor asked, leading her to the chaise.

"I must speak with you before the others arrive, on a matter of grave importance."

"Certainly! You know you can talk to me about anything." He took the seat next to her. "What is troubling you?"

Raven faced the duke and studied him intently. His eyes reflected concern, but not love. Though she had not expected to find love there, it would unquestionably make things easier, for without love, it was unlikely a man of his status would ever agree to a scheme as mad as marrying her while she carried another man's child.

Having little in the way of options at this point, she decided to proceed and pray for the best.

"Victor," she began, wringing her hands nervously in her lap, "I find myself in an unfortunate situation, and I desperately need your assistance to resolve it."

He took her hand in his gently. "As I said, *anything.*"

"Do not make promises you may not wish to keep once I reveal my entire story to you."

Victor's brows knotted in confusion, but he nodded, urging her to continue.

"You are my dear, dear friend, for you have stood loyally by me these last months. A lesser friend may well have believed me mad and avoided my company like the plague."

"I dare say you are more sane than anyone I know. And I assure you, it has been my good fortune to have become your friend." He shook his head with an impish grin. "First time I've ever been friends with a lady, if you know what I mean."

"You're truly a gentleman, and it is because I trust your friendship so completely that I feel I can confide in you. You must give me your solemn oath that you shall never utter a solitary word of what I am about to impart."

"You have my oath. Never a word. Now," he teased, rubbing his hands together in anticipation of a delicious secret, "what is it that I must never tell another soul?"

"I would like you to consider taking me as your wife," she said bluntly.

There was a long silence, and then suddenly the duke broke into thunderous laughter. "Oh, Miss Raven! You almost had me believing—"

Her hand came up quickly to quiet him. "I shall ever be grateful for your friendship, and I know I have no right to ask more of it than you have already given. But I am quite serious about marriage. And if you would consider marrying me, even though I suspect you do not love me, I would do whatever you asked of me in return."

"Of course I love you, but—"

"There's more, Victor," she cut him off. "I must leave Dahlingham at once. As you may well suspect, I have nowhere to go. You are my only hope of leaving with any dignity." Raven reached up and dabbed her eyes with her handkerchief.

With a tender brush to her cheek, the duke's gaze softened. "While I am flattered that you should think to bestow such an honor upon me, for your own sake, I must refuse you. Trust that I am the last person on this earth you should wish to wed. I am hardly husband material."

"Which makes you the very man I wish to wed, Victor," she sniffled. "It would be a perfect arrangement. We can still be friends, nothing more in private. I am not asking to be your wife in every way. Just for appearance's sake. You could have as many mistresses as you wish."

Standing abruptly, Victor walked to the fireplace, rubbing his hand briskly over his chin, until anger won out and he swiftly turned on Raven. "Why would you degrade yourself so, as to allow your husband a mistress?"

"Because—"

"I will always be your friend, no matter what. But *why* must you leave Dahlingham and why are you so intent on marrying *me?* Surely there are other, more eligible, men who would make finer husbands, and we could still remain friends."

Raven inhaled deeply, until the fullness of her lungs

stifled the tears that stung her eyes. "Victor, I . . . I do not have time to wade through the eligible young men of Ireland to find a husband."

He dropped to his knees before her, taking her hand once more, his eyes sparkling with amusement. "Of course you have time. You are hardly on the shelf."

"Victor, I am . . ." She closed her eyes and forced her confession to come. *"With child."*

When Raven opened her eyes, the duke had gone pale. His grip went limp and his hand fell away. Her hopes vanished, as she realized, with this revelation, he would never wed her.

Damn Castlereagh. Of course! He should have known! Why hadn't he seen through Raven's excuses for her illness? Why hadn't he recognized when things had become intimate between them? And where the hell was Castlereagh? Why hadn't *he* offered to marry the woman?

"I cannot marry you."

Raven blinked and the tears finally fell. "I never should have . . . I mean, it was unfair to think . . ."

The duke sat again beside her and brought her close. She collapsed in his arms and relinquished herself to weeping.

"There, there, Raven," he soothed, stroking her hair tenderly. "Everything will turn out for the best, I give you my word." Even if he had to put a sword to Castlereagh's back and force him in front of the priest, he would see to it that Raven was not shamed.

"It shall never be right," she sobbed. "I have made a horrible mess of everything."

"Have you told him yet? About the child?"

Raven sat up and dried her eyes. "There's no one to tell."

For a moment Brookshire was taken back. "What about the father?"

"I made a mistake, Victor, some time back, and I never allowed myself to make that mistake again. He does not love me, so he shall never know."

Victor's blood cooled with her admission that the marquess knew nothing of her predicament. And obviously, the woman was entirely unaware Castlereagh was in love with her. Brookshire stared intently into her eyes. "And you are certain of this?"

Raven scraped her teeth across her lower lip, then answered. "I am most certain."

"I beg to differ."

Her gaze collided with his, gold fiercely sparking amidst the green in her eyes. "How could you? You know naught of what lies in my heart or the heart of the man I speak of!"

Brookshire grinned. "I know much more than you believe."

"You know nothing," she hissed.

"*Hmmm* . . . perhaps you are correct. Perhaps I do not know that you are in love with the *Marquess of Castlereagh.*" He watched carefully as her mien took on a thousand different emotions at the accuracy of his words.

"You're mistaken!" Raven took to her feet, walked quickly away from Victor, and stared at the wall beyond her rather than into his eyes, lest he see the truth in her own.

"I have known for some time that you were in love with the marquess. In fact, from the first day I met you I knew. I know, too, that this child you carry belongs to him, for you are not the sort of woman who could give herself to a man you did not love with all your heart."

She confronted the duke with all of hells fire in her voice. "And what do you intend to do, Victor?"

"I think the more appropriate question is, what do *you* intend to do?"

The simple question stole her fury. "I—"

"Yes?"

Running her hand across her satin skirt, she watched the material shimmer in the lamplight and fought to retain her control over a situation that was going worse than she'd ever dreamed it could go. "I intend to get as far away from Dahlingham as possible." Then, lifting her chin, Raven squared her shoulders and looked him dead in the eye, adding, "With or without your assistance."

"If you would just listen to reason . . ."

"I will remind you that you gave me your oath. Please do not betray my confidence, as it would serve no purpose beyond ruining the lives of all concerned, Victor."

"But Castlereagh—"

"Even the marquess, for Priscilla would most assuredly make him pay dearly for his indiscretion."

"Priscilla? What has she to do with any of this?"

"I am not a lackwit, Brookshire. I am well aware Devan intends to wed her."

Victor covered his grin with his hand, knowing at this point his laughter would hurt her. "And do you believe Priscilla a fitting wife for the marquess?" he asked seriously.

"My opinion does not matter."

"Just answer me."

"Fine!" she snipped in exasperation. "I do not."

"Why, pray tell?"

"Because . . ." For a moment she paused, unsure whether she should continue, but finally blurted, "Because she does not love him."

She felt his eyes scrutinize her from behind. After a long hesitation, she heard him take a breath in preparation to speak again, and her body tensed while she awaited his words.

"And why do you believe this to be true?"

"Because, Victor, she clearly desires his wealth and position above his heart and soul."

"Do you love him?"

"It is not relevant." She walked farther away.

"Answer me."

Silence.

He walked up behind her and, taking her by the shoulders, turned her around so he could see the answer portrayed in those amethyst eyes. "Do you love him?"

Love did not even begin to describe all she felt for Devan. But little more than misery would be her reward for dwelling on it. "Enough, Victor. Leave me some dignity and privacy of my heart!"

"You must tell me, or I cannot help you. *Do you love Devan Castlereagh?*" he prodded without mercy.

Tears blurred her vision, and strangulating sobs shook her body. He would not stand down until she gave him what he wanted, and so she relented. "With all my heart," she whispered.

"Then you must tell him how you feel."

"I can*not*. And 'twould be of no avail."

"I am inclined to think otherwise," he said, reaching into his waistcoat and withdrawing a dusky blue silk handkerchief. He gently dabbed the tears streaming down her cheeks. "You must tell him you love him, and give him the opportunity to love you in return."

"Oh, Victor, how can I? It is obvious to me what he feels, and even if I thought there was any hope of him returning my love, Priscilla will be clinging to him the entire evening."

The duke roared and hugged Raven. "Yes, I can see where that might make things a bit uncomfortable. And knowing her as well as I do, I doubt she would allow you to get a word in edgewise." He kissed her forehead and then swiped the handkerchief lightly at her nose. "I shall occupy Lady Priscilla Coushite, so that you might have time alone with Castlereagh."

"She will not leave his side, Brookshire."

"Miss Raven, did I ever tell you that Priscilla and I have a past?"

She could only stare in response, stunned by his revelation.

Winking, he wrapped his arm through hers. "It is a lengthy and sordid history, I assure you, my dear."

"*Victor!*"

Her shocked expression made him laugh out loud. "I know. Even I am ashamed to admit it. Frankly, I have strayed as far from her door as possible the last several years, simply because I know Priscilla for what she is. And don't think *duchess* is not a position she and Arlington have long coveted. It was only when I made it clear I had no intention of marrying her that she directed her charms on poor Castlereagh and decided to settle for a mere marquess."

"What are you saying?" Raven leaned closer, her eyes sparkling with curiosity.

"What I am saying, dearest, is that Priscilla would drop the dapper marquess in a breath if she thought there was any hope of snaring me and all that goes with my dukedom. For you were correct in your notion that Priscilla does not love Castlereagh. She loves no man for the man, only what the man owns or stands to inherit, and the position it affords her in society."

Raven glanced down at her hands, and then met his gaze again, uncertain. "Please don't think me simple, Brookshire, but how does her fickle disposition fit into all this?"

With a wide grin, the duke placed another brotherly kiss upon her hand. "Oh, Miss Raven, there really isn't a devious bone in that outstanding body of yours is there?"

She blushed violently.

"And I love you all the more for it. What I am saying is it shall take but a few insincere words on my part to effectively have her willing to go wherever I might lead, for as long as I wish to lead her. So at my first opportunity, I will lead her into a rather fitting kidnapping."

"Where will you take her, Victor?"

"Somewhere . . . *private*. Do not fret. Believe me when I tell you Priscilla will enjoy every moment she is in my company. But that is not your concern. You have other things to concentrate upon."

Brookshire's expression turned wicked, bringing a giggle from Raven.

"And what is it I shall concentrate upon?"

"The marquess, Miss Raven. You shall hurry on to your chamber as soon as we are finished here, and you are to send Collette to watch and inform you of the precise moment Castlereagh has finished greeting his guests in the receiving line. Then you will make your grand entrance down the staircase that leads into the ballroom. He will most certainly receive you personally, and while he does, I will take care of Priscilla."

"It sounds lovely, but what if—"

The duke lifted her chin so that her eyes met his. His expression was tender and confident. "Trust me. He will have no choice but to do your bidding. I dare say, had I not loved you so much, my greed would have overcome me, and I would have accepted your proposal of marriage in less than a heartbeat."

"Truly?" she sniffled, her expression brightening somewhat.

"Absolutely. Now, my darling, go to your chamber and tend to those eyes. You must look your best when you enter the ballroom, and when he looks into your eyes, he must not see your sorrow—only your love."

Collette fell back in apparent shock when her mistress entered the room appearing in better spirits than she'd been in in weeks. "My goodness, he accepted! Felicitations are in order I suppose."

Raven ran to Collette and threw her arms around her. "No, he did not!" she grinned.

"And you are happy about this?"

"Collette, Brookshire refused to marry me, and I am deliriously happy that he did. He convinced me that I should not give up on my heart's desire so easily."

"What are you talking about?"

"I have spent these last months battling my heart and all that I feel. And in my denial, I have been prepared to leave all that I hold dear." She walked to stand in front of the full-length mirror, using a silk handkerchief to dab at her swollen eyes. "I will never love anyone the way I love Devan, and I shan't let him wed Priscilla without a fight."

CHAPTER TWENTY-NINE

Devan extended his white-gloved hand to the Earl of Stratforth, and then took the hand of his wife, bowing formally. "Good evening, Countess." Standing at his full height, he offered his best impersonation of a happy host. "Welcome to Dahlingham."

"Wouldn't have missed it, Castlereagh," Stratforth replied. He smoothed his slate gray mustache thoughtfully, then raised an inquisitive brow. "Do I understand correctly, that you've taken up with one of the Irish lasses?"

Devan's jaw tightened and he drew in a sharp breath. The earl was not the only peer prying this night. Apparently, word had spread quickly amongst the aristocracy of Ireland upon their return from London at Season's end that a woman now resided at Dahlingham. More precisely, a woman who was not one of *them*. And not a solitary person in attendance was not dying to get their first glimpse of the woman who'd set the Dublin gossips' tongues ablaze—though most, to their credit, were a tad more subtle than Stratforth.

"If you are referring to Miss Raven, Stratforth, there is nothing inappropriate regarding her residence at Dahlingham. She is my *ward*."

The two exchanged disbelieving glances. "Well, you simply *must* introduce us," the countess insisted.

Devan shrugged casually. "I would be delighted to

oblige you, but . . ." his voice trailed off.

"*But?*" they asked in unison.

"Victor is her escort this evening." His hands clutched at his side, until he felt his knuckles go as white as his gloves, but his forced smile remained trained on the meddlesome pair.

Leaning in, Stratforth's eyes narrowed. "Brookshire?"

"The same."

Brows knitted, the countess pouted. "But I assumed—"

Cutting her off mid-sentence, Devan's smile drew into a tight-lipped smirk. "You *assumed* wrongly. Now," he said, his patience at an end, as was his desire to speak further of Brookshire's claim to Raven that evening, "as there are no other guests in line to greet, it is time I saw to my other duties as host."

He left them standing there, mouths agape, and made his way across the ballroom and into the crowd. As he walked, his gaze darted from one end of the room to the other, but he saw no trace of Raven. Pulling his watch from his waistcoat, he checked the time. Surely she should have come down by now.

After an entire day of pondering the writings of Séamus Ó Lionáird, he understood that this ball—the ball that had long been a tradition of his ancestors, then his parents, and now himself—was the very ball where everything had gone wrong between Séamus and Mairéad. If his intuition and Úna's predictions were correct, she had no choice but to make her appearance at this ball. Nor did Victor.

The marquess accepted a glass of wine from a footman and, feeling closed in, moved out of the crowd, and stood near the entranceway, feigning an interest in watching his guests. But his thoughts remained where they'd been all day.

Séamus had made what appeared to Mairéad an indiscretion—his dance with Áine, and his proclamation of love. Mairéad had not realized it was she he spoke of. And she would not forgive him, even when he lay upon his deathbed. The young man had paid a high price for having not been courageous enough to stand up to his father and publicly denounce the loveless arrangement, in favor of a love match with a woman of whom his father would not have approved.

Mairéad had paid dearly as well, for she'd had to bear the burden of her pride, and her guilt became a yoke. At last she had fallen beneath the weight of it, taking her child to her grave with her.

Devan recalled how Raven, in her delirium, had sought his mercy—Séamus's mercy—in the churchyard. If he'd have only known then what he now knew, perhaps he could have delivered it to her and ended her torment.

After tonight, all would be as it should have been, he thought, swallowing the last of his wine. As it should *be*. And no matter the agony he would be forced to endure, he was determined it would be so.

He scanned the ballroom again. Priscilla was nowhere in sight. She'd been at his side through most of the reception, but he'd been preoccupied, and it had not been until that very minute he actually thought of her. Her constant chatter made it difficult to think coherently, so he was glad she had found someone else to occupy her for a time.

As he walked the perimeter of the ballroom, it occurred to him that there was one light in all this darkness. Tonight, once his debt to Coushite was paid in full, Devan fully intended to politely and effectively sever all ties to him and Priscilla.

"Devan!"

Speak of the she-devil. The nasal bleat of her voice made

him tense and scan the room for cover, but Priscilla was already on top of him.

"I've been searching all over for you," she whined. "Everyone is dancing except us."

He attempted to dissuade her. "I am not in the mood to dance, Priscilla. Here," he said, motioning for the footman, "have a glass of wine. It will do you good."

Shooing the servant away with an impatient flick of her wrist, she latched on to his arm and pulled Devan toward the center of the room.

Knowing she would cause a scene if he did otherwise, he reluctantly complied. *But then I will owe you no more,* he thought, with no small measure of satisfaction. Surely he could suffer something as simple as a dance if it would appease this self-proclaimed appendage and cease her wretched whining.

He could not recall a minuet longer than the one he danced with Priscilla. It seemed an eternity before at last the music ended, but mercifully, it did. He bowed politely and turned to search for a safe haven.

"Where are you going, Devan?" the mewling miss demanded in her most offended tone.

"The wine isn't doing the trick," he muttered under his breath. Then facing her again he said, "I need a brandy, Priscilla."

Her bottom lip protruded. "But it is a waltz."

A soft murmur rose suddenly through the crowd. Their gazes followed the direction of every other in the room.

And then he saw . . .

Her.

Lady Katherine stood beautifully poised at the top of the stairs, just as she had appeared that night at Dakshire House. Was this some cruel hoax? Or were his eyes playing tricks on him? he wondered, blinking in disbelief. The hair, the dress—everything was identical to Katherine.

Then suddenly, it was not Katherine his eyes drank in, but Raven—*his* Raven—in all her glorious splendor, descending the staircase, eyes staring straight into his.

Priscilla, too, obviously witnessed the stunning ebony-haired Irish beauty's descent, as well as Devan's evident admiration for the dark enchantress. All at once, without warning, she catapulted herself back into his arms.

Raven saw nothing or no one as she descended the staircase, save the Marquess of Castlereagh. For a moment she believed all was as Brookshire promised it would be, until Devan took Lady Priscilla in his arms to the waltz that was playing.

Her throat tightened, she felt the color drain from her cheeks, and then despair pricked her heart like a jagged needle. Cool satisfaction glittered in Priscilla's eyes when she recognized Raven's sudden hesitation.

Gripping the polished dark oak banister, she sucked in a deep, determined breath. Lifting her chin in blatant defiance of Priscilla's perceived victory, she turned her stare back to Devan, squared her shoulders, then continued her descent with the dignity of a queen.

Brookshire suddenly appeared at the foot of the stairs, his hand extended. "Keep your eyes on the prize, Miss Raven," he said with a less than troubled expression. In fact, the madman was grinning.

She lifted her hand into his and forced herself to return his smile as she pulled her gaze from Devan's.

The duke leaned into her ear as he led her onto the floor. "She is not cooperating, my dear, though I'm not altogether surprised. She's always been the inconvenient sort. Except for a brief encounter with her father, she's been attached to his side the entire evening, and I've been hard pressed to find my opportunity to snatch her away."

Victor bowed and gathered Raven protectively into his arms, while the sea of strangers surrounding her, for all their societal protocol, stared openly.

"Victor, why do these people gawk so?" she whispered, uneasy.

Laughing, he whirled her around, bringing her closer. "It is rumored amongst the *ton* that the marquess has taken a mistress."

"*What?*" Her feet quit moving.

"Keep dancing, dearest." He smiled encouragingly. "Very good. Now, where were we? Oh, yes. Polite society stands before you, certain you are the mistress our Castlereagh has been hiding away from them."

A flood of indignation coursed through her. "But how could they think?"

"What else could they think when the marquess left London during the peak of the Season, and has remained all but secluded during his stay in Ireland? His absence from society these last months, coupled with the scuttlebutt that a young and beautiful Irish girl occupies the chamber adjoining his, has given the *beau monde* reasonable cause for speculation."

The viciousness of such a hateful rumor blurred her vision and enflamed her cheeks. "There is nothing reasonable about it, Victor."

As if sensing a desire to run, the duke held her tighter. "Now, now, Miss Raven. Chin up and dry those tears," he assuaged, dabbing her eyes discretely with his handkerchief. "And do not blame the innocent. This, I've no doubt, was merely an attempt by a jealous Priscilla to shame him into removing you from the hallowed halls of Dahlingham. Not only will it fail, but we shall prove any indecent assumptions wrong this very night, shall we not?"

Raven sniffled as the duke whirled her around again. "How is it we shall do this?" she asked skeptically.

"The Marquess of Castlereagh has not taken his eyes from you since the moment you entered the room, fair lady. And judging by that grimace upon his face, I'd say he is none too pleased that you have bestowed the honor of this waltz upon me."

"In light of the fact that he has chosen to waltz with *her*, it is hardly his concern."

"What makes you believe he had any choice in the matter? Tit-for-tat, remember that."

"Meaning?"

"Since she made it impossible for me to prudently take her away from him, I shall have no other choice but to do it quite blatantly."

"I do not understand."

"That is only because your mind is not as perverse as mine." He grinned wickedly, rather like a serpent would grin if it could, she reckoned. "But then, it is not your worry. You concentrate on seizing the opportunity when it presents itself, while I seize Priscilla."

Before she had a moment to consider his words, Brookshire had pirouetted them directly next to Devan and Priscilla. Giving Raven's hand a reassuring squeeze, he then turned her loose without warning. Just as quickly, he wrapped his fingers around Priscilla's hand, pulling it away from Devan's arm.

"May I have this dance, m'lady?"

She attempted to shake off his grip, but to no avail. "My escort is the host of this ball, Victor," she hissed. "It is vulgar for you to cut him like this."

Paying no heed, the duke stepped between Devan and

Priscilla, and took her into his arms, quite against her will.

Priscilla visibly seethed when Lord Castlereagh still made no move to prevent Brookshire's interference. "Devan, are you just going to stand there?"

"There, there, Priscilla," Victor soothed, almost convincingly, while throwing Raven a conspiratorial wink before stealing her further into the crowd.

The most ghastly of expressions swept over Priscilla's face before she disappeared from view, and Raven giggled softly behind her glove. But then she remembered she stood in the center of the ballroom, *alone.* What does one do when one finds one's self in the center of a ballroom, *alone?* She glanced over her shoulder at the marquess, who did not appear to have the answer to that question, for he still stood where Victor had left him, seemingly as confused as she at that moment.

The answer provided itself quite clearly to Raven; when one is alone in the center of a ballroom, one removes one's self promptly. Eyeing the staircase, she inched her way toward it. But just as she gathered her skirt to make a dash across the floor for the stairs, a hand reached out and took hold of her arm. Startled, Raven halted dead in her tracks.

"It appears our partners have abandoned us."

The achingly familiar voice brought her around to face him.

Her captor swept into a low bow, rose and offered his hand. "My lady?"

She found her hand suddenly within his waiting palm. With a deep, flowing curtsey, she smiled timidly. "My lord," she whispered, the words painfully exquisite.

Enfolding her hand gently within his own, he pulled her toward him. The dancers parted as he led her back to the dance floor. The strings sang and she fell into his embrace.

Their bodies moved in perfect unison to the music that seemed to play for only them, and all time stood still as they whirled across the marble floor.

His dark eyes penetrated her heart with their tenderness. What was it she saw reflected there? Dared she believe it was *love,* as Brookshire and Collette insisted? Or would such foolish little girl notions merely serve to break her heart again?

A glimmer of a dream once forgotten rushed back, and in that moment, Raven knew that she had loved this man all her life. Nothing else could explain the intensity of her love, nor the emotions that flooded her with the slightest brush of his hand, or the warmth that enveloped her when their eyes met. Somehow, she had fallen in love with him in a dream dreamed long ago—in another time or another place, before her memories and her life were stolen from her.

A distant wind filled her ears, and the room began to spin around her.

He brought her closer.

Closing her eyes, she let her head fall to his chest. In his arms she was safe, if only for this moment.

The crotchety old voice filled his mind again. *"Discover the truth that lies within yer own heart—and hers . . ."*

Devan tilted her chin upward and stared into her eyes.

Raven's breath fluttered and his face blurred as tears welled in her eyes. She turned her head to hide her tears, afraid to allow him to witness the truth.

Far too soon, the waltz ended. The music faded, but still they clung to each other.

A sudden shove, and the realization that every eye was upon them, shattered the magic.

Lord Coushite stepped between Raven and the marquess.

The numbness was ripped from my body as I watched the

pain fill Mairéad's eyes. But I was immobilized in the chaos surrounding me . . .

Devan reached out his hand to her. "Raven."

The wind grew louder, and just as her legs began to buckle beneath her, Brookshire's arms went around her waist. Priscilla took Devan's hand then, and she and her father spirited him across the room.

Raven turned to Victor, suddenly filled with a terror she could not comprehend. "Take me from this place."

Before the duke could whisk her from the crowd, Collette moved up beside them and pointed, directing their gazes.

Lord Coushite's voice resounded throughout the ballroom. "I wish to raise a toast!" he boomed, lifting his glass high into the air.

Dah and Ó Seachnasaigh raised their glasses to each other, congratulating themselves on the union they believed about to take place . . .

"To the Marquess of Castlereagh, and my lovely daughter, Lady Priscilla!"

"Coushite!" Devan hissed. "You are making a spectacle of yourself!"

"Have a glass of wine, Castlereagh, and leave this to me. You shall thank me in the morning," the inebriated man slurred dismissively.

Priscilla clinked her crystal glass against her father's and slid her arm through Devan's.

Looking out across the crowded ballroom, he beheld Raven in Brookshire's arms. A sword in the gut could not have pained him more than the sight of the duke whispering in her ear as she rested her head lovingly on his shoulder.

Devan's hands balled into fists of immense rage, with a sudden, overwhelming urge to violently shake the duke's neck within his bare hands.

Then he realized, for Raven's sake, it had to be.

So be it! Let Priscilla have her title of marchioness. He'd lost Raven, and without her, nothing else mattered. Devan took the wine and lifted his glass.

Raven trembled as she watched Coushite lift his glass to toast Priscilla and Devan. It was only the steady support of Brookshire's arms that kept her to her feet.

"I'm so sorry, Miss Raven," the duke whispered, bringing her closer. "I truly thought—"

She let her head fall to the comfort of his shoulder, softly crying and sighed, "I-I know."

"Ah, Raven." Collette's voice broke as she placed a compassionate hand on her friend's arm. "This is all wrong."

Raven wished to disappear—to make this whole horrible night go away. How could she have ever believed he could love her? A sick, gnawing pain filled the pit of her stomach when Devan lifted his glass to accept the toast offered by Arlington.

He looked into Priscilla's icy blue eyes. Whatever their future, he could not proclaim it while watching the cold satisfaction that played in her expression. He closed his eyes, and with a sharply indrawn breath, held his glass higher.

"To the lady who shall be my wife," he said flatly.

Raven grew rigid with the marquess's proclamation. Victor continued to hold her while the sobs she fought to suppress shook her body . . .

★ ★ ★ ★ ★

But all I could think of at that moment was Mairéad . . .

Devan's voice rose. "A woman I love above all others . . . my every breath . . . my most sacred dream . . ."

Each word broke Raven's heart, again and again. And with every oath of adoration, a dream withered and died. In her mind, she saw again a rose, faded and failing in the despair of winter . . .

The words had fallen from his lips unbidden. What was he doing?

The sound of Úna's ancient voice whispered in his head. *"Look into your heart . . ."*

His heart . . .

The past and present collided.

Not Brookshire . . .

He stood taller, and this time, his voice sounded unfalteringly throughout the ballroom. "She is the only woman I shall ever love, and the future Marchioness of Castlereagh if she will have me."

"Oh, I will," cooed Lady Priscilla, who closed her eyes, and lifted her lips to receive the tender kiss that should follow such a heart-felt pledge of devotion . . .

The fractured seconds became an eternity. The ballroom was filled with a stone silence, and the breaking of her heart echoed inside her head.

Unexpectedly, the dark eyes of the marquess flew open, locking on Raven's. She tried to look away, but it was too late, for his gaze would not relinquish her.

"Raven."

A unified gasp rose through the crowd, and suddenly, all eyes followed the stare of the Marquess of Castlereagh.

"Devan!" Priscilla cried out.

But he ignored her. "Raven," he called resolutely, demanding her acknowledgement.

Raven slowly lifted her head. "My lord?" she murmured, bringing the back of her gloved hand up to wipe away the tears.

Never taking his fixed stare from her, he moved determinedly from the far end of the ballroom to the center of the floor where she stood and embraced her hand.

Her hand trembled within his. Her heart thundered madly. *This is a dream,* she told herself. Another cruel and merciless dream.

Falling to one knee, he looked deep into her eyes. "Will you marry me?"

The walls and the floor closed in around her. Her legs went weak and gave way, but Brookshire's arm held fast and secure, forcing her to remain in the scene being played out.

"I am asking you to marry me," he repeated, a desperate plea in his fathomless black eyes. "Be my wife, Raven."

Devan Castlereagh knelt before her, saying the very words she'd so longed to hear him say. But her voice failed her.

When no answer came, his head bowed low.

Removing her glove, she warily stretched forth her hand, still certain the man before her now was merely an illusion. But she felt the warmth of his flesh beneath her fingers, and he did not vanish into thin air. A tear slipped to her cheek. She cupped his chin until his tender gaze met hers once more.

"My lord, I will marry you."

CHAPTER THIRTY

Raven lifted the skirt of her dress and spun in graceful circles around her chamber. Lifting her left hand high into the last bit of setting sun that shone through her window, she gazed at the elegant band around her finger. The soft golden rays danced within the emerald stone and the tiny diamonds surrounding it.

She'd never dared believe such happiness existed! To have the love and name of Devan, Marquess of Castlereagh, seemed almost too wonderful to be real. All at once she stopped her spinning and pinched herself, and the resulting pain was utterly welcome.

"Raven, what are you doing?" cried Collette, entering the room.

"I'm deliriously happy, and I'm reveling in it!" Raven responded with giddy laughter, bounding toward her friend.

"Well, it is time to stop your dancing. Lord Castlereagh will come soon and you must be ready for him."

"Oh, I *am* ready!"

Collette grinned. "No, you are not. However," she said, walking quickly to the wardrobe, "I think this will help." From the collection of gowns and dresses, she brought forth a gown of white gossamer and a robe to match.

"I may as well be wearing nothing at all!" Gently stroking the sheer material, she marveled at its beauty. "It is . . . *scandalous*."

Disappointment marked Collette's expression.

"And, most likely, indecent." She pressed the soft fabric lightly to her cheek.

Collette pouted and all but stomped her foot. "You're not being fair. You haven't even tried it on."

Crossing her arms in front of her, she contemplated the gown in earnest. "I've no need to try it on," she said at last, meeting the maid's glare with a grin, "to know it is the most *beautiful* gown I have ever seen."

"You are positively evil," Collette growled in exasperation. "For a moment I thought I would have to tell Maime you refused it."

"What does your mother have to do with this?" Taking the gown from Collette's hands, she laid it out across the bed.

"It is her wedding gift to you."

"Mrs. Captain?" she asked, disbelief thick in her tone.

"I hardly believed it myself. But trust me, it is best we do not try to figure her out. I've failed miserably at the task for years. Besides, if you do not hurry, you will never get to wear it, for I expect him to be knocking at your door very soon."

"Then let's be about it, Collette." She angled around so her back was to the maid, allowing her access to the tiny pearl buttons that climbed from her waist to her neck.

Layers upon layers of dress and undergarments were removed and set aside. Then Collette held the gossamer silk gown while Raven stepped into it. When she at last turned to the mirror, she was gripped by a sudden flood of panic, as she came face-to-face with what the night would hold in store.

It is not as though you are intimately unacquainted with the marquess, she reprimanded her image, frowning.

But it would be the first time she would make love to him without fear of the dawn.

"Raven, you are shivering," Collette said softly, holding the robe.

"I–I'm fine," she lied, realizing her discomfiture was more than just a bride's nervousness. Pushing her arms into the sleeves of the robe, she kissed Collette's cheek. "Have I told you how much I love you for all you've done since I came to Dahlingham?"

"Have I told you how glad I am that you came to Dahlingham?" She looked Raven over from head to toe. "You are stunning." She laid an affectionate hand to her shoulder and smiled. "I shall leave you a few minutes to yourself."

Nodding, Raven watched as she disappeared into the corridor and the door closed behind her. Then she turned back toward the mirror.

Since the moment he knelt before her at the ball and asked for her hand, it had been as though she was part of a glorious fairytale. Now, everything was suddenly very real and impending. Devan was about to enter her chamber as her husband, entirely unaware he was soon to become a father as well.

Drawing a shaky breath, she walked to the dressing table, pulled the pins from her hair, and slowly stroked her tresses. How would he take the knowledge she was about to impart? Surely he would want an heir for his estate and title, and it was still early enough that few would dare speculate on the timing of the blessed event.

But they had never actually discussed children at any length, least of all *their* children. What if he was not yet ready for a child?

There would be time enough to tell him he would be a

father tomorrow, she decided. Tonight was her wedding night, and she must allow him to get used to his role of husband first.

The room had grown almost dark, and Raven lit the lamp on the nightstand, keeping the flame low, so it merely radiated a soft glow. Sweeping back to the dressing table, she took the bottle of rose water from the drawer. Closing her eyes, she smiled dreamily, imagining his lips upon her skin, and dabbed a drop of the fragrance in all the places she recalled the heat of his kisses.

A hand gently gripped hers, startling Raven. Her eyes darted to the mirror, and caught Devan's smile behind her.

"Please . . . allow me." He reached around her and dipped the tip of his finger into the rosewater, then set the bottle to the dressing table. Pressing his cheek to her hair, his finger trailed the fragrance from behind her ear and across her throat, while his other hand caught the sheer strand of the bow at her waist and tugged.

His lustful gaze roamed the reflection of her thinly veiled body. "You are beautiful," Devan whispered, brushing her hair from her shoulder, exposing her neck to his hungry kiss.

Beneath the translucent silk, the silhouetted shape of her body beckoned him with the promise of sweet communion, one of bodies and hearts and souls. He sucked in a deep breath, summoning control, then nuzzled his face into her riotous mane, tangling his fingers through hers. The faintest hint of roses mingled with her scent.

His trousers suddenly became two sizes too small.

Slowly, his hands glided up her arms to her shoulders, and he guided the robe down the length of her arms until it drifted to the floor at their feet. She tried to turn to him, but he firmly held her in place so he could continue to watch her every expressive reaction to his touch. His fingers traced the line of her jaw, then curled gently around her neck, finally resting on the rapid pulse beating at the hollow of her throat. Shallow breaths tickled his ear, and he raised his stare from the play of his hands to the reflection of her eyes in the mirror.

"Are you nervous, Raven?" he asked softly.

Lowering her eyes, she nodded.

Of course she would be anxious about this night, he thought. The last twenty-four hours had been something of a whirlwind for them both. Though taking her quickly to the marriage bed would go far in slaking his long-suffering desire, she deserved more. Tonight he would be tender and loving and erase any fears or doubts she might still harbor.

Devan pushed his fingers into her hair and massaged her scalp. He felt some of the tension drain from her body as she leaned back against him with a fluttering sigh.

"Did I tell you that I love you?" he asked, his hands finding their way to her shoulders, while he bit softly on her earlobe.

"At least one hundred times." She shivered when his tongue teased the inside of her ear.

He chuckled. "Then make it one-hundred and one. I love you, Raven." Catching the strings that laced up the bodice, he pulled until they let go. Then, hooking his fingers around the neckline of the gown, he eased it over her shoulders.

Her arms rose protectively, preventing the gown from falling lower. "D-Devan," Raven gasped, the look of resignation in her eyes replaced suddenly by panic. "The light."

Grasping her wrists gently, he drew them back. "The lamp shall stay lit, my darling," his words a pulsing whisper against her heated skin, "for I intend to feast upon every inch of you this night, with my hands, my lips, *and* my eyes."

The husky desire in his voice rendered her arms too weak to ward him off, and they fell limply to her sides.

A wicked grin twitched at the corners of Devan's mouth. "That's better." Again, his fingers ran beneath the neckline of her gown.

In silence she watched as he drew the material further down, exposing her body, little by little. As he stripped away her satin gown, so she felt her shyness being stripped away, until no part of her remained hidden from his inquisitive eyes and she reveled in it. His gaze roamed lasciviously over her, and her heartbeat quickened as she watched him watching her.

"Tonight there will be nothing to interfere," he promised. "The past and the future belong only to us."

Devan felt her shiver against him, and when he cupped her breasts within his palms, her breath caught, and then came out as a shuddering moan when his fingers and thumbs teased her nipples to hardened peaks. That soft moan of pleasure was like a hymn to his ears, and he slid his hands from her breasts and down the smooth curve of her narrow waist and hips, pressing her tightly to him. Raven's head fell back against his chest as his finger slipped into the warm haven shadowed between her thighs.

Swallowing hard, he held himself in check. "God, how I have wanted you."

"And I, you," she whispered, lifting her face to his, until her lips caressed his lips.

The agonizingly sweet heat of his mouth descended upon hers, his tongue stroking hers with a tenderness and yearning that brought tears to Raven's eyes. He did love her. She felt it in his achingly gentle kiss, in the trembling of his body pressed to hers, and the adoration of his hands. Moments ago, she had not thought she could love him more, but now she felt as though her heart would shatter with its fullness of love for this man. *Her husband.*

Raven melted against him as his hand embraced the tender folds of her womanhood and his tongue caressed hers in the same languid motion. His finger dipped smoothly into the honeyed paradise and she squirmed with intense pleasure. His breath broke off in a deep, guttural groan when he felt her tighten around his finger. Devan held her to him, all the while watching her reflection, mesmerized by the vision of Raven. Her breath came in short, panting gasps, her eyes fluttered and closed. Her body quaked and convulsed against him.

Gradually, her breathing slowed and when her eyes opened, she was confronted by the wry and knowing reflection of Devan's smile. A hot blush crept from her bosom to her cheeks and she glanced away from the mirror, embarrassed.

"Don't look away," he chuckled, nipping lightly at her ear.

Slowly Raven brought her gaze back to the mirror.

A particular solemnity now marked his expression. "I want you to see how very exquisite you are," he said, his hands lightly grazing the flesh of her throat and then skimming lower to her breasts.

Deep inside her, desire stirred once more, but not so much from his feathery touch as her awareness of the need that smoldered in his dark eyes when he looked upon her. Cupping her cheek, he brought her face to his and slanted his mouth possessively over hers. This time his kiss was ravenous, ardent, and each thrust of his tongue matched the rhythm his body now stroked hers. Every tingling nerve in her body was jolted by the rough passion in his hands' caresses.

Suddenly, Devan's hands quit their restless roaming and he dragged his kiss from her lips. Raven nearly whimpered and endeavored to capture his kiss once more, but Devan refused her. She glanced up. His stare was transfixed on the mirror.

Turning to their reflection, she saw the confusion drawn on his countenance. Then her gaze darted to his hands, splayed across the slight swell of her belly.

"Why didn't you tell me?" he asked, his tone flat, every muscle rigid.

Her lashes swept her cheeks and she looked away. "I'm sorry . . . I-I didn't know how . . ."

Taking her by the shoulders, he turned her to face him.

She brought her hurt gaze to meet his squarely. "You are angry—"

"*Angry?*" he all but shouted, causing her to flinch and shrink away.

She felt the beautiful dream her life had become turning quickly into her worst nightmare. "I know it was unfair of me to withhold the truth from you."

"Unfair is an understatement."

Tears burned her eyes, but she inhaled deeply to quell them. "And I-I—"

One finger placed beneath her chin cut her off. "It is unjust," he said, "that you have denied me these months of joy."

Raven blinked, not trusting her own ears. "*Joy?*"

Throwing his arms around her, Devan hugged her close. "What greater joy has any man than the knowledge that his child is nestled within the womb of the woman he loves?" He held her out away from him. "And to think mere moments ago I did not fancy I could be any happier!"

"Truly?"

"Haven't you been listening, Raven?" Suddenly, he lifted her from her feet as though she were weightless and whirled her about the room. "I can think of no sweeter gift."

"Devan," she giggled, bracing her hands against his shoulders, "you are making me dizzy and causing enough commotion that the servants shall gossip about this night for ages!"

"Let them talk, my sweet," he exclaimed as he carefully eased her down upon the bed. Stretching out alongside her, he propped his head on his hand and a broad grin revealed itself. "At this moment, I am surely the most contented and blessed man in all the world."

Raven twisted a strand of black silk around her fingers and gazed into his dark eyes. "Do you mean that?"

"I've married the most beautiful woman in the world," he said, laying his palm against her cheek and brushing his thumb over the soft curve of her lips, "and soon I shall be the father of the most beautiful baby in the world. She shall be as lovely as her mother, and I will see that she has everything her heart desires. She will be loved as no little girl has ever been loved."

"What if *she* is a *he?*"

Devan paused and considered it a moment, and then shook his head. "I will love all our children, Raven. But this one," he said, moving his head down and hovering over her belly, "shall be a girl. Mark my words." He placed little kisses across her skin, as though kissing the babe that lay sleeping beneath.

His elation was suddenly halted by the Minceir's tale, but he shook off his dread and vowed to himself that nothing would prevent *this* child—*his* child—from being born into this world.

The night before he'd kept guard at Raven's door. There

had been no weeping from nightmares and no midnight excursions.

He'd seen Úna that morning, lingering on the dirt road at the entrance to Dahlingham. She grinned, that toothless, weathered grin, as he'd rushed out to greet her.

"Ye did well, lad. Ye've given her peace at last."

"Are you certain?"

"Aye. And me, mine."

"Úna. One question. Am I . . . ?"

Úna nodded slowly. "Aye, Séamus."

Again she was gone, with no further explanation, and somehow he knew he would never see the old woman again.

He'd decided not to reveal the truth to Raven. The dreams were gone for both of them. The story of Mairéad and Séamus would only serve to confuse her. She'd been through enough.

Raven sat up on the bed. "Devan." Her voice brought him back.

"Yes, my love?"

He looked up into amethyst eyes that drew him in until he drowned in them, and then she pouted.

"You have her entire life to dote on her."

"And I shall."

"So you shall," she sighed. "But tonight it is your duty to indulge *this* female in her *every* desire." There was no misunderstanding her meaning, especially when she took hold of his hand and brought it to her breast.

Her heat coursed through his hand and laced through his body. "But of course," he relented.

"And . . ."

"And?"

Inching closer, she took hold of his shirt and dragged him to her. "To let her indulge you."

She captured his lips, her kiss savage in its hunger. She pushed against him, taking him down to the mattress, then straddled his body, her weight settling over him like a whispered promise. Her fingers hurriedly drew the buttons of his shirt through the buttonholes, and then she pushed the material aside, exposing his chest to the eager exploration of her hands and mouth.

All at once he felt the top button of his trousers pop and let go. Devan peered down the length of his body, catching Raven's grin before she clamped the material between her teeth once more and freed another button, and then another, until his hot flesh sprang free.

Her fingers lightly encircled his arousal and her tongue teased down his length and back again. Then her warm lips embraced him in the sultry haven of her mouth. Devan cried out in a deep groan of pure ecstasy and threaded his fingers through her silky midnight tresses, arching to her until the heat of her kisses threatened to bring him to release.

"Not yet," he growled. Threading his hands in her hair, he brought her to him, kissed her, and in the same motion, rolled her to the feather mattress beneath him. "Tonight, my love, my pleasure shall come from yours." Standing, he liberated himself completely of his trousers, and then, finally, his shirt.

When he came back down to her, he crushed her lips beneath the fiery intensity of his kiss, his long legs entangling around hers, and his hand smoothed down her stomach and through the soft curls. One finger glided into her and began an artful stroking while his tongue flicked over a taut nipple. Then it was two fingers inside her, delving deep, then withdrawing, with a steady, soulful cadence that soon had Raven breathless. Then he took possession of her nipple, drawing it fully into his hot mouth, suckling hard, until he had her poised at the top of a great cliff of ecstasy, flames of desire coiling and leaping within her.

Raven's hand came over his, driving him further, her hips rising from the bed, the fingers of her other hand tangling in the black waves of his hair. "Devan," she beckoned, her voice low and throaty.

He continued his ministrations, his length pulsating across her thigh, his fingers stroking.

"Devan," she whimpered.

He lifted his head and met her gaze with a lazy grin, before he came down over her and settled between her thighs.

She thought he was at last going to sate the quivering need he'd fueled within her, but just as her hips rose to his, he pushed himself away from her and sat up on his knees.

"Devan," she implored him, breathless, *"please!"*

"I–is it—" He stared down upon her, a look of sheer fear distorting his features. "I don't want to hurt you," he said.

Raven smiled a seductive smile. Her eyes were only half-open, cat-like, desire sparking dangerously within. The length of her hair fanned over the satin pillows and the soft glow of the candlelight radiated dancingly upon her skin.

"Devan," she whispered again, reaching for his hand and licking her full lips like a thirsty feline before she eased his finger into her mouth.

"Me thinks the lady a wicked wanton," he teased, returning to her, careful not to place his full weight upon her.

"I am wicked *and* wanton," she admitted, "and I intend to possess you completely."

"You already do."

"My lord . . ." she moaned, her voice beseeching. She parted her legs and raised her knees. Her arms slipped about his neck and she pulled him down to her. "I will surely die if you tarry a moment longer."

And he knew he would die if he did not take her. His flesh met hers, and Devan eased slowly into her and then withdrew. Raven pouted. Knowing how very much she wanted him to fill her made him smile as he thrust his hips forward once more, then pushed deeper, before drawing back, taunting her.

She writhed beneath him. He tasted the satin skin of her neck and inhaled the heaven of her scent.

"My God, I love you," he rasped.

He pushed further into her, feeling the warm, moist heat of her enveloping him, consuming him, inch by inch. Her nails dug into his back, the pain a welcome diversion from the aching in his loins. Her long legs wrapped themselves around his hips and locked him to her.

"Then show me, Devan." Her lips took his captive, she rose to him, taking him deeper. "Show me how much you love me."

He struggled to hold back, afraid of hurting her. But there was no cry of pain when her upward thrust sheathed him fully in the tight sanctuary of her body. Her body met his in a steady, sensuous rhythm, until he surrendered his fear and it was replaced with an immense need to ravage her. His kiss fused to hers and he gave in to her desperate pleas.

All at once, she emitted a hoarse cry as her body began to quiver and constrict around him. With a groan of combined agony and intense pleasure, Devan thrust once more and filled her.

Spent, he rolled to her side, breathless, bringing her against him, and they clung to each other, basking in the wonder of it all.

Raven kissed him softly on his chin and ran her hands

through his damp hair, gazing into his half-closed eyes with a sigh. Gliding the tip of her finger down the length of his nose, she smiled dreamily. "My lord, you were magnificent."

"And you, my sweet marchioness," he said, taking her hand and kissing the tip of each finger, "are more than any mortal man deserves."

In the soft glow of the lamp, she was exquisite, her body sparkling with dampness and her hair in dewy tangles across the sheets. Gradually, Raven's breathing slowed. She tenderly reached up and caressed his cheek, a tear threatening to fall.

"Why so sad?" He kissed away the tear that slid to her cheek.

"I expect I shall awaken and find this all to be no more than a beautiful dream."

"You are not dreaming." He cupped her face in her hands and brushed his lips to hers, once and then again. "This is real, and there is no one who can take this from us."

Raven tried to smile. "Promise?"

"My most sacred."

His hand smoothed its way downward until at last it rested on her belly. He grinned at the thought of the child growing beneath his hand, and it felt as though his heart would burst from all the love that filled him.

Then, beneath the tips of his fingers, he felt an area of her skin that was scarred, that he'd never noticed before. "What caused this?" he asked, running his fingers carefully over the small patch.

Her hand came down over his and stopped him from exploring it further. "It is nothing."

"You were wounded?"

"I do not remember it, Devan. Collette told me my dress

and hair had been burned when they found me at Dahlingham, and this scar is merely a reminder of a misfortune I cannot recall."

"Your hair?"

He saw Katherine as he waltzed with her, her hair falling well below her waist, and then again as the burning beam fell between them, cutting her off from him entirely. In his mind, he saw her attempting to escape through the flames, running away from him, the fire following in her path.

"Tell me, Raven, can you recall anything of a fire?" he asked, sitting up.

She sighed. "I cannot."

He eased back down to the mattress beside her and wrapped her in his arms. Nuzzling into the dark curtain of her hair, he told himself it was *impossible*.

CHAPTER THIRTY-ONE

"Collette!" the marquess nearly shouted, grabbing the maid by the arm.

"Lord Castlereagh, there is no time for this. Your child is about to be born."

"But is she . . . ? Her cries are more than I can bear!" He ran his hand through his hair and began to pace the corridor in earnest. "Is there not something that can be done to ease her pain?"

"Yes, my lord."

"Tell me. Whatever it is, I will see that it is done."

"As soon as this babe makes its way into the world, the pain will be over. Now please allow me to get the blankets and hot water Mam has asked for." With that, the maid fairly flew down the hall and disappeared down the staircase.

Christ! The waiting was unbearable. *How in the name of God has civilization survived, dependent upon something as barbaric as childbirth?* he wondered.

His pacing quickened. *Blast this infernal waiting!* Devan grappled his hand harshly over his whiskers, and rubbed his burning eyes. Raven had been locked up in that room with Mrs. Captain for more than a day, and Mrs. Captain had ordered him to remain outside his own chamber. Imagine, a housekeeper delivering orders to the lord of the manor! Unheard of, it was!

Damn and blast it. And *damn* again!

Devan paused outside the door. Raven's moans became increasingly more intense. His heart ached for her. But he was helpless. It was his duty to protect her, and there was not a bloody thing he could do.

Just then she cried out again, as though mortally wounded. *Enough!* He would not stand idly by any longer while his beloved was in such agony!

Throwing the door to the chamber open, there, on the bed, drenched with sweat, pale and gaunt was his beautiful Raven.

"Lord Castlereagh, this is no place for a man!" demanded Mrs. Captain.

"Like hell it is not," he ground out, moving fast to Raven's side. "My darling," he whispered, kneeling beside the bed, taking her hand, "I am here."

She seemed in almost a trance-like state, as though she did not fully hear him, or understand him. Raven moaned, long and anguished. She squeezed his hand, stunning him with a strength he'd never imagined possible in a woman.

"Mrs. Captain, what is wrong? Why is she in so much pain?"

"Devan!" The housekeeper stood up, planting her balled fists firmly on her generous hips, her foot tapping impatiently. "If you insist on remaining, you will concentrate on making her more comfortable, and allow her to concentrate on birthing this baby. Have I made myself clear?"

He nodded, uncertain how to respond to the woman's assertion of control.

"Now," she continued, returning to her seat at the foot of the bed, "wipe her face with that cloth and keep quiet. We don't have long to wait, and there will be plenty for you to do when the time comes."

Devan did as he was bid, and tenderly wiped Raven's forehead with the cool, damp cloth. Her grip tightened again. Her body stiffened. And the pain he witnessed in her tortured gaze tore his heart out.

This is absolutely savage in this day of modern medicine, he thought, running the cloth gently over her cheeks and down her neck.

Collette appeared beside the bed, a pan of steaming water in her hands, and fresh cloths draped over her arms. She smiled at the marquess. He almost smiled back, but Raven lunged upward.

"Bloody hell!" she screamed.

Devan grinned. It was the first words he'd heard her speak in hours.

Collette's hand came up to cover her mouth and stifle a giggle.

"Get this *bloody* baby out *now!*" she wailed, gnashing her teeth, her eyes untamed and angry.

"Sweet Mary and Joseph, the babe is coming!" exclaimed Mrs. Captain. "Collette, bring the water over here."

"What can I do?" Devan asked, rising to his feet.

Mrs. Captain dipped a cloth in the hot water, and wrung it out, applying it between Raven's legs.

"What are you doing, Mrs. Captain?"

"Never mind about me, young man. I helped birth you, and I'll birth this child. You get up on the bed behind her, and when I tell you, you push her forward. Collette, raise her legs."

"What the devil are you doing to me?" Raven demanded angrily, as they all took their assigned positions.

"Take her hands," the housekeeper instructed, "and get ready."

"Why won't you God forsaken demons answer me?" Raven yelled, struggling to free herself of Devan's hold and kicking her legs at Collette.

"Quit your blasphemy, young lady. If you want this to be over, you'll put your effort into pushing this child into the world, instead of cursing the people who can help you do it."

Again Raven cried out in agony.

"Now, Devan! Raven, push!"

"My God, you people are trying to kill me," Raven gasped, as her legs were pulled into the air and she was compelled upright.

"Again!" came the command.

Devan pushed his body against Raven's back, forcing her to sit up in the bed.

"I see a head!" Mrs. Captain shouted excitedly. "Keep pushing."

Her breathing was labored. "I can't."

"You must," Devan urged. "It will be over soon."

"I'm too weary."

The marquess brought her back down, and soothed her brow with the cloth. He knew she was tired, drained completely of her strength. "Raven, you are almost there. Do not give up now."

"One more good push, and we'll have ourselves a baby," added Mrs. Captain.

"Again?" Devan asked, indicating Raven.

Mrs. Captain nodded. "Last time, girl. One strong push."

Raven's face grew suddenly determined. He pushed her forward, and could feel the awesome power she exerted against him.

"Ahhh!" she cried out loud.

"It's a girl!"

Collette shrieked with excitement.

Devan eased Raven back into his lap and smoothed the hair from her face. "Did you hear that, darling? A *girl*. Just as I predicted."

He gazed lovingly into the eyes of his wife, that quickly lost their wild aspect. Her expression relaxed, and a slight, weary smile graced her lips.

"Our daughter," Raven whispered.

The babe let loose a loud and thirsty wail.

"And she's been blessed with her mother's temper," Mrs. Captain teased, as she bundled the baby in a warmed blanket and handed her to Raven.

Raven cradled the baby in her arms and sighed. Her body began to tremble, and her teeth chattered violently, though she was not cold. Her heart was filled with a gentle, all-consuming warmth it had never before known. She looked up to her husband, who still held her head in his lap, and smiled weakly.

"What shall we name her?" he asked, reaching his hand out to lightly touch the tuft of black hair upon the head of the nuzzling infant.

She stared into the hazy blue eyes of the tiny baby and pondered the question. Then, at last, she simply said, "Elizabeth." It was the only name that came to mind, and it somehow seemed to fit the little face that peered up at her.

"Elizabeth is perfect!" Devan exclaimed, his grin growing broader.

"Elizabeth . . . *Grace*," she murmured, her eyelids growing increasingly heavy.

At the sound of his mother's name, the marquess leaned his head down and kissed Raven.

CHAPTER THIRTY-TWO

Raven's eyes flew open. Fear surged through her and her heart beat so loud she could hear its frenzied thrumming. Darkness surrounded her, and her eyes darted about frantically in the blackness for something familiar. The rolling motion startled her. Then she sighed, letting go the breath that had caught in her throat as a result of the confusion and momentary panic, and recalled she was no longer at Dahlingham, but on a ship bound for England.

She reached over and cradled the sleeping Elizabeth to her. The baby made soft little grunts as she nestled close, hungry again. Barely two months had passed since Elizabeth was born, and it had been the happiest time Raven could recall.

She heard the rhythmic sound of Devan's breathing just beyond the baby, and her racing heart slowed. Just then, he rolled over, and his arm enclosed her in his embrace.

Raven smiled to herself. Little more than a year earlier she had wandered upon the steps of Dahlingham, in a state of delirium. She had fallen in love with this man the moment she laid eyes on him. She almost laughed when she remembered how certain she'd been that he'd despised her. Life had such strange ways of working itself out, for now she had no doubts whatsoever of his love.

Then her heart grew heavy again. All those months of dreaming of Mairéad and Séamus, and suddenly, the

311

dreams disappeared that night after the ball at Dahlingham. There had been nothing but sweet dreams since then—until now. Only moments before, she'd awakened from a dream as unsettling as any she'd ever had in Ireland. She saw a vision of herself and Devan surrounded by flames, and the fire grew hotter and higher, until it enveloped her. She heard herself call out to him, but she could not see him. She feared he'd perished, but then heard him call the name *Katherine*. And at that moment she was lost to him forever, for he sought another to save from the flames.

It was just a dream, she reminded herself, as the baby drifted off to sleep and her husband inched closer in his slumber. The rocking of the ship soon lulled her to sleep as well.

"Raven, wake up!" exclaimed Devan, showering her cheek with excited kisses. "It's morning, and you have a great deal to do."

Her eyes fluttered open. Just the slightest bit of sun shone through the long velvet draperies of their chamber, but it was enough to sting her tired eyes that were still as yet unaccustomed to the light.

"Come now, my darling little Raven. You have the entire Season to sleep late," he said, kneeling beside her. "But today you shall take charge of Winterbourne and must greet your servants for the first time as the Marchioness of Castlereagh. Up with you now," he laughed, pulling her to her feet.

"Oh, Devan," she yawned, sitting back down upon the bed, "it is barely morning!"

"You have a few moments to yourself. But I will be sending Collette soon to wait on you. I expect to see you at the table within the hour, full of vim and vigor," he teased.

"Yes, dear," she yawned again.

He kissed her cheek and then exited the chamber.

Stretching her arms out toward the cradle that sat next to the bed, she reached for the squirming child. "Hungry *again*, little one?" she sighed. The baby pushed at her bosom and she grinned. "Of course you are."

The journey from Ireland had been long and arduous. Spring storm winds blew across the seas, bringing with them ghastly waves. Unaccustomed to the bouncing and rocking of the ship, Raven spent the better part of the journey with her head in a pail.

Oh, why couldn't she have at least one day to herself before becoming the official mistress of Winterbourne Park? She pouted. Why must everything be so formal in London?

Gazing down at the nursing Elizabeth, she recalled their arrival at Winterbourne in the wee hours of the morning. A maid attempted to whisk the baby from her arms and up to a nursery on the third floor, one floor above her own chamber. Raven would have none of it, and set her foot down on the matter right from the start. But she somehow doubted she was going to have as much luck changing anything else about the stuffy old Winterbourne standard procedure.

Her lip trembled and she dabbed the mist from her eyes. She already missed Ireland sorely, and it would not be until September that she could return to her beloved Dahlingham.

She contemplated her plight and quickly surmised it would not be all bad, after all, she had her husband and their child, and Collette and Mrs. Captain had joined them. The time spent in London would be a busy time, full of society balls, and teas with the Duchess of Gloomy-mire or the Marchioness of Boring-shire. And she and Collette would spend their days visiting the shops in London and buy everything beautiful that caught their eyes. Yes, it would be a grand time for them, she reasoned. And she would do her best to be a fitting member of the *haute ton,* if for no reason but Elizabeth and her future as the daughter of the Marquess of Castlereagh.

Raven removed the babe from her breast and gently laid her back into the tiny cradle. "Sleep little one. Mama must prepare to play queen of the castle this morning. But later, we shall visit London and indulge our feminine fancies."

She took to her feet and threw open the gold velvet drapes to allow what little sun there was to break through the windows and fill the room. It was the first time she'd actually seen the grand appointments in the master chamber. Hand tooled rich mahogany wood trimmed the walls, and made the doors, and surrounded the marble fireplace. The walls were covered in the palest cream textured paper and the floors protected by an oriental carpet, embroidered and woven in greens and golds. The wardrobes, too, were mahogany, and built neatly into the wall, while ornate mahogany furnishings adorned the room.

Turning back to the bed, she admired the sheer ivory oriental silk draped over the canopy, gathered at each of the four corners by delicate emerald bows. A bone satin feather down quilt, embellished with tiny roses of golden silk thread lay rumpled.

A wry grin twitched her lips as she allowed herself a vision of the marquess stretched out lazily upon that bed. Perhaps London was not to be so difficult after all.

"Come, come," clucked Mrs. Captain upon entering the room with a barely audible knock to warn of her entrance. "It is time for me to take little Elizabeth and for you to get yourself ready to break your fast, missy." She scurried over to the cradle where the baby lay gazing up at the muralled patterns on the ceiling. "And how is my wittle eensy teensy Lizzie dis morning?" she cooed in the baby talk that was now a prominent part of the formidable woman's vocabulary, ever since she'd appointed herself governess.

Collette and Raven glanced at each other and fell into a hug to hide their laughter.

"Don't you two be cackling behind my back," Mrs. Captain declared, turning on them with a stern frown.

"Mrs. Captain, we would *never* do such a thing!" exclaimed Raven in mock righteous indignation.

Beyond her mortal control, Collette's giggles broke free.

"Uh-huh. Well, you just go on and laugh." She reached her arms out and brought the child to her hefty bosom, cradled her close, and headed for the door. "Don't you pay any attention to those dreadful women, Lizzie," she warned. "They just don't understand." And with her nose held high in the air, she disappeared through the door and down the corridor.

Raven shook her head in awe. "Who'd have thought?"

"I know," Collette grinned. "My mother never ceases to amaze me. But we do not have time to figure out that complex woman. We must be about our business and get you dressed and downstairs before Lord Castlereagh is thoroughly beside himself."

The maid brought out a morning dress of spotted muslin, of the palest pink, trimmed along the short sleeves and neck-frill in a delicate white lace.

"This should do quite nicely, Collette, for it is simple and refined, and shall serve as adequate attire for a day in London, don't you think?"

"You are going into London?"

"No, dear Collette," she corrected. "*We* are going into London with Elizabeth, and the three of us shall visit

Madam Boutrey's dress shop, take our luncheon at Tilly's Tea House, and then walk from Bond Street to Hyde Park and feed the pigeons, while the marquess tends to his affairs."

"If I didn't know better, Raven, I'd swear you've been to London before."

Raven pondered the comment for a moment and then shook her head. "No, of course I've never been to London. I must have overheard Devan or Brookshire speak of these places at one time or another, although I cannot precisely recall when. Oh, well, it matters not. Will you choose a fitting bonnet and have one of the drivers make ready the carriage? And take whatever you wish from my closet for yourself. In the meantime," she sighed, smoothing out the last of her curls, "I shall see to this business of greeting my staff and letting them know in no uncertain terms that Winterbourne Park is to be a cheerful residence during my stay, and I expect all stuffiness to disappear before I return from town this afternoon."

"Is it not the loveliest site you have ever seen, Collette?" Raven gushed, flipping the brim of her hat up, enabling her to see more of the city, and then went on without waiting for a reply. "I don't know what it is about England, but everything simply *feels* right here. Perhaps I shall insist Devan bring me back to England after the ball at Dahlingham."

Collette sat back in the leather carriage seat, and peered out her window. Raven did not need any comments from her. In her excitement, she made ecstatic gestures with her hands and rattled on, talking more to herself than anyone else. It was just as well, for Collette, who'd never been farther away from Dahlingham than the city of Dublin, was quite overwhelmed by the size of everything and the hectic pace of London.

Suddenly Raven screeched out, "Halt!"

Within moments the team was pulled to an abrupt stop in front of Madam Boutrey's. Raven laughed wildly, clinging tightly to the bundled Elizabeth, and holding the leather strap that hung from the carriage ceiling to keep her balance. Collette wasn't so prepared or lucky and nearly fell to the floor.

"I'm sorry," she laughed, opening the door herself, nearly knocking down the driver who'd stepped up to do the task. "Hurry, hurry, Collette! We've much to do!"

Regaining herself, she drew a deep breath before following Raven out of the carriage and into the dressmaker's shop. "Next time you decide to pull a stunt like that, *m'lady,* I expect some forewarning," she huffed as she reached Raven's side.

"Oh, Collette, don't be a bore." Raven frowned, handed her the baby, and proceeded to undo her hat and flip out her hair. "I must be fitted for a gown for some haughty-taughty society ball, and then we shall spend the entire day exploring London. The very least you could do is suffer me some pretense that you are enjoying this experience as much as I."

"Very well, Raven, but don't kill me in the bargain. That is all I ask!" A wide smile replaced the annoyance on Collette's freckled face.

Raven knew her friend had a devil of a time staying mad, and she loved her for her even temperament, knowing full well the woman was a saint to tolerate her flights of fancy. She gazed around the shop at all the beautiful swatches of satins and silks and wondered which color would suit her best. The pastels really did not flatter her porcelain complexion and dark hair nearly as well as the richer, deeper colors. She lightly rubbed a vivid burgundy between her thumb and forefinger, and held it up to her face.

"What do you think?"

"It suits you perfectly," came a shrill voice from behind. "My gracious, Madam Boutrey could not have chosen a better color for you herself!"

Raven's eyes darted toward the sound of the piercing voice that cut off Collette's opportunity to answer, and saw a gray-haired, portly woman fast approaching. The woman almost tripped over a bolt of fabric as she bounded toward them.

She put forth a fat little hand and beamed at them. "Madam Boutrey." Her eyes scrutinized Raven's features. "You remind me of someone, but I do not recall whom. I don't believe I've had the pleasure of making your acquaintance, my dears."

Raven studied the woman, and decided instantly that she would enjoy dealing with her. She recalled Mrs. Captain's instruction on the art of shaking hands, and offered her hand and an infectious smile in return.

"I am Raven, Marchioness of Castlereagh," she said, tasting the full flavor of the title.

"Of Winterbourne Park?" Madam Boutrey squealed.

"Yes!" Raven replied, imitating her strident tone, with a sly, teasing wink at Collette, who turned away just in time to avoid another giggling jag that was so common when she was with Raven and Raven sported such a silly mood.

"Then this must certainly be for the Gloushire Ball that you come. Heavens! You haven't given Madam Boutrey much time!"

"Oh, and I am sorry for the inconvenience, Madam Boutrey, but my husband and I have just returned from an extended stay in Ireland—in fact it was in the wee hours of this very morning. And certainly you can understand that I simply *must* have a new dress, as this is the first ball I will be attending as the wife of the Marquess of Castlereagh."

Collette lifted a disbelieving brow at the sticky-sweet tone Raven donned, as though she'd been a peeress all her life, and the manner in which the round little woman lapped it up.

"Of course Madam Boutrey understands." She clicked her tongue fretfully. "It wouldn't do *at all* to wear anything but the best of Madam Boutrey's originals on just such an occasion." She placed a finger gingerly to the side of her nose, contemplated the situation, and then said, "I will fit you this very moment. But if Madam Boutrey is to have this gown ready in time for your appearance at Gloushire, you must trust Madam Boutrey to design you the finest, most elegant gown in all of London, for there will be no time for any but the most minute of alterations."

"I trust Madam Boutrey's skill implicitly!" Raven gushed, in feigned seriousness, latching on to the way the dressmaker referred to herself in the third person.

"Wonderful! Madam Boutrey is available to fit you now."

Raven stood on the platform, in front of a long oval mirror, while Madam Boutrey measured her proportions. Her reflection threw witless faces back at Collette, who sat in the background holding Elizabeth, and funnier than the distorted faces was the perfect timing of a disarmingly innocent expression the moment the seamstress glanced into the mirror.

During the measurements, an older woman walked into the shop alone, looking neither to the left, nor to the right, and quietly sat next to Collette and, taking a book from her satchel, began reading. After some time, she glanced over at the sleeping Elizabeth and her somber face brightened with a smile.

"You have a beautiful child." She leaned closer for a better view. "My," she sighed, swiping a snow-white strand of hair back into place atop her head, "she reminds me of a child I cared for once."

"Oh, the babe does not belong to me," Collette corrected, pointing toward the mirror in the distance where Raven stood, "but my friend."

"Do I detect a bit of the Irish in you?"

"Yes, ma'am."

She lightly touched the child's hand and Elizabeth grabbed onto it in her sleep. "Ah, she's a strong one. What brings you to London? You are a long way from home."

"Aye, a very long way indeed. The marquess has just returned to London after spending the last year in Ireland, and I am the handmaid of his bride." Collette shifted her bundle closer to the woman. "It is my lady who has come to be fitted for a dress this day."

The old woman seemed so entranced by the tiny bundle that she found little interest in much else. Collette sensed a bit of sadness in her voice and wondered what it was about Elizabeth that would bring about such a reaction.

Before long, Raven was finished and after thanking Madam Boutrey for her understanding and good humor, she found her way to Collette.

"Are you ready for tea?" she asked, reaching for her hat. "We cannot dawdle all day, you know."

The old woman, at the sound of Raven's voice, peered up. Her eyes were filled with uncertainty and then shock, as she gasped and then exhaled, *"Katie!"*

CHAPTER THIRTY-THREE

"I am sorry, ma'am, but you must have me confused with someone else. My name is Raven."

"No, child. You are Katie as sure as I'm sittin' here talkin' to you!"

Raven felt great discomfiture beneath the scrutinizing gaze of the woman's pale blue eyes, and she could think of nothing beyond taking Elizabeth in her arms and running as far away from the shop as possible. "Come, Collette, we must be on our way," she insisted, drawing the baby possessively to her.

"Katie, girl, don't you know me?"

"Madam, I have never seen you before in my life. *Collette!*"

Raven did not tarry on account of her friend, but walked swiftly toward the door.

"Katie! How could you be forgettin' yer own Mrs. Pip?" the woman cried out, her voice broken with tears.

Once safely outside Madam Boutrey's dress shop, Raven scurried to the carriage, and the driver could scarce open the door before she leaped inside.

"Hurry along, Collette!"

"I'm coming. For pity sake, there's no need to get yourself in such an uproar over an old lady who meant no harm."

"I wish to return to Winterbourne *at once,*" the driver

321

was instructed in a tone that could not be mistaken for anything less than commanding. Then Raven turned to Collette, who sat across from her, utterly dumbfounded at her rash behavior. "There was something very odd about that woman."

"She was just a little confused."

"I do not know what it was precisely, but when she looked into my eyes, I felt as though someone had danced hard upon my grave," she said, shivering.

"Lady Windham! Lord Windham!" wheezed Mrs. Pip, as she tripped through the entrance of Windham Manor. Not even a footman was in sight, and she could run no further. So she stood in the center of the anteroom and let go a blood-curdling howl. *"Looooord Windhaaaaaam!"*

"For God's sake woman! What is all this infernal commotion?" grumbled the Marquess of Windham with his walking stick held high in the air when he appeared.

"Lord Windham, I m-must," she stammered, "speak to y-you and your wife immediately!"

"Elizabeth!" he shouted, turning toward the spiraling staircase, coming face to face with the marchioness.

Elizabeth withdrew a step, hardly accustomed to anyone—even the marquess—clamoring for her in such a heathen manner. "No need to shout, dear, I'm right here," she drawled. "What is the trouble?"

"Seems Mrs. Pip needs to talk to you. I'm going to the library for a smoke of the pipe."

"Oh, no you don't, my lord." Mrs. Pip fairly flew across the floor with a sudden rebirth of wind, yanking the sleeve of his smoking jacket to halt him. "You'll stay. And you'll be glad you did, I warrant!"

"Very well," he blustered, his cheeks turning a fiery

crimson, clashing with the snow white of his hair and mustache. "Unhand me, woman!" The marquess jerked his sleeve from her grasp. "Let's take this little crisis to the library. I've just received a shipment of tobacco I must try out, from a place called *Kentucky*."

Lady Windham blew a wisp of mahogany from her forehead, and with Mrs. Pip close behind, followed Lord Windham down the long corridor and into the stately library, where the marquess spent his *thinking time*. He motioned for the women to be seated upon a rarely used overstuffed chaise, while he took his place in a tattered and faded armchair the marchioness had long failed to talk him into replacing with a more fashionable piece.

Lord Windham dipped the pipe into a velvet pouch, and then packed the moist brown stuff into the bowl with his finger. He lit a taper, set it into the bowl and puffed until the tobacco accepted the flame. He inhaled deeply, concentrating on the flavor and ease with which the smoke went down.

"Ahhh." He exhaled the old smoke and took another puff. "Not bad, even if it is from that uncivilized society that calls itself *America*. United States indeed," he groused. Lord Windham then crossed one generous leg partially over the other and leaned back in his chair, clamping his teeth down on the mouthpiece of his pipe. He spoke only from the left side of his mouth, as the pipe occupied the right side. "So tell me, Mrs. Pip, what is it that has you all a-fluster this afternoon? Another squabble with Madam Boutrey over Lady Windham's dress?"

"No, my lord—something far more serious."

"I see." He nodded his head as permission to continue.

"My lord—and lady," Mrs. Pip said, acknowledging her mistress in the matter as well, "I went to Madam Boutrey's, just as you requested, late this mornin'. When I arrived, she was in the back of the shop with a lady, so I sat next to a young Irish woman to wait out my turn in line. I took a book, but the Irish girl held a babe in her arms, and I couldn't help stealin' a glance at her."

"A *baby?* Is that what this is all about?" he snapped.

"No, my lord, I'm gettin' to that." Mrs. Pip situated herself more comfortably and took a deep breath. "As I was sayin', when I took a close look at the babe, there was something mighty familiar about her. I says to myself, 'Self, that child resembles Katie.' "

Mrs. Pip paused for a moment to see how the sound of Katherine's name would affect the Windhams. It had been an unspoken rule in the house of Windham, ever since the dreadful fire little more than a year earlier, that no one speak the name of their daughter, lest the marchioness be set in a depression for days. She sat, seemingly unaffected, except for an uneasy brush of a stray strand of auburn hair from her forehead. A slight grimace marked his face, and his fingers began to tap on the arm of his chair. Both were telltale signs that there was not much time left before he began shaking his walking stick and stormed from the room with a string of curses.

"As I was sayin'," she rushed on, "come to find out, the Irish girl ain't the mum of the babe, and soon enough the mother strolls out, finished with her fitting." At this point Mrs. Pip turned to Lady Windham and took her hands. "I swear on my own life, the mother of that child was Katie."

The marchioness's face went colorless. "Mrs. Pip," she struggled to retrieve her composure after such a ludicrous statement, "at best it was merely a woman who resembled Katherine. Richard and I were there. She never came out of the fire, and no one could have survived it. Dakshire House burned to the ground."

"You've got to believe me!" Mrs. Pip pleaded, now turning to the marquess. "I raised that child! I know her better than I know my own heart, I do!"

The Marquess of Windham dug his stick into the carpet and struggled to his feet. But he did not shake it. Instead he merely looked her in the eye, cleared his throat as though he had not the strength to deliver an appropriate rebuttal, and flatly stated, "Mrs. Pip, I'll turn you out onto the streets should you dare utter a tale as ghastly as this again." With that, he walked slowly from the library, his walking stick thumping rhythmically down the corridor.

"Lady Windham, I didn't mean to—"

"I know, Mrs. Pip. We all miss Katherine more than words could possibly express." The regal marchioness dashed a tear, then closed her eyes for a moment, as though honoring the memory of her daughter with a silent prayer. Then her eyes fluttered open, and a half-smile formed where a frown had been. "I'm certain the woman favored Katherine, and in your desire to see her, her resemblance became stronger. But we shan't be upsetting the marquess anymore, shall we?"

Mrs. Pip's eyes lowered to the floor. She had been positive it was Katherine she saw in Madam Boutrey's shop. She swiped away a tear that fell to her cheek. Perhaps Lady Windham was correct, for she did grievously miss the child with the wild and romantic spirit.

Where was Papa? The last guest left her party more than an hour before. He'd gone, just as her birthday party was to begin, promising a grand surprise upon his return. That was hours ago.

The girl situated herself on the window seat, still in her pastel lavender party dress, made especially for the occasion of her birthday by Madam Boutrey's in London. She rested her chin sulkingly upon her hand, and forced her lower lip out in a dramatic pout. But Mama was busy writing a letter, and did not witness it, so it really didn't do her much good. It wasn't like Papa to keep her waiting for anything, especially on her birthday, and one as important as her thirteenth birthday, to boot! She sighed—loudly.

Her mother did not raise her eyes nor cease her scrawling, but took notice of her daughter's fretting just the same. "Darling, your father will be home soon. I really have no idea what this surprise is he has in store for you, but as ecstatic as he was when he left this afternoon, we can be certain it is a magnificent one. Now, why don't you write a letter to your cousin, Beatrice?"

Just as she was about to decline her mother's offer to write the letter, an activity the girl found utterly tedious, she heard the familiar sound of her father's walking stick thumping down the hall, toward the sitting room. She leaped to her feet, in a most unlady-like manner, bringing forth a wince from her mother.

"Papa!" she shouted, springing into his ready arms. "Tell me! What is the surprise?"

The marquess studied the child and knew he'd found the perfect gift. He handed her a box, wrapped in pretty paper.

"What is it?" she gasped, her excitement mounting.

"Open it and find out, Katherine!"

She flung the pretty pink bow to the floor, and ripped the paper from the box. She didn't even shake the box for a clue as to what lay inside. Within seconds the lid was thrown away, and the contents revealed.

"Boots, Papa? And breeches?"

"Breeches?" Lady Elizabeth echoed, at last taking her eyes from her writings.

"Ahem. Yes. Breeches."

The marchioness fanned herself with her hand and rolled her eyes, as if about to faint. "It is scandalous to the extreme, Richard! Our daughter cannot—I repeat, cannot—possibly wear those hideous things!"

"Oh, but she can, my lovely wife. And she will. Katherine assuredly cannot ride properly in a cumbersome skirt, now can she? I'll not have my daughter injured trying to race her blood."

"My blood, Papa?"

"Yes, my beautiful Katherine, your blood. He's waiting right outside the door for you, ready to ride, just as soon as you put on your riding clothes."

Mrs. Pip could not help her out of the party dress and into the riding attire fast enough.

"Oh, hurry, Mrs. Pip! I absolutely must see the new horse Papa bought me!"

"Quit yer squirmin', Katie, or else I'll never be able to undo these buttons."

"Can you believe it? Truly, can you?"

"No, and I'm quite certain yer mum will be havin' somethin' to say on the matter. You know she is not for a lady ridin' the back of any beast."

Pip blew a straggle of shimmering white hair from her face as she undid the last button and helped her change out of it.

"Oh, and breeches, Mrs. Pip. Are they not simply wonderful? I wonder what he looks like. The horse, I mean." Katherine wriggled into the tan riding breeches and fumbled to fasten them quickly, while the housekeeper readied the white linen shirt. "I'll bet he is splendid!"

"I would expect nothing less from your father. And mind your tongue, child—'bet' is not an appropriate word for a lady to be usin'."

Katherine slipped her arms into the sleeves of the man's shirt, and Mrs. Pip tended to the buttons. Then she hurriedly pulled on *the black riding boots, and turned to the mirror to witness her appearance.*

"I do not wish to be a lady. In fact, I shall never wear a dress again, Mrs. Pip. I rather believe I am more suited to this attire." Katherine ran her hands over the coarser, thicker material with admiration, and reveled in the freedom of movement they made possible. "What do you think?"

"I think your mum will—"

But Katherine broke her off, with a kiss to her cheek and a tight squeeze. "And I shall ride the blood every day, all day, and never leave Windham Hall, so long as I live."

"Now close your eyes, Katherine."

"Oh, Papa, must I?"

Of course she knew she must. Katherine's father relished moments such as this, when he could cater to her child-like fancies. He'd had a dreadful time with this particular birthday, having seen it as one step closer to her becoming a woman—a prospect he was not yet ready to accept.

She closed her eyes tight, and placed her hands over them for good measure. "All right, Papa," she yielded, going along with the ritual, "my eyes are shut and I cannot see a thing."

The marquess took her arm and led her out the door, down the front steps and through the lawn. By the time he halted, the butterflies raced madly in Katherine's belly and she trembled in her excitement.

"Now, Papa? May I look now?"

She did not wait for an allowance, for she heard the soft snort of the horse. Her hands fell away immediately, and there before her was the tall white horse she rode in her dreams.

Katherine flung herself into her father's arms. "He is beautiful! Thank you, Papa!"

He squeezed her firmly and kissed the top of her head. "Is he as handsome as the horse you've dreamed of, darling?"

She nodded.

"And what name will you give him?"

Katherine gazed at the tall white thoroughbred and thought a moment. "Hmmm . . ." she paused, pressing her finger to her lips, while inspecting the animal. "He looks rather like a warrior, does he not, Papa? I believe I shall name him Knight. Yes. He shall be my white Knight!" She turned then and looked into the tender hazel eyes of her beloved father, and threw her arms about his neck. "But you, Papa, you shall always be my prince," Katherine whispered.

CHAPTER THIRTY-FOUR

There could not have been a more beautiful spring evening for a carriage ride from Winterbourne Park into London. The dusk gathered, and a magnificent full moon was painted upon a canvas of deep pink and rich blue hues. Raven caught a glimpse of a falling star, closed her eyes, and made a secret wish.

She inched closer to Devan and smiled adoringly up at him. He was entirely stunning in his formal black and white ball attire. If anyone ever was suited to sit in the House of Lords, surely it was this man. She entwined her arm through his, leaning her head against his shoulder.

"Devan?"

"What is it, dear?" he asked, brushing her cheek tenderly with his white-gloved hand.

"How much longer do you think it will be until we arrive at Gloushire?"

"Quite some time. Why?"

The Marquess of Castlereagh gazed into her sparkling violet eyes that fluttered demurely, surrounded by tiny strands of ebony ringlets that fell free from a loose roll pinned securely to the top of her head. She was beautiful, he thought, in her gown of elegant burgundy satin and long white gloves that adorned delicate hands and slender arms. He had never known a woman with such natural grace and poise. His wife was certain to be the envy of all of London.

Tonight would be her first formal appearance in society. If anyone was born to be a lady, it was Raven.

"Well," she began, a slight pout hinting at the corners of her lips, "ever since we arrived in London, you have been ever so busy with your duties, and this fussy spell that Elizabeth has taken this past week has simply had me exhausted. This is the first time we've been completely alone in ages without any interruptions."

The marquess checked his pocket watch. "I'm sorry for neglecting you, Raven. A year in Ireland is a long time to be away from the country where most of my holdings lie, but I will make a concerted effort to spend more time with you. Is there something you wish to talk about?"

Her hand slid from his arm, down his waistcoat, and over his breeches. Devan experienced an immediate rise to attention.

"Conversation was not precisely what I had in mind," she nearly growled into his ear as her teeth bit at it teasingly.

Devan leaned down to take the kiss she offered, and fidgeted uneasily beneath her stroking. "Ah, Raven, but your dress," he rasped.

"We'll be careful," she whispered with a giggle, silencing his meager objection.

Raven's heart fluttered as she walked into the Gloushire ballroom, on the arm of the most handsome man in all of London—her husband. The dazzling smile she radiated as she was received by the hosts seemed to force the usually stoic members of the *beau monde* to mirror similarly cheerful expressions.

As beautiful as Winterbourne had been to Raven, nothing had prepared her for such a grand sight. Marbled floors, hundreds of sparkling crystal prisms in chandeliers to reflect the light of the candles and lamps, muralled ceilings, footmen and servants at every turn, and so many people dressed in their finest, most elegant fashions, were all enough to whisk the very breath from her.

The music from the string ensemble at the far end of the enormous room filled the air, as did the sweet scents of fresh roses and spice. Timidly Raven looked around the room, and felt quite awkward when she compared herself to the more worldly young women that surrounded her, with their flaxen, perfectly shaped curls, and porcelain aspects—tiny button mouths, turned up noses, pale eyes in various shades of gray and blue, and perfectly measured movements. She might have felt entirely out of place and utterly imperfect had it not been for the gentle squeeze Devan gave her arm and the loving smile that accompanied it.

He led her to a quiet seat at the far end of the room, and within moments a footman handed her a glass of champagne. From her seat she watched as each girl was whirled round the dance floor by several different men, seeming to range in age from early-twenties to ancient. Some of the gentlemen fat, some thin, some tall, most shorter than she supposed most girls would have liked, some with a mop of hair, and some with barely a wisp.

Whatever her past might have been, she was glad she'd never had to take part in such a ritual, only to be married off to the likes of the men displayed here.

The more she studied the spinning couples, the more she realized these affairs were no more than the women being herded in, much like cattle, in order for the yet unmarried or widowed male members of the *ton* to inspect. One giggling girl with a positively round face danced with a young, seemingly gauche gent, who truly appeared to be examining her prominent teeth, and at any minute Raven half expected him to pry her lips upward to check the color of her gums. She laughed out loud at the sight, leaned back in her chair, and continued to watch the crowd, conjuring up sordid stories to place with each face. How positively appalling Mrs. Captain would have thought her, but it was the most fun Raven had since her arrival in London.

Suddenly, a white glove interrupted her diversion, startling Raven. She peered up to see the marquess smiling down on her. "Would you care to dance, my lady."

She lifted her hand into his, and stood. Raven curtsied and with her head poised just so, batted her lashes flirtatiously, "Why yes, my lord, I would be honored."

Devan took her right hand, and placing his right arm around her waist, he whirled her easily across the dance floor.

The *haute ton* was compelled to stare at the couple who flowed together in a flawless unison of motion—the magnificent Lord Castlereagh and his lovely young bride. It had been rumored amongst the society set that the marquess had taken an Irish wife, much to the dismay of many of the unmarried misses. Someone whispered something about the manner in which the new marchioness resembled the daughter of Lord Windham—such a tragedy the girl had perished at Dakshire. Another commented on the nerve of the young marquess to have married a woman who could never truly be one of *them*. But no matter their views on the unlikely union, or the jealous gossip that buzzed throughout the ballroom, none could dispute the fact that the marquess and marchioness were indeed the epitome of the *beautiful people*.

It was two waltzes and a minuet before they left the floor, and every head turned to follow them as they made their way back to their seats. Someone sighed, thinking it romantic beyond words the way the Marquess of Castlereagh gazed into her eyes, his love so evident, and bowed to his bride—not for the members of the *ton* to witness, but obvious adoration.

Lord Richard Windham dipped the ladle into the bowl of champagne punch and filled a glass for Elizabeth. Though the Season had been in full swing for nearly a month, the marchioness politely sent her regrets to all invitations, including Almack's. He finally put his foot down and demanded they attend Gloushire—not because he particularly enjoyed the company of the majority of the *ton,* but because he could not stand idly by and allow her to seclude herself any longer.

Since Katherine's death, Lady Windham had lost all interest in the affairs of society. Those first months after the fire found her in bed most of the time, without even the slightest inclination to write a solitary letter or take tea with any of her peeresses.

The marquess understood well her grief, for Katherine had been the light of his life. But Elizabeth was his foundation and his reason for the very breath he breathed, and he would not lose her, too.

Perhaps the bit of spirits in the punch would serve to bring about a long absent smile and lift her out of the depression she'd been in since that day Mrs. Pip swore she'd seen Katherine in Madam Boutrey's. It did not escape his notice that the marchioness accompanied the housekeeper the day her gown was to be ready, and since his wife avoided going anywhere for any reason, her sudden desire to go to town could only have been a secret wish to find Katherine at the dressmaker's.

Lord Windham sighed as he filled his own crystal cup with the punch. He had to get her out of the corner in the back of the room she'd been sitting in all evening. He really wouldn't mind laying down his walking stick to waltz with his wife. It had been a long time since last they'd danced.

He turned then, to head back to his Elizabeth, but the punch splashed out of his cups and all down the front of his waistcoat, when he ran into . . .

"Oaf!" Richard thundered. "Of all the incompetent—" At that moment, his gaze locked upon most unforgettable sinister eyes. *"You!"*

"Excuse me, sir," the young man said. Then suddenly, his face reflected recognition, as well. Lord Castlereagh stepped back for a moment as if in shock at seeing the Marquess of Windham standing before him.

Windham glowered while intense anger coursed violently through him. *This* was the man who caused Katherine's death! Had *he* not taken her from her father's side that night at Dakshire, she would have escaped the flames!

Richard wished to place his bare hands around Castlereagh's neck and choke the life out of him. But before he could, a pair of lavender-blue eyes peered out from behind the man.

When the woman took her place beside Castlereagh and protectively wound her arm through his, Windham's blood ran cold.

The half-empty punch cups fell to the floor and shattered in thousands of crystal slivers. Richard fell back, barely staying to his feet with the aid of his stick. He blinked his eyes, unable to believe the vision standing before him.

"K-*Katherine!*"

"Whatever is this man babbling about, Devan," Raven murmured. "Why does he stare at me so?"

"Lord Windham, if you would allow me to explain," he said in a hushed tone, hoping to draw no more attention upon the situation than necessary.

"Richard?" came a voice from his right. Lady Windham moved to her husband's side, and as she did so, her hand came up quickly to her mouth in stunned awe. *"Katherine?"* she asked softly, directing the question to the woman across from her.

Raven could do nothing but stand there, beneath the scrutinizing stares of Lord and Lady Windham. She saw the tears that filled the woman's eyes, and realized she'd gone pale the moment she'd gazed upon Raven. And in turn, Raven was filled with an awesome and growing panic, as though these two people had it within their power to steal something precious from her. Her grip constricted on Devan's arm, a wave of cold fear enveloped her.

Devan spoke up, and Raven sensed more than a bit of tension in his voice. "May I present my wife, the Marchioness of Castlereagh."

"Impossible!" Lord Windham huffed.

"It cannot be!" The Marchioness of Windham looked as though she was about to faint, and fanned herself with her hand.

"Th-this is a cruel fraud, Castlereagh!" Windham shouted accusingly. "How dare you b-bring this—this—*imposter*," he pointed a reproachful finger at Raven, "into my presence."

The eyes of all of London burned through Raven. She wished she could run, but her legs would not move. Why would they glare at her with such loathing? She shut her eyes fast, so she would not have to witness any more of their disdain.

Each woman clung trembling to her husband. "Take me

home," they both pleaded at once. And for a brief moment, their eyes locked, and Raven felt the breaking of her heart.

Raven fairly raced from Gloushire, with Devan attempting to keep up while retrieving their wraps. Even back inside the carriage she did not feel completely safe from the wretched old marquess.

"Devan, who were those people?" She leaned her head against his chest, pulling his arm securely around her.

He did not answer, but she felt him bring her closer, and some of the dread was washed away by his comfort. Closing her eyes, she let the gentle motion of the carriage calm her.

In her mind, she saw the old woman from Madam Boutrey's again . . .

"Now, don't be streakin' yer face with them little girl tears, Katie! All we did was clean off the dust and trade them breeches and boots in for proper ball attire. It is yerself you be seein' in the glass, and you better get used to it."

"But Mrs. Pip . . ."

Mrs. Pip was a character in the strange dreams that had occurred over the last week, but it had not been until that moment that Raven had seen her face . . .

CHAPTER THIRTY-FIVE

"Yer folks 'ave been plannin' yer introduction into society for yer 'ole life, and I ain't about to let you let 'em down, you know. So buck up, girl, and let me finish yer hair. It's about time to be leavin'."

The warning tone of the thickly accented Cockney told Katherine that Mrs. Pip believed her to be on the verge of a childish temper tantrum. Yes, she wished to throw herself upon her bed and weep, but the housekeeper would not understand all the reasons for it—the very least of them childish.

Katherine carefully sat herself on the corner at the foot of the bed and resigned herself to Pip's tugging at her thick, unruly raven locks . . .

None of her dreams since arriving in London had made any sense. She heard voices and saw images veiled in shadows, but nothing had been clear about the dreams. Now suddenly, the voices had faces and names, as though a shroud had been lifted. And she saw her own face in the mirror . . .

"Yer nineteen, and a lady by birth, and there are certain things you simply cannot get out of—and this is one of them." *She began brushing through the waist-length tresses again, glancing now and then at the flickering changes on the girl's expressive face. "There is no sense in sulking, you know," she added at last.*

Katherine felt all chances of winning her argument fade abruptly away. Mrs. Pip was right. Better to make the best of it. Once this dreadful Season was over, she could return to the country and Knight.

"Devan," she whispered, tears streaming from her still-closed eyes. "Something is very wrong."

"Raven, what is it? You are weeping?"

"I am dreaming, Devan, but I am not asleep."

He took her hand. "*Shhh,* darling. Open your eyes, and everything will be all right. You've just had a disturbing evening," he soothed before turning again to stare out the window at the darkened landscape.

But Raven could not open her eyes, nor force the visions from her mind . . .

"Now, Katherine, darling," Lady Windham said, in her most elegant tone, as she carefully pushed the stray auburn curl that had fallen over her forehead back in place, "you do realize the importance of making a perfect impression during this first Season, do you not?"

"Oh, for God's sake, Elizabeth!" Lord Windham almost shouted, bringing about expressions of surprise from both Katherine and her mother. "Leave the child alone." With a sly wink, her father's gloved hand reached across and brushed Katherine's cheek affectionately. "My Katherine is the most beautiful and eligible young lady in London. There's not a member of the ton that will not be falling all over himself to be first in line with a proposal for our daughter." He smiled, his hazel eyes twinkling in the moonlight that seeped through the carriage windows. "I will merely have to see to it that he is worthy," he added under his breath.

★ ★ ★ ★ ★

"Katherine," Raven breathed softly.

At the sound of that name, Devan's head jerked around from the window he'd been staring out to confront her. "Why do you speak her name?" he inquired urgently, lifting her chin to witness tear-streaked cheeks.

Raven would not force herself to open her eyes to look at the marquess. There was something about the trance-like illusion that had come to her that she knew in her heart must be played out.

"It is my face I see, and they call me *Katherine* . . ."

Richard raised his walking stick into the air, as he did on occasions when stressing a point. "Our Katherine will not have any difficulty finding a suitable husband when the time is right. If she does not find one this year or the year after, then the ton *will just have to wait to attend our daughter's wedding." He boisterously cleared his throat and shook his stick with even more authority. "We're in no hurry. The king can wait as well."*

Elizabeth sat up even straighter in the stiff leather carriage seat. "Richard, you know how important this year will be!" She fanned herself with her hand, rolled her eyes and sighed dramatically, as if she were about to faint. "I have kept to myself and allowed you to hide our daughter away in the country, where she has grown up in a fashion outside the bounds of the society she ultimately shall live in and need to perform in. But the time has come for her to grow up and take her place in that society. I will not have her end up on the shelf. It will not do for my daughter to wait two years for a proposal!"

"Who calls you Katherine?" Devan demanded.

"The Marquess and Marchioness of Windham." She

swallowed the fear that rose in her throat. "I am with them at Dakshire House."

Devan fell to the floor of the coach on his knees. She marked a change in his breathing and his trembling grip strengthened before going limp and falling away from her hand.

But Raven could not tear herself away in order to comfort him . . .

Without warning, he turned in her direction, and before she could cast her glance elsewhere, his black eyes locked upon hers. Then it was too late to move her gaze away. An uneasiness swept through her and a rush of wind filled her ears. Her blood ran hot, then cold, then hotter than any fire she had ever known. A strange mixture of foreboding and longing filled her heart. She became weak, felt helpless, as his eyes bored straight through to the core of her soul, and threatened to steal it from her. A cry rose in her throat and lodged there. Katherine's hands began to tremble. She wanted to run, of that she was certain, but was it from him . . . or to him?

He extended his large, dark hand in Katherine's direction. His voice was velvety low, penetrating, commanding. "I will dance with the lady."

"You are there also."

"Raven, please stop this," he cried out, old guilt tearing at his gut. "However you heard about Katherine is not important. But do not torture me this way."

She reached her hand out and tenderly caressed the face of the marquess. His tears tore at her heart and she could hear the anguish in his voice. But she remained focused on the man in her mind . . .

He gazed deeply into her eyes, bending almost close enough to touch her lips with his own. "Tell me you cannot feel it, Katherine. I knew at that moment our eyes met that I have loved you my entire life. And in your eyes I see you feel it, too. Can you tell me you do not?"

The room became cloaked in a dream-like fog. Katherine steadied herself against the wall. She took his face in her hands, tears flowing from her amethyst eyes, and her voice shaken. "God help me," she wept, "I do feel what you, yourself, profess to feel. But have mercy, and take your hands from me, for I fear I have not the will to tear myself away from this moment. I beg you, prey not upon me, nor offer up false promises that speak to my heart!"

"There is nothing false in my words, and it is with only the most honorable of intentions that I seek your vow."

The room began to spin around her. The rush of wind grew louder. "Release me now, for I am in danger of relinquishing myself unto you, my lord," she cried out, as great, unexplainable sorrow overcame her and tears streamed from her eyes.

The Marquess of Castlereagh stood before her, still holding fast to her hands, showering them with soft kisses. "Yield your heart, Katherine. Say you will marry me. Give me your solemn oath."

"I—" With all her might she tried to withhold the words she knew could not be taken back once delivered, but she no longer had a choice or a will of her own. "I give you my . . . oath."

"Ah, my Katherine, the morrow be damned. I will not suffer you the opportunity to change your mind."

"We were to go to Scotland . . ."

Devan fell back against the wall of the carriage, his insides twisting, his heart breaking. "Why do you do this to me, Raven? Katherine is dead," he declared weakly.

"A fire . . ."

★ ★ ★ ★ ★

The flames raged around them. Devan pulled her sharply to the right, just as a beam fell where she'd been standing.

"We are going to die!" she cried.

"I shall not let you die, Katherine," he shouted over the thunderous fall of a section of the ceiling ahead of them.

Pushing her backward, he changed their direction, taking her hand and leading her away from the chaos. Just then another beam fell from above them, bringing down more of the ceiling. And once it had fallen, she was on one side of the heat, and he on the other.

"Devan!" she screamed, "Help me!"

"Hold on, Katherine!"

A spark ignited her gown, and Katherine ripped fiercely at the emerald satin, as the material fused to her skin. She knew then she would not survive.

Katherine called out to Devan, but there was no answer. Again she cried his name into the fire. And again, his voice did not come.

She opened her eyes then, and stared at the man who sat in a broken heap on the floor. "I did not perish," she said, reaching out for his hand.

He lifted his eyes, afraid to touch her. "H-how can this be?"

"You did not reply when I called for you. And I thought you had . . . I thought the fire . . ."

"But how?"

She closed her eyes again. "I remember a window, and I knew, somehow, if I could only make it to the window, my life would be spared." She paused then and took a deep breath before opening her eyes. "I do not remember anything else before the day I woke up at Dahlingham with Collette and Mrs. Captain."

Rising to his knees, he put his head into her lap and sobbed, clutching her gown within his fists.

She tenderly ran her hands through his hair and leaned over to kiss his head, finding comfort from the panic that had been building inside with each new frightening vision that filled her memory.

The carriage turned onto the long drive of Winterbourne Park. She gently took his head in her hands and raised it so to look into his eyes.

"I am *Katherine Windham.*"

CHAPTER THIRTY-SIX

Katherine snuggled the sleeping baby to her bosom, and took a deep breath to calm the nervous anticipation. "I am ready," she softly said, her voice filled with apprehension.

Devan took hold of the heavy brass knocker and rapped it loudly three times. They waited for what seemed forever. Again he let the knocker fall, again three times.

"For pity sake!" a voice shouted as the door flew open.

Mrs. Pip's mouth fell open and her eyes bulged out, as though she saw a ghost. Her hands came up to cover her gaping mouth, in terror or disbelief one. But she uttered not a word, silenced and paralyzed by the woman before her.

Katherine's face broke into a feigned pout and then a smile burst forth. "Are you just going to leave me standing out in the night air, Mrs. Pip? I would have expected at least a hug and an invitation to enter."

"*Katie?*"

Katherine nodded.

"Katie!" Mrs. Pip exclaimed, throwing her arms around her. "Come in, Katie, girl! Come in!"

The housekeeper practically yanked Katherine from her feet in her hurry to move her through the door and into the anteroom of Windham Manor, seemingly not noticing the marquess who stood beside her in the slightest.

Devan quietly walked in and closed the door behind him, and took Elizabeth from Katherine's arms while the

345

two women fell into tears and hugs.

"Oh, Mrs. Pip," Katherine wept into the soft fold of her neck.

"I've been lost without you. My goodness!" She abruptly pulled Katherine away from her shoulder, and peered into her eyes. "It *was* you! I've not lost my wits!"

Katherine shook her head. "I'm sorry I did not know you, Mrs. Pip. It's such a long story."

"Ah! You're here now, and that's all that matters!" She ran her hand caressingly across Katherine's cheek, but then pulled it back sharply to her mouth. "Oh, Lordy! I must wake yer par—"

"Who the devil would disrupt an entire household at this time of night?" a loud voice thundered, approaching fast.

Just as Lord Windham turned the corner he stopped dead in his tracks, obviously stunned by what he saw there. Within seconds, the marchioness was beside him, appearing quite pale.

"Papa?"

The face of the Marquess of Windham grew suddenly red, his eyebrows knitted together, and his teeth were clenched in fuming anger. "Get out! Get out, I tell you!" he yelled, raising his cane in the air and shaking it about madly while bounding threateningly toward the object of his ire.

Mrs. Pip stepped quickly in front of Katherine and shielded her defensively. "You'll not be throwing my Katie out on the streets, my lord!"

"Th-this woman is *not* Katherine," he seethed, halting just short of the housekeeper.

Devan stepped forward, handing the baby to Mrs. Pip, and then stood protectively in front of his wife. "Windham, I assure you, this young woman *is* your daughter. If you will just hear her out, I think you'll find—"

"What is it you want from me, you blackguard? Have you squandered your holdings on port and gaming hells? Is this some elaborate plan, to bring this—this woman into my home, and steal the inheritance that would have belonged to Katherine? I tell you, it won't work!"

Lady Windham took her husband's arm, gently lowering his cane. "Richard, I do not wish you to have an attack. Please calm down." Then she cast her eyes upon the woman who stepped up warily beside the Marquess of Castlereagh. "Young lady, there is nothing more in the world we wish than to have our daughter back. But we know it cannot be. So, if you will simply leave the premises, we will not summon the guard."

Katherine fought the tears that threatened her eyes. She realized the manner in which the marchioness endeavored to remain in control. Feeling wholly lost at that moment, and aggrieved that it should be she to cause her dearest parents more pain than they'd already suffered, she inched closer to Devan.

"Mama, please believe me. I am your daughter."

Looking into the lavender eyes of the young woman, identical to her beloved Katherine, Lady Windham finally lost the composure she'd struggled to maintain, and broke down in the arms of her husband.

"Now, s–see what you've d–done?" the marquess stammered.

"Papa, I can prove who I am, if only you'll allow me."

"Tell 'em, Katie. Prove you're who you say you are!" Mrs. Pip cheered from the corner of the room where she cradled the child, who'd somehow managed to sleep through the uproar and commotion. The marquess shot an acrimonious sneer in her direction, and Mrs. Pip immediately bit back her tongue.

"Mama, won't you sit with me?" she implored, brushing her mother's arm tenderly.

The marquess stepped forward, his patience waning. "I asked you to leave. I shall not ask again."

Suddenly, the Marchioness of Windham lifted her head and dabbed away her tears. "Richard, I wish to hear her out. If there is any chance—"

"This is ludicrous!"

"Thank you," Katherine sighed, trying to feign a smile.

As Lady Windham was led into the drawing room and to her chaise, Katherine took a seat across from her, in the chair next to the one her father usually occupied. She recognized the fury that raged within him by the violent coloring of his face. She'd seen it many times before, but never, she thought sadly, directed at her.

"Papa, won't you please sit in your chair?"

In silence, Devan took his stand behind Katherine's chair, wishing he could spare her such a difficult task as she was up against. But he knew, at that moment, all he could render was his presence as support.

"See there? She knows which chair belongs to you!" Mrs. Pip offered.

"Nonsense! Anyone could have figured out which chair is mine since my spectacles sit on the table beside it." Then he glared at Katherine and pointed his stick directly at her. "No, I will not sit down, because I intend to lead you out the door the moment my wife has come to her senses! And another thing—do *not* refer to me as *Papa*. I am not *your* father!"

"Katherine, let me take you home," Devan whispered, unable to watch her go through anymore. "Do not put yourself through this."

She patted his hand that rested safeguardingly on her shoulder. "No, darling. I am fine," she lied. Katherine's hands then began to wring themselves nervously in her lap. How was she going to convince them that she was, indeed, their daughter?

"What have you to say, young woman?" Lady Windham asked, searching her eyes.

"There was so much I planned to say. However," she said, her gaze lowering to the floor, "I-I really do not know what to say now that the moment has arrived."

"Of course you do not, for you've nothing to say that would prove you anything but a charlatan!"

"Richard!" The marchioness turned back to Katherine, who sat in the chair across from her. "May I ask you questions?"

Katherine nodded.

"You say you are Katherine. But I watched Dakshire burn to the ground, and Katherine never came out. How do you explain this?"

"I-I . . . the last thing I recall was being surrounded by flames, and spying a window. I can only presume that I made my escape through that window."

"And why would you not have sought out your parents? Where have you been this last year?"

"The next thing I remember is waking up in Ireland."

"Preposterous!"

"Enough, Richard. Allow her to finish," scolded the marchioness.

"As I was saying, I awoke in Ireland, at Dahlingham. I was told that I'd wandered onto the estate, and lay unconscious for days before finally opening my eyes."

"Why would you not have gotten word to your family at that time?"

"Because I didn't know I had a family. As difficult as it is to fathom, I'd lost my memory entirely."

Little by little, Katherine related the story of her time in Ireland. Lady Elizabeth listened attentively to every word, allowing only an occasional glimpse of emotion to steal into her eyes. Lord Windham turned his back on the whole situation, choosing, instead, to stare at the portraits on the wall.

"While I feel for your plight—"

"If a word of it is true," growled the marquess, still pretending to study the paintings.

The marchioness ignored her husband's impatient mutterings, shifted positions and shook out the hem of her robe. Katherine felt like a naughty child beneath the inquisitive gaze of the older woman, and looked to her hands that still worked fretfully in her lap.

Mindfully clearing her throat, she continued. "Your situation is certainly difficult, but you have given me no cause to believe you are not, in fact, the Irish maid you once believed yourself to be. Can you tell me anything at all that would lead me to recognize you as Katherine?"

When the baby began to fuss, Mrs. Pip brought her to Katherine, and the child immediately settled into the familiar comfort of her mother's arms.

"This is your child?"

"Yes, Ma—my lady. Her name is—" She stared down at the sweet face she cradled to her bosom. "Her name is the same as yours. *Elizabeth*. The day she was born, there was no other name that suited her so much. Even then, I hadn't truly forgotten you."

The revelation clearly unsettled the marchioness. "I'm sorry." She masked her emotions again and visibly stiffened. "That is not enough."

Suddenly Katherine could take no more of the strained politeness between herself and Lady Windham, nor Lord

Windham's biting remarks. She leaped to her feet, practically throwing Elizabeth into Devan's arms, and boldly turned on the marchioness.

"I will not allow you to continue to deny the truth, Mama!"

The marquess spun around at the impetuous conduct the woman exhibited. "Young lady!"

"And I'll not have any more of your set downs, Papa!" She shook her finger accusingly, much in the same manner he sported his walking stick. "You've become entirely cantankerous, and I am soon to lose my good humor!"

"I *never*—"

"Well, Papa, it is high time you did! What will it take to prove to the two of you that I am who I say I am? Is it not enough that I can name every surly face in each of these portraits?" she lashed out, indicating the portrait-lined walls of the ancestors with a wave of her arm.

"My family has always been very prominent in London. It means nothing!"

"Or," she continued, strolling quickly to pick up an ornate wooden box, decorated with precious stones of amethyst that sat on the end table, "Mama keeps her stationery in this? How about the fact that you received George in this very room, and fed him enough food and spirits in the grand dining room for six men, when he was still the Prince of Wales?"

She stormed across the room and grabbed hold of the marquess's walking stick. "This—this cane is the result of a bum knee that you injured when a horse's hoof shattered the bone." Then a light appeared where seemingly none had been. "The horse," she whispered, her eyes flitting up to the largest portrait on the wall, over the mantle.

She ran to the fireplace and stood before it for a long

moment, her eyes filling with misty memories. When at last she spoke, her voice quivered. Slowly her finger pointed to the portrait of a young Katherine beside the tall white blood. "He is my white Knight."

"I've had just about enough. Anyone could have known that!"

And in that instant, she turned around to face the man who had been so much to her all her life. Something in her expression softened his hazel eyes, and the glower nearly disappeared from his face.

"But you, Papa," she said, a child-like quality reflected in her hushed tone, "you shall always be my prince."

"My God!" he gasped, his shoulders slumping and his cane falling with a thud to the carpeted floor. "Katherine?"

She ran and threw her arms about his neck, just as she had done so many times before. "Papa!"

"Yes!" squealed Mrs. Pip, clapping her hands together.

"Richard?"

He clung to the girl for dear life. "Elizabeth, no one knew that Katherine whispered those words to me the night I presented her with the thoroughbred, except me—and Katherine."

Lady Windham fanned herself with her hand, appearing ready to faint. Devan rushed to her side and offered his hand. She accepted it hesitantly, and he carefully held her to her feet.

"And this," she asked, pointing to the tiny bundle, "is my grandchild?"

Katherine moved to stand next to the marchioness. "Yes, Mama," she smiled tenderly, pressing a gentle kiss to her mother's cheek, and then taking the baby from Devan, now awake from all the jostling around, handed the child to her mother.

Suddenly, in the distance, came the sound of the front door flying open and banging into the wall.

Lord Windham raised his cane again. "What in the name of—"

"*Devan!*"

Katherine grinned, while Devan rushed toward the ante-room. Within moments, Mrs. Captain and Collette followed him back into the drawing room.

"Who are these rude people?" Lord Windham demanded.

"*Rude?*" screeched Mrs. Captain. "I'll tell you what is ill-mannered, sir! It is the way I've been made to sit in a cold carriage in the wee hours of the morning, waiting for—" Her eyes shifted back and forth between Lord and Lady Castlereagh. "What was it you woke me up in the middle of the night to come here for?"

"Mrs. Captain, I'd like to introduce you to Lord and Lady Windham," Katherine began, her smile broadening beyond her control. "My parents."

"Your . . . ?"

Devan reached over and took Mrs. Captain by the shoulders to steady her. "Mrs. Captain, meet Katherine," he laughed, indicating the woman known to the housekeeper as *Raven.*

Mrs. Pip took little Elizabeth from Lady Windham's arms and walked away from the excitement, lightly bouncing as she went, in order to quiet her restless whimpering.

"Katherine?"

"K-Katherine?" Collette echoed.

The marquess roared. "Yes! Katherine! I'll explain it all to you when we get back to Winterbourne."

"But you cannot leave Windham Manor!" Elizabeth took

Katherine's hand and held it to her heart. "You must spend the night here."

"I agree," rumbled the Marquess of Windham. "Wholeheartedly, I might add!"

"Well, something's got to be done!" commanded Mrs. Captain in her most authoritative tone, marching over to Mrs. Pip and reaching out for the baby. "My wittle Lizzie is sweepy and needs to be fed, doesn't she?"

Mrs. Pip held fast to the child. "And who are you that you think you can steal *my* babe out of my arms?"

Mrs. Captain planted her balled fists firmly to her generous hips and scowled. *"Yours?"*

The Marquess of Windham, forgetting his walking stick, limped across the room and attempted to take Elizabeth from an unwilling Mrs. Pip. "She is *my* granddaughter. So if anyone should have the child, it is *me!*"

"But certainly I am to be her governess!" exclaimed Mrs. Pip, asserting her rightful place in the child's life. "After all, didn't I raise Katie?"

"Balderdash! I raised the marquess from the cradle, and it is my place to watch over my wittle Lizzie, isn't it sweetums?" she asked the baby.

Suddenly, Katherine felt herself being dragged away from the squabble. She looked over her shoulder to see Devan, wearing a devilish grin. He took her hand and led her around the corner into the dimly lit corridor.

"Happy?" he asked, pulling her into his embrace.

"Deliriously so!"

"I wanted you to myself for a moment," he said, tenderly nestling his face against her neck. "And I just wanted you to know that I love you. Raven, Katherine, it does not matter, so long as it is *you.*"

She lifted her lips to meet his. "And I love you."

"Do you think they'll notice we're gone?"

"I dare say it is doubtful."

"I believe that's far too much love and devotion for one small child to manage alone." He grinned wickedly then and pressed her closer. "Shall we sneak away for a while and see what we can do about getting Elizabeth a little brother to carry some of that burden?"

"I would love to, but . . ." She gazed into his dark eyes and felt a swelling blush wash over her. "You already saw to that, my lord."

"Are you saying—"

Katherine nodded. "But there's no reason we should not practice for a third." Then she smiled seductively at the marquess, and taking his hand, led him up the staircase.

A Note from Laura Mills-Alcott

About the characters:

All characters in *The Briar and the Rose* are fictitious.

When looking for a name for my hero, who was half Irish, I did a search on places in Ireland in order to come up with a name for my hero's title, and found the name Castlereagh. I loved the sound of the name, and so Devan became the Marquess of Castlereagh.

I later learned that in English history, there was a real Lord Castlereagh, Robert Stewart, the son of the second Marquis of Londonderry, who was named first Viscount Castlereagh, and later became England's Secretary of War. He died in 1822.

Devan is *no* relation to Robert Stewart, and the title Marquess of Castlereagh is *not* a real English title.

About the story:

As a long-time admirer of Dolly Parton's music, when I learned Dolly had a new live album coming out, I was first in line to buy *Heartsongs*. I immediately loved this CD because of its mix of traditional songs and original compositions, but then a song I'd never heard before began to play, and between Dolly's arrangement and the words, I had to stop and listen—*really* listen. The song was "Barbara Allen."

The tragic ending to Barbara and Sweet William's story haunted me for a long time after, and ultimately, I had to base

357

a book on the ballad of "Barbara Allen." After all, as a writer of romantic novels, I couldn't let their story end unhappily!

It is important to note here that the History at the beginning of *The Briar and the Rose* is, in reality, part of my story.

In the "History", I told you my research turned up "Barbara Allen's Cruelty," published by Thomas Percy in 1765 in his collection of poetry entitled *Reliques of Ancient English Poetry*. This was true.

However, I claimed literary license, and entirely made up everything regarding the Irish folktale "The Briar and the Rose," as well as the reference to Percy's diaries and his visit to Ireland, for the sake of my story. Séamus and Mairéad's story is, of course, based on the ballad, but the characters and the details beyond the ballad are products of my ever-vivid imagination.

Now that you've read *The Briar and the Rose*, I heartily recommend you listen to the ballad "Barbara Allen" that the story was based on.

Dolly Parton's version (on the *Heartsongs* CD) includes Irish lyrics sung by Altan. Dolly told me, "I grew up singing it ("Barbara Allen"). As a writer and singer, I took a few liberties as far as lyrics and melody just to Dolly-ize it. The result was an awesome and emotionally moving recording."

It was her version that called to me, fueled my imagination and is the basis for *The Briar and the Rose*.

Another of my favorite artists, Emmylou Harris, recorded a different version of "Barbara Allen" for the *Songcatcher* Soundtrack, which also includes a lovely traditional lead-in by Emmy Rossum. The *Songcatcher* Soundtrack is a wonderful sampler of the old ballads.

Thank you for allowing me to share *The Briar and the Rose*. I hope you enjoyed reading Devan and Raven's story as much as I enjoyed writing it.

Barbara Allen
Arranged by Dolly Parton

'Twas in the merry month of May
When rosebuds were a swellin'
Sweet William on his deathbed lay
For the love of Barbrie Allen

He sent his servant to the town
The town where she was dwellin'
Said my master's sick and he sent for you
If ye name be Barbrie Allen

Then slowly, slowly she got up
And slowly she went nigh him;
And all she said when she got there,
Young man I think you're dyin'.

Oh, yes I'm sick, I'm very sick
I hear the death wind howlin'
No better, no better I never shall be
If I can't have Barbrie Allen

I can't forgive that jealous night
Down at the Lockwood Tavern
You drank and danced with the ladies there
And you slighted Barbrie Allen

She was on her long way home
She saw the hearse a comin'
Lay down, lay down your corpse of clay
That I may look upon him

The more she looked, the more she moaned
'Til she fell to the ground in sorrow.
Sweet William died for me today,
I'll die for him tomorrow.

They buried her in the old church yard
And William's grave was nigh her.
On William's grave there grew a red rose
On Barbara's grave a briar

They grew and grew up the old church wall
'Til they could grow no higher
They lapped and tied in a true love knot
The rose wrapped 'round the briar

Dolly Parton 1994, Velvet Apple Music, Nashville, Tennessee, Used by Permission

Barbara Allen

Gaeilge translation by Proinsias Ó Maonaigh

(as it is sung by "Altan" in the recording of
"Barbara Allen" on Dolly Parton's "Heartsongs")

Sa Bhéaltaine san saol gan ghruaim
Is bláth na rós a'líonadh
Ar leabaidh'n bháis bhí Liam na luí
Óna Ghrá do Bharbara Allen

Chuir sé giolla fa na déin
Go d'tÍ'n áit a raibh a conaí
Tá'n maistir i le'an's leatsa a'dréim
Ma's tusa Barbara Allen

D'éirigh sí go mall s'go reidh
'S go mall a thriau sÍ chuige
Sé'r dhúirt sí leis ar theacht chun tí
A fhir óig, tá tú siothlú

Ó Táim i léan
Táim lag gan bhrí
Tá síon an bháis ag éagain
S'ní biseach 'tá i ndán domh choí
Muna bhfaighmse Barbara Allen

Translation © 1994 Proinsias Ó Maonaigh, Used by Permission

361

Barbara Allen's Cruelty
From *Reliques of Ancient English Poetry*, Thomas Percy
(1729-1811)

In Scarlet towne, where I was borne,
There was a faire maid dwellin',
Made every youth crye, wel-awaye!
Her name was Barbara Allen.

All in the merrye month of May,
When greene buds they were swellin',
Yong Jemmye Grove on his death-bed lay,
For love of Barbara Allen.

He sent his man unto her then,
To the town, where shee was dwellin';
You must come to my master deare,
Giff your name be Barbara Allen.

For death is printed on his face,
And ore his hart is stealin':
Then haste away to comfort him,
O lovelye Barbara Allen.

Though death be printed on his face,
And ore his harte is stealin',
Yet little better shall he bee,

For bonny Barbara Allen.

So slowly, slowly, she came up,
And slowly she came nye him;
And all she sayd, when there she came,
Yong man, I think y'are dying.

He turnd his face unto her strait,
With deadlye sorrow sighing;
O lovely maid, come pity mee,
Ime on my death-bed lying.

If on your death-bed you doe lye,
What needs the tale you are tellin:
I cannot keep you from your death;
Farewell, sayd Barbara Allen.

He turnd his face unto the wall,
As deadlye pangs he fell in:
Adieu! adieu! adieu to you all,
Adieu to Barbara Allen.

As she was walking ore the fields,
She heard the bell a knellin;
And every stroke did seem to saye,
Unworthy Barbara Allen.

She turnd her bodye round about,
And spied the corps a coming:
Laye downe, laye downe the corps, she sayd,
That I may look upon him.

With scornful eye she looked downe,

Her cheeke with laughter swellin;
That all her friends cryd out amaine,
Unworthye Barbara Allen.

When he was dead, and laid in grave,
Her harte was struck with sorrowe,
O mother, mother, make my bed,
For I shall dye to morrowe.

Hard harted creature him to slight,
Who loved me so dearlye:
O that I had beene more kind to him,
When he was live and neare me!

She, on her death-bed as she laye,
Beg'd to be buried by him;
And sore repented of the daye,
That she did ere denye him.

Farewell, she sayd, ye virgins all,
And shun the fault I fell in:
Henceforth take warning by the fall
Of cruel Barbara Allen.

Barbara Allen
Francis J. Child collection, Child Ballad #84

In Scarlet town where I was born,
There was a fair maid dwellin'
Made every youth cry Well-a-day,
Her name was Barb'ra Allen.

All in the merry month of May,
When green buds they were swellin'
Young Willie Grove on his death-bed lay,
For love of Barb'ra Allen.

He sent his servant to her door
To the town where he was dwellin'
Haste ye come, to my master's call,
If your name be Barb'ra Allen.

So slowly, slowly got she up,
And slowly she drew nigh him,
And all she said when there she came:
"Young man, I think you're dying!"

He turned his face unto the wall
And death was drawing nigh him.
Good bye, Good bye to dear friends all,
Be kind to Bar'bra Allen

When he was dead and laid in grave,
She heard the death bell knelling.
And every note, did seem to say
"Oh, cruel Barb'ra Allen"

"Oh mother, mother, make my bed
Make it soft and narrow
Sweet William died, for love of me,
And I shall of sorrow."

They buried her in the old churchyard
Sweet William's grave was neigh hers
And from his grave grew a red, red rose
From hers a cruel briar.

They grew and grew up the old church spire
Until they could grow no higher
And there they twined, in a true love knot,
The red, red rose and the briar.

ABOUT THE AUTHOR

LAURA MILLS-ALCOTT's first love was music, and she began her writing career at the age of eleven, when she wrote her first song. After graduating high school, she moved to Nashville, and some of her music was published.

Though she wrote her share of love songs, Laura's favorite was the story songs—the modern day equivalent of the old ballads. However, she often found herself frustrated when attempting to fit a single title novel into three verses, a bridge, and a chorus. So one day she decided she'd try her hand at writing a book. "After writing the first paragraph," she says, "I was hooked."

In *The Briar and the Rose*, she combines her love of music with her love for romantic novels and history.

Laura and her work have been featured in *Romantic Times Magazine*, on the "Talk America Radio Network", and most recently, she acted as a consultant for the daytime talk show "The Other Half" on a segment dealing with romance novels.

Laura currently resides in NE Ohio with her three beautiful children, two dogs, and too many cats.

She enjoys hearing from readers. Readers may write to Laura at:

Laura Mills-Alcott
P.O. Box 457
Orwell, OH 44446
Visit Laura's website at The Romance Club:
  www.theromanceclub.com/authors/lauramillsalcott